SOMETHING WICKED THIS WAY COMES....

I hung up my black apron and realized it had been a good shift as I sneaked half my tips into Lolita's jar. Lo deserved it. She brought a friendly, fun vibe to the bar. All I did was pour and serve with a smile, touching my patrons to steal away their emotional energy.

Suddenly my hand froze on the tip jar, my senses tingling. The feeling was so mild, I almost mistook it for my own guilty excitement at finally being able to feed off my patrons. But the sensation built, and I knew what it was.

A demon is coming.

Praise for *Confessions of a Demon*

"Way-fast read, intensely built world, tortured hero, kick-ass heroine—what's not to like?"
——Jennifer Stevenson, author of *Trash Sex Magic*

"A fascinating, utterly original demon world, teeming with conflict and intrigue. I fell in love with Allay and her struggle to keep her humanity despite the forces aligned against her. Mesmerizing and addictive, *Confessions of a Demon* is urban fantasy at its best!"
——Jeri Smith-Ready, award-winning author of *Wicked Game*

CONFESSIONS OF A DEMON

S. L. Wright

A ROC BOOK

ROC
Published by New American Library, a division of
Penguin Group (USA) Inc., 375 Hudson Street,
New York, New York 10014, USA
Penguin Group (Canada), 90 Eglinton Avenue East, Suite 700, Toronto,
Ontario M4P 2Y3, Canada (a division of Pearson Penguin Canada Inc.)
Penguin Books Ltd., 80 Strand, London WC2R 0RL, England
Penguin Ireland, 25 St. Stephen's Green, Dublin 2,
Ireland (a division of Penguin Books Ltd.)
Penguin Group (Australia), 250 Camberwell Road, Camberwell, Victoria 3124,
Australia (a division of Pearson Australia Group Pty. Ltd.)
Penguin Books India Pvt. Ltd., 11 Community Centre, Panchsheel Park,
New Delhi - 110 017, India
Penguin Group (NZ), 67 Apollo Drive, Rosedale, North Shore 0632,
New Zealand (a division of Pearson New Zealand Ltd.)
Penguin Books (South Africa) (Pty.) Ltd., 24 Sturdee Avenue,
Rosebank, Johannesburg 2196, South Africa

Penguin Books Ltd., Registered Offices:
80 Strand, London WC2R 0RL, England

First published by Roc, an imprint of New American Library,
a division of Penguin Group (USA) Inc.

First Printing, December 2009
10 9 8 7 6 5 4 3 2 1

Copyright © Susan Wright, 2009
All rights reserved

 REGISTERED TRADEMARK—MARCA REGISTRADA

Printed in the United States of America

PUBLISHER'S NOTE
This is a work of fiction. Names, characters, places, and incidents either are the
product of the author's imagination or are used fictitiously, and any resemblance
to actual persons, living or dead, business establishments, events, or locales is
entirely coincidental.
    The publisher does not have any control over and does not assume any re-
sponsibility for author or third-party Web sites or their content.

If you purchased this book without a cover you should be aware that this book is
stolen property. It was reported as "unsold and destroyed" to the publisher and
neither the author nor the publisher has received any payment for this "stripped
book."

*This novel is dedicated to
my loving husband, Kelly*

ACKNOWLEDGMENTS

I would like to thank Jessica Wade, my editor at Roc, and my agent, Lucienne Diver, for their dedication in making this novel the best that it could be.

1

It was the usual Friday night at the Den on C, the neighborhood bar in New York City I had managed for almost a decade. That was a long time by human standards, but then again, I wasn't a standard human. I was something more—or less. The jury was still out on that one.

A group of pool-playing coeds had stopped by after hanging out at a beer garden in the East Village, but they were starting to trickle away as the midnight rush eased off. Some would end up in the chic bars popping up just to the south on the Lower East Side, leaving behind the regulars, mostly older Latino men and a smattering of working-class guys covered in ghostly drywall dust. A few crowded tables of arty hipsters still filled the back, where everyone was loudly talking over one another.

I swung open the front door wide to catch the mild night air of early spring, trying to ignore the metallic tang of exhaust. A few streets below Houston was Delancey Street, where the lights were much brighter and the avenue opened up wide to accommodate the steady flow of cars over the Williamsburg Bridge. The congestion always got worse late Friday night, choking the streets with fumes and honking horns as too many people tried to get in and out of Manhattan at the same time.

I could see my own reflection in the narrow glass pane; the light from the aluminum shade overhead cast a speck-

led pattern across my face. Wisps of dark hair touched my
forehead, cheeks, and neck. I had tried to stay faithful to
my original, human appearance, a heart-shaped face that
was pretty enough, capable looking rather than delicate.
I had aged myself over the years to look like I should—
twenty-eight this spring.

Behind me, the opening strains of "Kiss Me," the original version by Six Pence None the Richer, with its tinny
drums and silly, sweet vocals, came through the speakers
hanging high in the corners. I knew the words by heart:
"Kiss me, beneath the milky twilight / Lead me out on the
moonlit floor. . . ."

It lifted my heart for a moment, like the song always had
ever since the year I'd been turned. But that touch of minor
key, the slight note of sadness, resonated much deeper than
it should have. It meant so much more to me—all that I had
lost; all that I would never be.

I knew better than to try to ignore my regret. That made
it worse. The pain that came with the past was something I
just had to endure.

Since I became a demon.

"Possessed" is the correct term, I reminded myself. *I'm
possessed by a demon.*

I was a human-demon hybrid, the only one alive. No
longer sustained by food or drink, I lived off emotions—
any would do, but my preferred elixir, the feeling I'd do
anything to provoke, was the simple yet all-powerful feeling of respite: relief from sorrow or pain. That was why I
was known as Allay.

Plenty of people came to my bar looking for a little release from their pain. I provided all of the usual services
bartenders typically give their patrons: I served them drinks
and listened to them when no one else would. And when it
was really bad, I would pat their hand and steal away some
of their pain. But taking energy from people, even the bad
feelings, caused an imbalance in their system. I took only

enough to make them feel better, and then for my reward I would sip a drop of their brief contentment.

I had to be careful, for their own good, not to go too far. When people were drained of their emotional energy, they could turn schizophrenic, manic, or so depressed they killed themselves. Some people became physically ill and died.

I wasn't sure, but I thought emotions were the seat of the soul. That was why they radiated so much energy.

But how can you recognize a soul when you don't have one?

When the song was over, I decided it was time to call it quits and spend some quality time with my patrons. I could afford to hire only one bartender a shift, so I tended bar during the busy hours, along with restocking, dealing with salesmen, maintaining the books, and cleaning up the puke from the bathroom floor when my janitor and all-round handyman, Pepe, couldn't make it in.

The Den on C was narrow and deep like most of the other storefronts along the avenue, with a scarred mahogany bar along one side. There was enough space to put two tables against the front windows and a few next to the bar. In the back, there was an old pool table that I had refelted a few years earlier. I thought the bar's best feature was the floor, with its tiny black and white hexagon tiles. It made a pleasing old-fashioned pattern in spite of the cracked and missing tiles. My customers liked the bar-long mirror hanging from the ceiling that let them see behind them without turning around.

With my demon insight into people's emotions, I could have talked my way into a bartending job anywhere in the city. Every week a new hot spot opened up for the celebrities and party girls who clattered over the narrow cobblestones in their spiky heels.

But I felt comfortable at the Den. They needed me here. When I found the bar, Alphabet City was still riddled with crack dealers and the gutters were strewn with empty vials and dime bags. But there were also vibrant murals decorating every long brick wall—images of trees, cars, people, animals, and exaggerated renderings of city buildings in hot tropical colors. The lower facades of the old tenements were painted bright red, turquoise, and green, and the air was usually pungent with the smell of cilantro, fried plantains, and roasted pork. Now the neighborhood was full of trendy bars and restaurants, and bakeries that sold cupcakes for five bucks each.

I hung up my black apron and realized it had been a good shift as I sneaked half my tips into Lolita's jar. Lo deserved it. She brought a friendly, fun vibe to the bar. All I did was pour and serve with a smile, touching my patrons to steal away their emotional energy.

Suddenly my hand froze on the tip jar, my senses tingling. The feeling was so mild, I almost mistook it for my own guilty excitement at finally being able to feed off my patrons. But the sensation built, and I knew what it was.

A demon is coming.

Nobody else in the bar could tell. But one of the cats who had adopted the bar as home suddenly rose to his toes in the deep window frame. Snowplow's back arched and his tail puffed out like a Christmas tree, tapering to its Angora tip. He was a misplaced purebred, but to me, he was the best demon-alert device in the city—and his sirens were blaring. As he leaped onto the bar, his claws scattered napkins, and a couple of people snatched up their glasses as he dashed down its length.

"Watch out!" Lolita said as Snowplow's final leap took him up into the duct leading to my second-floor apartment. She scooped up the overturned gin and tonic the cat had knocked over. "That was a good one. At least seven feet, maybe more."

Customers at the bar were complaining loudly while I hurried over to the open door. I needed to figure out who was coming. From this position, I could retreat upstairs to my fortified apartment, if I needed to. I hated to abandon my patrons to a hungry demon; they were all I had other than Shock. But I might have to in order to call in reinforcements. As the very last resort, I could call Vex for help.

Not that I'd ever had to resort to that.

Lo wiped up the spill with a wet towel as Carl, one of our regulars, bitched, "That stupid cat leaves white hair all over me, and I don't even touch it. Now it steals my drink?"

"Shut up—you'll get another one." Lo's sly smile took the sting out of her blunt order. Carl smiled sheepishly in return as he brushed at his mismatched shirt and baggy jeans. He liked it when women told him what to do, and both Lo and I in our different ways had figured that out early on.

Lolita was my rock, always there for me for the past five years. She was tall and voluptuous with an hourglass figure and a lusty swagger that caught everyone's eye. Lo took full advantage of the sensual charge she ignited in both sexes, flirting indiscriminately. She was open to all kinds of relationships, but she was slow to slap a label on anything or create expectations that couldn't be met. She liked no pressure, and not pressuring other people. That meant she rarely let people go, not for good, and the interlocking family she maintained openly and honestly included a number of relationships that continued to meander and grow organically. One of them was sitting right now at the end of the bar, chatting up the prettiest girl in the place; Boymeat was Lo's friend, her former playmate, and younger brother in her family of free spirits.

Lolita was just as vulnerable to demons as anyone else, but having her at my back made me feel safer. Especially this time; I didn't recognize the approaching signature formed by the unique energy waves that radiated from each demon. The signature, getting stronger, resembled Shock's distinctive buzz, but it was much more chaotic and jarring. It reminded me of Pique, the latest horror to invade my territory and feed off my people.

If Pique was coming that fast, it couldn't be good. He was constantly on the move, like a shark, stirring up trouble, provoking people to feed off their irritation. Even worse, Pique liked to drain his victims of all their emotions.

A yellow cab pulled up outside. The signature was much clearer—a buzzing, tingling feeling that ran along my skin. It rose in intensity until it abruptly broke off. Then the buzzing restarted, rising again.

It *was* Shock's signature. She was the most important person in my life. Shock had always been a demon, whereas I had started out human and made my transformation into demonhood as a teenager. She became one of my first friends after I had been turned, and she was the only demon who'd never tried to hurt me or take anything from me. Shock had the same progenitor as Plea, the demon who had turned me, so among demons we were considered siblings. Everyone at the bar thought she was my half sister, born of the same mother but with different fathers. That explained our last names and why Shock was so petite and blond whereas I was brunette with a classic California tan.

But I could tell from Shock's signature that something was wrong with her. Very wrong. She was *pulsing*.

The cab door flung open and Shock's familiar slender figure appeared. With her men's sleeveless undershirt and loose jeans, she looked like a kid from the neighborhood. Her white-blond hair stood only an inch high over her sharply defined face, but her rounded breasts and hips left no doubt that she was female. Her expression was oddly blank as she staggered jerkily between the parked cars. She cut through three people who separated for her without a word, glancing back curiously.

"Allay . . . ," she croaked.

Shock's pulsing energy made me instinctively bristle, ready to defend myself. This wouldn't be the first demon who had imitated Shock's appearance in order to get close enough to try to steal my energy.

I was fixated even as I wanted to run. "Is that really you, Shock?"

"Help me," Shock whispered.

Shock never asked for help. She was the one who helped people. She was an emergency medical technician, saving lives as she soaked up the stunned, pained emotions of the people she scraped off the streets. I couldn't believe this vibrating creature with the shaking hands was Shock.

Abruptly she stopped short, just out of arm's reach. One hand held on to the doorframe, and she clutched her stomach with her other arm. She looked ready to collapse.

Never let another demon get within touching distance. That was the first advice Shock had given me when she tracked me down in Southern California. Within months after I had absorbed Plea's essence, word of my existence had quickly spread within the demon world. Vex, the head of my line, had first sent Revel, then Shock, to fetch me to live in safety in his New York City territory. In exchange for his protection against the other demons, I had to do things for Vex, things I didn't like. But I didn't see any way around it. His influence kept most of the other demons away from me, though I still had to deal with rogues—the demons who didn't do as ordered by Vex and Glory, the progenitors of the two existing demon lines.

Only Shock was careful to stay more than arm's length away from me at all times. I always had to make the first move to get closer to her, even when it was something as simple as sitting down on a barstool next to her.

The fact that she was swaying out of reach, keeping her distance, was proof enough for me.

"Shock! What's wrong with you?" I reached out and drew her into the bar.

Shock stumbled against me, her hands clenching involuntarily into fists as her entire body spasmed. "Upstairs now, Allay. Or there's gonna be fireworks."

I looked over my shoulder and down the street as cars flowed by. It was hard to sense other demons when Shock, with her abrasive signature, was so close to me. "Is someone after you?"

Shock shuddered hard, clenching her jaw until she couldn't answer. Everyone in the bar was watching, except for a few yahoos in the back shouting over their pool game. But for now the most animated expression was mild interest. Patrons staggered in dead drunk often enough that Shock's condition wasn't remarkable. The Den was known to give away cups of great coffee after midnight.

Lolita came out from behind the bar. "Need help?"

"I'm not sure." I half dragged Shock farther into the bar, toward the inner door that led to the stairs to my apartment on the second floor.

Lo approached and took only one look at Shock's rigid expression, blurting out, "That looks like an overdose. I'm calling 911."

"Shock doesn't do drugs. You know that." I couldn't let Lo call the EMTs. Demons could make their bodies appear any way they wished, but Shock was somehow losing control of herself. "I'm taking her upstairs. Maybe she's just been scared by something," I added to appease my bartender. "Maybe . . ."

Lolita shook her dark curls. "*Rape?*" she mouthed in concern, taking Shock's arm to help her.

I gave Lo a stricken look over the top of Shock's hunched head. The way she was holding on to herself, shoulders tight, knees together, it did look as if Shock had been violated. But a human couldn't have hurt her—it must have been another demon.

Drawn to my surprised distress, Shock latched on to my arm. Her aura flared as she tried to stop herself from absorbing my energy, but her favorite emotion was too tempting.

"I'll take her up!" I insisted, pulling Shock away from Lo. "Stay with the bar, Lolita."

Lolita glanced back at the now avidly interested patrons. The music was drowning out our words, but clearly there was something wrong with Shock. I felt the tottering of the semiprofessional wall I had erected to keep everyone from asking questions so I wouldn't have to lie to them. I liked being their confessor, but for that to work, my own life couldn't intrude.

Lo turned to face everyone, her hands on her hips. Though she reveled in breaking down boundaries in every way possible, she protected my right to privacy. "You're supposed to be drinking, not gawking at us," she called out to Jose as she returned to the bar, asking if he wanted another.

The door to the stairs closed behind me, shutting out most of the sounds in the bar. It was a good thing demons were strong, because I had to drag Shock up every creaking step to my apartment door. As soon as it slammed shut behind us, I demanded, "Shock, what's wrong?"

Shock stuttered, hardly able to move her lips, "Birthing . . ."

"You're not going to—"

"Split. In two." Shock grimaced at me, her face rippling with the pulsing of her aura. "Not safe. The demon . . . It'll attack me."

"Holy shit." I couldn't think of anything else to say, so I repeated myself several times as I helped Shock across the slanting floor of my kitchen. It was big enough to hold an old-fashioned Formica-topped table with matching green vinyl chairs, and had a frosted window over the sink facing an airshaft. There was a coffeemaker for when I had visitors, but no microwave, toaster, or any of the usual food clutter that filled ordinary kitchens. The back of the counter was lined with a row of books, with a few piles on top. I

kept only the barest essentials in the refrigerator as cover—
some cheese, bottled goods that wouldn't spoil quickly, and
several bottles of soda that were years old.

I dragged Shock through the arch into the front room,
which was strewn with odds and ends, the comfortable
clutter of daily life. My place had never been renovated,
so the battered tin ceilings and exposed pipes were thick
with paint, and the plaster had buckled and cracked over
the lathe. There was no bed because I didn't sleep, so I put
Shock down on the old red sofa. She didn't look good, but
I didn't know whether this was normal; I had never seen a
demon birth before.

Shock's last offspring was Stun, born fifty years ago. He
made my skin crawl every time I had to deal with him, but
since he was one of Vex's minions, I had no choice. It bothered me to think that a creature like that had come from
Shock.

I was determined to avoid birthing a demon at all costs.
I consumed only the bare minimum I needed to survive,
never building up reserves. Not only did it make me a less-
tempting target for other demons who wanted to absorb
my energy, but it made it impossible for me to overdose
and birth another demon into the world.

When a demon absorbed too much emotional energy, it
split in two, giving birth asexually. The original demon was
basically unchanged, while another fully grown demon was
created. New demons were born with memory traces from
their progenitor, and the basic knowledge about the ways
of the world, other demons, and how to feed off the energy of human emotions. It had been difficult for me, with
Plea's knowledge clashing against my seventeen years of
human memories. I had eventually coped by walling off
those unsettling thoughts and feelings—visions of myself
hurting people, giving in to ugly desires, surrounded by
reaching hands. Those thoughts made me feel tainted,
inhuman.

But my body seemed the same; in that way nothing had changed. I listened to my own heartbeat for hours in the early days, feeling the blood pulse through my veins, cutting myself to watch the red rivulets flow down my skin until my flesh miraculously healed, digging deeper despite the excruciating pain to see muscle and the glint of bone, over and over again, until I wearied of examining my own body from the outside in. Other than the way I healed, the only thing that felt different was that my appetite was now focused on emotions instead of food. Laughter was like sugar cookies, cynicism like a tart lemon, and comfort like a bowl of warm stew, satisfying to my heart.

I had asked Shock what her body felt like, and she said it was the same. She was even more fascinated by her humanlike yet ephemeral body. She had a habit of clasping her wrist to feel her pulse race when she was pumped up on adrenaline.

I eyed her nervously. "How much longer?"

"Almost there." Shock panted, curling into fetal position. "You got any energy? That'll help. Over with faster."

I gently clasped her hand so she could draw what she needed. The aura around our hands flared orange with my fear.

Shock writhed on the sofa, her feet kicking the cushions as her back arched. I didn't need to turn on the light—a pearly glow filled the room as energy shed off her like the tail of a comet. Surely every demon within a few blocks could feel her signature now, amplified by the impending birth.

With a spike of panic, I realized I hadn't bolted the door behind us. What if the door hadn't closed below? What if Lo came upstairs when she heard Shock's strangled cries? But she was holding on to me so tightly that I couldn't let go.

Shock released my hand the instant before energy exploded from her body. The shock wave thrust me back against the wall. Cracks radiated away in the plaster where I hit. I couldn't breathe; I could only stare.

Shock was flat on her back, nearly rigid. The lustrous glow swelled so brightly that the outline of her body grew fuzzy. I almost had to turn away; it hurt my eyes, but I couldn't stop looking. I was born human, so it was hard for me to remember that I was a being of pure energy now. Demons looked exactly like humans, felt like real humans, so it was easy for me to forget my true nature.

This—*this* made it real. The veil of flesh ripped away as Shock's body split apart.

The brilliant glow shattered as the upper part of Shock rose from the sofa. But Shock still lay there, twisting in agony as the light-filled shadow tore from her flesh.

A brand-new demon stood up before me. As the blinding light began to fade, the last remnants of energy burned off in its creation. The new demon looked like Shock. It was naked, sexless, but the slender form and short white hair were Shock's.

I gaped, looking from the demon, back to Shock.

"Allay . . . ," Shock mouthed. She tried to sit up but fell back, depleted.

The demon turned to Shock and took a step back to her. Every moment, it was looking less like Shock, its features blurring and reshaping, the hair darkening, growing, then curling. It was expending energy with every shift, but it seemed much stronger than Shock, who struggled to sit up.

The demon was close to Shock—too close. Shock was having trouble shielding herself, trying to tighten her remaining energy to protect her inner core. My skin prickled as if chilled as my own shields instinctively snapped into place. Usually I was more lax, but not when another demon was anywhere nearby.

To distract the demon from Shock, I peeled away from the wall. "Get away from her."

The demon whirled on me like a cornered animal, dropping into a defensive crouch. I froze, locking eyes with it. *Shit! That thing's about to jump on my face!*

This was a demon in its most primeval form—shapeless, a parasite driven by hunger, ready to do whatever it took to survive. But an arc of recognition shot between me and the tensed creature before me. Because of my background, I was as different as I could be from this demon, yet I was formed from the same material. We were the same at the core.

At least now it was focused on me instead of on Shock.

I took a slow sidestep, careful not to advance or retreat but taking control of the situation by making the first move. That was when fear hit me in the gut. The demon's signature finally penetrated the persistent buzzing of Shock's signature. It was a shiver down my spine, making me yearn to look over my shoulder to catch the eyes that were watching me, following me, waiting to do the worst things imaginable to me. . . .

"Petrify," I said. That was the demon's name, his true nature. My palms were sweating as I radiated exactly what he wanted—fear. I had been feeding Shock a steady stream of panic ever since the poor girl had arrived, so that was what this demon craved.

Some help I am! Why didn't I pour love into her? Or calm?

Petrify, his hands opening and shutting, took a step toward me, compelled as he was to touch me, to soak up my fright. But I couldn't let him—he would steal the little energy I had left.

I stumbled toward the kitchen, drawing him away from Shock. His facade was still wavering, but he was quickly gaining more control, conserving his energy for an attack.

Shock managed to push herself to her feet. "What are you waiting for, Allay? Take him. You need his essence."

It took me a second before I realized what she was saying. "You want me to consume him?"

"Go on, Allay. It'll be easy to slip past his shields. He doesn't have much control."

I stared at Petrify, who stopped his advance. It was true that his aura was fluctuating, his energy flow chaotic. Maybe it would be easy to absorb his power and expose the core that kept him alive. Then I could steal his essence for myself, just as I had inadvertently stolen Plea's essence ten years ago.

Yes. The longing swelled inside of me until it made my heart pound. I had felt this need growing for a long time, but I had tried to deny it. I couldn't hide from it any longer.

That hot fire of life will make me immortal.

Well, at least it would keep me alive for a couple of centuries. That was how long it took to burn down the candle again, to reach the final waxy puddle where our demon flame began to gutter and go out. I could feel it happening inside me and knew if I didn't take the core of another demon soon, I would wither and fade away. That is, if a stronger demon didn't kill me first. Then the spark of my essence would renew his life for another two centuries.

Plea had last consumed a demon 188 years before I had taken her essence. From the first time I'd heard about this catch to demon immortality, I had hoped the clock had been reset when I was created. I had enough problems to deal with. But the odd, growing urgency inside of me, forming a tight knot in my stomach over the past few months, was unlike any other. I knew instinctively that I needed to take another demon's essence soon, or I would begin a rapid decline and eventually disappear into a puff of nothingness.

The craving suddenly overwhelmed me. I reached for Petrify, unable to resist that animating spark buried deep inside of him. Our hands met, fingers interlacing like lovers.

Power fluctuated between us. He tried to pull the fibers

of my being into him, but I wrenched back. This was different from the everyday desire to fuel myself. This was life or death.

The influx of his energy hit me like a lightning bolt. I felt as if I could crush the slight man in my arms, as if I could leap into the sky and fly. Demon energy was nothing like human emotions, which suddenly seemed pale and insignificant next to *this*—this glorious power. . . .

I breathed out, relaxing into myself for a rare, compelling moment. This was what it meant to be a demon, to consume one of our own. No wonder some demons were addicted to demon energy. Some made sport of specifically hunting *me*.

This time I was doing it—stealing his essence, his soul. As I stared into his eyes, the impossible suddenly seemed perfectly reasonable. I could kill him, just as I had killed Plea, though that had been a terrible accident.

Perhaps I'd been afraid that I couldn't beat another demon, that if I tried, I would lose. Then I would finally and truly die. That fear had kept me running from demons ever since I had been possessed.

Now I realized who would triumph was a matter of will. My will had been as bendable as a reed. But now I felt like a different person, like Allay the Demon. It was as if the secret powers I had collected were nothing but matchsticks, and this was lighter fluid. It was pure, unadulterated energy—*all mine*.

Actually, it was Petrify's. Before that, it had been part of Shock. Petrify hadn't existed a moment ago. What did it matter if he disappeared now? If I crushed him like a cockroach because he meant nothing to me or to anyone. If I devoured him like—like a killer. Like a cannibal.

"No." I shoved Petrify away from me.

He scuttled off, but Shock managed to trap him between us. "Don't let him go," Shock said. "You have to finish him off, Allay. You're almost done."

I shook my head, clutching the countertop behind me. "No, I won't. I'm not going to lose the last bit of humanity I have."

Shock was wobbly, but she blocked Petrify from getting around her. Now that he was weakened, it was easy. "Go on, Allay. You'll be exactly the same. Without him you'll die."

I stared at Petrify, who was slightly hunched over and shaking, leaning against the wall. He was trying to gather together what was left of his energy.

"I would be different. I'd be a murderer."

"It's not murder!" Shock protested. "It's . . . how it has to be. How it's always been."

I shook my head. "I'm not going to kill your offspring, Shock. Now move aside. He can go out the bedroom window."

"You're letting him go?"

I gave her a hard look. "You don't eat your own."

"I'm not going to take a demon until I have to. Like you, right now."

"It's not that urgent."

Shock shook her head. "You think so? Because it seems to me it's getting that way. Besides, if you let him go, someone else will snap him up. The new ones go quickest."

"Maybe. But it won't be me."

Petrify had been listening, and he wasn't as frightened anymore. In the bedroom, he snatched up a pair of sweatpants and a T-shirt and hurriedly pulled them on, as if he expected me to deny him. I dragged the chaise lounge away from the window in the bedroom, and pushed the old wooden frame as high as it could go.

A titanium lock secured the gate at the wide lock plate. I had installed the heavy-duty gates made from three-quarter-inch iron, the strongest I could find. Soon after I had moved in, a demon had broken the window and tried to force its way inside, but a can of mace had burned its eyes and given it a seizing cough, just as it did with humans. After that, I turned my place into a fortress of steel to make sure no demon could sneak up on me again.

The lock was stiff, but I wrenched it open and swung the gate out. The backyard was very narrow, made of concrete with a drain in the center. "Jump down and go that way." I pointed. "Then into the yard behind that one. You'll find an open lot with a fence on the next street."

Shock sighed behind me. "Word will spread fast. It always does after a birth."

"Get out of the city," I told him. "Stay away and don't come back until you have to."

Petrify swung his legs through the window and glanced back inside at me. "Why are you helping me?"

My flip retort—*I'm Super Demon, champion of poor and oppressed fiends everywhere!*—died at the sight of his big, soulful eyes. Now he looked much darker than Shock, an elfin man with shaggy hair. Despite his appalling signature, he wasn't that bad.

"I'm trying to be humane," I said honestly.

"But you're a demon."

I sighed. "Yeah, I know."

Self-preservation reasserted itself and Petrify ducked out the window, then poised on the sill, judging the drop. His feet made a soft thud as he hit the ground. I locked the gate again and pulled the window back down so it was partially open to let in the night air. The flowers on the acacia next door smelled so good.

Then I turned to Shock. "Is that why you came here? To give me your offspring?"

"Yes. Plus I knew that birthing another demon so quickly would weaken me. I was afraid he would turn on me while I couldn't defend myself."

"He almost did."

Shock shook her head. "I still don't understand why you didn't take him, Allay."

I watched the shadowy form climb over the fence. "I just couldn't . . . kill him." I turned away from the window. "Did you really think I was going to eat your child, Shock?"

"He's not my child, Allay. He's my offspring. There's a big difference, and besides, I don't see what that has to do with anything. You need to take a demon. Soon."

I shook my head, suddenly unable to speak. I could still taste it, that overwhelming desire to steal Petrify's essence. The hunger burning inside of me was much stronger now that I had gotten a taste of what I needed. I had almost given in to my worst demon urges.

"I didn't mean to make you feel bad." Shock shoved both hands into the front pockets of her baggy jeans. She always dressed down when she wasn't in her EMT uniform. "I want to help you, Allay. I don't want to lose you."

"You demons just want me because I used to be human," I said as a joke, trying to lighten the mood.

But Shock was serious. "To be honest, maybe I was fascinated with you because of that in the beginning. You know you're different. I could really feel it when you were feeding me. You taste like that last burst of energy a human releases. . . ." She glanced away, aware that she was admitting to having drained someone. "So sweet, but passing. They say people get the same high from drugs. But you have it all the time. You radiate it. It's really compelling."

It was nothing I hadn't already figured out. But I hated to think that my human-tainted energy was why Shock kept coming back to see me. "Lucky for me, my godfather sends his finest to watch over my nonexistent soul."

Shock was standing awkwardly in the archway. "I think it's love. I don't know anything about love; what demon does? But I can see it in you, how you treat people, how you care about making things right. You hug me and I want to hug you back; I want that feeling. But I don't know how."

My throat closed up. She was warped, vulnerable, and

inhibited. But she was reaching out—trying. I appreciated that.

"You hug great." I smiled sadly. "The more you do it, the better you get."

Shock didn't move. She was always hesitant to touch me because of her instinctive fear that other demons would try to steal her energy, so hugging definitely didn't come naturally to her. I had to go to her and put my arms around her. She hugged me, surprisingly hard and long. It was the first time I tried to let go before her. I squeezed her tighter for a few moments more, sinking into that safe, familiar feeling. It had been so long since I had felt like that . . . the last time I'd felt so human.

2

I used to be an ordinary girl living an ordinary life in Orange County. But a month before my eighteenth birthday, I'd accidentally been possessed by a demon. It happened over spring break during my senior year. I'd lied to my parents and gone to a rented beach house with my friends in San Diego. It wasn't the first time I had lied to them— I'd been sneaking out of my room since I bought my first junker at sixteen. I saw no harm in soothing my parents' fears so I wouldn't have to deal with their worry. I took care of myself.

But on the last night of my vacation, there was a pimply-faced dude at the bonfire who wouldn't leave me alone, so I told my friends I was going back to the hotel. They were right behind me, packing up the towels and saying good-bye to everyone. But it turned out to be an important few minutes, because on the boardwalk in a vast shadowed space between the lamps, I stumbled on a man attacking a woman.

I didn't know what was happening at first, and thought maybe they were making out. The guy had his arms wrapped tightly around her, and there wasn't any noise— the woman didn't call out for help or protest. That was why I didn't see them until I was almost on top of them. I felt the impact of their feet hitting the boardwalk as they struggled, and the woman beat feebly on his back with her

fist. Then her arm dropped as if she were too weak to fight
back anymore.

I didn't even think about it; I ran right into the guy,
hitting him in the side as hard as I could. He spun away
from the woman and slipped on the sand, hitting his back
against the railing. He disappeared over the edge, falling
down to the beach.

I skidded on the sandy boards, sprawling down and
scraping my hands and knees. From below, not eight feet
away, the would-be rapist shot me a look I could barely
see in the darkness, only a wild-eyed glare of animal rage
that turned my insides to mush. I thought I was a goner,
but the guy was too far below to climb back up. He loped
off into the shadows down the beach, probably looking for
a staircase.

In a panic, I scrabbled over to the girl. She had collapsed
onto her back, her arms and legs akimbo, as if she couldn't
even curl into a protective ball. I didn't know it then, but
Plea was a three-hundred-year-old demon. The guy I had
pushed off the boardwalk was another demon who had
drained her of all the energy she had collected from her
human prey, from feeding off their emotions. Without that
protective shell of energy, her essence lay exposed.

I couldn't see the pulsing white core nestled in her belly,
that magic bullet of demon immortality her attacker had
tried to steal from her.

But when I touched Plea, her essence, the unending
flame of life, passed into me. In that instant, my old life was
over and I became the demon Allay.

My physical body was transformed into pure spirit; a
replica of what I had once been, a simulation of flesh that
still bled and felt pain. Yet with a thought I could change
how I looked, willing myself into being. I no longer slept or
ate or drank. I would never get sick and die the way other
people did. I would never grow old.

It was completely disorienting. I felt the same physically,

though I no longer experienced hunger in the same way—
I wanted emotions instead of food for sustenance. And I
couldn't sleep, which was maddening. I felt as if I were on
a constant coke binge and couldn't stop, could never stop,
and I revved myself higher and higher, compelled to touch
people to suck off their feelings, surviving by instinct rather
than conscious thought.

But the worst thing was the memories, those glimpses
into Plea's life, her secrets, her knowledge, her experiences.
All fragmented into puzzle pieces, and I could see only a
few pieces at a time, which was next to useless for helping
me figure out what was going on. It was from these scant
clues that I knew I was now a demon like Plea had been.
I got flashes of mythology; in various times we had been
considered angels, devils, vampires, ghosts, ghouls, goblins,
spirits, fairies, the *daevas* of Zoroastrianism, the Hopi *pow-
aga*, the *narakas* of Jainism, and the jinn or genies of Islam
created out of fire two thousand years before the creation
of Adam. We were the *kuei* that Chinese Taoism used bon-
fires, firecrackers, and torches to ward off; the *oni* and *tengu*
the Japanese believed to possess spirits.

At first, I truly thought I had gone mad. I ran through
the streets babbling about things I should know nothing
about. When the authorities came and wrapped me in a
straitjacket, I told them they were doing the right thing,
that I was possessed by a demon named Plea that needed
to be exorcised. I kept asking for a priest, though I had
been born a Protestant and attended relatively few church
services in my life.

When my parents arrived at the county psychiatric ward
with their sad, shocked eyes, my mother's red-rimmed from
crying, they sat and spoke in hushed tones on the other side
of a scarred table. It was like a slap in the face. I had never
caused any trouble, always got good grades, and had good
friends, as I successfully kept the more unsavory aspects of
my experimentations from them. They never met my first

real boyfriend because he was a senior while I was a fresh-man. They never knew about my late-night visits to parties at UC Irvine.

At that moment, knowing I had to "protect" them, I somehow managed to get hold of myself, and talked my way out of there with the help of my parents. I confessed to a drug experience gone bad, and claimed I had learned my lesson. *No more acid for me, I swear! Never again. I'll go home and be a good girl.*

Then I struggled to live the lie that I was still Emma Meyers of Fountain Valley, California, celebrating my birthday with people who suddenly seemed as if they were strangers. But I was the one who was different. I was now "Allay," because Plea's final emotion had been relief to see a girl rather than a demon looming over her. She thought she was going to survive, but instead I took her life without meaning to. That's why my strongest desire was to touch people who felt relieved and to absorb their emotion.

Over the years, I had tried to keep a relationship with my parents, my sister, and assorted cousins, but they were now firmly convinced I was addicted to drugs. To them, noth-ing else could explain my bizarre behavior. Even worse, demons were attracted to them when I visited. I finally gave up holidays at home, and having to pretend to eat and sleep. I told them I didn't want more from my life; that I couldn't be around them right now. I hoped it would be dif-ferent someday, but it was hard to explain why I didn't have any serious relationships and why my sister's talk of having babies and getting promoted left me cold. I was stuck like a fly in amber.

Who was brave enough to confess to their mother that they had been transformed from a nice, God-fearing girl into a demon? No, it was better that they thought I was a loser than some unworldly creature.

No doubt Shock had had other motives when she had dropped by my bar every few days over the years. I figured she was under Vex's orders, so what difference did it make that it was also because my hybrid energy was alluring? A real bond had grown between us, and at this point in my life, she was the only family I had left.

And here I was, standing in my living room, holding a demon close.

"My sister," I murmured as we finally separated.

Shock was nodding. "That's why I wanted to give you my offspring, Allay, because you need it. You can't die. I can't lose you."

I couldn't argue with her now. "You should rest, Shock. You look like you're about to fall over. I think you should stay here. It isn't safe for you to go out again tonight."

Shock reluctantly nodded in agreement. She preferred hiding away in her brownstone apartment in the heart of the Village when she wasn't working the streets. Her current persona had "inherited" the place when her last persona, a butch spinster, got too old to work as an emergency room doctor. It wasn't an easy charade to pull off, but Shock had done it for almost a hundred years. That was why most demons lived in cities; it was simpler to disappear in the crowd.

"I'm definitely feeling punky," she admitted. "That one came too fast."

"You should control yourself better at work." Shock skimmed a little energy from everyone, like I did. Perhaps she'd made a mistake, gone too far without realizing it. I knew better than most how seriously she took the "Do no harm" motto of a physician. But every shift she handled people who were boiling over with pain and terror—a lot to absorb on a daily basis. She had always loved medicine, starting back when leeches were a doctor's most reliable remedy. She was still enthusiastic about the little buggers and how they could bring down swelling and bruises better than any modern-day remedies. I thought their being slimy slugs was enough reason to move them out of the realm of medicine.

I left her lying on the sofa and made sure to lock both bolts behind me. Demons were strong, but not strong enough to rip the hinges off my door.

I took a few deep breaths before descending, firming my shields around myself. I usually didn't bother unless I felt another demon coming. But after that blast of energy from Shock, I had to be ready to defend myself. There were a few cannibalistic demons living in the city: Bask was addicted to demon energy, and dogged me on a fairly regular basis. Goad was also known to prefer demons. They were bound to be drawn here tonight.

I also had to prepare myself to face Lolita and my patrons; it wouldn't do to rush down looking as if I had just banished the monster my sister had spawned.

"How is she, Allay?" Carl called out as soon as I came through the inner door of the bar. The bolt clicked as it shut behind me. I shouldn't have doubted my security system.

"She's fine. She's gone to bed." I tried to smile it off. "It happens to the best of us."

They laughed, as they wanted to. It was too late to be getting all serious. Then I noticed Savor at the bar.

It was a nasty shock, since I hadn't sensed the demon's arrival. But Savor had a very light signature; a slight humming in the back of my throat and a mouthwatering sensation. I hadn't noticed it in the clash between Shock's and Petrify's signatures. Now Petrify's signature was rapidly fading away.

Savor was wearing one of his male personas—a man who went by the name Sebastian. He was short and slender, in his mid-twenties with black, artfully spiked hair over his prim face. But that knowing smirk and sarcastic drawl were enough to put anyone in his place.

Savor was leaning over the bar, holding out a chocolate for Lolita. She tried to take it from him, but he pulled it back, chiding, "No, you'll nibble at it like a squirrel, like you always do. You have to eat the whole thing to get exactly the right burst of flavor."

Lolita opened her lips obediently, ready for anything. Savor delicately popped the chocolate onto her tongue. Her eyes widened with delight as she bit into it and chewed.

Savor stroked the back of her hand, soaking up her pleasure at the taste. Bright yellow eddies of delight swirled around their skin where he touched her. I knew it would taste as sweet as that chocolate.

I stomped over. "What kind of poison are you feeding my bartender, Sebastian?"

"It's good." Lolita slurped as she tried to swallow and speak at the same time.

Savor raised one brow at me. "See, she likes it." His hand was still resting on hers, absorbing her enjoyment.

I grabbed a towel to wipe the bar, moving it between them so they had to let go. Lolita rolled her eyes at me, then grinned at Savor. She sauntered off to the other end of the bar where Boymeat was laughing at her, having watched the entire thing go down.

I was going to have to say something to her. I had tried to avoid it, knowing that Lo wouldn't take kindly to my interference. But Savor was getting out of hand. This was my territory, my people. I didn't like his coming in here and feeding off them.

But I had no choice. Savor worked for Vex, just as I did.

I followed Lolita to where we could speak alone. Lo's voice lowered so no one could hear. "What's with Jamie?"

Shock's current persona was "Jamie Shoquille," so her nickname could be Shock. Everyone called her that, including her workmates. But Lolita had gotten into the habit of calling her Jamie because it got Shock's attention. Shock was so emotionally distant that Lo had made a game of trying to loosen her up.

"She's not hurt. She was scared more than anything." I touched Lolita's arm to reassure her. I absorbed hardly more than the waste cast off from her radiant energy, her worry about Shock, about me, and the residual pleasure from eating the chocolate Savor had given her. Thankfully, there wasn't anything special she was feeling for Savor.

At my reassurance, a jolt of relief quickly flowed through her. Unable to resist, I took a tiny bit, like a sip of pure delight; it satisfied me like nothing else could.

It made me feel like a filthy parasite, like Savor. He was watching us, glancing down pointedly at my hand. He probably thought I was marking my territory in front of him. I pulled away as if I'd been burned.

"Poor thing," Lo said. "Is she staying here tonight?"

"Definitely. If you see her, don't let her leave."

Lolita rubbed my shoulder comfortingly. "Are you sure you don't want to report this, Allay? This guy who did it— he could hurt someone else."

I had to force the lie through my lips. "It was a misunderstanding with a patient at work. They'll handle it."

"That doesn't sound good."

Now I was going to have to cover myself. "Don't tell her I told you. You know how Shock is about her personal stuff."

"It runs in the family." Lo gave me a quick squeeze.

I refrained from soaking up more relief from my friend. It was bad enough that I was lying to her; I didn't have to steal her emotions, too. "Sorry," I muttered reflexively. "It's been a rough night."

"You can go back upstairs to your sister. I'll take care of closing." Lo knew I didn't like to be pressed when I was upset, so she turned to start cleaning the shelf under the rows of liquor bottles behind the bar.

I didn't want to go back upstairs. I was revved up on the supercharged demon energy I had taken from Petrify. "No, thanks. I should let her rest."

I set off like a golf cart with an eight-cylinder engine, moving faster and burning brighter with power than ever before. I felt like I was high—on top of the world, and whatever I did was right and good.

It was probably mistaken for nervous energy as I wiped down tables, picking up some stray glasses and settling the chairs back in place. The bar would be clearing out soon enough. I calculated every move to bring me in contact with the patrons. I touched their arms as I bid them good night, gave them little nudges along with my quips, and was big on leaning into people as I took their order.

I didn't really need to feed, but a surprising number weren't happy despite their outward cheer. I lingered with them, reasoning that it was better to absorb a little bit of their negative emotions since that offered them some relief. Some customers came back night after night without understanding they came because I made them feel better.

Like most demons, I could feed on any emotion. For the dump truck loads of shit I had to absorb, I got to taste only a few drops of ease. But I would do anything to create those precious drops. So rather than an altruist, as too many called me, I was a hypocrite at heart, seeing only the comfort they found with me and not what I took. It was selfish in the extreme. And I could never forget it.

That was what made me a demon.

All the while, I avoided Savor. He was the only demon, other than Shock, allowed in my bar. I was Vex's bagman, and Savor was his messenger; Savor's job was to drop off the discreet envelopes of payola that I passed on to local, state, and sometimes even federal officials. The enormous Prophet's Arena would never have been built in Brooklyn right on the East River if the church hadn't paid off the commissioner of the planning and zoning board. His driver still picked up an envelope on the first of every month.

Vex's empire was his religion, the Fellowship of Truth. He'd started it right after World War II, posing as the first and now-dead prophet of a philosophy that was more libertarian than spiritual. The current prophet was Dread, Vex's firstborn and most loyal demon—they had been working together since the fifth century. Without the draconian personal restrictions that Vex's older religions had tried to impose on people, the Fellowship was growing at a respectable rate. Believers emphasized personal responsibility over everything else, and judgment by none. The church's ultimate carrot was the promise of immortality gained through individual perfection. The fact that none of their followers had attained such a state didn't matter—the promise of it seemed enough to inspire hundreds of thousands to join the Fellowship.

I knew the other side of the church, the one that had no qualms about subverting laws and blackmailing people to get whatever Vex wanted.

I wasn't proud of what I did. I hated it. But it was the price I paid for Vex's protection. After I came to the city and took my job at the Den on C, the demon attacks subsided to a manageable trickle when I gained his support. As the head of his line, he had more power than anyone in the demon world other than Glory, both of whom had been born from the ancient demon, Bedlam. Through Vex's influence, I was mostly left alone. I was human enough to be grateful for that.

So I stayed at the Den. A savvy owner would have closed it long ago and transformed it into something more profitable. But Michael Horowitz was my benefactor, the most important person I had ever won over with my demon persuasion. Michael gave me the use of the apartment upstairs and the freedom to do whatever I wanted with the bar, as long as I managed everything. It was one of a number of real estate investments he owned, while he managed many more. He wasn't like other business people I dealt with— Michael cared about me. Aside from work, he made sure I was doing okay, and he bustled in like a doting gay daddy to fix anything I needed.

Most things I was able to take care of myself. I regularly had to cajole city authorities into allowing the rickety old building to remain open, and once I'd resorted to asking Vex to pay for necessary restorations to be done on the facade rather than letting the building be condemned.

I'd thought about asking Vex for money to buy the bar from Michael, but it would put me even more in his debt, and besides, I couldn't reconcile myself to being a permanent blight on the community. Even with Vex's protection, demons were drawn to my hybrid energy. But when they couldn't get to me, they ended up preying on my neighbors instead. It was the reason for the high crime rate in the area. Gentrification had moved in from every direction, but within the radius of a few blocks, my territory still contained too many closed and empty shops. Thanks to me, it was one of the last pits of decrepitude in Manhattan.

After the bar closed in the wee hours, I usually spent the rest of the night inside my apartment. If the other demons knew I rarely went out, then there was no reason to hang around.

That was the price I paid for living the illusion of being human. I could give up the act and stop endangering the people I lived among; I could leave my friends and the bar, and isolate myself, just as I had given up my family for their own good. I could become a wanderer so nobody would suffer because of me.

But what sort of life was that? I wasn't that big a person. I needed my home and my people. So I sacrificed my demon-self instead. At least, I tried to. I avoided demons, except for Shock.

This included avoiding Savor when I could. He was looking up into the long mirror hanging over the bar, watching me with an amused expression. I usually didn't have to talk to him to do my job; he deposited the envelopes of dirty money through the mail slot into the foyer of my apartment.

But Savor seemed to take a perverse joy in forcing me to treat him like an ordinary patron.

I went behind the bar and pulled down the crystal bottle filled with an emerald liqueur. I found a large brandy snifter and filled it almost a third of the way. "Sebastian, you aren't drinking. I know how much you love this."

"Sorry, I don't have any money." He patted his pockets blandly. "I'll have to pass."

"I insist. It's on the house. For bringing Lo chocolate."

Next to him, old Jose muttered something about bringing candy for booze next time. Savor stalled; he didn't want the drink. It burned energy for demons to process food or liquids, and was a real drain on the system. "That's not the glass it's supposed to be served in. You're ruining the bouquet," he protested.

I picked up the snifter and poured the contents into several shot glasses, filling them to the brim. "How's that, Mr. Silver-spoon-up-his-ass?"

Savor grinned and passed two of the shot glasses to the guys. Old Jose knocked it back in one swig, then grimaced at the sticky-thick consistency. Savor sipped his. "Hmmm ... lovely. Is this a celebration in honor of the recent birth?"

Thankfully Lolita was in the cooler and couldn't hear him. I leaned forward. "You felt it?"

"I was coming off the bridge and I felt it. You should be careful, Allay. A blast of energy like that is like sirens calling the hounds home. I wouldn't be surprised if you see a few more of our people hanging around tonight. You'd be better off taking Shock home and getting out of here."

I snorted. "As if I were going to take advice from you. Shock is safe upstairs, and that's where she's staying."

Savor shrugged. "Do what you want. I'm only trying to help."

"Why would you help me?"

He pursed his lips as if he were giving me a mock kiss. "We're on the same side, you silly child."

"You mean demons versus humanity? In case you hadn't noticed, I'm on the side of the humans."

"Ha-ha. No, I mean the whole Vex versus Glory drama."

"That has nothing to do with me."

"You think? Because from where I sit, you're quite the prize for Vex. He's got the only human-demon hybrid alive in his tight little grip."

That irritated me. As if I were his pet guinea pig. "I work for him, just like you do. And whether I like it or not, I'm a sixth-generation Vex demon. I'm part of his line."

"Unlike me," Savor added, so I wouldn't have to. Savor was the only demon alive who didn't know who his progenitor was. Two hundred years ago, moments after he had been born, his progenitor had shoved him overboard into the Indian Ocean. He wasn't even sure what kind of ship it was, but it was moving so fast that by the time he recovered, he couldn't sense his progenitor's signature. The shock had distorted his memories, so he didn't have much to work from, and he was reckoned damaged by all the other demons. None of them had stepped forward to claim him, so he was a free agent. It was only recently that he had begun working for Vex. I almost envied him his freedom—almost.

"At least I know what it means to be a Vex demon, though you obviously don't," Savor added.

"Don't I?" I gestured bitterly to the inner door that separated the bar from the foyer and staircase, where undoubtedly Savor had deposited a packet of money for me to pass on.

He waved that away. "Oh, that's Dread's stuff. He's the businessman; he handles the administrivia. Vex doesn't care about Manhattan real estate and privacy laws. Vex is busy stirring up wars and making enemies on a much larger scale than you can imagine."

"So I'm only a penny-ante accomplice. Not a true minion of evil. I guess I can live with that."

For a moment, something flashed deep in his eyes, a frustration that he couldn't voice. Then it was gone. "Don't sell yourself short, sweetheart. Nobody expected you to live this long, you know. Not only are possessed humans more unstable than new demons, but you've got that amazing taste." He touched the back of my hand so quickly that I couldn't move away in time. "Succulent, delectable, not demon and not human, but the best of both, distilling the essence of each into one fragrant bouquet. How can we resist it?"

"That's it." I picked up his mostly full shot glass of liqueur and poured it into the sink. "You're cut off."

Lolita emerged from the cooler in time to hear me. "Allay! Stop picking on Sebastian. He's not drunk." Her glance took in the old man who was leaning on the bar with his head nearly touching the scarred mahogany. He was definitely drunk. "Time to go home, Jose. Your wife is waiting for you."

Savor got up to leave, taking the hint for a change. Lolita sounded apologetic as she bid him good-bye and thanked him for the bite of chocolate. "There's more where that came from," Savor promised. His slinky walk was effete as he headed out the door and gave us both a flip of his hand in farewell. Lo was epicurean in her tastes, sampling all kinds of people, including the occasional woman. But the one time when Savor had asked her out—to my shocked annoyance—I'd been relieved when she had laughed it off as a joke.

I barely waited until he was gone, unable to contain myself. "Lolita, don't encourage him. You can't trust him."

"You say that, but you never say why. I like Sebastian. If he asks me out again, I'm going to go."

"Lo, you shouldn't go near him. He's a wily, slimy little bastard."

She considered it, as she considered everything. "I . . . don't think so. I think he's sweet. And a little lonely."

It was true that Lo's intuition was almost as good as a demon's. I didn't know anyone who was better at assessing people so quickly.

But I couldn't begin to tell her the truth about how wrong she was about dating a demon. If she had sex with him, he could accidentally suck off too much of her emotion and leave her a slobbering mess. Was I going to have to get tough with Savor? If I had to, I would. I would do whatever it took to keep him away from my people.

3

I was completely frazzled by the prospect of Lo dating Savor. It ruined whatever enjoyment I had left in the demon energy I had stolen from Petrify.

Forget that Savor was just using Lo to get to me—there was no such thing as love when it came to demons and humans. How could there be love when everything was a lie?

Nobody knew me, so I was lonely in spite of the people I surrounded myself with. I wanted a partner to share things with, to struggle with, to learn and grow with.

But it was impossible.

So having Savor come around here and seduce my bartender was too much for me to handle. It pushed my buttons in a very personal way.

I washed the glasses roughly, thinking of what I could say or do to Savor that would make him back off.

I was so distracted and my senses were so overwhelmed by Shock's buzzing signature overhead that I didn't feel Pique approaching until he was very close. He was brandnew, and had been around only a few weeks, but already I hated Pique's irritating signature—a grating, grinding sensation in my bones that rubbed me raw. It was even worse than his unwashed smell.

Last weekend Pique had targeted a green kid from Iowa who came to the Den. When his friends left as he unsuccessfully tried to pick up a girl, he had to walk home alone. I left the bar to Lolita's care and followed them. I didn't like the guy, who was too frat-boy privileged for his own good, but he'd been drinking at my bar, so he was my responsibility.

I had to provoke Pique to get him off the kid, and he'd taken the lure and chased after me, leaving his victim woozy but undamaged by his assault. Pique would have sucked him dry and left him for dead if I hadn't stopped him.

Pique had chased me through the city that night, catching my trail after I lost him again and again. I finally jumped on a subway train heading south and managed to fool him into getting onto a different train. Our eyes had met as my train pulled out, leaving him behind, and I knew he hadn't given up the chase.

As I hurried over to the window, Pique appeared around the corner across the avenue heading uptown. A line of traffic passed between us; then I saw him again in the shadows, leaning against the metal shutter rolled down over the front of the hairdresser's across the street. He stared intently back at me.

He must have felt Petrify's birth. I shouldn't have been surprised that he, a born vulture, was the first to arrive, sniffing after fresh meat. Pique looked innocuous enough; too puffy, too pale, with a round, doughy face and an old-fashioned haircut. Behind thick-lensed glasses, he sniveled as if from allergies, and his long shorts hung awkwardly from his hips. His sneakers were huge.

Pique might look like a harmless computer geek to everyone else, but I'd seen the truth when he came after me. He was so frenzied that night that he'd ripped my shirt trying to get hold of me to steal my energy.

I had used the Aikido techniques I had perfected to deflect, disengage, and find his leverage points to unbalance him. Then I ran. I was very good at running—and healing. Pique broke my arm that night, but I didn't care whether he broke my arms and both legs; I would run home, anyway. Pain didn't matter when I could repair myself later.

Pique would certainly go after a new demon like Petrify while he was vulnerable in his newly minted, nearly drained state. He might even try to go after Shock.

I glared across the street at Pique, clenching the towel. I wanted to confront him and drive the beast away. Who did he think he was coming into my territory and hurting my people? With the energy I'd taken from Petrify coursing through me, I felt as if I could beat him. It felt right to try.

Pique pushed his glasses up firmly, as if he were making a decision. He waited for several taxis to pass by, then started across the street. Some guy shouted after Pique, shaking his fist in the air. That was Pique, pissing off people everywhere he went.

"Trouble, Lo!" I called over my shoulder, hurrying to the door. I put my hands on the worn jambs.

Pique came straight toward me, apparently not concerned about anyone else. This was exactly why I worked for Vex: so he would keep demons away from me.

"You can't come in. You're not welcome at the Den," I said loudly enough for the patrons inside and some passersby on the sidewalk to hear. They were walking toward the bright lights of Houston and barely noticed the argument. One guy quickened his steps to get out of the way.

Pique's head was hanging slightly and he peered at me through his Coke-bottle glasses, making his eyes seem larger and more protruding. I hoped Petrify wouldn't be such a nasty demon as Pique, but if he was, it was my fault for being so frightened during his birth and imprinting that fear on him.

Pique kept coming forward.

I shouted over my shoulder, "Lo, call 911."

The police couldn't stop a demon, but they could certainly help run interference. Surely Pique had enough sense of self-preservation that he wouldn't reveal his true nature.

I stepped forward out of his line of attack, moving away

from the door and to one side, the classic Aikido defense. As he tried to close the distance, I lightly pushed down his outstretched wrist with both hands. He resisted, stepping back as I took another step forward. Spinning in a full circle, I brought his hand up again, twisting it around into an armlock. With the slightest pressure, I pushed him down on his back away from the door of the bar.

I'm sure it looked easy, but it took good judgment and timing to do Aikido right. Demons usually went for the brute-force approach. We were stronger and faster, maybe because it didn't matter if we ripped up our bodies. We might appear to have the organs and bones and digestive system of a human, but we were really a three-dimensional copy, like solid ephemera.

As Pique grabbed at me again, I turned slightly and deflected his arm away from me. Then, fueled by all that demon energy I had stolen, I took a step closer and punched him in the face three times, flattening his nose.

A human would have dropped down to the ground, but Pique took it with hardly a shake of his head.

Aikido moves technically weren't supposed to include offensive maneuvers. I couldn't have punched him if he hadn't been attacking me. Yet my punches left me open when, instead of going down, Pique grabbed my wrist and his fingers sank in.

He had me. He was pure determination, wanting only to steal my energy—and the demon essence at my core.

I'd been too cocky and caught off guard when my punches hadn't flattened him. As I was a creature of pure will, shock at my own stupidity made me vulnerable. My shields slipped.

He started ruthlessly sucking up my emotions.

I could barely breathe because of his pungent stench. It was truly amazing how dirty a person could get in the city in only a few weeks. I figured Pique used his smell to bother people. It bothered me.

I launched myself at his head, diving over him. He toppled backward, rolling onto the sidewalk as we both went sprawling. But his hold on me didn't break. He instantly repaired his nose, ignoring the wet blood on his upper lip and chin.

If I were a human, I would have been drained within minutes, a husk left to rot from within. But even with all of Petrify's energy, I had little more time than that to fight him off.

Lolita appeared in the doorway, her voice higher and faster as she cried into her cell phone, "He's attacking her! You have to get here fast!" I heard her give the address.

Pique didn't try to fight back as I kicked him, struggling against his one-handed grip. He kept spinning as I grabbed the back of his hand and tried to twist it away. Lo dived into the fray and flailed her fists, hitting Pique squarely in the chin. But his only concern was hanging on to me so he could continue to drain me.

I should have retreated upstairs and called 911 the second Pique moved toward the bar. I had installed a reinforced steel door on my apartment for exactly that reason.

Now I wished I hadn't sent Savor packing. There was at least a fifty-fifty chance he would have helped me.

My aura was flashing luridly as I tried to resist Pique, with my first red flush of anger shifting to a frightful orange. I was going down in flames. What if I couldn't last long enough for the police to pry him off me?

Would he really consume my essence and make me go up in a puff of smoke in front of all these witnesses?

It appeared that he would. I could just imagine the *New York Post* headline: BARTENDER SPONTANEOUSLY COMBUSTS ON LOWER EAST SIDE.

"You're a psychopath, You can't do this," I hissed at him, desperate to break through. Pique didn't respond. He never spoke. I wasn't sure whether he could.

From the midst of the crowd that was gathering around

us, a man stepped forward. He bent over me, reaching for Pique as Lo tumbled away again.

I caught sight of his angry expression; he was a dark-haired man, of mixed Mediterranean heritage. I figured he was in his mid-thirties. I had never seen him before, but he looked like the kind of tough guy who had lived in this neighborhood his entire life, long before the hipster boutiques and cafés arrived.

He broke Pique's hold on me with a savage twist. I could feel the power behind his grip. "Let go of her."

It sounded like both bones in Pique's wrist broke. He screamed, more in frustration than pain.

Released, I scrambled backward, trying to gather the shreds of my shields around me. I ended up pressed up against the worn wooden paneling on the front of the bar. Lolita was sitting dazed on the curb, her curly hair standing on end and her lipstick smudged. She looked more angry than hurt.

A few of the patrons were hanging out the open front windows above me, shouting encouragement to our savior. The tall, dark-haired man with big muscles had managed to subdue a demon, something I'd never seen before.

He clearly radiated possessive pride, determined to keep his neighborhood clean. I could feel it even from a few feet away. He smiled slowly, cracking his knuckles. Still, there were no sirens. "You gonna do something about it?" he asked Pique.

Pique glanced around at the audience gathering on the street and finally came to his senses. He sniffled at the remnants of blood running out of his nose, luridly painting his mouth and chin red. Then he leaped up with surprising agility, and darted off.

I was about to sigh in relief, but the neighborhood hero took off after him. "No, don't," I called after him. "Let him go!"

At the corner, the guy grabbed Pique and they spun out of sight. Sirens finally sounded in the distance.

I had trouble standing up, but Lolita joined me, supporting me. Her alarm and flushed feeling of victory poured
into me; I was grateful for the sustenance. Pique had taken
everything I had stolen from Petrify—and more.

I rubbed my arm where it was swollen and bruised from
the tightness of Pique's grip. He had latched on so fast. He
had almost killed me right there on the street in front of
everyone. One mistake, and my life had almost ended.

*If that man hadn't broken Pique's hold, I would be dead
right now.*

I swayed, pulling away from Lolita to run to the corner.
What if Pique was draining him?

Lo wasn't the kind of girl who hung back. She caught up
with me in a few steps. "Watch the bar," I ordered.

"Boymeat's got it."

I nodded, knowing he could be trusted. So we rounded
the corner together. The sirens were getting louder.

"Where are they?" Lo asked.

I strained to see, but in truth I dreaded what we would
find. Third Street was much darker and narrower than Avenue C, with the trees blocking the intermittent streetlights.
Lo squinted her eyes, searching down the sidewalk, but I
could feel Pique's signature fading away; he was near Avenue B at the other end of the block. He would soon be out
of range.

My shoulders sagged in relief. Pique was leaving.

A slight scuffing drew my attention to the stairway down
to the Chinese restaurant. The tiny window was dark, and
the door was shuttered under the stoop that led to the apartments on the upper floors. I almost dismissed it as some
drunk peeing down there again. But the shape was wrong.

"Is someone there?" It definitely wasn't a demon. There
was no signature.

"No problem," came a deep if rather breathless voice.
"Nothing to worry about."

My eyes widened at Lo. "That's the guy."

"You think?" Lo asked.

"That's his voice."

I ran down the steps. In the shadows at the bottom was the man who had forced Pique to let go of me. He was sprawled uncomfortably in the tiny space, his head leaning back against the wall. The smell of burned peanut oil and ammonia made me wince.

"What happened?" I touched the leg he had braced against the bottom step. Despite the canvas dungarees, his pain blossomed out at me. But he was quite good at controlling his response to it, grimacing rather than crying out loud as he shifted.

"I fell down the steps. Like a dumbshit." He pushed himself up. His leg moved away from my hand as he drew his feet under him.

"Don't stand up!" I tried to keep him down. "You must have hit your head."

He touched his hairline; blood glistened on his fingertips. "Yeah, once or twice."

"You should have let him go."

"You're welcome."

I realized how ungrateful I sounded. "Thanks for helping me. Who are you? I haven't seen you around here before."

"Theo Ram," he said, wincing.

The sirens were right on top of us. Lo called down helpfully, "The police are here."

"Great." We sighed together, in decidedly uneager tones. I gave Theo Ram a harder look. "What? You don't want to deal with the cops?"

"Not particularly. I want to go home and forget about this."

I took hold of his arm to help him, since he was determined to stand up. He tried to shrug me off, but I needed to know what he felt. He wasn't panicked, like a criminal would be. He was angry at himself, humiliated by his fall, and hurt far beyond what he intended to admit.

It was a heady brew. Pique had siphoned off so much from me that I really needed the energy, but this guy was particularly tasty—irresistible. He was hurt and needed help.

I responded like a flower to the sun; I wanted to make him feel better so that his relief poured into me, filling me as if nothing else mattered. Then I could have blessed peace, if only for a moment.

"Thank *you* . . ." I tried to remember to breathe.

He gave me an odd look. "Anyone would have done it."

My hand tightened, helping him up the steps despite his protest that he could do it. I soaked up as much of his potent emotion as I could, in all decency, allow myself to take, but it felt as if I could hardly hurt him; there were deep wells of feeling in this man. I was glad Pique hadn't gotten hold of him.

The police car finally pulled up, blaring with lights and noise. The cops saw the curious onlookers at the corner and the gesturing patrons leaning out the windows of the bar, and came straight to the corner to meet us.

Theo squared his shoulders and faced the inevitable. I wasn't scared of cops—I knew what the police wanted. As long as you were polite, cooperative, and honest, they would go away quickly. At least I had two out of three going for me. It wasn't my fault that I would never be able to be fully honest with anyone again.

I handed over my driver's license and told the police that an obnoxious guy had caused a disruption last week in the Den. When I refused him entry tonight, he had grabbed my arm. I showed them, having faded the bruises thanks to my savior's energy, leaving my arm only reddened.

Theo patted his pockets when the cops requested his ID, but his wallet was gone, making him swear under his breath. Lots of demons were thieves, living off the spoils of their victims. I had seen Pique rifling through a backpack the other day.

In response to their questions, Theo said he lived up on Tenth Street and Avenue D, across from the Jacob Riis Houses. He didn't have an accent, like most people born and raised in Manhattan. He said he drove a cab, and the cops gave the first sign of interest when he said he didn't work for a company, that he drove his dad's car under his medallion, reciting the number absently.

I felt bad about the grief the poor guy was going through. But I had the presence of mind to move us down the street so we stood in front of the bar. If any other demons showed up, I could get upstairs quickly.

Lo handed over Pique's glasses, which she'd found on the street, and confirmed what had happened; then she went in to close down the bar with Boymeat's help. I described Pique for the cops and agreed to come to the station house and look at pictures tomorrow morning. It set a good example for the community to report crime, and it let the other demons know that I would use the legal system against them whenever I could.

"Looks like we should call an ambulance for Mr. Ram," one cop said.

Theo raised his hand slightly. "Nope, I just need some shut-eye."

The black cop handed over a thick square of gauze to press on his bloody forehead. "I'd drop by the emergency room if I were you. That was some set of stairs you fell down."

"I'm okay," Theo insisted, holding the pad firmly to his head.

By the light streaming out of the bar, I got my first good look at the man who had saved me. His strong-boned face and dark curling hair made him look Greek or Italian, with startling gray eyes fringed by black lashes. His hair would have been gorgeous if it was longer, flowing like the statues at the Met. He was a bit weather-beaten and worn beyond the events of the evening, as if he were used to working hard. I liked his steady gaze—as did the cops, clearly—and his frank way of speaking.

All I could think about was touching him again.

It was quite the surprise. It wasn't just a desire to feed on him. I was attracted to him. I thought that part of me had dried up and blown away a long time ago.

When the cops kept insisting despite his refusals, I offered, "Come inside. My sister is an EMT. She'll make sure you don't need stitches on that cut."

"Who's your sister?" the black cop asked.

"Jamie Shoquille."

"I know Shoquille," the cop said. "Shorter than you, with platinum blond hair?"

I smiled and nodded brightly. "She's here now."

The cop rewarded me by urging Ram, "You should let her sister take a look. I don't like releasing you when you're still bleeding like that."

Theo tried straightening up again, but something was clearly wrong with him. The gauze pad was getting redder. Faced with a long wait at the emergency room or a quick look-see upstairs, he had little choice.

"Sure, if that's what it takes," he agreed.

The cops gave me the police report with the case number on it, reminding me to come in tomorrow to see if my assailant's records were in their files. Theo also got a report number for his stolen wallet.

Theo was limping as we headed into the bar. I held the door open, then shut and locked it behind him. Lolita had ushered everyone out, so there was nobody left but Boymeat. They were both out in the backyard spraying down the plastic honeycomb mats. All I could hear was Boymeat's voice, probably bitching about some girl who had just broken up with him even though he already had another one waiting at home for him.

"Wait." I left Theo leaning against a table near the door to my place. Running across the room, I slid behind the bar to fetch the enormous first aid kit that Shock had given me in case one of my patrons had an accident. Untying my black apron, I left it folded by the cash register for tomorrow.

Lo appeared in the doorway and saw Theo. "What's he doing here?"

I gestured vaguely in his direction. "He's hurt. I'm taking him upstairs so Shock can take care of him."

Lo stepped closer and lowered her voice. "Are you sure that's a good idea?"

"You don't trust him?" I wanted some alone time with this guy so bad that I almost didn't care whether he *was* dangerous. That was one of the benefits of being possessed; no man could make me do anything I didn't want to. I was too strong, and if worse came to worst, I could drain a man of his emotions until he could hardly move.

Lolita was clearly swayed by his heroics, but she hesitated. "Shock may not want to see a guy right now, not after what happened tonight."

"Are you kidding?" I held up the big red case. "This is exactly what Shock needs to take her mind off things. Believe me, I know."

But I wasn't telling the whole truth, and Lo knew something was up. I gave her a quick, one-armed hug. "Don't worry, Lo. It will do us both some good."

I couldn't tell my friend that this poor wounded man had exactly what I needed—he was in pain and I could comfort him. I longed to touch him, to take his suffering away and feel the deep peace that came when hurt and care were left behind. If I could feel that way even for an instant, then everything would be all right.

I was a junkie in need of my fix. I had almost killed and been killed today. I deserved this midnight snack, and I was going to take it. After all, I wasn't going to hurt the guy. He would come out of it feeling great. I could sense what a man needed, and I gave it to him. *You want space; I can give you space. You want to be touched; I can touch you.* Most men were fairly simpl? that way. If you gave them exactly what they wanted, without their having to say a word, they fell in love with you. Not that I wanted anyone to fall in love with me; I just wanted to please this succulent man for a little while so I could get what I needed.

I'd gotten good at striking these kinds of bargains between my human and demon self. At least that was what I told myself—again and again.

"Okay, I'll lock up when we leave," Lo agreed. "If he does anything, you yell for me. We'll stay for a while and have a beer."

I normally would have heeded Lolita's warning, but nothing was going to keep me from diving into these deep waters. She didn't know that I couldn't be hurt, not in the usual ways. "Thanks, Lo, I owe you one."

But as I returned to Theo's side, the sight of the reddened gauze now self-sticking to the wound on his forehead bothered me. His steady gaze was also a bit unnerving. I was taking advantage of him, no matter how much I gave back in return. I almost repented and ordered him to leave.

"I think I do need some help," Theo said.

He was sagging, so I put his arm over my shoulder and held on to him around his waist. That did it. The manly smell of him was sublime, solid, and real. In one touch, I knew he felt vulnerable in a way he hadn't felt in a long time.

"Come on," I murmured, unable to resist him. I was going to have this man, even if only a taste, before I let him go.

4

When I unlocked the door that led from the bar into my foyer, the first thing I saw was the narrow manila envelope lying on the cracked tile floor. Savor must have slipped it through the slot in the front door while he was here.

Shit. I forgot about that.

Well, that was what this guy was for: to make me forget about everything. *Seems to be working so far.*

Steadying Theo with one hand, I swiped the envelope off the floor, tucking it into the back waistband of my jeans. He noticed, but didn't say anything. I could have left it lying there, given the two industrial-grade steel doors on the ground floor protecting my apartment. But I wasn't willing to take any risks with thousands of dollars. I didn't know how much it was, and I didn't care. I never liked being responsible for it.

As we turned to go up the stairs, Theo tried not to lean on me too hard, but he was hobbled by his hurt leg. Clutching the first aid kit in my other hand, I slowly went step by step. He grabbed on to the railing and helped pull us up. His cheek was nearly resting on my hair, and I thought he took a deep breath of it. We were snug against each other from hip to shoulder. He had the body of a working man in his prime, lean and hard under my hands. To my surprise, that spurt of all-too-human desire hit me again. It reminded me of things I had left behind. . . .

I opened the vaultlike upper door to my apartment and helped him inside. Theo gave the double steel door a surprised look.

"Some people seem to think I'm rich," I explained. Kicking the door closed behind me, I shot the bolts with two quick turns of my wrist. "Shock? We have company."

I helped him over to one of the vinyl chairs, and he leaned with a sigh against the generously curved back. Then I went to the archway that separated the two rooms. Shock was lying on the sofa, her eyes hooded.

I ran forward. "Shock! Are you all right?"

Shock muttered irritably, rolling away. For a second, I was afraid she was dying. But one touch revealed that she still had plenty of energy left after birthing Petrify. Shaking her gently, I tried to get a coherent word from her. But she appeared to be unconscious.

She was in the stupor that immediately followed fissioning. I had heard of the danger—another demon could steal your essence without a struggle while you were in a stupor and your shields were down.

Yet Shock trusted me enough to stay here. I patted her hand, slipping her a bit of my love.

"Is everything okay?" Theo called from the kitchen.

"It's fine. Much better now." I quickly stashed the thick envelope in the drawer of the table at the head of the sofa. It had code words written on the front. "My sister's had a hard night."

He appeared in the archway. "What happened?"

I didn't want to lie to him. "She'll be fine. She just needs to rest." I rejoined him in the kitchen and firmly led him past the bathroom to the bedroom in the back.

A pillow was lying on the rug and the chaise was pulled into the middle of the room, where I had left it after letting Petrify out the window. I decided to pretend that was where everything belonged.

Guiding Theo toward the chaise, I righted the lamp that

had been overturned on the small table and switched it on. An overstuffed chair sat in the corner between groaning bookshelves, and a daybed lined with pillows was against the far wall. The three windows had seats built in, with more bookcases underneath.

Theo winced as he sat down on the chaise. He pulled up one leg of his khaki pants, carefully feeling the tender area on his knee. "Not a scratch. Just strained it, I guess." He groaned as he tried to flex it.

"Lie back." I opened the kit on the low table and dug about, so eager to feed off this luscious man that I didn't even feel guilty. That would come later, in its own due time.

I couldn't help myself. When I was very low, it was impossible to resist the need to feed. I kept myself that way too much. Shock often complained about the feebleness of my aura. She once told me she wanted to shove a plump, angry guy at me and order, "Eat!"

But I had no choice. I was already too tempting for hungry demons. Look what happened when I revved up my reserves—Pique went for me in my own bar. If I stuffed myself, I'd start attracting demons from the Midwest instead of from just the eastern seaboard.

I pulled out a couple of wet wipes. "I need to clean the blood off your face to be sure that big cut is the only one."

He reached out to take the wet wipes. "Here, let me." He carefully cleaned all around the gauze patch on his forehead, then down to his cheeks and jaw, wiping up the blood.

I gently pushed him back until he relaxed on the cushions. The lamp cast a warm light as I leaned over him, examining his face minutely. From the stubble on his cheeks and chin, I guessed he had shaved yesterday morning.

"No other cuts." I took his chin and tilted his face to the other side. I soaked up his weariness and took the edge off the throbbing purple pain. It was rich and juicy, making my mouth water.

Theo closed his eyes, implicitly giving me permission to touch him. I turned to the kit again. "I'll have to take off that gauze to clean the cut."

He opened his eyes. "It's stopped bleeding; just leave it."

"I have to clean it or it'll get infected. And the scab will stick to the gauze."

"I don't want it to start bleeding again."

"Stop being a baby. I have butterfly bandages. That's what you should close it with or you'll get a bad scar." I pushed back his hair to examine the gauze. I felt his irritation, along with the deeper hues of pain. This guy wasn't used to taking orders or lying around on a chaise. I could feel a driving energy that powered those deep emotions. "The cut goes into your hairline on the upper edge. I'll try to do this gently."

He gave in reluctantly. Using a cotton ball soaked in water, I wet the edges and slowly peeled back the gauze and cleaned the wound.

To keep him distracted, I asked, "What's it like being a cabbie?"

His brows drew together at the question, then stopped at the tug of pain from his forehead. "About what you'd expect—dealing with traffic and too many people."

"There aren't many independent cabbies left in the city. Your father must be one of those genuine old-timers who's seen it all."

For the first time a ghost of a smile appeared. "You said it. I used to drive around with him after school, and I sometimes think *I* saw it all before I was twelve. But there're always surprises."

"So you grew up in the city?"

"Right here in this neighborhood. My parents moved to a house in Middle Village when my sisters were still in high school, but I kept the old apartment on Tenth Street. Pop still drives in the mornings, and I take the late shift. I was just coming home from dropping off the cab when I saw that guy attacking you."

The J train that went into Queens was down several blocks on Delancey. "That's a long walk."

"I don't mind. It's better for the neighborhood."

I silently agreed; if Alphabet City had easier access to subways, the poor people would have been displaced a long time ago. "Brace yourself for the peroxide," I warned him.

I sucked in my breath in sympathy as the peroxide sizzled and stung his forehead. The twinges were lessening every time I touched him, as I absorbed his pain. To me, it was a feast.

When the cut was thoroughly cleaned, I dabbed it dry and applied several butterfly bandages to keep the edges together. He raised his hand to feel it, but I brushed him away. "Don't get it dirty."

I went to get a hand mirror and gave it to him. "Thanks," he said as he looked at his forehead. There was a rounded purplish bump with a two-inch gash in the middle. It looked bad, but if he didn't have a concussion, it should heal fine.

"Do you have a headache?" I asked, putting away the supplies.

"Not at all, strangely enough. I guess I'm lucky." Sighing, he lay back on the chaise and closed his eyes again.

There was music coming from downstairs where Lolita and Boymeat were hanging out. I figured I should go join them and let the poor guy sleep, since that was what he needed.

"Here's a cushion for behind your back." I brought over a soft, round pillow, but he had trouble sitting up. "Your ribs are hurt. Why didn't you say something?"

He winced as he lay back with the pillow in place. "It's no big deal."

"Let me see." I pushed up his T-shirt, my palms brushing against his stomach.

He tensed, and our eyes met. He felt vulnerable. It resonated more intensely than anything else I had felt from him.

I sank to my knees, instinctively putting my head lower than his, making myself less of a threat. My hand rested on the tightened muscles of his stomach. "Let me see," I repeated softly.

All of his defenses were raised, but he took a deep breath and relaxed back as I told him to. I slowly slid his T-shirt up his chest. Where my hands grazed his left side, shooting pain cut through him. I skimmed off the worst of it, dulling the throbbing as I absorbed the radiating energy. I stole only a feathery brush of his relief.

"You've got a bad bruise here." My finger outlined the blue and purpling flesh. "I should probably tape your rib cage."

I got out the wide tape and helped him sit up so I could wind it around his middle. He had tight abs and a strong chest, toned through years of manual labor, softening only slightly with age. His shoulders weren't overbound by muscle—he had the smooth movements of a runner rather than a weight lifter—but his biceps bunched thick when he bent his arms. There was a dusting of dark hair between his pecs and much lower down, below his belly button.

He kept glancing into my eyes, which still had the flecked green and brown irises I was born with. Most demons would have turned them into a striking green, and they would have made their skin smoother and their breasts larger or smaller. Though I had tried to remain faithful to my human form, it was inevitable that I had perfected myself in hundreds of small ways—sculpting my body and face into what I wanted to see. But I didn't want to be a parody of myself. I wanted to be myself, as impossible as that was, so I kept my eyes their human color.

As I cut the tape and smoothed down the end, Theo reached out to touch the wisps of dark hair against my cheek.

Surprised, I looked up at him.

"You're being really nice to me," he said. "You don't even know me."

"You saved my life tonight."

He smiled. "That's a fish story—it gets bigger with the telling. That guy wouldn't have done much more than knock you around." His hand brushed my arm where I had left the bruises unhealed. "Are you hurt?"

"No, not at all." I glanced away. "Don't mind me. I'm always a fool for the big gesture. I guess it's my one and only romantic streak."

"I'm sure you have others."

I shrugged, feeling as if I had taken advantage of him enough. It was depressing that a stranger had saved my life, and I couldn't even convince him of that. "Do you want to rest here for a while? Or would you be more comfortable on the daybed?"

"This is fine."

"Is there somebody I should call to let them know you're all right?"

"No, nobody's expecting me."

I arched a brow. Why didn't this lovely hunk of a man have a wife or at least a girlfriend waiting for him? "Nobody at home?"

"No," he insisted.

I almost pressed him, wanting to understand. But he was resistant, tensing up after all my hard work to relax him. I owed him his privacy, at the very least.

I reached over and turned off the light shining in his face. That left us in the comfortable shadows cast by the small lamp next to the daybed. The tiny shade was mostly gold, the color of happiness.

I went to his feet and began unlacing his worn leather shoes. Theo reached out to stop me. "Don't; they're so dirty."

"You think I can't handle a little dirt? I work in a bar."

The corner of my mouth twisted up as I drew off his left shoe. Then I unlaced the right one, taking my time, like a mock striptease, pulling the bow untied.

He laughed weakly. "Making fun of me?"

"Not really." As I pulled off his shoe, I let my finger slide over his bare ankle, diving deep into his emotions, as I asked, "Hasn't a girl ever undressed you before?"

His instant response washed over me; a wave of pure passion. He was suddenly raring to go, even as banged up as he was, practically pumping out testosterone as the driving, aggressive engine that powered him shifted into high gear.

So that was why he didn't have a woman waiting at home for him. He was the kind of guy who'd probably had hundreds, maybe even thousands of women. He wasn't likely to settle down with one girl and start doting on babies, not when he was out driving around in a smorgasbord every day.

"Is that what you're doing? Undressing me?" His invitation was clear.

Without thinking, I shot back, "Are you offering me the chance to be another notch on your belt?"

He jerked back, as if I had punctured the air out of him. I had ripped off the soothing facade he used to protect himself and had said the truth out loud. It wasn't a nice thing to do. It made people feel bad when they had to face their own shit.

I was supposed to be making him feel good. I owed him that for taking his energy.

Apologetically, I settled a chenille blanket over him, then knelt down to check on his head wound. I smoothed the creases in his forehead, stroking back his hair. I didn't take any of his emotions; I just wanted to touch him. I wanted it to be pure, without any taint.

Without warning, I felt his confusion and despair flooding out. I couldn't help sensing it, even though I tried not to feed. Such terrible pain. It seemed everything hard and ugly and cruel had been his to bear.

A silent cry of agony rose inside of him. He hated his weakness; he struggled against everything he felt. But for a moment he truly felt alive again, even if it was too much.

"It's all right," I murmured, stroking his hair. "It'll be all right. . . ."

He turned, taking my hand in his so he could kiss my palm. His lips were hot against my skin. "You don't know that."

I was reeling. "I know you're not a bad man. I can tell, believe me."

My hand trembled, trapped between his palm and his lips. Theo spilled his relief into me, his eyes burning.

Like a molten river of gold, the precious feeling filled me up, the combination of his urgent need for absolution and the comfort he found in my touch. I wondered how this poor man could have erred so badly to need such solace. He didn't know what true evil was—how could he, when he didn't know about demons?

I cupped his warm cheek in my hand. His skin was hot and moist against mine, so human and alive. After I had been possessed, my flesh had perceptibly cooled. I was drawn to him like a snake basking on a sunlit rock. The image was repellent but true nonetheless. I was a dark creature living on the fringes of existence.

Yet here and now, I felt human again. I savored each slow kiss he left on my palm, one after another. His satisfaction sent pulses of delight through me, awakening my body.

It had been too long.

I hesitated, wanting to be sure before I leaped. But I had nothing to lose—nothing left to lose.

Leaning forward, I kissed him, wanting to feel his lips against mine. I sank my hand in his thick black hair, the ends curling around my fingers. His lips were full and firm as he kissed me slowly, savoring my plump lower lip and licking the tip of my tongue.

His fingers grazed my cheek, running along the hollow. His other hand went around my back, pulling me in closer until I was leaning into him, one hand against his hard chest.

I was as giddy as a teenager, back when I was kissing my boyfriend for hours on the beach, when everything lay ahead of us. Nothing had been so monumental as our budding love and fierce attraction for each other. He had been my first lover, though the reality of our short relationship hadn't turned out nearly as wonderfully as the illusion I had created on the beach.

A little illusion can be good for the soul....

I wanted the feeling of wonder and promise that a man's touch could give me. In this man's arms, I could be a girl again.

I didn't have to deal with the consequences. There wouldn't be any. This guy would be off and running come tomorrow morning. I could have him here and now, and not have to deal with anything else. I was capable, even ready, for so much more. But the lies involved made it impossible.

So that left me with this.

"Hmmm ... ," I murmured, relaxing against his chest as we kissed.

As if he had been waiting for that signal, Theo pulled me up onto the chaise, so I lay with him, our legs intertwining. His hands ran down my sides, curving in at my waist, then down to my hips. He pulled me into him, against the rigid shaft that lay against his belly.

My eyes opened wide—he was raging hard already. His torrent of passion was emerald green, the true color of fertility and desire. His need burned my fingers, but his lazy mouth and gentle caresses were under strict control, as if he didn't want to scare me with his urgency.

I flung myself into him, losing myself as he bucked up

against me, his teeth biting down on my lip. I moaned, my hands pressing his shoulders to hold myself away from his chest, not wanting to hurt his damaged ribs. But he ran his arm up my back and pulled me close to him. It caused a flare of pain and I soaked it up. There was so much more desire and need inside of him that it seemed insignificant.

"I must have you," he whispered into my mouth.

I almost came at his words, spiraling into bliss. Nothing else mattered but him; his hot fingers tugging my T-shirt over my head; his calloused hand against my breast, squeezing the nipple until I gasped, then dropping lower to my belly. I cringed, instinctively protecting my core, but I didn't want to stop him. For a moment it didn't matter that this wasn't really my flesh, that it was a simulation of what I used to be.

Most men told me that I was beautiful, but Theo didn't. He seduced me with a touch.

He unfastened the buttons of my jeans, pulling them so they softly popped apart. His hand ran underneath the denim, burning across my tender skin. I raised myself up so I could slide them down, rolling away to kick free my legs. I helped him pull off his T-shirt, stopping him from raising his arms because of the tape around his chest.

Then he unzipped his pants, and his cock strained from the dark hair at his groin, reaching to his belly button. I couldn't help myself; my hand brushed over the deep cut of the muscles above his hip, then down his heavy thigh as I pulled off his pants, my fingers coming within a hairbreadth of the shaft. He moaned.

Theo drew me down to lie against him, our bodies rubbing from our chests to our bare feet. His gaze went down to my right shoulder, to my tattoo. It was an ouroborus, a stylized circle. It wasn't obvious at first, but if you looked carefully, you could see it was a snake eating its own tail. The tattoo was inked on the front of my shoulder, only a couple inches across. I could have created it there myself, but I had gone to a real artist not long after I had arrived in New York and got it burned into my skin. It belonged to the human part of me.

He gently kissed the tattoo as his hands pulled my thighs open against him. He rubbed himself against me, making my energy pulse in a different way, grounding me in my body even as I couldn't help but feed, as his emotions poured over me.

Just rubbing against each other felt better than I had imagined, far more intense, sweeping me away in a flood of sensation as every nerve fired off. I still felt his need, but an animal urgency of my own was taking over. I rocked with him, matching his rhythm.

"I don't know if I can control myself." His head arched back as he tried to loosen his grip, to slow down.

I bent and kissed his chest, licking the salty sweat from the hollow at his throat. He buried his face in my neck as the tip of his cock pressed against me, barely entering me. He pushed in slightly, enough for me to feel how thick he was, making me cry out wordlessly as he teased me into opening for him. Like rich, crumbling earth, like deep, still waters, it cut to my very essence.

"Do you want it?" he murmured.

"Oh, yes . . ."

He pushed into me as I sank down on him, letting him fill me. I was so ready for him, that with his second thrust he buried himself to the hilt. I forgot everything—Shock in the next room, Pique attacking me—and writhed in abandon. All I cared about was moving against him, his strong hands bracing me as he steadily pumped into me.

Nothing else mattered but the feeling of being satiated, filled to my depths, fired with exhilaration as I'd never felt before.

I let go as I climaxed, my orgasm shattering all perception. All I felt was power, a roaring column of power that I rode on, shooting into the heavens.

When I returned to myself, I was panting, collapsed on
Theo's chest. A low laugh started to build inside, making
me shake until I finally laughed out loud, limp yet strangely
energized.

He was breathing hard, too, and was sheened with sweat.
I usually never perspired, not unless I drank something and
was struggling to expel it. But now my skin was moistened
and flush.

And just like that, I remembered that I was lying to him.
Every second I pretended to be human was a lie. Guiltily, I
remembered how the power rushed into me as I came. That
had never happened before. I hoped I hadn't hurt him.

I raised my head, examining him anxiously. He looked
spent, but it had been a long night for him. He was smiling
slightly.

For a moment I thought he would kiss me, but he tucked
a wisp of hair behind my ear. He was still inside of me, as
deeply as he could be, looking into my eyes.

Suddenly it was too close, too intimate, given that I
didn't even know him. This was why casual sex was crazy;
you found yourself in the most vulnerable and revealing
moments with a stranger, a blank slate. But that also made
it intoxicating. . . . He was exactly what I needed him to be.

Too bad it was over.

5

By the time I disentangled myself from Theo, he was asleep.
I covered him with the blanket and backed out of the room.
I liked watching his face, with that slight smile of content-
ment. He looked younger now.

But I couldn't sit there all night watching him and day-
dreaming about love. Only needy codependent psychos did
that with a guy they had just met—or rather, needy codependent *human* psychos.

So I grabbed a change of clothes and went to the front
room to check on Shock. She was the same, out cold but
with her eyes weirdly half open. Her aura was not as strong
as usual, and her shields were clearly down. I kept telling
myself that she would be fine tomorrow.

I settled in an easy chair across from her with a book
in my hand, but I couldn't read. My entire body still tingled. When I shifted, rubbing my thighs together, it sent a
zing right to my core. Everything, including Theo's terrible
need, inspiring such urgency that he had to have me, was
exactly what I'd needed. His face, his hands, those heavenly
abs with a hint of extra flesh over his hips, just like a man
should be . . . *yum.*

Everything had felt bigger and more intense; my feelings, my response . . . I had never felt that way before. My
lust had been like a bolt of lightning, searing everything
else from my mind.

Maybe it was because he had saved my life. Maybe it was because I had been so close to killing Petrify. Despite all the energy I had consumed, I still felt a deep, burning need inside that said my time was running out. It was as if I were desperately grabbing for what I could get. I had forgotten the constant struggle to live, and for a moment simply lived.

It had been sublime, worth every second of grief that would follow when I couldn't have him again.

I had fed off him; it ruined everything. Even if he was capable of it, I couldn't have a real relationship with him. Better to say good-bye now and still have the memory of us. I thought about it all night, and that was the only conclusion I could come to.

When the night was over, I was still sitting there with a book dangling from one hand, torturing myself with flashes of what could have been—and worrying about what to do next. I had almost killed Petrify. I had really wanted to. I needed to take another demon in order to survive. But I couldn't. That was a problem I'd have to solve sooner rather than later.

Eventually the sky brightened with the dawn, and soon afterward the buzzer sounded, ending my little masochistic game. Theo groaned and shifted on the chaise as I peeked into the shadowy bedroom. But he didn't wake up.

I punched the button to the speaker. "Yes? Who is it?"

"Delivery from Dag's," replied a scratchy voice.

I pushed the button again. "I'll be right there."

I had already changed into a tank top with a white flowered skirt. I slipped on a pair of red flip-flops and left the door cracked open, ready to return on the fly if need be. I was worried that Shock might wake up disoriented and feed off Theo. I wanted to be able to hear him if he called out for help.

Eddie, the delivery guy from the grocery store, was waiting patiently at the door to my foyer. He carried two big boxes of bagels inside as I unlocked the door into the bar. I couldn't let him into the bar directly because the metal shutter was down, covering the windows and wooden front door. It made the interior of the bar darker than usual, but a pretty, dappled light shone through the rear windows, casting shadows on the pool table. I didn't bother to turn on the overhead lights.

Eddie set the two boxes down on the bar, talking in his slow, slightly monotone way about the nice weather. His parents had moved here from Guatemala when his older brother was a baby, and he now was the tallest in the family. It was his pride, as he'd declared dozens of times.

Twice he carefully counted the money I gave him. I snagged five dollars from my tip jar and handed it over, telling him, as I always did, "This is for you and your family."

"Thank you, Miss Allay." He was one of the few humans other than Lo who said it the demon way, A-lay instead of Al-ly. "I'll see you next week."

I got the bagels every weekend and gave them away for free in the afternoon with a Bloody Mary. I had started the slightly twisted tradition when I first came to the bar.

Eddie stopped to give Snowplow his obligatory pet. Unlike Lolita, Snowplow had no loyalty—he indiscriminately loved everyone, except demons, who walked into the bar. He patronized me when there was no alternative, unless I happened to be busy wrestling with a keg or arguing with a salesman, and then he suddenly had to have pets from me *now*. I indulged him because nothing could radiate pleasure quite like that cat when he was petted exactly when and where he needed it.

I walked Eddie back through the bar, touching his shoulder as I mentioned that he should check out the tulips across the street, sipping the sunshiny glow of his response. Eddie loved flowers.

From the foyer, I opened the steel-reinforced front door to let him out. The sounds of passing cars and people talking were growing louder as the morning brightened. A dozen sparrows flew from the sidewalk into the tree in front of the bar as Eddie returned to his van. They had been eating some crumbs he had dropped on the curb. I stood watching as Eddie got into the van and the birds flew back down to peck at the dirty concrete. The house sparrows were tiny, brown-striped birds, much like the wild tabby cats who roamed everywhere in the city.

But my enjoyment of the fresh morning was shattered when I caught sight of a man across the street. Tall, lanky, and handsome in a haggard sort of way, Phil Anchor was a one-time famous journalist who had come to fetch his payola. He was wearing an old leather jacket paired with expensive leather shoes, as usual.

The fat envelope I had stashed upstairs must belong to him. He would give me the code words and I was supposed to hand it over to him. Phil wasn't the first guy who'd come to my bar to fetch dirty money, but he was the most enduring. Most cheaters and scam artists sent messengers to the bar, but Phil always came himself.

Phil ran to the center of the street and stopped awkwardly to let a car go by before crossing all the way. His smile, showing off his straight, white teeth, was boyishly charming, despite his being in his late forties,.

But then his gaze slid off mine, maybe because I stopped smiling, abruptly reminded of the real world. In the bright light of day, his hair was lank and greasy, and his pale skin seemed dried and leathery. His neck was also wrinkled, showing his age. That must bother him. He'd always been vain about his looks, relying on women throwing themselves at him.

When I first met Phil, there had been an instant spark of attraction. But sanity required that we keep our hands off each other. He was working for Vex, like I was, and he was even more deeply compromised because of his prominent, public position. I don't know how much of a temptation

I had been to him—I'm sure it was some—but now I was glad we hadn't been intimate. As the years went by, he had grown bitter.

"You look gorgeous, gorgeous," he rasped, holding up his hand to block the mellow morning light. "I lost my sunglasses last night. Could you let me in?"

"You look like shit, Phil," I said honestly. "Been up all night?"

He shrugged as I let him into the foyer. I'd left the door to the bar still open, and he ducked inside, sniffing. "It's been a tough one. I could use a drink, if you don't mind."

"Sure, help yourself. I'll be right back."

I ran up the creaking stairs to my apartment. Peering into the darkened bedroom, I could see that Theo had rolled over, dropping the blanket to the floor. He was still asleep, and I decided not to bother him by replacing it.

A quick glance showed Shock was the same. I grabbed the envelope and checked the code words. Tucking it into my back waistband, underneath my tank top, I went downstairs.

Phil was downing what appeared to be his second shot of whiskey, my best brand. He was standing behind the bar as if he owned the place. That cockiness had suited him when he was on his way up. I wondered if he ever admitted to himself that he was now in a terminal dive.

I didn't know how Phil felt, because I never fed from him. He avoided even the slightest touch. I wasn't sure whether it was because he didn't want to cross the line between us, or whether he was that way with everyone. But his aloofness, and the mystery of what he was feeling, had made him particularly intriguing back in the day.

"You should take a rest between binges," I reminded him. Cocaine had once been an accessory of his affluence, but now I was afraid it was getting to be the most important thing to him.

"I'll sleep later. I have to finish a story."

"For the *Times*?"

He grimaced. "No, the *Post* again."

I shouldn't have asked. "At least it isn't *AM New York*." That was the free paper they left in stacks in the subways and on the street corners.

"They just bought my piece on alternate-side parking." He looked at the bottle as if debating whether to have another shot.

I slid it away from him. I couldn't have another repeat of the day he passed out when he came to get his bribe money. I'd had to roll him under the pool table to sleep it off. That wasn't good for patron morale.

His blue eyes were dull without the sheer force of will that made them sparkle. "Your boss is the devil himself. I don't know how you live with yourself."

"Whoa." I held up both hands. "Don't blame me. I'm just the post office. You can pick up your checks in Brooklyn, if you'd rather hike over the bridge."

"Maybe I should."

That stung. "What's wrong with you, Phil? I've never done anything to you."

He glared back at me, making me nervous. Phil relied on being charming; it was his main weapon. But there was something ugly in his tone and the way he faced me—fueled by the whiff of desperation.

My fingers braced against the worn leather of the barstool as I readied to defend myself. I had never been scared of Phil before; it had never occurred to me. Some of the guys I had to deal with were intimidating. But not my old flirt-friend, Phil.

"Have a little pride," I told him, using the word "pride" that was my half of the code that had been written on the envelope of cash. "Let's get this over with."

"I forgot the code words." His hand scrubbed at the stubble on his chin.

I sharpened my eyesight and saw there was a lot more gray in his beard than before. Desperate and deteriorating—it was not a good combination. "Then we don't have anything to talk about. You know the rules, Phil. Your drinks are on the house—"

His hand slammed down on the bar. "Just give it to me!"

The cats took off like shots, skittering around the corner and back into the storage room. My shoulders hunched until the din died down. It was at times like this I was glad I was a demon. He didn't know who he was dealing with. Even if he was in a drug rage, I could survive anything he did to me, though it might really hurt.

But when he took his hand away, there was a USB storage device lying on the bar. It had an orange tip and was about the size of my finger.

"There. My life's blood, my future trussed up on a stick for your prophet. Your man of God. The biggest hypocrite of the Holy Rollers with their prostitutes and gay boys who don't have the guts to be honest about themselves." His voice was rough as if he were about to cry, and he kept raking his hand through his greasy hair. "You don't know what I had to do to get that. I swear, if I saw him now . . ."

I had to know if he was telling the truth. What if the USB device was blank, and Phil was shaking me down for drug money? Then again, how would he even have known I had a packet of money waiting for someone?

I patted his hand, saying, "I understand exactly how you feel." He pulled away, as I expected, but not before I sampled a good surge of his emotions—anger, frustration, humiliation, and the endless need to fill that empty hole inside of him. He didn't want to give me what was on that USB storage device, but he felt forced into a corner. He thought he had to do it.

I scooped it up and pulled out the envelope of money. He glanced down at the code words written on the front. "Yeah, right. You say 'pride' and I was supposed to say 'organic.' How could I forget that?"

I lifted my shoulder in a half shrug. "It happens."

The whole thing was so sad and sick, with the smell of him stronger now that he was burning with adrenaline—like booze and sweat.

"Come on, I'll let you out." I walked him through the side door into the foyer.

He didn't stop until his hand was on the front door. His gaze dropped to my ouroborus tattoo. "I haven't seen that in a while."

I suddenly remembered Theo slowly kissing the circle on my shoulder. A wash of residual pleasure shot through me.

"You haven't been around," I managed to say. I used to see Phil every month, but now he came only a few times a year. "Maybe that's a good thing."

Revving up a smile, he said, "Sure. That's better than admitting I'm next to useless." His words fell flat, and he knew it.

"Don't worry, we're both in the same boat." I felt sorry for him, but there was nothing I could do to help. He wouldn't let me make him feel better. He never would.

I bolted the door behind him and closed the one that led into the bar. There was no sound from above. Theo was up there, sprawled out on my chaise, ripe for the picking. If only I could go upstairs and pull him onto the daybed for a proper lovemaking session, nice and slow this time, to forget all this for a little while longer . . .

If only . . .

I ran up the steps and pushed open the door. The light streaked through the front windows, looking exactly the same, but the door hit something.

Pushing harder, I saw Theo's legs sprawled on my kitchen floor. He was naked, wearing only the white bandage around his ribs.

6

"Theo!" Kneeling next to him, I gave him a slight shake. He didn't respond, lolling unconscious.

"Shock?" I hurried into the front room. Shock's foot was resting on the floor, but she was still out of it. "Shock! What happened?"

I hated to think the worst—that Shock had hurt Theo. But it was hard not to. I shook Shock a lot harder than I'd shaken Theo. "Tell me, Shock! What did you do?"

Blinking languidly, Shock mumbled, "Huh?"

"Shock, what happened?"

"Demon. . . ." Her fingers flexed.

Her nails had blood on them.

I stood straight up, every sense alert. "Demon? Here? I don't feel a demon."

Shock slumped back into her stupor. I rubbed her fingers, and the blood came off on my own hand. It had the distinct scent of demon, as if it were slightly fermented. Shock's aura was also weak, much weaker than before.

My heart was pounding as I ran back and closed the door, locking it. I checked all the windows, and saw the gates were intact. I even looked in the closets and under the daybed, just to be sure. But nothing was out of place.

Where did it go? How did it get in? The front door was supposed to lock automatically when it shut. Maybe someone had been standing nearby as I let Phil inside. I hadn't stepped outside; anyone could have been huddled in the doorway to my neighbor's house or in one of the cars at the curb. If a demon was quick, it could have caught the door before it closed.

"Phil . . . ," I said out loud.

Phil could have let the demon inside. I couldn't remember if I heard the bolt click behind him as he went into the bar. I ran up the stairs so fast to get the money. He could have waited until I went inside my apartment and let a demon inside. I couldn't figure out how a demon could get upstairs without my seeing it, but Phil had been standing behind the bar, making me keep my back to the door.

Why would Phil do it? For the money? That was the obvious reason, since the man didn't appear to have any loyalty. Phil had been waiting outside for me to open up. He might have come across a demon drawn here by Petrify's birth. The demon bribed him, like everyone bribed Phil, to let it inside my bar. That would explain why Phil had been so aggressive toward me—he felt guilty.

As he should! Phil didn't know how close he had come to death himself, dealing with evil like that.

Whoever the demon was, after it fed from Shock, it must have snuck back downstairs and let itself out, while I was inside the bar talking to Phil. Shock wasn't shielded, so it would have taken only a few minutes.

Any longer, and Shock would be dead. I was almost sick to my stomach at the thought of Phil trying to take another drink. If I hadn't stopped him and kicked him out . . .

The most frightening part was that I hadn't felt a signature. Shock's signature was so invasive that as the hours had passed, I had basically shut down my ability to sense it rather than go mad. But even when I was actively trying to sense around Shock's signature, it was difficult— like yesterday, when Savor came to the bar without my knowing it.

Regardless, it was my fault for being so careless, when I knew Petrify's birth had painted a huge target on us.

I returned to the kitchen to kneel down next to Theo. Checking his pulse, I found it strong and steady. He was fine—it appeared the demon hadn't taken any of his energy. Shock had been the target.

"Theo? Are you okay?" I stroked his cheek, and only then noticed a huge red knot on his cheekbone. A black streak smeared under his eye, the beginnings of a black eye. "Oh, no . . ."

Theo licked his lips, groaning. Anxiously watching him, I felt awful. *How could I let this happen?*

Most men would have been uncomfortable waking up naked on the floor in front of a woman. But Theo smiled up at me as he opened his eyes, and for a moment I remembered how it felt to have him inside of me. I was the one who blushed and glanced away.

Then he winced and put his hand to his cheek. "Who was that guy? Please don't tell me it was your boyfriend."

"Of course not." I waved that off. "What happened?"

He rolled onto his side, shaking his head slightly to clear it. Propped up on his elbow, he looked even better than flat on his back, as the muscles in his chest and arms flexed. His penis was heavy even when relaxed, lying on his thigh. He had dark curls at his groin, and a dark line of hair down the middle of his chest, but otherwise his dusky flesh was smooth.

I forced my gaze away. *This isn't the time for that.*

"I was going to the bathroom, but the front door was open," Theo explained. "I heard voices down below. Then this guy burst in and punched me." He gingerly touched his cheek. "That's all I remember."

"Was it the same man from last night? The one you pulled off me?"

He frowned at her. "No, this guy was darker, with black hair. Latino, maybe."

It could have been Pique, but in a different guise. I wasn't used to being on full alert in my own home. I didn't like it.

"You didn't see him?" Theo asked.

"No. I was busy with the delivery guy." I didn't want to go into who Phil was.

"I hope you don't mind my saying this," Theo said kindly, "but from the looks of things around here, you need some muscle. Don't you have someone watching out for you?"

"I can take care of myself."

His admiration was clear. "I bet you can." He shifted his eyes down to his taped chest. "But it seems to me that people are getting hurt."

I swallowed. "I'm doing the best I can."

He touched my knee through the thin cotton of my skirt. "You can ask for help."

"Ask who? You?" I met his eyes. "Why—are you a part-time bodyguard?"

He seemed surprised. "I have been. But I'm not sure if I'm what you need. . . ."

It was an awkward moment, and suddenly I wasn't comfortable with his being naked on my floor. He must have gotten the same feeling, because he gave me an apologetic grin as he got up.

I left him to get dressed as I checked on Shock. She didn't rouse this time. I clasped her hand and focused my fear and confusion into her. It was just the sort of feeling that Shock loved.

I shuddered at the sight of blood under her nails. Another few minutes and Shock would have died.

As Theo washed up in the bathroom, I fed Shock. She never opened her eyes or said another word. When Theo reappeared, I gently detached my hand from hers and met him in the kitchen.

"How's your sister?" he asked.

"Not as improved as I'd like. But she'll survive."

He made a faint attempt at a smile, as if he didn't

know what to say to that. The streak under his eye was darkening.

"I'm really sorry." I wasn't going to lie to him and say I had no idea who hit him. Actually I had some ideas, and all of them involved demons. "Thank you for helping me last night."

"That sounds like good-bye." He sounded disappointed.

My shoulder lifted. His gaze stopped on my tattoo, but again he didn't ask me about it. Instead, he said, "I'd like to see you again."

I couldn't stop looking at his black eye and the huge cut on his forehead. It didn't matter what I wanted; I couldn't keep using him as a human shield against demons. "We both know, for our own reasons, why this was a one-night stand."

I could tell I was right because he had to look away, in a rare moment of discomfort.

The silence stretched out until I started to feel uncomfortable. "You can always stop by and have a drink on the house," I offered.

"I don't drink anymore."

"Ah, that's why I've never seen you before."

It was cold, awkward, but I couldn't help it. I was too upset by the thought of a demon sneaking past me. It was time for him to go—he was a distraction.

Theo wasn't being very warm and inviting, either. But on top of all of his intimacy and avoidance issues, a punch in the face could do that to a guy.

I went to the front door. "I'll let you out."

He gave one last glance around my place, then followed me into the stairwell. I pulled the door shut and listened for the bolt click. As I went down the stairs, I concentrated as hard as I could through Shock's now-weakened signature, but I couldn't sense any other demons.

I opened the bottom door and stood propping it with

one foot. There were a number of people sauntering past on the sidewalk, heading to Sunday brunch with friends, running errands, out for a holiday. Still no sign of any demons. I hoped Theo would get home safely.

He paused on the stoop. "Are you going to the police station to check mug shots this morning?"

"I'm supposed to." I didn't add that it wasn't likely. I was too spooked to leave the bar. "Are you?"

Theo nodded. He leaned over, and I tensed. But he kissed my forehead, touching mostly my tousled hair with his lips. "Take care, Allay."

I was surprised that he said it correctly. He must have heard Lolita last night. "You, too."

He gave me a shy smile, then headed off. I watched him until he turned the corner. For some reason, I didn't want to go inside and close the door. It felt as if it would be the ending of something that had barely gotten started. Thwarted dreams—that was my life.

That, and danger.

I closed the door and made sure it locked. With fear skittering at my feet, I ran upstairs to my apartment. Only when the door was shut behind me did I feel safe.

And empty.

I rejoined Shock and sat down on the edge of the sofa. After all these years, I shouldn't feel sad. But there was no getting around it.

I'm not fit to love a man like him. Not fit to love a man, period.

I laced my fingers with Shock's. She didn't rouse, but I felt the slight drawing sensation as she consumed my sorrow.

I lay down on my side, facing her. Her head was propped on the same cushion. Her face and body were smoothed out, with none of the fine details she usually gave her guise. Her porcelain skin suited her apparent youth, but right now she looked unfinished, like a doll in the making.

"I'm sorry," I whispered, holding Shock close and pouring my love and concern into her.

Eventually, I had nothing left to feed her. I sighed and gently untangled our fingers. Shock didn't resist, but she shifted and tried to open her eyes, murmuring something. I stroked her short blond hair, bending close and whispering, "You'll be all right, Shock. I'm going downstairs to open up the bar. I'll be right back."

Shock's aura was stronger now, and mine was much weaker. I needed to feed. And it was time to get to work. I hoped Shock would wake up soon.

I pulled away from her reluctantly, my white-flowered skirt flaring out. Then I quickly searched my place again, being more thorough this time. Paranoid, sure, but I relied on being able to sense demons before they got close to me. I had to be more vigilant from now on.

Pepe arrived not long after I raised the metal shutter halfway up. He ducked to get under and opened the front door of the bar. It was made of old wood that matched the cherry panels on the front, with carved leaves and flowers on the lower sections. It didn't matter if the door was weak, because the metal shutter protected the entire front of the bar when it was down.

"*Cómo está?*" I asked.

"*Bien, bien.*" Pepe was a stolid, middle-aged man with four kids and a wife in Bushwick. He worked a couple hours a day doing the heavy cleaning in the bar and any odd jobs that I needed. He was also the super of his building and several others in Brooklyn. He was as reliable as a metronome, and several years ago I had given him the key to the padlock on the shutter in case he needed to come early to clean.

On the blackboard, Boymeat had written the afternoon special—*Bagel Free with Bloody Mary*—and illustrated it with a grinning cartoon queen holding a bagel. Below it Lo had written, *Drain in backyard clogged.*

"Pepe," I called into the back where he was getting the broom, "do you have time to snake the drain in the backyard?"

"*Sí*, no problem." He emerged with the push broom, as I started picking up the chairs and overturning them onto the tables. We went through the ordinary morning bar prep, as I filled the ice bin and updated the inventory sheet while Pepe mopped up, then went out back and ran a metal snake through the drain. In the spring it got clogged with flowers falling from the neighbor's tree, and in the fall it got clogged with berries. The debris landed on the concrete and got washed into the drain no matter how much I kept it swept. But I loved that tree—it hung so gracefully over my yard and was the first thing I saw through my back windows.

Everything should have felt normal, but it didn't—not after last night. I kept running upstairs to check on Shock, but she was always fine. But despite that, the slow-burning hunger in my core was a reminder enough of everything that had happened, unsettling me.

So when my daytime bartender came in, frowning in spite of his iPod earbuds, I was glad I wouldn't have to try to be cheerful for him. Darryl was an intense young man who took college courses at Hunter in the mornings and worked until seven p.m. at the bar. I put on my tiny black apron and helped out with the prep work of cutting up lemons and limes.

Darryl was quickly followed by a stream of sleepy-eyed people with laptops under their arms or in their backpacks. Almost all of them ordered the special, but a few just drank coffee. I guess they liked my bar better than the chrome-and-glass-walled Starbucks on Avenue B. Ever since I had gotten wireless Internet service, the afternoon crowd had tripled.

I worked the room. At the back corner table, I rested my hand on the shoulder of a regular called Clem as I asked, "Another Mary?"

He shook his head, feeling a brief flash of guilt for taking a table while he wasn't paying for drinks. But I didn't mind that he was one of many who nursed a drink for two hours. I needed to have lots of people around so I could feed. "In a few minutes," he promised, absorbed in reading his e-mail. He felt excited, defensive, and aggressive. I sucked it in—not my favorite brew, but potent enough.

I moved on to an angry college-aged girl who was so absorbed in the article she was reading online that she didn't hear my question until I touched her. She was repulsed and fascinated, a sharp pungent mixture. I craned to see the title of the story—it had something to do with PETA.

The two tables at the front were taken by couples reading the Sunday *Times*, one gay and one straight. At the straight table, the man was mulling over an article in the real estate section; his wife jealously obsessed about something while she pretended to read about Fiji in the travel section. The gay couple were tired and a little bored, trying to figure out where they were going to eat.

Old Mrs. Marquez was in her usual spot, eating a bagel and cream cheese with her vodka on the rocks; a special—hold the tomato juice. I didn't mind the black hairs on her lip or the way the skin on her neck waggled. She was a remarkably contented woman, and her energy was just the pick-me-up that I needed. I kept circling around to rub her rounded back, soaking up her simple pleasure.

It was an all-you-can-eat demon buffet, and I went back for seconds.

I worked my way through the room until I returned to Darryl, who was leaning over the bar, asking a patron with a laptop to search Craigslist for roommates-wanted posts. I went behind the bar to serve drinks while he was busy with that. I couldn't blame him. From what I'd seen, finding a livable place was one of the hardest challenges in the city. I would rather worry about his problems than my own.

When Darryl was done e-mailing responses to a few of

the ads, I asked him to watch the bar while I went up to check on Shock. She was still out cold, but it was barely twelve hours since she had fissioned. I couldn't remember how long the stupor was supposed to last, but it couldn't be more than a day. Her aura looked strong, so I didn't feed her again. I left a note by the sofa telling her to come down-stairs when she woke up. I would feel much better when she was awake and able to shield herself.

As I walked back down into the bar, I felt the first tingles in the back of my throat, announcing Savor's approach. My hand went to my pocket as I remembered the USB device. It was still there. Savor must be coming to fetch it.

At least I felt him coming this time.

Darryl called me over. "Do you mind if I run down to Stanton Street to see an apartment? It's only two blocks away. It sounds like a good one."

I wanted to talk to Savor without his overhearing, any-way. "Yeah, but get back here quick, okay?"

He ran out, much more enthusiastically than when he'd come in to work. In the doorway, he paused to let Savor in. Savor was wearing yet another new guise; a woman this time, with smooth, dark skin and intricately braided hair that ended in beads swinging against her shoulders. Savor's personas were usually skinny, almost emaciated, and this one was no different. Her clothing was basic Old Navy in subdued colors.

Savor met my eyes with a saucy grin. I had to smile. She changed personas like some people changed their clothes.

"You almost look glad to see me," Savor said quietly as she sat down at the bar.

"I'm marveling at your creativity. You reinvent yourself so much, I sometimes wonder if you know who you are."

Savor smiled, and in her eyes I could see Sebastian and some of her other favorite personas. Yet her flirty expres-sion was entirely feminine. "It's easy for me. I'm the one on the inside."

"You just keep the rest of us on our toes." I broke off to fix two more Bloody Marys and open a couple of beers. Savor read her paper and sipped the shorted beer I poured for her.

When I returned to her end of the bar, I lowered my voice. "I had trouble last night after you left. And a demon sneaked inside this morning and attacked Shock. I didn't feel his signature. I think he came in the front door while Phil was here."

If I had any doubt that Savor knew about the attack on Shock, it was gone in the deeply interested flash in her eyes. "What happened to Shock?"

"She's okay. She's still sleeping off the birth. The demon only got to her for a few minutes, but it was enough to make a real dent in her aura."

Savor pressed her lips together, humming to herself. I'd clearly given her something to think about.

"You know something," I realized. "If it has to do with Shock, you'd better tell me."

"It's not about Shock, specifically. Everyone knows about it, including her. The only one who might not know is you, Allay. You keep yourself in such a bubble. You really should make more friends. Among demons, I mean."

"You mean this has happened before?"

"Many times. Haven't you heard about the mystery deaths? There're more and more all the time. They say that thousands of years ago, one or two demons would disappear every century. But in the past decade alone, there have been nine unexplained disappearances. Usually it happens in a demon's first year or even earlier. But Malaise disappeared last fall. She was more than seven hundred years old. She was living in Rikers Island, stirring up trouble among the prisoners. Then suddenly she was gone."

"Do you think it's some kind of natural phenomenon? How could a demon's energy just drain on its own?"

Savor gave a slow shrug. "At one time, that was the

general opinion. That demons can become unstable some-how and spontaneously implode. But no one's ever seen it happen."

"So it must be another demon doing it. As far as I can tell, you all prey on one another like flesh-eating bacteria."

"Don't be crude—"

I turned away to serve a patron, and checked on every-one at the bar. I didn't want to fight with Savor. I had to find out what she knew. "You were saying?" I asked when I returned to her end of the bar.

Savor let out her breath in a huff. "Do you really want to hear this?"

"Like my life depends on it."

She thought I was teasing her, but I was serious. I waited until she finally gave in. "Statistically twice as many Vex demons have disappeared, so Dread thinks Glory's behind it."

"Glory? Why would she care about new demons? She's . . . she's . . . like Madonna. Hasn't she got bigger things to worry about?" Glory lived for sensation, passions, and excess. She followed the peaks of society, unerringly choosing the hottest city in the most exciting country of the time, reveling in luxury and the arts. She had moved her entourage to Harlem right before I arrived and had profited immensely from the real estate boom in that part of the city.

"Vex agrees with you. He thinks it's absurd that Glory would break their détente by killing demons in his line. Much less her own. But the rising number of disappear-ances is becoming a problem. Especially since Malaise went *poof*. She was a major Glory demon, part of her inner circle."

"So who does Vex think it is?"

Savor smirked. "Everyone knows, that's the best part. Vex thinks *Dread* is behind the deaths. His own second-in-command. He figures Dread is killing off the competition within his own line. Vex even questioned a few of us who do odd jobs for Dread, to find out if we knew anything about it. Dread was humiliated when the word went around." Savor broke off to laugh, a sharp bark of appreciation for the joke.

"I'm sure Dread doesn't think it's funny."

Savor gave me the most condescending look. "Oh, my poor child. You don't know how many of us have suffered under his hand."

If Dread was behind the attack on Shock, that was really bad. Pique, I could handle. But Dread was my boss, the number two demon in the Vex line. And Vex was the only thing that stood between me and a constant barrage of demon attacks.

Shock was also under Vex's protection. If Dread had turned on her, she was in serious trouble.

With a sinking feeling, I remembered that Phil worked for Dread.

"Do you think Dread is the one?" I asked.

Savor took her time before she replied. "I don't know. I do know Dread is seriously on edge. Last week Vex stated in front of several witnesses that Dread had convinced him that he's not responsible. But the harm's been done. Not to mention the blow when Lash left him. You do know about that?"

I gestured at all the papers lying in patches of sunlight cast on the tables and bar top. "How could I not?"

Lash was Glory's firstborn, not much older than Dread. Lash and Dread had been a couple for almost sixteen hundred years, symbiotic in that they fed only from each other. It was one of those perfect love matches that so rarely happened among demons, their strongest desires syncing together perfectly. In their current personas, Lash's role was the devoted wife of Prophet Thomas Anderson, active in social circles and charity causes. She had retained her blond beauty, but appeared to be in her late fifties. Then last

month the headlines had blared the whole tawdry affair—
the prophet's wife had left him for a local jewelry designer,
a known playboy twenty years her junior. Shock had told
me that Mark Cravet was really Crave, a century-old Glory
demon, known to be Glory's special pet. The public only
knew that the prophet's wife had abandoned her holy husband and marriage for a man who would never marry her.

"More humiliation," Savor said knowingly. "Dread's
been so tight lately, he vibrates—"

A slight bump came from the ceiling. Instantly I pic-
tured the sofa, directly above me. Listening intently over
the music, I thought I heard scuffling up there.

Without a word to Savor, I darted across the room. I
didn't even remember there was nobody manning the bar.

By the time I got upstairs, I couldn't hear anything
through the door. The key was shaking as I unlocked it.
Swinging it open, I looked on the floor with a terrible flash-
back of Theo lying there unconscious.

7

Instead of there being a naked man on my floor, the black rope ladder that I used as an emergency exit was hanging from the tiny skylight into the center of my kitchen. Black motorcycle boots with scarred leather toes were disappearing through the skylight.

I stifled my scream with both hands as the boots jerked and were gone in an instant. I was left standing there, looking up at the open skylight in disbelief. How did that man get inside?

The intruder wasn't a demon; that much I knew. With one glimpse, I could see his faint human aura. And he didn't have a signature. The energy emanations I picked up were perfectly human.

Glancing from side to side and seeing no one else, I quickly climbed up the rope ladder after the intruder, my heart racing. But there was nobody on my roof. The guy must have gone up the side of the three-story tenement next door. The two big dogs a couple yards over were barking loudly, raising the alarm.

I looked down between my feet at the kitchen. Nobody was there. But I half expected someone to jump out at me any second.

I grabbed the hinged skylight and closed it as I climbed back down the rope ladder. The top was shaped like a pyramid in heavy wrought iron. It served as an escape hatch to the roof, with the rope ladder usually coiled neatly inside the casing. I could unhook the ladder with a broom handle and have a quick emergency exit out of the place, if I needed to.

The three holes that should have held a heavy steel pin were empty. I didn't see the pin anywhere. How long had it been missing? Maybe that was how the demon got out this morning, leaving itself a convenient way to get back in. I ran back down and grabbed a fork from the drawer. With a little twisting, I was able to wedge it into one of the holes. That was good enough for now.

Leaving the ladder hanging, I hurried into the living room.

"Shock!"

She looked odd, as if the air had been let out of her, making her skin too large for her body. She was hardly breathing, and her aura was silvery white.

With a flash of terror, I remembered that when Plea died, she had been crumpled in on herself like Shock was now. It only took one touch, and Plea's body had instantly decompressed, imploding into nothingness as I absorbed her essence.

The demon had come back for Shock. If I hadn't heard the thump and run upstairs, it would have killed her. Straining as hard as I could, with Shock's signature now sickly low and muffled, I still couldn't sense any other demons nearby.

But I could feel Shock's essence, calling to me. Her core was exposed and vulnerable, ready for the taking, like beautiful music that lured me forward, never ceasing. It promised to soothe that deep ache I'd been living with, to lift me to salvation—

I wrenched myself way from the very thought. I could never kill Shock!

Determined, I held out my palms near her skin without directly touching her. I lowered my shields and let my emotions flow freely, channeling my alarm into her. It wasn't as good as making physical contact, but Shock absorbed the energy like an empty sponge.

It was the best I could do until I was sure I wouldn't inadvertently steal her life force with a touch.

But I kept looking over my shoulder, waiting for a demon to leap out at me. Shock was trembling on the edge of death, so I couldn't stop feeding her to search my apartment more thoroughly as I desperately wanted to. Chills kept going up my spine as I expected a demon to come crashing down the skylight or through my window at any moment. I kept thinking it must be Petrify nearby, and I was confusing my own fear with his signature.

Who was the intruder in the black boots? An accomplice? A minion? It wasn't the demon; I'd never heard of a demon with a signature so mild that you couldn't sense it while you were in the same room.

It took too long, but slowly pale colors began to appear again in Shock's aura. Her skin wasn't as wrinkled anymore, or maybe it was my imagination. I definitely didn't have enough reserves to bring her all the way back, and I couldn't risk letting a human touch her when she was so close to the edge of death.

I needed a demon I could trust—an oxymoron, if there ever was one.

We were both under Vex's protection, but what if Dread was behind the demon deaths and he had turned on Shock? It seemed like a bad idea to take Shock into Vex's complex in her current defenseless state. Any demon could steal her essence with an innocent tap, and I didn't trust my ability to be able to defend us both.

Savor was downstairs, but she was not a demon I trusted—not in any way. Besides, Dread had her under his thumb.

That left Revel, our progenitor. He was also a Vex demon, but after a millennium, he had gained his own measure of independence. My lips drew back in distaste at the thought of going to him for help. I had personal reasons for hating the first demon to seek me out after I had been possessed.

Since I'd moved to the city, Revel had reached out to me in every way possible, inviting me to his house in the Hamptons during the steamy summer months, offering me money to buy the bar, and regularly sending me keys to luxury apartments where I could live in comfort. It had become a boring ritual for me to refuse his latest offer. But it was the only power I had, come to think of it.

I couldn't stay here, not when my defenses had been so easily breached. I looked warily back at my kitchen and the sunshiny bedroom beyond.

Shock was near death.

I made up my mind. I bent over her, murmuring, "Don't worry, I'm taking you to Revel. He'll help us."

As I lifted up Shock, I finally remembered the bar. The cash register was sitting there unattended. I wondered what Savor was doing right now.

I wrestled my phone out of my pocket and speed dialed Darryl. He picked up on the first ring. "Hey there, I just left. You won't believe this place—"

"I can't talk. I have to leave now. Get back here as soon as you can." I flipped the phone shut on his surprised exclamation so I could carry Shock down the stairs. She was oddly rigid, not like someone who was unconscious. Her body had grown denser as it shrank in on itself, and she was stiff as a board.

Bracing myself in the foyer, I threw open the door and lifted Shock through. As I got my balance, Savor burst out of the door of the bar right next to me. "What's going on?"

"Don't touch her." I swung Shock around so she was on the other side of me. At the same time, I glanced down at Savor's feet, clad in brown sandals, not motorcycle boots. Actually Savor was the only demon who had an airtight alibi—me. But that could have been part of the plan, Savor keeping me talking while another demon invaded my place and attacked Shock.

And that again pointed back to Dread.

Savor took in Shock's condition with one practiced glance. "Who did it?"

"I don't know! I didn't feel anything. Did you?"

Savor shook her head thoughtfully. "No, only Shock. Weak as she is. And I'm known for my range."

I couldn't tell if she was lying. She was such the adept actress, able to become exactly who she needed to be on a moment's notice. "There was a man with the demon, wearing motorcycle boots. They climbed in from the roof."

"Another mystery death." Savor examined Shock again. "A near-death."

"I don't have time to chat about it, Savor. I have to go, so would you please leave now?"

"Allay, you have such a terrible opinion of me. When did I ever do you wrong?"

"You're trying to seduce Lolita. You know I hate that."

"You take things too seriously. I'll make sure no one steals the liquor until Darryl gets back, like I've been doing." In a huff, Savor ducked back into the bar. Only then I remembered the USB device in my pocket. But I didn't have time to waste calling her back.

As I dragged Shock to the curb, our auras crackled in muddy colors where we touched.

Everyone was staring curiously.

That was when I saw Theo hurrying toward me. I couldn't have been more surprised. He reached out in alarm. "Allay. What's wrong—"

"Stay back," I ordered. I turned slightly to keep Shock away from him. "Don't touch her."

I was thankful that he stopped. I doubted Shock was going to implode with his touch, since I was already carrying her. But I couldn't risk turning him into a demon and losing Shock at the same time. That would be too tragic.

Theo put his hands up as if showing he had no weapon. "What happened to your sister?"

"What are you doing here?" I countered, looking pointedly down at his feet—I couldn't trust anyone. I would be looking for those black motorcycle boots everywhere I went from now on. But Theo was wearing the same old shoes I had pulled off him last night.

"I just went to the station house, and the cops told me you hadn't come in yet to look at the mug shots. I was worried something had happened." He was hovering too close. "Let me carry her for you."

"No." I shifted Shock well out of reach. "If you want to help, flag me a cab."

Theo instantly stepped into the street and raised his arm as a series of full cabs went by. I finally had a reason to be grateful for gentrification since it had brought cabs to my neighborhood.

An empty cab pulled up, but there wasn't much space next to the parked cars, so the door couldn't open completely. "Move back," I ordered.

Raising his brows, Theo took a step back, standing next to the fender. I silently blessed my strength as I muscled Shock's stiffened form into the cab. She bent oddly at the hips and waist. I crawled in over her to sit in the middle, slamming the door shut so Theo couldn't get in.

He protested, but I called through the partly open window, "Thanks."

I leaned closer to the thick Plexiglas that separated us from the driver, who was looking a bit alarmed. Then the door behind the driver opened. You weren't supposed to get into cabs on the outside.

"What are you doing? No, get out." I tried to stop Theo as he started to climb in. "You can't come with us."

Theo sat down on the seat, physically shoving me over, so I jostled Shock into the opposite door. She rocked stiffly.

He shut the door firmly behind him. "You need help, Allay."

"I'm going for help."

The wide-eyed cabdriver looked over his shoulder, his voice rising higher. "No trouble. No trouble."

He was about to kick us out. Theo lifted his palms up as if to placate both of us. His voice was low. "Let me do what I can, Allay."

I was so paranoid, for a second I wondered if he might be part of the demon attacks. But it didn't add up. Why would he save me from Pique if the goal was to kill Shock? Surely I was Shock's last line of defense.

His black eye reminded me of how much I owed him already. And he had seen the demon in my apartment the first time. Maybe he could be useful. As long as he didn't try to touch Shock.

"All right." I leaned forward, speaking through the pivoting money drawer. "Take us to Park and Sixty-eighth Street."

With the driver still muttering, the cab lurched forward. I laced my hand with Shock's. There was still no response from her. I took a deep breath, letting my adrenaline-fueled panic empty into her. That was Shock's preferred emotion, so it would sustain her best.

The rapid drawing down of my own energy made me feel as if I were sinking. Yet there was an undeniable sensuality in pouring myself into another demon. I had never fluctuated so high and low so fast—it was quite the rush. I could see how some demons got addicted to it.

On my other side, Theo's thigh was against mine, warm through my skirt. His hands were clasped tightly in his lap, and his jaw was clenched.

Trying to shake off the hypnotic lure of feeding Shock,

I asked, "Why did you come back? Most guys would have run after what you've been through."

"I thought I might accept your job offer."

I blinked a few times. "What job offer?"

He cleared his throat. "You need a bodyguard. I can't keep driving the hours I've been doing, so I have plenty of time to help out."

A short, disbelieving laugh escaped; then I realized how insulting it sounded. "No offense, but every time you've come up against these guys, you weren't exactly the winner."

"Ouch . . ." His drawn-out enunciation could have put Savor to shame.

I had to smile, in spite of the situation and the panic in the pit of my stomach. Shock and the bar were the only things I had. "Thanks for offering, but I'm not going to risk anyone's neck for mine until I know what's going on."

He did that manly thing of not answering, because then he could pretend he hadn't heard me say no. But I didn't call him on it. Even if it was only for a cab ride, it felt good to have someone on my side.

The cabbie turned onto First Avenue and began a mad dash up the edge of the island, weaving in and out of traffic. For once I didn't tell him—*I'm not in a rush!* This time I was in a rush, hurrying to beg help from the last person I wanted to be indebted to.

We drove through the dregs of my neighborhood plastered with graffiti and strewn with trash, then the East Village, filled with young people out enjoying the weekend. Around Stuyvesant Town, north of Fourteenth Street, baby carriages reigned. Then there were the ten-block-long NYU Medical Center and Bellevue Hospital, where Shock ended up too many nights in the company of cops and bloody patients in handcuffs. We were passing through the stratified realms of Manhattan, laid down like layers of sandstone through the centuries.

North of the Midtown tunnel was the boxy tower of the United Nations. For security reasons, traffic channeled into a tunnel several blocks long that whisked us by the UN, safely unseen. When the cab emerged from the tunnel, large upscale apartment buildings filled the blocks, with plate-glass windows for boutiques, banks, and restaurants lining the avenues. Between the behemoths, the one-way cross streets of the Upper East Side had narrow town houses with tiny manicured gardens, lush with flowering vines and trees. Each facade was pristine, with the elaborate cornices and window bows a testament to wealth.

As the cab turned left on Sixty-seventh Street, heading deeper into the moneyed neighborhood, I tried to prepare myself. Shock absorbed my nervousness as easily as my other emotions. I stroked her cheek, glad to see it was indeed growing firmer and rounder. I was grateful that Theo wasn't asking questions. Our silent ride had given me enough time to bring Shock back to life.

I checked my cell phone, and there was a text from Darryl saying, *Back, all ok*. I texted back, *Stay alert*. My bartenders knew I took safety seriously, and I encouraged them to be quick to call 911 if they needed help. Hopefully by removing Shock, I had taken away the target at the bar and the demons would leave my people alone. Hopefully Savor had moved on to other haunts.

With that settled, it was time to dial the dreaded number. It rang several times; then an accented female voice answered, "Fortunay residence."

I swallowed. "Please tell Giles that Allay is calling."

"*Certainement*," she replied.

There was a long wait as we sat at a traffic light. Then Revel's voice came over the line. "Allay, what a pleasure to hear from you."

"I'm sure." I had to force myself to say it. "I need your help, Revel. Shock's been hurt."

There was a slight pause. "Where are you?"

"Two blocks away."

"Good. Go to the entrance on Sixty-eighth to the underground parking garage and tell them you're here to see me. They'll send you up in my private lift."

I rolled my eyes. Of course Revel would have his own elevator. I hung up, instructing the cabdriver to circle the block to go down Sixty-eighth Street.

A few minutes later, I found out that money could buy a lot of discreet service. I said the name "Giles Fortunay," and the cab was instantly waved inside the concrete-columned parking garage by a security guard. Without a word, a white-gloved valet directed us to an interior sidewalk. The elevator door opened as we pulled up.

Theo paid the cabdriver as I struggled to get Shock out of the car. She was looking much better, filled out instead of crumpled in on herself. But that made her more flexible, so it was harder for me to lift her. I pulled her from the cab, and her feet bumped against the edge of the curb.

Theo grabbed Shock's legs, lifting them up. "Let me carry her," he said quietly.

The valet was headed our way, so I let Theo carry Shock. At least she now looked like an unconscious human instead of a mannequin. Shock's head fell against his chest as Theo settled her in his arms.

I held her hand as I walked beside him, continuing to feed her, though I was starting to feel light-headed. Shock shifted and moaned, the first signs of life she had shown since I had found her. Theo kept looking at me instead of Shock, but I was too busy willing the colors of her aura to strengthen.

"You really would do anything to help her, wouldn't you?" Theo said.

"Anything." My voice caught.

The penthouse button was already lit on the panel. The door slid closed and we started up. It was an old elevator with polished wood trim, parquet floor, and narrow proportions that suited a more modest era.

As the elevator ascended, the tingling sensation of Revel's signature got stronger, making my heart beat faster in spite of myself. It felt exhilarating, like being on the verge of jumping out of a plane or succumbing to orgasm.

I hated it, and everything it reminded me of.

The elevator bypassed the lobby and went straight to the top, pinging through the numbers like a countdown. It was, of sorts. I hadn't seen Revel in five years, not since the last time he had dropped by the bar. I had ordered him to leave, loudly, in front of everyone. But he had maintained his cool, laissez-faire attitude, smiling and waving at the confused regulars on his way out as if he were leaving a charity benefit and the paparazzi were recording every second.

I had never been to Revel's place before, though Shock had forced me to memorize his address and phone number in case of an emergency. As badly as Revel had treated me, I was fairly sure he didn't want to kill me or Shock.

That was more than I could say about any other demon.

With a final, refined ping, the elevator eased to a stop and the door slid open silently. I went first, stepping into the vestibule.

My first impression was that we were high up in a vast space, a marble cathedral filled with diffuse light. We looked down on a two-story gallery with three stained-glass windows placed high in the wall. A heraldic shield was centered in each window with twining leaves around the outside edge, blocking the view and much of the afternoon sun. The carved marble arches around the windows were supported by double stone columns. Next to the grand staircase leading down from the vestibule, there were two matching arches overlooking the gallery.

"It's a museum," Theo muttered. Musty traces of old parchment, wood, and oil paint permeated the air.

One of Revel's flunkies was standing at the top of the staircase leading down to the floor of the gallery. "Good afternoon. My name is Ki. If you please wait, Mr. Fortunay will be with you shortly."

Ki appeared to be of East Indian ancestry, with his skin like creamy coffee. He had delicate bones like a girl's, with slender ankles that showed between the bottom cuff of his black suit and loafers. He folded his hands and stood at the head of the stairs blocking further entry, all the while smiling pleasantly as if he saw people carry unconscious girls into the apartment every day.

Theo continued holding Shock as if she weighed nothing. I scuffed my flip-flops on the black and white marble floor, laid in a pattern that resembled the coffered ceiling with its dark wood beams and white plaster roundels. A high-backed wooden bench to one side and a chair with a fili-greed carved back set a medieval tone. Down in the gallery, the walls were filled with stylized paintings in arched frames showing three-quarter figures on gold-foil backgrounds, each one lit by its own light. Even the bronze chandelier was ancient, filled with fat, white candles ready to be lit.

But high up along the cornice, moveable cameras aimed down at us. I realized if I had misjudged Revel, all of us were in trouble.

As if reading my mind, Theo murmured, "Are you sure this guy is your friend?"

I shrugged, admitting my doubt. "You'd better get down here now, Revel," I said directly into one of the cameras, "or I'm leaving."

I silently counted off ten seconds before Revel appeared through a side door of the vestibule. Of course he had been watching us. That was his favorite thing to do.

Revel's persona was a dashing young Frenchman with longish dark hair and the flippant manner of a man of leisure. Everything about him was perfect—his smooth complexion, his vibrant blue eyes, a slight dimple that appeared when he smiled, and the compact yet powerful physique of a race car driver.

He quickly joined us, giving me a look of concern as he pretended to check Shock's pulse, assessing her energy levels. I almost believed he was worried, but then again, Revel was good at acting as though he cared. His current persona was much younger than when I had first met him as "Jacques Fortunay," the supposed cousin of Giles. Jacques had passed into graceful middle age, and a few years ago Revel had created Giles to transition into. I wasn't surprised that he preferred young personas, though he trotted out the older ones whenever he needed to cash in on society favors.

This persona was consistent with the Fortunay mold. His skin was tanned beautifully, and his dark hair curled to his shoulders. His vibrant eyes could speak volumes, as could his sensual, full lips. Even his mannerisms were the same— that sly smile, the way he crossed his legs at the knees, the lazy tilt of his head.

"How long has she been this way?" Revel demanded.

"Half an hour, give or take. She looked worse when I found her. A lot worse."

Revel pinched Shock's cheek and the back of her hand, noting how long it took for the dents left by his fingers to disappear. "I don't think she's in any immediate danger."

"No," I said, glancing at Theo, "or I would have taken her to a hospital."

I didn't take Shock's hand again. I was depleted enough already and I needed to have my wits about me.

Revel took a long look at Theo Ram, head to toes in that cool, judgmental way of his. "Who's doing your heavy lifting, Allay?"

"I'm her bodyguard," Theo said assertively.

"No, you're not," I told him.

Revel's amusement was clear. "So you've finally acquired a staff. Well, it's about time." He saw me tighten my lips, and he quickly waved a finger. "Bring her down here."

Revel's signature was tingling very strongly. Either he had just fed, or he was excited by our arrival. He led us down the steps and through the galley. Huge double doors were opened with a slight flourish by Ki. Inside was a two-story-high reception room with a coffered ceiling supported by square wooden columns and a formal arrangement of antique furniture. A vast expanse of maroon rug was monogrammed with a huge *GF* in the center, about as pretentious as you could get. I thought the four windows along one wall were the best part, offering a breathtaking view over the tops of the intervening town houses toward Central Park. The mass of leaves spread out, flashing silver and green in the afternoon breeze.

Theo laid Shock down on a brocade sofa. I sat down next to Shock, keeping myself between her and Revel just in case he got any ideas.

Revel shooed Ki out, then took his time settling himself on a nearby chair. He was eyeing Theo as if trying to figure him out. Theo wasn't giving anything away. He stood at Shock's feet, his hands clasped in front of him and his legs braced apart, watching me instead of Revel.

There was no way I could explain my past with Revel to Theo. I had first met Revel within weeks of returning home from the insane asylum, when he was posing as Jacques Fortunay. I was sneaking out of my parents' house at night, unable to sleep, and scammed my way into all kinds of Hollywood and Beverly Hills nightclubs and parties, making myself look more glamorous and beautiful. "Jacques" was exotic and exciting with his European background, a big art collector who lived in a Malibu beach house—every California girl's dream. The tingling feeling in the pit of my stomach whenever I was with him sealed the deal.

Revel soon told me that he was a demon, too, and I

was so infatuated with him and happy to find another of
my kind that I didn't even care that he had lied to me.
He showed me how to survive, teaching me self-defense
moves and enrolling me in my first Aikido class to make
sure I could protect myself when he wasn't around. He explained the origin of modern demons to me: Vex was born
from Bedlam around AD 300 and Glory some fifty years
later, when the Roman Empire still ruled both the Eastern
and Western world. But the demons were kept locked in
coffinlike boxes by Bedlam, ready to be consumed when
he needed to regenerate himself. Together, Vex and Glory
broke free and killed Bedlam; without the ancient demon
controlling the emperors, the great empire soon split apart
and fell to the invading tribes of the north.

Since Plea was a Vex demon, that meant I was, too.
When I'd found out that Plea had been Revel's offspring,
I realized he was the same as the man in Plea's memories.
The memories of him were the only ones I could stand, and
Revel taught me how to block the rest out at will. He explained demonhood so reasonably, taking a soothing philosophical view born of his thousand years of experience.
Were demons really cast out of heaven by God? Were we
brothers to the angels as some claimed? Or was our existence a physiological function of quantum physics and the
human body? We might even be aliens from another world
living as parasites on humanity.

I didn't realize it then, but Vex was laying his claim on
me, keeping all the other demons away by sending his most
loyal people to form a protective screen around me, giving
Revel time to seduce me. When I begged to meet another
demon, Revel took me to see Mellow, an innocuous fel-
low who lived in Venice Beach and worked as a masseur. I
was shocked to discover that the tingly feeling I felt around
Revel wasn't love; it was his energy signature. The sensation that Mellow evoked in me was like being stroked; my
eyes wanted to close as I drifted away.

Revel didn't know how much that shook my faith in him. My gut wasn't really telling me that he was the man for me. But I still trusted him, and believed he was my salvation.

I didn't bother to graduate from high school. Maybe some girls could be possessed by a demon and keep up their GPA, but I wasn't one of them. Instead, I moved into Revel's beach house in spite of my parents' protests. I stopped returning their calls.

I was a girl when I met him and a woman by the end of the summer. Revel was ruled by sensation, as were all demons, but he indulged in the more sensuous passions. He had been born after the demon Storm overfed on a young nun who wallowed in religious visions; but since hysterics were few and far between since the Middle Ages, he had learned to make do with the more common ecstasy of sex.

He was openly bisexual, the consummate exhibitionist and voyeur, and orgies seemed to spring up around him naturally. I had indulged in all sorts of erotic explorations with his encouragement. To my knowledge, he hadn't been unfaithful. He had soothed my petty jealousies and seemed to truly love me.

It finally unraveled when Revel planned to return to New York that fall. He asked me to come with him. Living in the city sounded glamorous and freeing. I had to get away from LA to put some distance between myself and my past life, which was still going on exactly the same as if I had never existed.

The day before we left, Revel insisted that I attend my Aikido class. I wanted to blow it off like a typical teenager. "You need it," he kept saying. "If a demon attacks you when I'm not around, you won't be able to defend yourself."

Exasperated, I had brushed him off, saying, "I pushed that demon off Plea before I was turned. Now I'm much stronger. I can take care of myself."

"You were just lucky that sand was so slippery. That's

why you were able—" Revel broke off, realizing he'd said too much.

It was his own reaction that made me realize what he'd said. "I never told you that."

"You must have," he insisted, but it was weak.

Revel had refused to say more, so I was forced to go through the whole dreary charade of figuring out the truth myself. In the end, I went to Mellow, who revealed what the others already knew—Revel was the demon who had attacked Plea.

He was the reason I had been possessed. He had tried to kill Plea, his own offspring. Some demons consumed their own offspring immediately at birth, and some actually overloaded on energy on purpose every two hundred years, birthing their own pet demon to consume. The thought repulsed me, like eating babies.

But Revel had hunted down Plea when she was several centuries old. Years later Shock told me it had been revenge. She was the one who would know.

Needless to say, there was an ugly scene after I found out. I screamed and cried, but Revel never lost his cool. That more than anything told me what I needed to know: He didn't care about me; he just wanted to control me.

He had seduced me because Vex ordered him to. It was all a lie. He had done it to get me to move to New York and live under Vex's protection. He had manipulated me as though I meant nothing to him.

Now I was finally asking for his help, and Revel acted as if he always knew this day would come. But I wasn't playing one of his games. "Could you keep Shock here and take care of her until I find a safe place for us? And promise you won't tell anyone about it?"

"Why? Did that shack of yours finally burn down?"

"For all intents and purposes, yes."

Revel shifted his eyes to Theo, saying discreetly, "You're not giving me much to go on, Allay."

"I'm not giving you anything—except a promise that if you hurt Shock, I'll kill you."

He hesitated, but I held firm. I didn't want his help contingent on how much I told him. Revel was notorious for his information network of human and demon spies; he always knew what was going on, and he shared that information to get more. I wasn't going to have my troubles become his currency. He had to agree on my terms, or at worst I could move Shock from hotel to hotel until I figured out an alternative.

"*Allay*," Revel chided with a mocking smile, "there's no need for threats between us. Of course I'll take care of Shock. I would do that for Shock's sake, if not yours."

I was relieved, but I couldn't quite manage to thank the bastard. I wouldn't kowtow to him, not in any way. He needed to respect me in order to fear the consequences of hurting Shock.

Revel went to the door and pushed a button, murmuring a request. As he returned across the expanse of rug, a burly man appeared. "Bring Shock to the Green Room." Turning to me, he said, "Come along and you'll see that we'll take care of her properly." To Theo, he added, "You can stay here."

Theo stiffened, but I needed to be able to speak honestly to Revel. "Do you mind waiting, Theo? I'll be right back."

"Of course," he said, taking a step back to let the security guard pick up Shock. Her head lolled.

I glanced back at Theo as I followed Revel out of the room. It was an awful thing, but he was my canary in a coal mine. If something happened to him, I would know that it wasn't safe here for Shock. Unfortunately, all I had now was the word of a pathological liar.

8

Through the door in the corner of the ornate reception room, there was a spiral stairway leading up to a long hall-way to our right. Two young people in shorts at the top of the stairs were arguing good-naturedly about when they were going to play a game of tennis.

As I followed Revel down the hall, we passed another living room, more intimate in scale. A young coed was reading in one deep window seat, and a guy who couldn't be much older was playing a handheld video game in the other. The wood smelled of old-fashioned beeswax, and I imagined there was a sea of white-coated servants working feverishly behind closed doors to maintain this place.

At the end was a long wall of tempered glass, with shouts and laughter echoing inside. Several naked people were splashing in the lap pool, which was paved in tiny glass tiles of blue, green, and white. A mural bordered the pool; a vast expanse of golden countryside dotted with cypress trees and vineyards.

Down another short hallway was a pretty guest room of modest proportions, with a pale green rug and bedspread, and white satin wallpaper. It was probably one of the more ordinary rooms in the penthouse.

Revel dismissed the guard with a wave. "I'll send one of my harem to feed her. Michelle has a toothache; that should be to Shock's taste. Or maybe I should send her a boy—she's hopelessly heterosexual."

Maybe he was trying to remind me of the few bisexual experiences I had shared along with him. But those days were ruined, though he acted as if I were silly for thinking that way. "Just feed her, Revel. And don't let anyone get to her. I don't know when I'll be back."

"Where are you going?"

There was no doubt in my mind—I needed to see Vex. I needed to know whether Shock and I were still under his protection. I needed to find out if Dread was behind these attacks on her. "I'm going to see Vex."

He dropped his flippant tone. "What for?"

"You think I'm going to confide in you?" I let out a short laugh.

"You should, you know. Listen, I'll tell you what I've heard. Shock birthed another demon, and the rumor is that she had him at your bar. Petrify was last seen near the New Jersey docks. If he was smart, he grabbed a slow boat to Taiwan. I have reports that Pique was on his tail, but nobody's caught sight of him since."

"*Pique* again," I repeated grimly. "Who is he? Where did he come from?"

"Nobody knows. Nobody's claimed him." Revel seemed very interested. "Pique isn't talking. The first sighting of him was on the west side of Manhattan a few weeks ago."

"He must belong to somebody. He's been hunting around my bar a *lot*. And last night he attacked me, right on the street in front of everyone. He would have killed me if it weren't for that man out there."

Anger flashed over Revel's face. "I told you that bar isn't safe, Allay! You should have security around you at all times."

I didn't want to get into that again. But his reaction seemed genuine, which surprised me. He was always calculating cause and effect; he didn't usually get this upset unless he was putting on an act. And this wasn't an act; I could sense his frustrated concern without even touching him.

Suddenly I did want to confide in him. I was trusting him with Shock's life. I had to make sure he was on my side. "It gets even worse. Today a demon got inside my apartment—twice—and both times I didn't sense him. He's the one who attacked Shock. When he didn't kill her the first time, he came back to finish her off."

That made him pause. "Shock doesn't fit the profile."

"What do you mean?"

"There have always been mysterious deaths among our people. Surely you know that? Even the earliest Sumerian records include citations of demon 'begets' and consumption, but not all were accounted for. We can't hide it when we take another's essence—that pearly glow lingers for days and gives it away. But demons have always disappeared without explanation."

"I'm not sure which is scarier, a demon I can't sense or the chance that I could implode without warning."

"I think it's a demon who can stealth himself. The only time I heard of a near-death like this was Slam, back in the fourteenth century. He was a new demon, barely a decade old. He came to me one night in as bad shape as Shock. He said he was attacked by a demon he didn't sense until it turned on him. And he was standing right next to him. A few days later, Slam disappeared. I never did find out who did him in, and I searched out everyone to be sure. There weren't nearly as many of us back then."

"So this stealth demon might come back for Shock, now that she's been targeted?"

Revel gave me a long look. "It happened that way with Slam. Most demons just disappear, and we're left wondering."

"Like Malaise. Shock's also an older demon who's suddenly been targeted. Why?"

Revel had completely dropped his affected mannerisms. "I've kept close track of demon genealogy since I was born, and I've researched every scrap of writing from before then. There're a few things almost all of the demons who disappear have in common. They're young, rarely more than a decade old. Lately they've been even younger, under a year. They're also the more vicious sort, the ones who fatally injure humans. Malaise was definitely hurting her victims, and she lost her head when she found such a rich vein of her preferred emotion in the modern prison system. But Shock helps people, so it doesn't fit."

I remembered what Shock had said about the last dregs of human emotion. And she kept overdosing on emotions and birthing new demons. She was getting that energy from somewhere.

But I had to stick to the important point. "How can it be possible for a demon to appear and disappear without warning?"

"Isn't that what the bogeyman does?" Revel shook his head with the patience of a man who thought he knew the truth. "It must be a demon who has a very mild signature. There are a few around—yours is very light, Allay. If someone wasn't expecting you, I bet you could sneak up on another demon, maybe even into the same room."

"Then why did Vex accuse Dread of being the demon killer? He has a really strong signature."

Revel gave me a proud smile, as he did when he was teaching me something. "So you've heard about that! Very good, Allay. I almost despaired of your ability to navigate the complexities of demon culture."

I didn't want to admit I'd only gotten around to asking these questions when Shock's life was hanging by a thread. "Vex must know more than he's let on."

"Allay, you must let me make the arrangements if you want to see Vex. You can't walk in off the street and demand to see him. Will you leave it to me?"

"No way, you'll take forever doing it. And you'll get too involved. I'm leaving now."

"Now? But it's Saturday."

I looked down at Shock. "It's important."

A servile young woman entered and whispered in Revel's ear. "Apparently your man has wandered into my library."

"I'm ready to go." I leaned over and kissed Shock on the cheek, giving her hand a squeeze. "You take care of her, Revel."

"I will." There was something in his voice I didn't recognize. I hoped it was sincerity.

I followed Revel upstairs to the library, a large room lined with wooden glass-fronted display cases. Ki was standing nearby, with Theo seated in one of the leather chairs waiting for us.

A sweeping glance revealed the depth of Revel's collection. I knew he collected art, but I hadn't realized the extent of his investment in manuscripts. They were displayed in climate-controlled cubes scattered around the room. Next to the double doors lay an old book, open to a delicate parchment page.

I scanned the spidery, Old English words that listed the seven categories of demons:

Fates control destiny

Imps cause mischief

Succubi incite lust

Hordes bring conflict

Fiends tempt the saintly

Familiars instigate witchcraft

Guardians lend comfort

The descriptions did contain a kernel of truth. Since each demon sought out and devoured a particular emotion, that made them fall into certain patterns. Demons who craved anger, such as Pique, were Hordes causing conflict. Revel, with his constant partying, would be considered a Fiend, tempting the saintly. Shock and I would be considered Guardians because we helped people, Shock by taking away their physical pain, and I by making them feel better in any way I could.

Theo came toward me, as I nodded shortly, letting him know everything was all right. "Let's go."

But Revel stopped me. "Don't rush off like this, Allay. You need a chance to eat. You're looking famished, darling, and you need to be strong right now."

He was offering to feed me. Our auras fluctuated where he touched my arm, flaring brighter. Invasive green tendrils curled from him into my aura. My mouth watered at his sticky sweetness.

I peeled Revel off me, not bothering to hide how much I shuddered at his touch. It brought everything back with full force. There was pain deep in his eyes, but he was so expert at the wounded-male look that it was far too overdone. Besides, I'd been shunning him for a decade; he couldn't pretend to pout because I still felt the same.

Theo's eyes widened at my overt rejection. He moved between us, taking my hand and tucking it under his arm. "I can take care of Allay."

He let my palm rest on his forearm, so it was easy for me to draw off his emotions. Theo was jealous, surprised at his own reaction, but wanting nothing more than to get the better of Revel. It made me feel a feminine twinge of pleasure knowing Theo would get right into Revel's face if he had to and make him back off. I soaked it up, my lips parting.

Revel tried to brush it off lightly. "What on Earth could *you* do?"

Theo simply stroked my hand where my aura was flashing as I fed from him.

Revel's eyes narrowed. "How much do you know?"

"Nothing," I said hastily. "He knows nothing."

"The lady obviously needs protection," Theo said.

"That's what *I'm* saying," Revel said impatiently. "Allay, you know I can help. You can't go alone, and you'll need me to deal with them properly."

"I've dealt with them for the past ten years, Revel."

"Yes, but now you're upset, Allay. If you make *him* upset"—Revel gave me a particular glance rather than say Vex's name in front of Theo—"he could take everything away from you, including that bar you love so much."

That stopped me. "Michael owns the bar, and he would never cave to any pressure—"

Revel was shaking his head. "The church owns the Den, Allay. Vex bought it the week after you started working there."

"But Michael . . . he would have told me."

"He can't, not according to his management contract."

I took a deep breath, shaken by the news. "Why didn't you tell me?"

"You've refused to listen to anything I have to say. That's why you have to listen now. I'm going with you, and you can't say no."

I lifted my chin. "*No.* You can't order me around, Revel. Just take care of Shock, or I'll make you pay for it."

I tugged Theo's arm, heading toward the door of the library. I was already feeling stronger from his steady input.

But Revel tried to stop me again, saying, "Allay—"

I jerked away from his outstretched hand as if he were about to burn me. "Don't push it, Revel. Just take care of Shock."

Without another word, I marched down the spiral stairs and through the vast reception room. Theo followed silently while Revel trailed along behind us. In the stained-glass gallery, I ran up the flight of marble steps and stopped in front of the elevator doors.

Theo stood very close to me while I warily watched Revel. My aura was pulsing a dull red, like emergency flashers warning of danger ahead.

Revel glanced up at a camera and jerked his chin. The door opened as if by magic. I stepped inside, turning outward to face Revel. I stared him down until the door closed on us again. Even then, I didn't move, very aware of the cameras in the tiny space. Revel was such a voyeur, he would probably replay the tapes he had made of me later. The old ones, made back when I trusted him, and these new ones he'd gotten today. It made me feel sick.

The unobtrusive doorman had a taxi waiting for us by the time we crossed under the short green canopy to Park Avenue. Once we were in the cab and I'd given the driver my destination in Brooklyn, I sat back with a sigh.

Theo must have recognized the address. "The Fellowship of Truth. That's where you're going?"

I nodded. I knew I shouldn't take Theo with me to the Fellowship complex. It was too dangerous. But he had been useful with Revel, and I had Shock's life in my hands. Sad to say, I had to use every tool I could to save her.

Theo took my hand in his, startling me. I could feel how he admired the way I had stood up to Revel, refusing to back down. He was also confused about the suddenness of his own protective feelings about me. I skimmed off the edge of his strong emotions. I hadn't tried to provoke him into feeling more for me, so it was all the sweeter.

"Don't you hate not being in the driver's seat?" I asked, gesturing to the cabbie with my chin.

He grinned, abashed. "Yeah, I'm not used to the backseat."

I could feel that driving determination under his other emotions, and knew he would be going even faster than this driver, zipping in and out between cars as if he owned the road. There was something a little heady about so much tightly wound energy, and I fed from him with a rare abandon.

At one point during the long cab ride back downtown,

my phone buzzed with a text message. It was from Revel:
See Dread at PC.

I told him to stay out of it! If I had wanted to forewarn
Vex that I was coming, I would have called him myself.

.I leaned forward and said, "Take us to the Prophet's
Center instead." To Theo, I explained, "Fortunay got me an
appointment with the prophet. I had wanted to speak to his
nephew, Tim, first. I know Tim."

Tim Anderson was Vex's persona, not Dread who wore
the guise of the prophet. What if Dread was responsible for
the attacks on Shock? He could be running interference
between me and Vex.

I dialed Vex's number, but it went straight to voice mail.
"It's Allay," I said, mindful of Theo sitting next to me. "I'm
on my way to the Prophet's Center to see your uncle. I hope
you'll be there soon, because I'd much rather talk to you." I
hung up, hoping Vex would get back to me quickly.

As our cab crossed the Williamsburg Bridge, I looked
back at my neighborhood in Manhattan. The redbrick towers of the projects thrust up from the treetops, blocking the
view of my bar. But I knew exactly where it was. I briefly
toyed with the thought of calling the bar. Darryl would be
worried, but I didn't have anything reassuring to tell him.

As I looked into Brooklyn, the biggest building to the
north of the bridge was a hulking white cube called the
Prophet's Center. It was an old factory, seven stories high
with rows of enormous windows spangled with tiny panes.
A fuzz of green on top proclaimed that most desirable of
New York real estate, the roof garden.

The Fellowship had taken over six other large buildings on the surrounding blocks, mostly former warehouses
that had been transformed into offices that administered
the church and its various businesses—real estate management, an investment firm, even a biomedical research
facility. There were also apartments for some of their employees, including Vex and his closest demon companions.

Vex had moved his headquarters into Williamsburg in the early seventies when he was the original prophet. With his support, the neighborhood had eventually blossomed into one of the trendiest places to live in the city. I didn't know much about the religion, just what everyone else knew. Fellows (or truth-speakers, as they were also known) were required to take complete responsibility for their own actions and feelings, empowering themselves in order to achieve their life goals. They were pioneers of biofeedback where they learned how to control the autonomic functions of their bodies, and they were one of the first to offer EST-like workshops to build leadership skills.

The cab curved down and around too quickly, back under the bridge to get to the Prophet's Center. I paid the driver before we stopped, and looked at Theo. His eye was black underneath and slightly swollen on his cheek. The tumbled curl of hair on his forehead mostly hid the white butterfly bandages. I felt it necessary to ask, "Are you sure you want to come with me?"

"This guy owns your bar, doesn't he?"

"So I'm told."

"Then you should have some backup. Someone on your side."

He was right. "Okay. But stop telling people you're my bodyguard. I can't afford you."

"I come cheap."

He said it so fast, I had to grin. So did he, a little embarrassed. We really didn't know each other, but in a strange way we did. I suddenly had a sharp craving to make love to him again, slowly and properly. What would one more time hurt? He was too tempting to let pass by.

"It's nice to see you smile again," he said.

"It's been a rough day." I squeezed his hand, then let go. "Let's hit it."

We were so close to the river that a murky, fishy smell wafted down the few short blocks. Up above, the constant rush of cars speeding over the metal roadway of the bridge drowned out all other sounds.

A plain double glass door served as the entrance to an industrial-chic lobby with painted ducts and exposed conduit lighting on the ceiling. The acoustic tile on the walls barely damped the echo off the concrete floor, painted dark red. There were groupings of low benches and tables, adhering to the church's civic-minded philosophy of including public space in commercial buildings. This lobby was cramped compared to the other buildings in the complex—on my first meeting with Vex, I had waited in the conference center's atrium, which had trees three stories high inside. Vex didn't seem as eager to have a lot of loiterers in the building where he and Dread actually lived.

Still, there were a dozen people around drinking coffee, reading, and working on their laptops. Since they were mostly locals from Williamsburg, the place could be considered trendy.

I couldn't sense Vex in the building, and I hadn't sensed him in the other church buildings we passed. Barely within range, I could tell Dread was on an upper floor on the south side of the building; he had a slippery, sliding signature that made me feel off balance. On the north side, there was another demon signature, but it wasn't Vex's. The pressing, squeezing sensation made me draw in my breath, as her name came to me—Zeal. When Shock talked about Vex and Dread, Zeal's name was most often mentioned. She had a prominent role in the church as the minister of action, interfacing directly with their followers, feeding off their devotional frenzies. But I'd never met her.

I went to the desk by the elevators, cordoned off with a filigreed bronze enclosure that looked extremely strong. Demon-proof, one might say. I gave my name to the security guard. "I have an appointment with Prophet Anderson."

The guard checked his screen, quickly clearing us. We each had to stand in front of the computer cam so our picture could be taken. When we approached the bronze gate, it opened automatically. The guard explained that a face-recognition program would allow us access to certain parts of the building, and the doors we weren't supposed to go through wouldn't open for us.

The elevator also pinged open at our approach. It was sort of creepy, as if our every move were being watched. The Fellowship of Truth approved of modern technology, especially advances in medical science. They agitated for laws that improved the quality of life and they placed no restrictions on medical advances, including abortion, gene splicing, cloning, and stem cell research. Vex had run the Catholic Church under the Borgia empire, taking on the role of various notorious popes with Dread by his side. But I couldn't reconcile that history with this permissive religion. The Fellowship was all about free choice.

As we walked into the waiting room on the fifth floor, a small woman of Asian ancestry was there to greet us, smiling. I was surprised to see she was wearing pink braces—she was in her mid-twenties, at least. But with her bangs, upturned nose, and tiny, graceful hands, she exuded vivacious charm. I wondered if Dread made the poor girl work every Saturday.

"Hello, my name is June. I'm Prophet Anderson's assistant." June directed Theo to a comfy chair with magazines on the table next to it, and said, "You can wait here while Ms. Meyers sees the prophet."

"Allay," Theo asked quietly, "do you want me to come with you?"

"No, you can wait." I was glad when he didn't protest, even though he probably wanted to meet the notorious prophet of the church-of-anarchy. But Theo couldn't hear what I had to say to Dread.

"Let me see your phone," he said.

I handed it over, and he keyed in his number, waiting to hang up until it rang. "Call me if you need anything."

"I'll be right back," I promised.

He handed over my cell, letting his fingers brush against mine. I took in the bright spark of his attraction, savoring it. Was it the girl or the demon inside of me who wanted him? I couldn't deny that I thought about pulling him against me, pressing my eager mouth to his, wrapping my legs around his hips. . . .

I forced myself to walk away as Theo remained standing, watching after me. I was lucky he had saved me from Pique last night. Shock was also lucky, or she wouldn't have had me to stop the demon who attacked her this morning.

Leaving him there exposed and vulnerable felt wrong. But I had Shock to worry about. If something happened to him, then I should find the nearest exit. I had already pinpointed the location of the stairwell in the corner farthest from both demons as the one to take if I needed to escape.

As I approached the double doors at the end of the corridor, Dread's signature was more distinct than Zeal's. Close proximity made me stagger a bit as if the floor of the hall tilted downward. I felt as if I were sliding, about to lose control. It was uncomfortable, and I struggled to dampen the effects, to block it out as I did with Shock. I wondered if sensitive humans could also sense it, and if they were unnerved by the sensation.

June opened the door and announced, "Ms. Emma Meyers, Prophet Anderson."

I stepped into the big corner office while June left, shutting the door behind me. Through one wall of windows, I could see just over the top of the roadway to the huge, flat-topped Prophet's Arena south of the Williamsburg Bridge. The East River made a big curve there, with the piers and towering loading cranes of the Brooklyn Navy Yard clustered around the small bay behind it. In the distance, the Manhattan and Brooklyn bridges spanned the river to downtown.

The other wall of windows looked directly at Manhattan, with the thick, blue-gray torrent of the river rushing by in front of us. We were higher than the old Domino Sugar refinery on our side of the waterfront, and beyond the river were the East River Park and project towers. That was Alphabet City, my neighborhood.

"Nice view." I was glad the towers of the projects blocked my bar. I'd never considered that they might be able to see me from over here.

Dread, aka Prophet Thomas Anderson, stood behind a desk made of clear Lucite, with only a phone, laptop, and a leather pen case on top. The long wall had a built-in display trimmed in black, with white interior squares that held awards, citations, and photos of the prophet with important people. The shrinelike centerpiece was a photo of Dread with his arm around the shoulders of the original prophet, Dale Willams. That was Vex's former persona. Right now, Vex was off somewhere being the new prophet's wayward young nephew, Tim—or maybe someone else altogether.

From the black shiny floor to the careful lighting and sparse office equipment, I guessed this was not where Dread actually worked. This place was for show.

"Nice to see you again, Allay." Dread's persona was an urbane, Ivy-league man in his late fifties; tall, strong, with silvery short hair and the lightly bronzed skin of an outdoorsman. There was something both warm and dignified about him, but all I could feel was his slippery signature that put me off balance.

"Actually, I want to see Vex."

"Vex is out of the country right now. He's not due back for another few days. Perhaps I can help you?" He didn't sound too encouraging.

A few days! I couldn't wait that long. "I need to speak to Vex. Can't you get hold of him by phone?"

"No, I'm afraid that's impossible. He's deep in some rough country. You'll have to make do with me."

I tried not to shuffle my flip-flops as I crossed the vast

expanse to his desk. I had met Dread only a few times in the company of Vex, usually when he gave me orders on code words and procedures for my job. Other than that, I dealt directly with Vex whenever I needed something, which was rarely.

What if Dread was lying to me about Vex? He was far too smooth to be trusted. He was wearing a very expensive suit, and his white shirtsleeves were closed with cuff links. But he didn't have a tie, and his shirt was open a couple of buttons, showing off a few curly silver chest hairs. Shock had laughed once about how Dread had created his current persona with premature gray hair to help establish his authority within the church. She said his personas were always rigidly correct—the perfect knight, the devout monk, the finest courtier—but he had never assumed the leadership role until recently when he became the Fellowship's prophet, while Vex had taken a minor role as his nephew.

When I reached the desk, I wasn't surprised when Dread didn't offer me his hand. That was a human custom; demons rarely shook hands. It left the weaker demon vulnerable to a sneak attack.

Dread sat down, gesturing for me to take the chair in front of the desk. The two chairs on my side of the desk were organic in shape, with wings for armrests and a higher curve for the back. Mine was upholstered in nubbly white fabric and was surprisingly comfortable. But I didn't settle back, resisting its lure to relax.

Dread consulted the laptop screen. "Revel said a demon got into your bar today and attacked Shock."

So much for telling him myself so I could see if his surprise was genuine or not. "Yeah, but I didn't sense his signature."

"Perhaps it was Shock's new offspring. Or any other demon, for that matter, with a subtle signature that you didn't recognize. Shock was there, wasn't she? Her signature can be quite . . . harsh."

I didn't want to admit to him that I had shut down my sixth sense the first time it happened because of Shock's presence. "The new demon is Petrify, and he sends cold chills right up your spine. It's not easy to miss."

Dread smiled in understanding, but there was something tight about his lips and the stiff way he moved. "Of course."

He was patronizing me. Personally, I didn't care. But I had to shake him, to make him listen to me.

"Our agreement is that you keep me safe. Pique attacked me at my bar last night, and he would have killed me in front of everyone if Theo hadn't intervened. Today Shock was attacked twice inside my place. What's the use of working for you if this is all I get?"

Dread smiled tightly. "Speaking of working for us, I believe you have something that belongs to me. Savor said you didn't complete the handover."

My hand went to my pocket to the USB device that Phil Anchor had given me so reluctantly. I was lucky it hadn't fallen out in one of the cabs. I was almost tempted to lie and say I had lost it. But Dread would order Phil to make another copy, and he would have to go through the hell of turning it over again.

I pulled out the storage device. "Phil dropped it off this morning." Dread reached for it, but I didn't pass it over at first. "I left a message for Vex, but I haven't heard back yet. What are you going to do about these attacks on me and Shock?"

"I'll send Stun over to scare Pique off your territory. Meanwhile, you'll be safer staying here in the center until Vex gets home. I'm sure he'll want to speak to you."

I didn't like the sound of that. Dread was anything but welcoming. Maybe Dread *was* the attacker. He was cold as ice.

No wonder his wife had left him. I had felt sorry for him seeing all the tabloid stories that gleefully described how she was openly doting on a much-younger man, and how her affair with Crave had been going on for months, right under Dread's nose. This wasn't the first sex scandal that Crave's persona, jeweler-extraordinaire Mark Cravet, had been involved in. Right before 9/11, Crave had been part of the celebrity trial of the season when a TV actress successfully sued him for breech of promise and got a huge settlement. I didn't know then that he was a demon. Now that the prophet's wife was involved with him, the blogs and gossip columnists were going wild as they cut the sanctimonious prophet down to the level of ordinary men.

"There's a loft you can use upstairs," Dread added without a drop of graciousness.

"I'm not staying here. I'll come back when Vex gets home, but thanks anyway." I pushed up out of the deceptively comfortable chair, swaying from the effects of Dread's signature as I stood. I wasn't going back to Revel's, that was for sure, and my bar wasn't safe anymore. I would have to figure out where to go.

Dread rose and came to the corner of the desk to stand too close to me. "Vex's orders are that I protect you. I can't do that if you leave the center."

Is that a threat? I almost asked. He was waiting to see what I would do, as if he didn't care either way.

How can I trust him? That was the real question. Dread spoke for Vex, so defying him meant defying Vex. Whatever Vex's misgivings about Dread, his second-in-command still held his premier position, controlling the Fellowship empire as the prophet. But Dread could be the demon who was responsible for the attacks on Shock.

Vex knew I was here because of my message. I could call back and tell him I was waiting for him. Even if I should fear Dread, surely he wouldn't do anything to me here.

But I wanted proof. "Okay, I could use a place to stay," I said, just to see how he would react. He was so close to me that I managed to brush the back of my hand against his fingertips as I started past him.

Energy arced between us—he felt a burning, deep humiliation, staining him violet to his core. He felt betrayed, a sacrificial lamb, a laughingstock in front of people who, trembling, used to obey his word. A bright ribbon of bitterness wound through him, wrapped with jealousy and thwarted passion.

Suddenly his eyes weren't so shuttered. Rage blazed up in him, distorting his features. "Don't touch me!" He grabbed my wrist, his fist so tight that I gasped. He pulled hard on my emotions despite my shields, tasting my determination to protect Shock no matter the cost.

"I almost died last night!" I hissed into his face. "Shock was almost killed today. I have to know if I can trust you."

Through his grip, his suffocating blanket of humiliation overlay something buried deeper. He was armored in arrogance, yet there was a yearning budding inside of him, resonating with the even-larger void inside of me. Although Dread was powerful with his reserves stoked high, his essence was beginning to run out. He would have to take another demon; otherwise, within a few months, he would begin to wither and die.

"You've got the same problem as me." I now wished I hadn't touched him. The need to rekindle could make demons lose their minds. One time a demon got run over by a truck when he tried to get hold of me to steal my core. I didn't wait around for him to resurrect and resume the chase.

"Yes," Dread agreed, his upper lip twitching in distaste.

I tugged on my arm, and he seemed to remember himself as he let go of me. I thought it would break the connection between us. But it felt as if a wall had been breached. He felt my sympathy—*how could I not, being stuck in the same predicament?* Plus, he could sense that I never intended to hurt him when I touched him.

"For the first time in my life, I have this problem," he added bitterly.

My heart leaped. Maybe there was a chance for me. "How did you get this old without having to take another demon?"

"I did consume a demon, every two hundred years, regular as clockwork. My wife and I birthed demons for each other."

Ick! "Oh, really," I said faintly.

"We were everything to each other." His voice was tight, but his anger and frustration blazed out. But beneath it all was a despondent wail. I could feel it even though I wasn't touching him. "She gave Crave her offspring. He's not even one hundred fifty years old. He doesn't need it, and she knows I do. They say she took the offspring he birthed." His jaw ground for a moment. "That's our ritual. Our bond."

It sounded awful, but his pain was real. "I'm sorry, Dread."

It took a few moments for him to regain his composure.

"It'll be all right," I told him.

Dread clung to his proper facade. "I'm supposed to say that to you."

I smiled at him, feeling sorry for him now that I was fairly sure he wasn't going to attack me to steal my essence. I felt even more sorry for myself. Dread would have no hesitation in consuming a demon once he got hold of one. My problem wasn't going to be solved so easily.

But right now, my biggest concern was to figure out who was trying to kill Shock and stop them. That was far more important than my need to replenish myself. But at least I had found something in common with Dread. If he wasn't behind the attack, I needed to get him on my side so he would help me fix this situation fast.

Dread actually smiled at me, his well-honed preacher expression practically insisting I trust him. I watched him get on the phone, setting everything into motion so that I could stay at the Prophet's Center. The poor man didn't realize he had the illusion of control, but little else.

9

As we left Dread's office, he told me, "You'll have to go back downstairs and register with the security system."

"Why?"

"Since you're going to be staying here for a few days, you'll need to be scanned so I don't have to keep approving your presence in the center."

I wondered if he was telling the truth. What was it about the man that made me doubt every word he said? Regardless, it would be impossible for Dread to do away with me quietly if I was on record in their security system. Clearly, it made sense to cooperate. "Fine, let's get it over with."

As we rounded the corner, Theo stood up, waiting for us to rejoin him. I told him, "I'm going to stay here tonight. But I have to go down and log in officially."

Theo nodded, but Dread hardly glanced at him, asking me, "Do you want me to send for Shock?"

"No, she's fine." I wasn't going to tell him where Shock was. After a few moments, I added, "Thank you, anyway."

Theo caught my eye, letting me know he understood that I didn't trust the prophet. It was probably obvious to Dread, too. Things cooled perceptibly between us, and Dread didn't smile at me again.

Without another word I went back downstairs to the security desk and went through the process of having my driver's license scanned into the computer.

When the guard reached out a hand for Theo's ID, Dread said blandly, "That's not necessary, Martin."

"He's leaving, anyway," I agreed.

"Not yet," Theo said quietly, to me alone.

"I'm fine now, Theo. Don't you need to get to work?"

"It's my day off. I know you can take care of yourself, but I'd like to keep you company for a while. Then I'll go home."

Still I hesitated, so he took my hand, letting me absorb his determination to support me, to do whatever I needed, to be my rock to stand on. I took what he offered, an instant pick-me-up. "All right, you can come settle me in."

Dread merely smiled, as if it were only to be expected—many demons had an entourage of humans who gave them sustenance. He expected me to feed off Theo before I sent him away. Dread led the way back through the gate, which opened automatically for us.

Reaching the sixth floor, we found the elevator vestibule enclosed by more decorative bronze walls with a sliding gate that looked like a vault. Dread lifted his face to the camera, and the gate quickly slid open. I could imagine it shutting even faster if someone unauthorized tried to slip past.

Dread showed me into a spectacular loft on the northwest corner of the building. A wall of windows had a sweeping view of the river and Manhattan. To the north, the low brick buildings of Williamsburg and Greenpoint were oddly punctuated by slender, postmodern apartment towers, with the tallest ones near the waterfront. Farther upriver, the end of Roosevelt Island supported the cream lace struts of the Queensboro Bridge. From this vantage point, all of the Lower East Side and Midtown, complete with the Empire State Building, spread before us. I had to walk right up to the window to look south, where the sweeping cable and blackened stone supports of the Willamsburg Bridge loomed beside the Prophet's Center.

The loft looked as if it had been designed by someone who had been paid a great deal of money. Earth tones predominated, perhaps to contrast with the stark urban vista, with shades of beige and green accented by splashes of russet and gold. The bedroom was an open loft along the interior wall with a floating staircase leading up. Underneath was a long galley kitchen separated from the living space by a marble-topped island with four stools.

"Welcome home," Dread announced. I gave him a sharp look, but I didn't want to openly contradict him. He added, "This is one of our VIP suites."

I wandered around the loft, peeking into the door in the corner that led to the bathroom. I was at a loss for what to say. "Nice. Very nice."

"The kitchen is fully stocked," Dread explained, glancing in Theo's direction. "The maid will come in to clean and refill the supplies. You don't have to worry about a thing. Just press this red square." He showed me the touch screen mounted in the wall next to the door. "June will answer anytime day or night, and can get you anything you need."

"Where's the camera so I make sure she sees me?"

Theo didn't bother to hide his grin. But Dread took my question seriously. "There aren't any cameras in here. The Fellowship would never violate your privacy. It goes against everything we stand for."

"Sure," I agreed pleasantly.

He glanced at Theo again. "We have a Fellowship circle tomorrow morning. I'd take it as a favor if you attended with me, Allay. Once you get to know us, you'll understand the strength of our commitment."

Huh? His invitation came out of nowhere. Why was Dread putting on the prophet act with me? Was it for Theo? I must have looked completely dubious. I gestured to my smudged white tank top and low-slung skirt. "These aren't exactly church-going clothes. I think I'll have to beg off."

Dread got even stiffer, as if he didn't like being contradicted. "The Fellowship embraces everyone, regardless of how they look or act."

"How generous of you," I managed to say. For him to push me this way, I must have made a bigger impact on him than I thought.

"We wouldn't be the church of the people without the people." His joke fell flat when I didn't smile. "I'll pick you up tomorrow morning at ten thirty."

Dread didn't wait for my answer. He gave me his professional preacher's smile, and left. The door closed behind him with a whisper-smooth click.

Theo let out his breath in a rush, turning around to look at the loft again. "Whew! You didn't tell me you were some kind of bigwig. Talk about rolling out the red carpet."

"I'm not; I'm nobody. I don't get it." I paced over to the windows, my arms crossed tightly.

"They must have had some reason to buy your bar. Looks like it might be payback time," he said carefully.

I absently agreed. "Might be. I had better call Darryl and tell him I'm not coming home tonight."

Theo went into the bathroom while I called both the bar and Lolita on her cell to explain that I wouldn't be coming home for a couple of days. They were worried about me, but I lied and said I was fine, that Shock just needed me to take care of her until she was better. Apparently, Savor had kept his word and had watched over the bar while I was busy dealing with Shock. Great. My debts to demons all over the Greater New York area were multiplying like crazy.

When Theo emerged, he sat quietly in a chair in the corner, gazing out at the currents in the river. Heavy-laden barges plowed by from time to time, pushed by tiny tugboats. Long trails of white foam separated in a V in their wake. Empty barges sat much higher in the water than the full ones.

After I finished talking to my bartenders, I paced

through the loft. The setting sun cast a pink glow on the high scudding clouds, as I tried to think of what else I could do. But waiting for Vex to return seemed like the smartest move. Vex was the only one who could give me a straight answer about what was going on.

Finally I plopped down on the sofa, staring at the flaming sky and the dark mass of buildings across the silvery swath of river. Theo came to sit next to me and silently took my hand. I needed sustenance. Badly.

His palm felt hot on mine, but I didn't feed from him. Not yet. I held his hand lightly, taking comfort from the simple act.

We sat together in the fading light. It felt good to relax with each other. I couldn't remember the last time I had watched the sun set with a guy.

He was so comfortable with me that it brought a lump to my throat. I was engulfed by a natural feeling much like my own signature, like a gentle swell of water lifting us up and carrying us along.

Then I realized he was reining himself in, as if he didn't want to feel too much. I took some of his conflicted emotions to give him some ease. It was a bittersweet feeling; it was so good it almost made me forget I was using him again. Then I abandoned myself to the pleasure of feeding.

I don't know how long we sat there, but it was full dark with a glorious view of the light-spangled skyline of the city, when I finally tried to pull my hand away. "It's time for you to go, Theo."

His fingers tightened convulsively, as if he were hanging on to me to keep me from plummeting away. "I can't."

I shook my head. "You aren't staying here, Theo."

"Allay, you can't trust the prophet. He's completely focused on you, as if he wants something from you. He never even looked me in the eye."

"You should have seen how grudgingly he invited me to stay here. He's only doing it because he knows I'm a good friend of his nephew." I couldn't tell Theo that Dread acted that way because I had deliberately connected with him, to get him to help me.

"I don't think so. What if this is a setup? What if he's manipulating you? If only for your sister's sake, you should have someone else involved who knows what's going on."

My protest died on my lips. He had hit on my biggest fear—what if the people who were supposed to protect me were trying to kill me and Shock? I had to protect Shock.

"You need someone you can trust, more than Fortunay," he said, as if playing his last card. "That guy is shiftier than a Ferrari. And he has your sister."

I looked at him with new appreciation. "You're right, Theo. But I don't know what I've gotten myself into, and it could be dangerous for you. Deadly, even. I can't take that responsibility."

"I'm responsible for myself, just like you are for yourself. I've never met anyone with more determination than you. But any Marine will say you need a buddy at your side during combat." He rubbed his blackened eye. "Even one who's fallen a couple of times."

I smiled, leaning closer so I could brush his hair away from his forehead to look at the cut. "It's not so bad. But you'll probably have a scar there."

His arm circled my shoulders, pulling me in closer. It felt good when he touched me. "I don't care," he whispered.

He was telling the truth. I put my hand on his chest, smiling up at him. Feeding on him in the darkness was simple and almost sweet. But the feel of him under me aroused other, more intense stirrings. I wanted to press myself on him, drink deep of his heady spirit, satiate myself until I was filled.

There was a knock on the door, and I instantly jerked away. We both sat there, blinking at the door as if expecting someone to walk in. After a few moments, the knock came again, louder this time.

Theo went to open it. A woman, even taller than he, was braced at attention outside. She wasn't a demon, but the deadly focus that emanated from her was the next-best thing. I took in her short hair—nothing to grab in a fight—and her broad shoulders under the khaki uniform shirt, and knew she would be a lot to tangle with. Her stance said she was well trained, and her ramrod straight back screamed military, maybe Special Forces.

I was instantly on alert, shaking off the logy, sensual feelings caused from cuddling with Theo. I hurried over to meet them at the door.

"I'm Montagna, security chief of the Prophet's Center," she introduced herself crisply. Montagna gestured to a much shorter man who was pushing a rolling cart piled with shopping bags. "Delivery for Emma Meyers."

I peeked around the door. "What the hell . . . ?"

I retreated as the porter pushed the cart inside. "Where do you want it, Ms. Meyers?" Montagna asked.

"Anywhere." I gestured vaguely to the foyer. "I don't care."

Montagna stood back, checking us out while the porter briskly unloaded a dozen bags prominently marked SAKS FIFTH AVENUE. He stacked them in two rows, nearly filling the space along the wall by the door. Montagna gave them a last steely look, and the door shut behind them.

Theo looked through the peephole until they disappeared. He tried the handle, and it turned. He opened the door slightly to be sure it wasn't locked, then closed it again. He seemed relieved, but with the level of automation in this building, I didn't doubt any door could be locked the instant Vex or Dread ordered it.

I looked down at the array of bags. "How did they get it here so quick? By helicopter?"

"I doubt they do this for all their VIP guests," Theo said.

"You think?" I asked sarcastically. The mood was completely shattered.

I bent down and peeked between the layers of tissue. It contained an entire wardrobe, including boxes of satin undies of various shapes. Damn them, even the bras were the correct size.

A white card was sticking up from one of the bags. It had *Emma Meyers* written on the front. I plucked it out and ripped open the note—*I'll be back tomorrow afternoon. Sorry I missed you today.*

It was signed *V.* It wasn't Vex's handwriting, but I had no doubt it was written by his orders.

So this was Vex's doing. It was too much. What did Vex mean by this? Was it a message to Dread? To me?

I stepped away from the bags. "You know what? I'm going to take a long, hot bath and try to forget about all this."

Theo nodded. "I'll rustle up something for us to eat."

I gave him a grateful look, squeezing his arm in a wordless apology for snapping at him. I should have sent him away, but I was unnerved by Vex's extravagant gesture. I remembered how hard I had to work to convince him to "loan Michael" the money to fix the structural problems on the facade of the bar. It wasn't like Vex to toss presents at me—that was what Revel did. *I don't like this.*

The bathroom door was under the stairs, a big loftlike space with plenty of room between everything. It was a sensualist's delight; the Fellowship encouraged its members to indulge the senses. Absolute autonomy required that they know and accept themselves in every aspect, good, bad, excesses, and inhibitions. The church said there were many paths to knowledge—emotional, spiritual, and physical.

The steam shower had pulsing jets spaced around the marble and glass enclosure. The towels were thick and warmed by the rod, and the floor tiles were heated from below. The cabinets were filled with toiletries, unopened packets of makeup, hair accessories, and every beauty appliance imaginable.

Since Vex had built some of the most notorious palaces

in history, I wasn't surprised by the luxury. Impressing potential allies was apparently a time-honored tactic.

I decided to take a bath in the large Jacuzzi tub under one window; that would give me plenty of time to hide away. I could hear Theo in the kitchen, whistling as he prepared a meal I wouldn't eat. The last thing I wanted to do tonight was to play hide-the-food with my napkin.

I pulled aside the sheer curtains so I could see the night view, and lowered the lights. The water filled quickly, and when I undressed and slipped in, the frothing from the jets hid most of my body.

Theo called through the door, "Food delivery."

He probably wanted to join me. But I had to be alone to deal with the food. Already preparing words to get rid of him, I called, "Okay, come on in."

Theo glanced down at the tantalizing glimpses of my body among the ripples, his eyes crinkling in appreciation. I barely responded. This was the part I hated, the maneuvering, the lying so he wouldn't find out. This was why I should have sent him away.

He set the plate on the ledge next to me, along with a glass of dark red wine. It was a light meal with assorted cheese, crackers, lots of fruit, and small crusty rolls.

"Take your time." Theo headed out. "I'm going to hit the couch."

Startled, I gave him a real smile of gratitude as he closed the door. He was being awfully accommodating, making it easy for me to let him stay. There was no pressure, no explanation required. It was exactly what I needed.

But it wasn't fair to him. I was lying to him, creating a relationship that wasn't true. I felt guilty as I flushed the nice plate of food down the toilet. He deserved better. He was a good guy who said what he felt. His eyes told me more than most people did when they spoke out loud. I knew exactly how much he had doubted Dread's intentions with every knowing glance he gave me. When he looked at me in a certain way, was it admiration? Lust? Or just his way of assuring me that I wasn't alone?

When he had put his arm around me on the couch, pulling me against him, it had been electrifying. How could one touch ignite me like that? His firm hands were so confident that they belonged on me, so sure in drawing me closer. If the doorbell hadn't rung, I would have kissed him, and maybe more.

No wonder he wouldn't go away. Our bodies blazed up whenever we got close, and he was definitely getting possessive. Without a doubt, the maiden-in-distress routine was a powerful aphrodisiac. It wasn't fair to ensnare him while feebly saying, "No . . . no . . . go away. . . ."

I have to make him leave.

I was in over my head. I'd stumbled into the midst of a demon power struggle, and as little as I cared about that, I needed help finding out who had attacked Shock—and making sure it didn't happen again. It wasn't right to use Theo as a human shield.

I wrapped a thick white robe around myself and left the steamy bathroom. Putting the empty plate in the dishwasher, I couldn't miss the huge pile of shopping bags gleaming under the spotlight in the foyer. The rest of the loft was dark, illuminated only by the lights of the city.

Before I met with Vex, I needed to find out if it was true that he owned my bar. But I didn't want to call Michael from here if they were watching me. It could get Michael into trouble.

Is Dread looking at me now? Did he watch me bathe . . . like Revel, the consummate voyeur?

Revel had been proud when he showed me his surveillance system in the Malibu house that he used to watch his entourage and listen in on what they were doing. He loved it all; the sex, the fights, the lies, the secrets told. I spied on them, too, and on one memorable occasion stroked him to orgasm as we watched.

I couldn't let a demon control me again. I had to make my own way, or I was sunk.

I was willing to bet that Dread was full of shit and there were cameras in the loft. It was time to make a statement to both him and Vex. They might own the bar, but they didn't own me.

I drifted closer to Theo. He was sleeping on the couch, his head buried in a soft cushion. He had pulled off his shoes and T-shirt, and flung himself down wearing only his jeans.

I could make my point with Vex and Dread while I also dealt with Theo. Much as I needed some quality backup, it wasn't safe for him to get caught up in this. But I'd hooked him so thoroughly, I doubted anything would make him walk out on me now. I would have to aggravate him to the point where he'd give up and go away when I ordered him to.

I pulled the tie on the belt of my robe, letting it fall open. My reflection in the windows flashed skin with every step. Theo didn't stir.

It wouldn't be enough to deny him sex—he probably wasn't expecting it, considering that he hadn't pushed himself on me in the bathroom. I had to taunt him with it, then deny him. I had to be such an unbearable cock tease that it pissed him off to no end. A high-testosterone man who had possessed a woman once didn't take kindly to not getting her again, especially when she was dangling herself in front of him.

Sad to say, more than once I'd used the same technique to get rid of obsessed lovers. I couldn't help it that I could tell exactly what they wanted, and that I felt compelled to give it to them so I could sip the flow of their contentment. Unfortunately, that drove men wild. If you gave them what they wanted, they got addicted.

And if you wanted to get rid of them, all you had to do was fluctuate between being crazy needy and a raging bitch. That made even the most determined men go away. I would rather have been adult about ending my relationships, but a few men had hovered around the bar too long, waiting and hoping for me to come back to them, unable to understand why I didn't want to see them again when we were "perfect" together. That was disturbing. I couldn't let anyone watch me too closely, or they would discover I was different.

But I could certainly show Dread a thing or two. The way he acted tomorrow morning should tell me if he was lying about the cameras. Then I could call Michael to find out why he hadn't told me Vex owned my bar.

I sat down on the couch, leaning back against Theo's thighs. One arm was flung over his head and the other trailed off the edge. The glow from the city lights edged his cheekbones and chin, casting a deep shadow across his face.

I touched his cheek with the backs of my fingers. He was looking pretty beat-up on my account. It hardened my resolve to send him away.

Theo shifted under my touch and slowly opened his eyes. He drew in his breath, seeing the slice of chest and belly my open robe exposed.

My fingers ran down his jaw to his mouth, shifting back and forth over his lips. His head tilted back, pulling away, as if it were too much.

I expected him to put his arm around me as he did before, drawing me in so tenderly. But he closed his eyes, as if willing himself not to reach out to me. He was holding himself back.

Bending over, I kissed him. His lips responded with such passion that it surprised me. He finally moved, clasping my arm, sending a surge of his desire through me in verdant plumes. My thighs shifted, squeezing together in anticipation.

His mouth was a delight; soft, tender kisses in spite of

his rising heat, as if promising devotion with everyone. We kissed as if there were nothing else in the world.

Finally I pulled away. His fingers pressed my arm, but he didn't try to draw me closer. We were both breathing faster, sitting next to each other.

I hesitated, drawing out the moment, expecting him to tip over the edge. When he made his move, I would shut him down and stalk off as if I were offended, then rinse and repeat. After a few hours of that, he'd be sick and tired of me.

But in fact, I kept dwelling on the idea of his pushing me down and taking me from the top this time. . . .

Biting my lip hard, I forced myself to remember why I was doing this. It wasn't fair to him. I had to let him go.

Time to go for broke. My hand slid down his belly to brush against his jeans, tight over his straining cock. He tensed in response. I undid the buttons, freeing him. Stroking him, I rocked against his body, watching his face.

He bucked under my hand, so thick I almost couldn't close my fist around him. He stretched and clenched at every stroke, every scrape of my fingernails, driving him higher, deeper. . . .

His hand tightened around my arm, as a deep growl rose inside him. Still he said nothing, did nothing. How could I tease a man who devoured every drop I gave him so gratefully and never asked for more?

"What do you want, Theo?"

Instantly he replied, "Whatever you want."

My eyes opened wider. "Now there's a blank check."

"Not really—you'd never cash it."

I hesitated, realizing it was true. I didn't like taking anything from anyone. How could he understand me so well in only one day? I was supposed to be repelling him, not making him fall in love with me.

I stroked him firmer, feeling him so hard in my hand. He was raging with desire, pouring into me through my palm.

A kaleidoscope of colors—passion, pain, frustration, joy, fear, and sorrow; how could one man feel so much? His emotions overwhelmed me, carrying me along in spite of myself.

The last sane voice in my head reminded me that if I wasn't the most selfish bitch in the world, I would keep torturing him instead of pleasing him. I would drive him away.

I let go of him and rolled back to rub my moistened nub. My intake of breath, my shifting body lying on his, made him draw in his breath. His abandoned cock jerked between us as I slid my fingers back and forth across myself.

I tilted my head against the couch, letting the sensation fill me up. He was so warm and strong beneath me as he held me against himself.

My body pulsed, sending a white-hot light flooding through me. My quick climax caught me by surprise, but I went with it, anyway. I tensed against him, and he moaned along with me, though his sound was more of yearning than ecstasy.

When I finally relaxed against him, my hand brushed his cock. He wasn't touching himself. Through the waves of desire radiating off him, I followed the purple path of pain to its source.

He thought he deserved to suffer. He thought he wasn't good enough for me.

That broke through my haze of pleasure. Questions hovered on my lips. How could he possibly think that? But shared secrets would only deepen our intimacy. It would bind him to me. I had to lure him on, and then reject him.

Still breathless, I pushed myself farther down the couch. I leaned back, spreading my legs slightly. My fingers stroked the silky dark hair on my mound. "I'd like to cash my check now, please."

The scent of my flesh drifted up, moist from my arousal. The frank lust in his eyes was almost too much for me. I reached out for his hand, pulling it to me. His fingers found my clit, rubbing lightly across it.

I arched my back, my eyes closed, as he slid off the couch and moved between my legs. He kissed the inside of my knee, his lips hot against my skin, and trailed his mouth inward. I spread my legs wider. His palm burned across my thigh, searing me with his feelings; he wanted to join with me, become one with me.

He buried his face in my mound, as his hand held my belly, the very core of me. His other hand slid under my buttocks, lifting my hips. I writhed beneath him, crying out until it was too much.

He eased off to let me breathe as he kissed up to my belly button, then back down, teasing me until his lips brushed across my nub again. He flicked his tongue across me, refusing to let me squirm away as my orgasm built.

My fingers buried in his thick hair, tightening and pulling as he strained against me. It felt so good, like nothing I'd ever had before. Then all thought left as I abandoned myself to the pleasure.

My aura seemed to explode like a splintered prism.

When I finally relaxed, he drew away slowly, carefully, until I loosened my fingers in his hair. I must have hurt him; I had been tugging so hard. His breath was fast on my thigh, and then his warmth was gone. I heard him fall back on the rug.

When I opened my eyes, he was watching me with that now-familiar pained expression. His cock was still firm, jutting from his opened jeans, and from his flushed and heavy breathing, he seemed ready to die if he didn't climax.

But he wasn't making a move. He was lying there instead of trying to take me. How could I reject him if he didn't pursue me?

I wanted nothing more than to pull him on top of me so he could drive himself deep inside of me. I wanted to be filled by him, get fucked insensible. I wanted to cuddle against him for hours, letting him touch me everywhere, kiss me everywhere. . . .

This isn't working out quite like I planned.

It took every ounce of will for me to push myself to my feet. I took a few unsteady steps away, trying to think of something, anything to say. At least Dread had seen a thing or two if he was watching.

"That will be all." I wanted to smack myself, it sounded so stupid. But my brain seemed to have stopped working.

He groaned in response.

Tottering over to the steps up to the loft, I sneaked a look back. He was still lying on the rug, one arm flung over his eyes. He was exposed by his open fly, his jeans splayed back over his belly, but he didn't cover himself. He was twisting slightly as he shuddered, so primed and ready to release that he couldn't contain himself.

I hurried, hoping he would at least masturbate. He deserved some relief, but I couldn't give it to him. I had to push him away so he would be safe.

10

I didn't even pretend to sleep. I was hoping Theo would come up to the loft so I could reject him properly. I didn't bother lowering my voice as I called Revel to find out how Shock was doing; she was improved, though she wasn't up and moving around much yet. She had come within a hairbreadth of being consumed.

Then I paced around the loft and turned on the television, making plenty of noise, waiting for Theo to make some kind, any kind of advance toward me so I could be a bitch. But a peek into the living room below showed that he had crawled back onto the couch and though he rolled every now and then, indicating his sleep was interrupted, he never tried to come upstairs.

It was frustrating. I wondered if I was being played. I could sense his true nature and there was nothing meek about it—he was a driven, balls-to-the-wall kind of guy. Why was he being so accommodating, so selfless? We met only last night; he couldn't be that infatuated with me already. Could he?

Every emotion I felt in him said he was falling in love with me.

Theo got up with the streaks of dawn lighting the sky, and quietly puttered around the kitchen. This time I stayed quiet, as if I were asleep. I heard him fix some eggs, which he ate standing up at the counter; then he carried his second cup of hot tea into the bathroom.

I heard him take a shower in the hydro-chamber, turning on the jets full blast. I wouldn't mind trying that, but not with him in the bathroom. Since I had flubbed it so badly last night, I didn't want to risk trying the old bait-and-switch again. The cold shoulder was my safest choice at this point.

I waited until ten o'clock to come down. He was watching the sky over the city, sitting there patiently. The bruise on his cheek had darkened, but the smudge under his eye wasn't as bad today. He was wearing the olive drab T-shirt again. His hair had curled tightly as it dried.

I could barely meet his eyes, I felt so guilty about using him. I should have been used to it by now, justifying myself with the pleasure I was giving him in exchange. Some men paid a lot of money to be treated this badly. But he didn't want that, so it sucked in every way possible.

I wrapped the robe more tightly around me as I knelt down and rifled through the shopping bags. There were shiny, high-heeled shoes with tiny straps, and filmy dresses, some with plunging necklines and tight waists and others more conservative. I tossed them aside, digging deeper.

Theo held up some sheer silk hose I had dropped onto the floor. "Are you sure you don't want these?"

"I wouldn't be caught dead in nylons."

"They're stockings."

"Whatever."

I grabbed a few things that looked like they would do, and headed to the bathroom. Theo had fixed some hard-boiled eggs and bacon, the aroma of which was drifting from the warmer, and I quickly scooped some onto a plate along with a banana. I gave him a quick wave as I disappeared into the bathroom. Then I flushed the food down the toilet.

I had chosen clothes that clearly weren't intended to

make an impression. My black hip-hugging slacks flared at the bottom over patent-leather Mary Janes, and my dark purple T-shirt had a scoop neck and cap sleeves. With my face sans makeup, as usual, and my hair spiky from being wet down, I looked the same as I did any other day at the bar. All I needed was a black apron and I was set.

When I emerged, Theo smiled. "You ain't nobody's 'Pretty Woman,' are you?"

For the first time I met his eyes, grinning in return. It was hard to push away a guy who got me so well.

"We're the same that way," he said with satisfaction. "I can't handle people who depend on others to take care of them—who let someone else make the decisions. You don't let yourself get jerked around."

"Is that why you're being so accommodating? You seem like you're really dominant, but you haven't tried to impose yourself on me at all."

"I believe in dominating myself and my own desires, not others."

I shivered. How could I not like it that he gave me exactly what I wanted? I was used to doing that for other people, not getting it from someone else. I could sense his aggressiveness, his desire to fix everything, and that sense of constrained power was very sexy.

There was a polite knock on the door, and Theo went to answer it. It was Dread's assistant, June, wearing traditional church-going garb, complete with heels, flowery dress, and gold cross with the distinctive flared arms of the Fellowship of Truth. Her long black hair was pinned back with crystal pavé dragonflies.

"Good morning—" June's cheery greeting broke off when she saw the jumbled clothes and boxes on the floor. "Oh! I'll call and have someone put these things away for you."

"I'll do it later," I said.

June's impossibly pert nose kept her from looking angry,

but there was a line between her delicate brows. "No, really, I insist. The prophet would be upset if he knew I wasn't taking care of you." Unable to keep her eyes off the mess, June added, "The prophet is in the Evergreen Chapel. If you'll come with me, I'll take you both there."

I glanced at Theo. "I'm sorry, but Theo has to be going now."

"I don't have anything else to do," he said mildly. "I'd love to join your circle," he added to June.

"We'd be glad to have you." June sparkled in that special way petite, pretty women have. With her bangs and pink braces, she could have passed for fourteen. "Have you joined our circle before?"

"I've attended a time or two." Theo was polite but not too friendly.

I butted in. "I really think you should be going now, Theo. I'll call you later."

June, focused completely on him, didn't even glance at me. "Our circle is open, Theo. Feel free to join us before you go."

He was looking at me instead of at her. "I think I will."

I didn't try to hide how angry I was. I should have kicked him out sooner, before June came, but who knew she would interfere? I thought it would be easier to send him on his way if we were both on the move.

As we walked through the hallway to the elevator, June chatted brightly about the Fellowship, explaining how it had transformed her life. Two years ago, she had decided to move to New York from Washington to devote her life to the truth. But the expert way she told her story indicated she wasn't as green as she appeared to be. People probably trusted her instantly, figuring she was as defenseless as a kitten. But she couldn't have survived as Dread's assistant unless she was sharp and on her toes.

June addressed her remarks to both of us, and Theo responded nearly as infrequently as I did. But I noticed that

June caught his eye a few times, smiling a little longer than necessary. It was done so deftly that she thought I didn't notice.

The Evergreen Chapel was hung with sheer green draperies on every wall. On the far wall, a large gold cross was mounted in a niche much like an altar. The upright spindle was thin and pointed, but the arms flared like a Greek cross.

There was no sign of the concrete floors and exposed ducts that characterized the rest of the Prophet's Center; instead, the recessed lighting cast a warm glow. Plush carpeting surrounded a dark green marble slab in the center. It was knee-high, vaguely coffin-sized, with rounded, polished edges. Many Fellowship circles were held without the altar, but in the very heart of the church they upheld tradition.

The distinct scent of incense seemed designed to subdue the clash of expensive perfumes in the room. There must have been two dozen people dispersed in small groups speaking quietly with one another. They were of various ages, a few nicely dressed couples, a clutch of employees and their families, and several young hipsters from the neighborhood. There were no other demons present, except for Dread, who was decked out in a very expensive charcoal suit.

When Dread saw us, he raised one hand, beckoning us over. I could sense his intense interest in me, even stronger than yesterday when I had connected with him. He ignored Theo as he greeted me. Did that mean he hadn't seen what we did last night? Or had he seen us and was so coldly arrogant that he felt compelled to treat Theo as insignificant?

After all that, I was no closer to finding out if I had privacy in the loft. I needed to find a way to call Michael without anyone listening.

Dread immediately ushered me forward to the center of the room to stand next to the altar. In his sonorous prophet-voice, he announced, "I would like to introduce Emma

Meyers, the friend I've told you about. She is very close to the spirit, so we must all encourage her devotions."

I tensed up, feeling trapped in the midst of so many curious eyes, including Theo when he heard my real name. What was Dread doing? I tried to smile, but I must have looked alarmed.

June smiled and called out, "Welcome!" along with the others. I was soon surrounded by people greeting me and shaking my hand. They were excited to meet someone new who had been singled out by the prophet himself. Some were too eager, smiling too fiercely, talking too intently, and when I touched their hands, I could tell they were trying to woo me for their own purposes. I didn't mind—greed and selfish desire were energy just like other emotions, only they didn't taste as good.

My smile was rather fixed, and I kept my replies short in answer to their questions of where I lived, what I did, and what my bar was like. One of the younger, nice-looking men assured me that he would come by soon to check out the Den.

Theo shifted away to the outer edge of the room, keeping a low profile. June joined him, fingering the Fellowship cross at her throat. She asked him something, but they were too far away for me to overhear. She seemed to be flirting with him, moving her hips, leaning forward to touch his arm in emphasis.

Soon enough the circle was called and everyone joined hands around the slab of marble. I was even more shocked when Dread took my hand. I almost jerked away, but I didn't want to completely alienate him.

It was a test. He didn't try to feed from me, and I didn't want to feed from him. He felt my wariness, my spike of anger at being forced to touch him, unable to refuse in front of everyone. He was taking his time searching me out, to see exactly what I was made of. A couple of times I almost called it quits and let go, but I had nothing to hide. I was suspicious of his motives, yet I needed his help. I also felt a deep sympathy with his need to rekindle himself; on the most basic level, we were in the same boat, and he couldn't help but see that.

I consoled myself by absorbing the fanaticism pouring off the woman next to me. Cherie was a former supermodel, now in her mid-forties. She was rarely seen in print ads anymore. Cherie had found the Fellowship to great fanfare two decades ago when she was on top of the world, and she had been a celebrity fixture of the church ever since.

It looked like she'd had work on her face, and her makeup was too overdone, especially the foundation. Her arms were painfully thin, and I held her hand very gingerly as I skimmed off her devotion. She had plenty to spare. She was practically boiling over with faith.

The circle started with the chant. Each person said a word in turn, going clockwise around the circle, letting the different voices meld into each sentence. "Through freedom lies truth; through truth lies freedom."

Theo and I alone were off a few beats. It went on for quite a while, changing in content but not substance, as I picked up the rhythm. Many of them became tranced by the circular speaking, rocking in time, their eyes rolling up into their head. It was classic group manipulation, reaching for the ecstatic, and right up Zeal's alley. Zeal must have been attending a different circle.

I let Dread have the full brunt of my boredom as the circle wore on. He knew I was tolerating the proceedings like a circus horse being put through my paces. I would do whatever I had to in order to protect Shock, and if that meant I had to be polite and pretend to please his fanatics, so be it.

The one thing I really didn't like was that Theo was across the circle holding hands with June. She appeared to be in rapturous delight. Theo met my gaze occasionally, letting his eyes crinkle. I kept telling myself to stop, that I was supposed to drive him away from me. But he was the only one who seemed to feel the same way I did.

I tried my best not to think about him, so Dread wouldn't pick up on my feelings.

When the chanting stopped, we continued to hold hands through the truth-speaking. Not everyone spoke, but those who did dwelt on the freedom they had gained through the Fellowship to be themselves, to express themselves without fear. I knew they were proselytizing to me. They said they felt accepted in a way they hadn't been before. One man described his life before he joined the church, when he worked long hours to give his family whatever they wanted. But his health deteriorated, he hardly knew his kids, and he hated his job. After finding the Fellowship, he quit work and went back to college to get his degree in social science, intending to fulfill his dream of helping people. He admitted it had been a struggle and his marriage had been destroyed, but he was finally grappling with personal issues that he had ignored for decades.

One young woman spoke about how she used to let boyfriends push her into doing things she didn't want to do. She thought she had to always say yes in order to be loved, and through the church, she realized she had the personal responsibility to set limits for herself. Her voice broke a few times as she described the violence she had suffered, but she had been "uplifted" by the church and it had changed her. Now she was the one who decided what she did or didn't do, and her life and career had blossomed as a result.

It seemed more like group therapy than a religious service, except for the mindless chanting. Even worse, I got the feeling they were trying to outdo one another to impress the prophet.

Then Dread asked if anyone needed to be sustained. One woman stepped forward, letting the circle close behind her. She had spoken earlier about her estrangement from her daughter, and had seemed miserable, unable to articulate a bright side to her troubles like the others. She went to the marble altar and lay down on it, her head at the end near the gold Fellowship cross on the wall.

Dread finally let go of my hand to step forward. It was such a relief. Now I could feed off both Cherie and the woman next to me, who was in a lot of pain from her lower back. Pain was a good thing to take, so I sucked it down, hoping to give her some relief, as well.

At the altar, Dread placed his hands palm down, one on top of the other, on the woman's forehead. Quietly the group chanted in unison, their voices melding into a continuous drone. The woman's face twinged with each indrawn breath. Dread drew off her agony as hard as he could without hurting her. They stayed frozen in that tableau for what felt like a long time until the woman sighed and indicated she was ready to get up. Her aura wasn't as poisonously dark now. But it was depleted more than I would have dared.

With a final benediction from Dread, the circle finally split. I didn't have to hold Dread's hand again. And Theo let go of June's hand. I tried to shake off the vaguely sadomasochistic fog of absorbing at the same time Cherie's rapturous devotion and the pain from the other woman.

Now that the worst was over; it was much easier to talk to everyone. I tried to ask questions about the church so they wouldn't keep probing me; this was my old bartender's trick. Since Dread was feeding from them, clasping everyone's hand reverently, I did the same, freely soaking up the euphoria created by the circle. Touching people in the right way created intimacy, very compelling for the demons who learned how to do it properly. Vex had founded this church on touch, relying on the circle of hands to inspire closeness among the fellows.

But that didn't account for the almost-worshipful way they looked at me. They, including their celebrity, Cherie, gathered round as if they didn't want to miss the chance to talk to me. My casual touches seemed to encourage them.

I had lost sight of Theo in the crowd, when Dread finally appeared to extract me from their admiring embrace. Lowering his voice so only I could hear, Dread said, "Vex won't be back for another few hours. But he asked me to show you around." He steered me to the inner door.

"You talked to him?"

"Early this morning. He's flying back now."

June appeared behind us with Theo in tow. Dread nodded in approval. "Come on, I'll show both of you around the Fellowship complex."

I wasn't sure what kind of game he was playing. He was fooling Theo and June—and all of these other people—about who I was. But why?

I wanted to get rid of Theo before Vex came back. But I also wondered if Dread's little act had something to do with the wild sex I'd almost had with Theo last night. I needed to know for sure. If there were no prying eyes in the VIP loft, then I would be able to call Michael before I saw Vex.

So I agreed, and Dread proceeded to give us the grand tour. The Prophet's Center had dozens of finely decorated meeting rooms and reception halls, along with offices for the senior staff. The third floor had an airwalk linking the center to the building on the next block that housed administrative offices. The church also had a large publicity firm, dedicated to creating educational programs about their philosophy. Recruitment was well organized with banks of cubicles that mobilized truth-speakers to direct action in their communities. Local chapels could apply for monetary support for infrastructure and marketing materials to expand their circle.

Then we went outside and walked down to another white building that had a towering gold cross with flared arms painted on the side facing Manhattan. We stepped into an expansive lobby with an indoor playground for the community. It housed the Fellowship's law library and legal assistance program that served grassroots and national campaigns against a variety of "big brother" laws—from the radical, such as eliminating penalties for recreational drug use and supporting the right to assisted suicide, to the socially conservative, such as backing the National Rifle Association's stance on assault weapons, and the Southern Baptists' attempts to abolish separation of church and state.

Some people protested the apparent contradictions in such causes, but there was a simplicity at the heart of the Fellowship; it was all about personal responsibility. Dread explained that their impact on America had been significant and was growing. They advocated drastically downsizing government and waste by setting up a system of "pay for what you use." Their ideas included a citizens' tax to pay for firemen and policemen; property tax to pay for water and sewage; businesses to pay for schools, local streets, and public areas; cars to be charged via wireless devices to drive on highways and across bridges to pay for maintenance. They also called for the abolishment of income tax and the draft. The popularity of the church had surged during the late 1960s and early 1970s, and again more recently during the Middle East wars and economic recession. Dread pointed to welfare and health-care reform as two of their most successful projects.

I would have gotten more caught up in our philosophical discussion, but Dread seemed to be going through his spiel on automatic, like a salesman extolling the virtues of a used car. I kept looking for the hidden hook in all of his pretty words.

He pointed out other buildings that housed the church's newspaper publisher, real estate management company, one of the largest Internet service providers in the Northeast, and assorted other businesses. There were little storefront restaurants and shops everywhere. I could imagine how busy the streets would be tomorrow when all of their employees returned to work on Monday.

The tour definitely impressed me. The church was a juggernaut on the roll, catching speed. What exactly was it intended to crush?

I couldn't get over that I was a part of all this; a hidden, corrupt part of it, but part of it nonetheless. The tour concluded on the roof of the Prophet's Center, in the garden that was at least a football field long. From this vantage point we could see another park on the roof of the Prophet's Arena not far south of the bridge, on the edge of the Brooklyn Navy Yard.

The payments that had allowed that massive building to go up on the waterfront had passed through my bar.

Dread deftly separated Theo and me. June insisted on keeping Theo with her while a late lunch was served on a small iron table. June had been overtly flirtatious with him during the tour—at one point she had slipped her arm around his waist as she pointed down at a scaled three-dimensional map of the Fellowship complex. But Theo stayed by my side whenever Dread drifted away, and I was certain that he had no interest in her.

Dread took me into the long greenhouse, where we disappeared from their sight among the extravagantly lush plants and flowers. I was finally feeling more comfortable around him, despite his having stayed firmly in his prophet role for the past couple of hours. Maybe that was because I was getting used to the odd sliding sensation of his signature, so it wasn't as disorienting.

I took advantage of having him alone to ask the most important question, "Have you found out who attacked Shock?"

"Not yet. I've checked everyone in our own line, and it's not any of them. That leaves the rogues, of course, and all of the Glory demons."

"Do you know of any demon able to hide its signature?" I asked.

"No, that's impossible." He was irritated. "I think you'll find that Shock's signature merely masked a lighter one. Vex will talk to you about it when he gets here."

Maybe our tour of the church, bringing Theo in tow, had been designed to keep me from pestering him for answers that he wasn't ready to give me. But he wanted to talk to me about something; otherwise he wouldn't have brought me here where we could speak candidly. I raised my brows, looking at him expectantly.

He turned away, uncomfortable, as he fumbled with his phone, checking a text message. Then he finally looked up. "What are you going to do about your problem?" For a moment I didn't understand; then his hand moved to his belly as if covering his core. "How are you going to replenish yourself?"

"Frankly, I haven't thought about it. I'm too busy trying to figure out which demon got into my bar without my sensing it."

"You must have felt the need growing for some time. You're even more depleted than I am." He hesitated again, but couldn't help himself. "How can you withstand the urges?"

At his hungry, searching look, I wanted to take a couple steps backward. It was dangerous to tread this ground. He could lose control and turn on me; he could try to steal my essence for himself. I shouldn't have held his hand for so long during the church service. Even fully shielded, it may have been too tempting.

But he was opening up to me. I needed his help, and the only way to get it was if he trusted me. So I had to be honest. "I ignore it, I push it away, bury it in ordinary hunger. I stay too busy with people so that I can't think about it. It's not that hard—I've walled off that part of my life for a long time, along with Plea's memories."

"You don't use the memories?" He seemed very surprised. "My wife and I compared everything—she knew Glory and I knew Vex, and it gave us an advantage—" He broke off, his mouth working slightly as if the pain of speaking of Lash were too much.

"You must have made a good team. You were together for eons."

Dread nodded, and the benevolent mask of his persona slipped to reveal a broken man unused to expressing his true emotions. His hands were gripping each other so tightly that his fingers were white, as if he were barely holding on, fighting to get the words out. "Why him? Why Crave? He's a filthy *incubus*! She used to laugh at him, the way he sweeps women off their feet, then runs away and toys with them until they're obsessed with him. A stupid little game, the same one every time. And *my wife* . . . is with him now. Feeding him now. Giving him her offspring, when by right it belongs to *me*."

He was red in the face, his voice raised, as spittle flew from his lips. Suddenly he looked like a demon, demented beyond reason.

"Maybe she made a mistake," I suggested gently. "Maybe he convinced her she was different. But once she realizes she got caught up in spite of herself, it will be over. Then you can fix what's gone wrong between the two of you."

His fingers clenched as if wanting to throttle Crave, or perhaps his wife. "I would make her crawl every step of the way from Harlem; then I'd turn her away at the door."

Yikes. Vindictive much?

Carefully, I said, "It couldn't have been perfect between you for sixteen hundred years. People make mistakes. They change and grow. Haven't you ever hurt her in some way?"

"Always, but I did it because she wanted it. This is different. She hurt me. She didn't even tell me the night she left. She disappeared without a word. I made a fool of myself trying to locate her, only to be told that she was in *his* home, under *his* protection. She won't even see me."

So that was where his deep humiliation came from. Lash had turned the tables on him, and he couldn't handle it.

Dread paced away a few steps, unable to contain himself. "She refuses to sit in the same room with me, even with others present. I asked Glory to intercede, but Lash won't speak to me, despite her urging. Why is she rejecting me like this? I've done nothing but take care of her and give her what she needs."

It seemed to me the loss of control had stunned Dread more than anything. He was fumbling, unsure of where to turn. "I'm sorry," I said.

"She's been spreading rumors, lies about me. . . . Vex was furious. I'm not sure if he believes me."

Awkwardly Dread reached out and took my hand. His aura flared as he gave me his hurt and frustration, as well as his gratitude that I was there for him, listening to him, as he finally spoke his pain. His energy was dark and saturated—midnight blue and bloody purple, with a vein of burned ochre, as relief from my presence began to thread its way through him.

It was powerful, hitting me like a punch in the face. It was the kind of demon power I could get drunk on. Taking Petrify's energy had made me too cocky yesterday. I needed to keep my head. But I was gulping him down as fast as he let me, feeling the supercharged energy coursing through my body.

Yet I was relieved when his phone rang, interrupting the intensity of the moment. He released my hand. I had to steady myself against a planter.

His posture straightened when he looked at the number. "Yes, of course," he said crisply into the phone. He listened again, and agreed. "I'll do that now."

He closed the phone. "Vex's plane just landed. He'll be

here shortly. But he's asked me to show you something very special before he gets here. Your friend can't see it."

"Does it have to do with the attacks on Shock?"

"Yes, we think so."

"Good." I was ready to get some answers. Together we rejoined Theo and June. Theo gave me a slight smile, his eyes lighting up in relief at the sight of me.

I still didn't know whether Dread had seen me with Theo last night. He was coldhearted enough that he might discount humans entirely, so it didn't matter what I did with Theo. True, he had been nice enough when he answered Theo's questions during our tour of the complex, but he never gave any indication that he thought Theo was any more than a feed bucket to me. I had tormented the poor man for nothing last night. It was time to cut the cord before big daddy arrived.

"I'll have to say good-bye now, Theo," I told him. "Thank you for everything you've done for me."

June made a slight sound of disappointment to hear that Theo was leaving. Dread shot her a chiding look, and she very prettily apologized. "I'm sorry; I didn't realize Theo was going so soon."

"I can stay," Theo said easily.

June's expression brightened, but I shook my head. "I have to go see an associate of Mr. Anderson's."

June immediately jumped in, "I can take him down to your loft, Ms. Meyers. We'll wait there until you're done."

"Let me wait for you," Theo offered.

I didn't want him with June, and I didn't want him here when Vex came back. The fewer live bodies that got in the way, the better. But I also didn't want to get into an argument about it in front of Dread. In spite of our intense moments of connection, I didn't trust Dread. I didn't want him to know that Theo was important to me.

Theo held my gaze a moment longer, as if checking to

be sure I was okay. I smiled reassuringly. "Okay, I'll be back later."

"Much later," Dread added. He smiled to take the edge off his words, but I didn't like it.

But I had to try to work with him. It was no worse than plastering a pleasant smile on my face with irritating patrons.

June tried to take Theo's arm as they headed to the stairwell. I wondered if he would be able to scrape her off if she was truly determined to take him down.

I'm jealous, I realized. I'd been doing my best to distance myself from Theo all day, but I felt connected to him even across the room, joined together by every understanding glance.

It was past time for him to go home.

But first I needed to see what Dread had to show me. It looked like the gates were finally opening and I was going to get some real information.

I followed Dread down one flight to the top floor of the Prophet's Center. He escorted me into a windowless media room near the elevators. Inside we sat down in one of the rows of overstuffed red chairs that swiveled and reclined back. The lights dimmed and I stared up at the big screen mounted on one wall.

"Zeal made this," Dread explained. "She's a genius when it comes to marketing and PR. She really knows how to grab the target audience in the guts."

The computer graphics had a slick professionalism one expected from Madison Avenue, making it resemble a news show. The honey-voiced announcer explained, *"You are going to witness a true miracle in this program, proved to be real by cutting-edge scientific research."*

As far as infomercials went, it hooked me. The announcer was a sultry brunette, and she introduced the new Electromagnetic Resonating Imaging (ERI) machine by circling it and pointing out its features. It was a large white oval with rounded edges and an inlaid panel on both sides. Someone stepped into the arched opening while a white-blue light bathed them. Using graphs and clips from various scientific experiments, she showed how the advanced ERI recorded the minute energy emanations from people using a high-frequency, high-voltage, low-amperage electrical field.

A key point was that the frequencies exactly matched the color spectrum. The ERI wasn't the same as heat-sensing equipment, which assigned colors for the various temperatures. People actually emitted color depending on the frequency of the particular emotional energy, but it was too weak for the human eye to see. By reading the color and intensity of the aura, the feelings of a person were revealed, making the ERI a far more reliable lie detector than traditional methods. There was also a thirty-percent success rate in pinpointing locations where the energy was disrupted by physical flaws, such as malignant tumors starting to grow long before they were visible on X-rays.

"It's being tested by the FAA now for use as airport metal detectors," Dread explained to me, while the announcer continued speaking in the background. "Nobody can sneak anything past the ERI. The energy is distorted in very predictable ways by metal and plastic, making objects stand out. But this technology is fairly cheap to reproduce. Soon every government building and corporate headquarters will have banks of these. They'll not only be able to spot weapons, but also people who are angry and aggressive."

"That's amazing. Did you develop this?"

"No, it was some guys out of MIT. But once we caught wind of their research, we were able to duplicate the technology fairly easily in our biomedical lab. Now watch this next part."

Shots of various people in the ERI showed similarities in human energy patterns, concentrated around their torso. The machine produced images of auras that were much stronger than I could see with the naked eye, with fine, swirling gradations between the colors.

When a monkey was placed under the arch, its aura was slightly different. Instead of the rainbow-through-a-cloud blanket of human aura, his aura was thinner, hugging his skin. Dogs and cats also had a weaker aura.

Then the announcer's voice grew serious as she said, *"And now I give you the Prophet of the Fellowship of Truth, Thomas Anderson."*

Up on the screen, Dread walked on camera, giving the watching audience his patented cheery wave. He chatted with the nubile announcer, explaining the church's philosophy that when a person accepts the Holy Spirit without reservation, looking only to the inner guidance of that Spirit, they are granted immortality and will never die.

"That's some promise," I said to Dread. "Too bad it's not true."

Dread shrugged. "It doesn't matter. The fear of death is worse than death to most people."

That cut too close to home for me, so I shut up. The video went to a different shot, inside a laboratory. Dread stepped into the arched opening of the ERI machine. I sat forward as the machine hummed. But this time, instead of the fuzzy aura, his outline looked hard-edged, as if the energy filled him rather than surrounded him. The ERI showed three-dimensional cuts of Dread compared to other people. The human aura formed a shell around their bodies, while Dread's body was filled with colors that were shifting much faster than the humans', brighter and more sharply defined.

At the very center of his torso burned a soft, white orb. His core, his essence—captured in all its pulsing glory by the machine.

"We look different." The implications crashed in on me.

"Demons carry our energy within. It's our substance; we're spirit formed into flesh."

"But when I look at you, you have an aura, just like humans do!"

"That's the radiant energy that our eyes can see. For humans, their biophysical processes emit the aural energy, whereas for us, we are nothing but energy held together by our core."

On the video, Dread was smiling compassionately, his trademark preacher's smile, looking as harmless as he could. *"I have been transformed into spirit form. You can be, too. Come find the truth."*

The video ended abruptly, trailing off into a series of screen-sized numbers. "What happened? What's next?"

Dread shrugged. "It's still in production. We need a number of other things before it's ready for release."

"You're not going to show people that. You're proving that you're different, a demon."

"No, Allay, I'm filled with the spirit," Dread corrected. "A holy man who will live forever, set free by the truth. Amen."

"You can't be serious."

Dread leaned closer. "Science has caught up with us, Allay. We knew this would happen eventually, ever since machines began looking inside of people. It was only a matter of time before our differences were discovered. The ERI has done it. Every demon we put inside shows the same vessel-like quality. Humans look like they're wearing colorful blankets. Someday very soon we'll no longer be able to hide. We have to dictate the terms under which we make ourselves known."

My mouth opened. "You're going to turn us into saints?"

"It's safer than being demons. You don't know what it's like being the brunt of a witch hunt. But if we position ourselves on the side of angels, we have nothing to lose and everything to gain."

"How so?"

"People will do anything for immortality. Even without proof, without anyone ever actually defeating death, our truth-speakers give the Fellowship their ten-percent tithe and complete allegiance. They trust us. All of this," he said, gesturing to the complex of buildings around them, "is nothing compared to what we—what you—could have."

"Me? What do I have to do with this?" I wanted to run away just thinking about it.

"As a possessed human, you're unique. You can prove you were human, but now you're different. You have a past, pictures from when you were a child, report cards, immunization records, friends and family who will testify about who you are."

That sounded even worse. "I'm not that person anymore."

Dread lifted one shoulder. "It's not my idea to bring you into this. I told Vex that I should be the first demon to expose myself. I've built my credibility for the past thirty years, especially after I became prophet of this church. I put together this video as a proposal for how I'd go about it. But Vex thinks the problems in my backstory, the fact that I sprang out of nowhere, would lead to wide-scale doubts. It could ruin everything if the real truth about demons became known. So he wants a possessed human, you, Allay, to be the first demon who comes out."

"You say that as if all I have to do is kiss a girl at a party! Even with that machine of yours, people are going to think it's a trick, computer generated, manipulated to look different. No one will believe it."

"Everyone will believe it. First you have to prove we're different. Then comes the indisputable scientific proof." Dread got up and went over to the wall. There was a Fellowship cross hanging there. He unhooked it and spun it lightly in his hand. "Have you noticed how sharp the edges are, Allay? We say that's because the truth cuts like a knife."

Suddenly the way he was holding the cross made it look like an axe.

"We have to kill a demon publicly so everyone can see you come back to life," Dread explained. "We have to make it perfectly clear that you've survived what a human can't, so it has to be as dramatic as possible."

I put both hands to my neck. "You want to cut off my head?"

11

I got up and cautiously backed up the aisle from him. "You must be out of your mind."

"Spoken like a true human." Dread rolled up his sleeve, sliding it past his elbow. "Watch this."

He expertly twirled the cross-axe in his hand, then swung it hard at his outstretched arm. The blade cut through his wrist, hardly snagging on the bone, striking off his hand. A spurt of dark blood shot out after the falling hand plummeted to the floor.

I almost choked, my stomach clenched so hard.

Dread was shaking, his body reacting to the trauma he had inflicted on himself. But he was smiling throughout. Blood streamed out of the blunted end of his arm, pouring onto the crimson rug. He dropped the axe and clenched his fist around his arm, cutting off the blood flow; he grimaced only when some drops splattered on his fine white shirt.

My hands were over my mouth. The sharp alcohol scent of demon blood was strong.

Even standing back, I felt the shock wave of pain radiating out from him. But within a few moments, a ghostly hand appeared where flesh had once been. I looked from it down to his splayed fingers on the carpet. They were becoming smoky and insubstantial.

It took only a few minutes, and the hand on the carpet faded away in front of my eyes, while Dread's hand returned to normal. Only by squinting could I see the blood on the red carpet. But the smell still filled my nose.

Any humans who saw it would doubt their own eyes. That was what I wanted to tell myself. I could hardly believe it, and I had seen too many serious injuries heal on my own body.

"See?" Dread asked. "Being beheaded is easy—you don't feel a thing."

"How do you know? Have you ever been beheaded?"

He gave me a look. "I've been told by reliable witnesses."

"That's what I thought. What if it kills me?"

"Impossible. When you die, your core becomes impenetrable to protect your essence until your body can regenerate. That's why you can't kill a demon's body and then steal his life force." He smiled. "If it makes you feel any better, I'll go first. You can lop off my head and see how it works. A few minutes of discomfort are a minor price to pay for what we'll gain."

"Power. Over people." I crossed my arms.

"Power to make their lives better. Power to help them find their own path, and free them to follow it. Vex and I have been planning this for a very long time, Allay. We never meant to move this fast—we barely have a million members now. You can join the church, and we'll raise you through the ranks to become one of our leaders. You'll be publicly associated with the Fellowship, and then when we're ready, we can launch the Revelation."

I shook my head, at a complete loss for words. It was inconceivable.

Dread knew I wasn't buying it. Undaunted, he wiped the cross-axe down with his handkerchief and neatly hung it back on the wall. He rolled down his sleeve and put his coat over his healed arm.

Then he tilted his head. "Vex is coming."

I hadn't felt Vex's signature in a few years—a halting

sense, as if walls had sprung up around me, blocking all momentum. His signature was a strength when it came to dealing with other demons. They couldn't help but be affected by it, and it tended to slow them down enough so they listened and usually obeyed. Glory's demons followed her because of her charisma and charm, while Vex compelled his line into obedience, controlling them through money and influence.

Naturally he had an ulterior motive in helping me.

I would have preferred some time to absorb everything Dread had told me about their plans, but he took me straight down the hall and into a giant loft on the top floor. It was directly above the guest loft, which was a little unsettling. It was different from mine, very modern with shiny black wood floors and brushed-nickel panels on the walls. There were two raised platforms, one supporting a white grand piano and the other had a long glass table with twelve chairs around it. The décor was formal, obviously made for entertaining, with touches of whimsy in the decorative clocks and artwork from various eras. There wasn't much of a kitchen hidden behind a hanging bamboo screen along the wall.

"Is this Vex's place?" I asked.

"No, mine." *And Lash's*, he didn't add. But he didn't have to.

"Who plays the piano?"

His jaw clenched. "My wife."

I didn't mind giving him a dig, not after his little performance with the axe. Dread was closed off to me again, his shields buttoned up so tightly that I could barely sense the annoyance he was feeling at my questions.

The door to the hallway opened and Vex walked in. He looked like all the other young slackers who went skateboarding on the steps at Union Square with their pants hanging too low and their beards scraggly. His brown hair fell into his eyes and iPod earphones were slung over his shoulder.

I took a deep breath as Vex's signature served to counter Dread's sensation of sliding, canceling each other out nicely. Perhaps that was one reason they made such a good team.

"Hi, Allay. I'm sorry to hear you're having some trouble." His apologetic grin gave the impression of including me in the joke.

I stared at him. "Funny, nobody ever told me you owned the Den."

"You came to the city to be under my protection. What did you think that entails?"

So much for calling Michael to confirm the bad news. "I didn't know everything I was agreeing to when we made our bargain. Did you always plan to chop off my head to cement your religion?"

Vex raised his brows at Dread. "What did you say to her?"

Dread held up his hands to slow things down. "I gave her all the facts, like you wanted. She deserves to know that I offered to be resurrected, so she doesn't have to do it. I still think that's the best way to go, Vex. I know how to deal with the media, with the kind of intense questioning we're going to be faced with."

"It's time for you to leave, Dread," Vex said flatly. Dread almost protested, glancing at me as if he didn't want to leave me alone with him. It seemed possessive, the way he was reacting.

"I'll see you later, Allay," Dread assured me, almost as if we had made plans to get together for dinner. But we hadn't. Could his solicitousness be a consequence of his opening up to me? Or did he have his own plans for me? That was something to deal with later.

As Dread left his own loft, I realized I had plenty of proof that the two old partners were definitely at odds with each other.

I stared at Vex. "Are you going to answer my question?"

Vex grinned as if he were enjoying himself. Dread's little outburst didn't seem to bother him a bit. "You weren't even born when I started the church, Allay. But of course I always intended to feature a possessed human in my Revelation."

"Why not take Dread up on his offer? Or some other demon, if you don't trust Dread anymore."

Vex didn't rise to my bait about Dread. "I've thought of this from every angle, and there's too much risk in using a demon. If it's discovered that we're fundamentally different from humans, that we exist as a separate species, we'll be hunted down systematically and destroyed."

I scoffed at that. "There's no way humans can kill us."

"They can lock us in a box and never come near enough for us to touch them." For the first time, his expression was grim. "Believe me, Allay; you don't want that to happen."

He was remembering his years of imprisonment by Bedlam, kept ready for consumption whenever his essence was needed by his progenitor.

"We have to provide proof that you were once human, evidence that will satisfy everyone. We have to make it irrefutably a religious miracle, in the name of all that's good. People will flock to us once we show them they don't have to die. We'll bring spirituality back from the dust. We'll give people faith and hope again."

"Admit it, Vex. You were looking for a possessed human, and there I was. That's why you wanted me to come to New York."

"Honestly, I didn't expect you to last very long, Allay. No one did. And I wasn't ready to launch the Revelation ten years ago. We've experimented some, making possessed humans specifically for this purpose, but they all went insane and had to be extinguished. The difficulty of the transition has long been a problem. Hybrids are notoriously unstable.

We think you survived because you were young, but not too young. A blank slate is most easily written over."

"Thanks," I said sarcastically. I wasn't going to tell Vex that I was convinced the madness overcame humans because demons can't sleep. That had almost been my undoing. For the first few years, I tried over and over again to sleep. I would lie down and rest, meditating until I thought I was almost drifting off. It got to where I could do that for hours, but ultimately it never satisfied my yearning for sleep, that blessed unconsciousness. To leave everything behind and wake to a new day—you don't know how important that is until it's gone. Now I lived with continuous, never-ending awareness. Humans can't handle that. Shock had told me that sleep deprivation isn't just a physical problem—it's physiological, a need of the mind as well as the body.

"I gave you freedom," Vex said proudly. "I kept the other demons away, so you could do what you needed to do in order to stay sane. I hoped you would survive intact. And look at you. You're authentic, human, perfectly centered."

"You make me sound like Frankenstein. As if you cooked me up in your basement."

"Your making was an accident," Vex said. "But I gave you the chance to survive. Now I'm giving you the truth. I couldn't until now, for your own good. If anyone found out my plans, they might have preemptively killed you to stop this from happening."

"I still don't get why I'm so important in all this," I said doggedly.

"You're asking why don't I simply impersonate another human? Do away with someone and quietly take that person's place? It's been tried before, but never very successfully. First, there's the physical aspect—we never sleep, and it's difficult at best for us to eat and drink. Think of all the daily habits built around eating and sleeping, Allay. There has to be some explanation for such a drastic change in behavior. But if there's any disruption in our resurrectee's life, that could unravel the scrutiny that's sure to follow.

"And there's something else. No demon truly understands what it's like to be human. I've surrounded myself with humans for hundreds of years, but there are fundamental motivations that I don't understand, reactions that are purely based in the physical being of humanity. You still think like a human, though you're a demon. The way you react, the way you move your body. Those things create energy, a distinctive human energy. That's why your demon spirit still tastes so human. That's why you're able to integrate yourself so well into the lives of those around you. Most demons draw away from people when we aren't feeding from them; it's an instinctive thing. But you want to be near them even when you're not feeding."

"So that explains it." Shock hadn't been nearly as informative.

"Subconsciously, humans sense we're different. They know on some fundamental level that we're the *other*. Whenever we've tried to replace a human with a demon, the humans around the demon know in their gut that something is different. It makes them uneasy, makes the hair rise on the back of their neck, and it casts doubt over everything. Don't you remember how it was with your family? And you know how to act human. We can't have that happening after our Revelation. You're a known entity; nothing will change after you reveal yourself as immortal. Everyone can vouch you're exactly the same—except for the important fact that you have proved you can't die."

I stuck to the only thing I had. "They'll say it's fake, done with mirrors and computer-generated illusions."

Vex straightened up, lifting his chin. Right before my eyes he transformed in an instant. His clothes remained the same, but the man who wore them was different. His earnest, clean-cut face and neat hair were familiar from old newsreels and photos. "Do you know who I am?"

It was the man who had founded the Fellowship of Truth, young and vibrant even in black-and-white footage. Now he was standing before me in living color, breathing and speaking in that resonant voice. Before Billy Graham and Jerry Falwell, there was the first God-fearing Southern boy.

"Dale Williams," I said.

"After your resurrection is proved, Allay, and your background is fully investigated and confirmed, then I will reveal myself. Dale Williams has returned to Earth; only now he's of the spirit. There was extensive proof of my death; we made sure of that. Yet here I am alive, now immortal, bringing the revelation of truth to the people."

So that was why he didn't want Dread to be the first demon to out himself. Vex intended to return to the helm of his church. If Dread was in a dominant position, that would be impossible for him to do. No wonder Dread was frustrated—he had tasted what it felt like at the top, and he liked it.

"I'll doubtless survive a number of assassination attempts," Vex said, "some of them of our own devising so proof of my immortality will be abundantly clear."

"But people can't become immortal. It's a lie."

"We're offering hope—that's what people need, Allay. They want to live forever, but they know they can't. Most people can't stand thinking that when they die, they're snuffed out as if they never existed. So we give them hope and help lead them down a righteous path. We help them prosper and grow, so humanity prospers and grows, by encouraging people to be more independent, to fulfill their own desires. As the years go by, other demons associated with the church, such as Dread and Zeal, will come out. Even if discrediting information does emerge, we'll be able to counter it through the groundswell of support for the church."

"What about the demons like Pique? He's going to end

up getting caught by an ERI somewhere. That's a nasty association for your church."

"We can eliminate any problems in that area. I'm already working on that."

"Does that include Shock?"

"Of course not, Allay. I trust you enough to share with you my greatest endeavor. We'll shape civilization together. We can make advances as we did during the Renaissance, the Enlightenment, and the Industrial Revolution. You'll be instrumental in helping us take the next giant leap for mankind."

I stared at him. Was that all I was? A cog in their master plan to control the world? "I don't want any part in this."

Vex was still smiling. "I'm sorry, Allay, I thought Dread explained. Glory must be behind the attacks on you. Lash left for a reason, we know that now. She discovered our plans and told Glory. They've decided to kill you to stop our Revelation."

Glory. Now that was one demon I hadn't suspected yet. "If Glory is out to get me, then why did that demon attack Shock instead of me?"

"The best way to get to you is by removing the demons around you. We're positive that Pique is a Glory demon, operating under her command. When his frontal assault didn't work, she sent in a covert team."

"The stealth demon? The one who killed Malaise? Then you don't think Dread has anything to do with it?"

"No." Vex sounded flustered. "He may have killed one or two of our demons, though I don't have any proof. He says he didn't. But I know he's not responsible for the string of recent deaths. Or the attacks on you."

I wished I could be so sure. "Dread doesn't want me involved in this," I reminded him. "And neither do I."

"You're the key, Allay. Glory won't let you hang around on the street now that she knows what you can do. No, you're either dead—along with Shock—or you're with me."

"That sounds like an ultimatum."

"Not one of my making." Vex, exactly like the spoiled kid of a wealthy man, gave me an insolent smile. I got the distinct impression he also wouldn't let me "hang around on the street" any longer. He needed me for his Revelation, but if I wouldn't cooperate, he might just kill me himself.

"I'd like to think about this." I put my fingers to my temples. "You've given me a lot to consider."

"You're free to do whatever you want, though I can't guarantee your safety if you leave the complex. I'd rather not see you get murdered by Glory after you've come this far." He smiled at me. "Take your time thinking about it. I'm here if you have any questions."

Theo was on his feet the instant I opened the door. June was nowhere to be seen, and the pile of shopping bags and scattered clothing was gone, as well.

I slammed the door behind me as if I were being chased. My hands splayed back against it as if holding it to ward off intruders.

"What's wrong?" Theo demanded, running up to join me.

"Nothing." I moved away from the door. "I was just . . . spooked by something."

"What?" As I kept on walking to the windows, he stayed with me. "Allay, what did they do to you?"

I pushed the hair off my forehead to cool it. "They didn't do anything to me."

"Someone frightened you," he pressed. "They must want something from you."

He took my hand and I soaked up his concern and his burning desire to help. I clung to him, trembling. Vex had planned this all along. He would use me to legitimize his religion, then use the truth-speakers to undermine govern-

mental authority, ensuring their allegiance lay solely with
the Fellowship of Truth.

By comparison, Dread was merely vain and greedy,
wanting to boost his own power with the church. Vex
wanted to change the world. He wanted to take control of
people's hearts and minds again, as he had controlled them
for centuries through his influence on the Catholic Church
and the various rulers of the feudal nations.

Lop off my head, and everything would change. Mysti-
cism would be reborn with a vengeance as people reached
for the impossible for themselves.

"It's too big," I finally whispered.

Theo put his arm around me. I felt as if I were standing on the edge of a precipice. All of my fear crystallized
into my gasping words. "Maybe he means well. . . . Maybe
it would help. But it's a lie. I hate lies. They're toxic. They
ruin everything."

His head drew back, as if I had hit him. "Let's get out
of here, Allay. You don't have to stay. You don't have to do
whatever it is they want."

"You don't understand. I'm trapped. There's no way
out. They'll use me and twist me around until they get what
they need. I have no choice."

"Can't you negotiate with them, mitigate your involve-
ment somehow? Give them a little and get what you need
in return?"

"Believe me, this is a one-way street—to hell, if I'm any
judge. Once you burn someone on a cross, there's no going
back."

His arms tightened around me. "Allay! What are you
talking about?"

I pushed against his chest, wrenching away from him.
"Enough with the questions. You never ask me questions.
That's one of the things I like about you."

Theo was standing there with his arms open, desperately
wanting to hold me again. The pain in his gray eyes made

them nearly black. "You don't have to do what they say, Allay."

I stared at him, realizing that everything was over. There was no way I could go back to the bar and my cherished routine. That life now looked like a sham, a semblance of normalcy that had hidden the corruption beneath. It was gone, gone because Vex had always intended to use me this way.

"Allay . . . talk to me. Let me help you figure this out."

I couldn't. There was no way I could explain it to him. I padded over to the front door and pressed the button on the intercom. When June answered, I said, "I've changed my mind. I want to go up to the gardens."

"Of course, Ms. Meyers. I'll come and get you," June replied.

"No, don't bother. Just tell security to let me through the doors."

"Certainly. Hold a moment, please."

I glanced over at Theo. "I need some time to think."

Theo nodded silently, as if he didn't want to drive me farther away.

June came back online and said, "Ms. Meyers? You're authorized to go anywhere in the complex. Will there be anything else?"

"No, thanks."

I took my finger off the button, staring at the intercom. "It appears they trust me."

Theo nodded again without speaking; he looked upset.

"I'll be back soon," I promised as I walked out the door.

12

I could sense Vex on the floor above, at the opposite end of the long building, but there were no other demons in the Prophet's Center. Dread must have gone off somewhere to sulk.

Instead of using the elevator, I went to the stairwell. The door opened automatically when I looked up at the camera. I had to go up two flights to reach the roof; as I passed the locked door leading to Vex and Dread's floor, it gave me the shivers.

When I stepped onto the roof, I felt much better. The open sky and evening breeze scattered the cobwebs from my brain.

Time to blow this place. I had come up to weigh my options, but there were no others. I had to fetch Shock and get the hell out of the city for a while, as far away from Vex as I could get; otherwise he would ensnare me in his megalomaniac schemes.

With one last look at the view from Brooklyn, I knew it was time to test Vex's word and see whether he would let me walk out of here.

I ran down the stairs, back to the VIP suite, calling out for Theo as I entered. But he wasn't there. I gave a quick search of the place, noticing that someone had put the clothes away in the closet and drawers in the loft. Where could he be?

I doubted he tried to follow me to the roof; Theo wouldn't be that intrusive. And he wouldn't leave without saying good-bye. He couldn't go anywhere else in the building because of the automated security cameras.

Vex. It had to be Vex. That meant Theo was in danger.

I ran back to the nearest stairwell and dashed up to the next floor. As I burst through the door, I saw two men struggling in the farthest end of the hallway. They disappeared, stumbling into a room.

I gave a piercing scream at the sight of Vex attacking Theo.

They both popped back out into the hall, looking wide-eyed down at me. Theo took advantage of Vex's surprise, shoving him away so hard that the demon fell back into the room.

I ran toward them, so furious that my sight was tinted red by my aura. Vex was feeding on Theo. How dare he— Theo was mine. But the flaring energy as it flowed out of him was as distinctive as the northern lights.

He had lured Theo up here to get his hooks into him, probably to try to manipulate him so he would help Vex get his slimy mitts on me.

"How stupid are you?" I said to Vex, reaching Theo's side. Fortunately, he was okay. He stood up, a little shaky on his legs. He put one hand to his head as he glared at Vex. He made a move toward the demon, but I stopped him.

"Hey, I didn't do nothing. This dude threatened me," Vex protested hastily, clinging to his persona of a skater.

Theo shifted as if to go for him again. "You better leave her alone."

I gave Vex a hard look as I tugged on Theo. "Save your energy. It's not worth it," I told Theo.

I took his hand, and without a word Theo accompanied me to the elevator. When I pressed the down button, he asked, "We're leaving?"

"Yes. I shouldn't have come here." I still held on to his

hand, my fingers digging in tightly. He was more angry than hurt, but he didn't know how close he had come to being the main course.

"Good." He briefly stroked my arm, clearly hoping it would be that easy.

I could offer no reassurances. We were silent as the elevator dropped down to the first floor. But we bypassed the lobby and continued on down to the basement. Theo hit the red button for the emergency stop, but the elevator kept sinking. It was being remotely operated. We couldn't control where it went.

"I should have known it."

"Somebody doesn't want us to leave," Theo said.

We hardly had time to react. His arm went around me as the door slid open.

A group of security guards were waiting for us in the underground garage. Montagna stood in front, more than six feet of solid woman breathing hard. It looked like they had arrived at a dead sprint.

Montagna was holding her truncheon in her black leather gloves, ready for action. "Let her go! *Now!*"

With a jerk of her head, the guards rushed the elevator, forcibly separating us. I felt the first hands on me, and lost it, fighting back much harder than Theo. Using Aikido moves, I toppled them, even though they were all bigger than I was. I wasn't gentle about it. One of the guards screamed when I twisted his arm, the snap ringing out. I waited for the next attack, but none came and I spun, seeking action. The rest of Montagna's gang were converging on Theo.

That was when I realized they were after Theo, not me. I quickly sidestepped the next guard, shoving him hard into the back of the elevator. These were fragile humans, but even fighting full-out, I didn't have the skills to take on so many trained guards.

The guards pulled Theo from the elevator and wrestled him to the ground. Montagna and a big bear of a man stood between me and them, holding out their arms to stop me from going around. The guard with the broken arm backed toward a wall; white with pain, he was making a wheezing sound.

"Stop it!" I shouted, shoving Montagna aside. My strength surprised her, making her spin away. I reached the bald guy who was leaning over Theo, one knee in his back. "Let him go!"

I pushed him hard, and he fell forward, still on top of Theo. Montagna caught my waist from behind, pulling me off them. "Stand back, Ms. Meyers!" To the bald-headed dude, she ordered, "Cuff him."

I broke her grasp even though it tore at my flesh, and would cost me some serious bruises. "I said, let him go! You can't do this."

Montagna reluctantly stepped back, palms up as if under orders not to harm me. "He assaulted Tim Anderson, and made threats against the prophet. We have it on tape."

It was a lie, or maybe she believed the story Vex had concocted against Theo. I ignored her, trying to shove the bald guy off Theo's back. "He's not fighting you. Get off him!"

Theo was cuffed now, so at Montagna's nod, they finally moved back. I knelt on the floor at Theo's head.

Montagna reported into her walkie-talkie. "We've got the perp."

Through the static, I heard, "Take him to—"

I touched Theo's hair, and he turned his head to look up at me. There was a scrape down his cheek, and it was streaked with dirt from the cement floor.

"Don't," Theo croaked.

I looked up at the goons, my hands splayed protectively against Theo's back. "Call the police. We'll deal with this the right way. But first you're taking off these handcuffs."

"That's for the prophet to say." Montagna was unmoved. She stood at Theo's feet, ready to leap into action at the first sign of resistance. "This isn't about you, Ms. Meyers. I'd stay out of it, if I were you."

I had the sinking feeling that Montagna was used to getting her own way. I couldn't fight all of them. Vex had sent so many because he knew I would try.

Taking a deep breath to calm myself, I reached out with my senses. I could no longer feel Vex in the building. He had cut and run, leaving me at the mercy of his goons. But Dread had returned. It felt like he was just entering the Prophet's Center.

Montagna nodded to the guards, who lifted Theo under the arms. He staggered on his feet, as if they had knocked the wind out of him. His face was scraped raw and the sleeve of his T-shirt was nearly torn off.

I helped support him with one hand against his chest, feeling his harsh breathing. *This is my fault. I should have escorted him out last night. Instead, I used him like a gigolo.*

It had been selfish and cruel to expose him to this. But having him around made me feel . . . safe. I had wallowed in that beautiful illusion, even though it had done nothing but hurt him. Every day I had known him was written on him in blood.

"No, Allay—," Theo started to say.

"Stop talking. Get moving!" snapped Montagna, cutting him off.

"Where are you going?" I demanded, as they dragged him away from me, closing ranks around him. One of the guards helped the perspiring man who was gingerly supporting his broken arm. "Where are you taking him?"

"Detention until we get further orders." Montagna's mouth hardly moved. She apparently wasn't used to this much trouble. "You can't come with us, Ms. Meyers."

They dragged Theo around the corner and into a smaller elevator. He was struggling with them now. He opened his mouth to say something, but one of the goons jabbed him expertly in the solar plexus. Theo bent over, choking.

I grabbed the door of the elevator, but they were packed in, with no room left for me to shove my way inside. Montagna grit her teeth and carefully hit my fingers with her truncheon. I felt something crunch, and the pain spasmed in my fingers, making me let go.

"If you don't take me with you," I threatened, "I'll go find the nearest policeman and report you for kidnapping."

"Better ask the prophet about that, Ms. Meyers," Montagna said as the door slid closed.

Theo lifted his head at the last moment. He twitched his head as if warning me about something. Then I was standing alone in the basement.

This was *very bad*. I knew it from the second I saw Vex feeding on Theo. The truth was—Theo was just another casualty in Vex's pursuit of power.

I was doomed. I'd been caught when I came to live in the city under Vex's protection, and the trap had finally sprung.

Vex probably thought he would be able to pressure me into cooperating with him. Boy, was he wrong. I dialed his private number.

He answered on the first ring. "Allay, I'm glad you called. I want you to see the security tapes of what happened—when your friend Theo showed up at my door and started shoving me around."

"Likely story!" I snapped. "How could he get through the security cameras unless you let him? I bet you taunted him about me. Did you tell June to tell him we were lovers? Some nasty story about how I'm involved with the prophet's nephew? Then you invited him up so you could finish him off."

"Allay! I swear I didn't start this. I thought you loosed him on me. I never intended to hurt him."

"Your goons just beat him up and dragged him off!"

"All of this can be solved right now, Allay. We'll figure this out. We can work together and then you won't ever have to lie again. You can tell everyone you're different and stop pretending to live like a human. You would never have to change that persona that is uniquely you. Forever."

I couldn't speak for a moment. He was offering me the impossible dream, to be completely myself, honest with my friends and family about who I was. . . . I might even be able to have a relationship with a good man like Theo, someone who wouldn't hold my differences against me.

"Very seductive . . . but I'd be selling snake oil."

"You don't have to decide now. The only reason I told you this soon is because Glory made a move against you. Let's talk about it more. You can give us your suggestions— the Fellowship is open to incorporating a broader social message in our reforms. We can look deeper into our projections and research, while you help us refine our policies. There's no rush; we'd do everything on a timetable that you're comfortable with."

"So you'll protect Shock and me while I'm making up my mind?"

Vex's voice was soothing. "If you stay in the Prophet's Center, I can protect you. Next week, after I deal with the Glory situation, then it may be safer for you to go home."

"I'm not staying here," I said flatly.

His voice matched mine. "Then I can't release your friend, not unless you stay." Vex clicked the phone, ending our call.

I punched the elevator button and waited for it to return. It was impossible to tell which floor the elevator had taken Theo to.

When it finally returned, I stepped inside. Dread was now on the third floor, if I was any judge. I could be walking into a stupid game of good cop/bad cop. But I had to try to convince him to release Theo. Clearly, Dread and Vex weren't joined at the hip anymore, so there might be some crack I could slip a wedge into.

When I reached the right floor, I hurried down the corridor to find a way to the west side of the building. Dread was in a conference room.

The palace boardroom had not been on our tour. The compact jewelry-box layout featured blue satin panels between beveled mirrors, capped by a gold-leaf ceiling painted with cherubs. I felt as if I had stepped back into the time of the *Queen Mary*.

Actually, it was more like the *Titanic*. *Time for me to make like an iceberg.*

Dread sat at one end of an elaborate table. He had a pile of folders at one hand and an open laptop at the other. He was concentrating on something on the screen.

"Ah, Allay. They said you were coming up." He pushed the computer closed and gestured for me to take a seat next to him.

I went closer. "Tallying up what I owe the Fellowship?"

Dread was still pointing to the chair. "Sit down so we can talk about this, Allay. I'm sorry things have gotten out of hand. It was Vex's orders, and I told him it was a mistake."

I sat down. Perhaps Dread was willing to negotiate. "You can order his release. You're the prophet."

"Allay, I've seen the tape of him attacking Vex."

I waved my hand at him. "You know Vex had something to do with it. This reeks of a setup. He lured Theo to his room and then tampered with the evidence. Do you have footage of Theo's going up there?"

Dread narrowed his eyes. "Strange enough, no. My people aren't sure how he got onto the secured floor."

"It was Vex," I said triumphantly. "He's lying to both of us."

I knew I had hit him smack in the middle of his doubts. But Dread had been Vex's man for too long. "I can convince Vex to let him go if you agree to cooperate with us."

"I haven't decided yet. Vex said I could take my time thinking about it."

Dread considered me for a few moments. "Look at it from his side, Allay. He's afraid you'll be killed if you run around on the streets in your current state. Maybe Glory doesn't want you dead, but at the very least she wants to stop you from helping Vex. He'll do anything to keep you here in the complex, even if it makes you angry. You're too valuable to him."

"Then why doesn't he lock me up instead of Theo?"

"He thinks you'll come around and cooperate with him. Once you realize you'll be the most powerful person on Earth."

I took a deep breath. Person? I wasn't a person anymore, and that was the critical thing these two demons were forgetting. Lies were my life. I'd say anything in order to get Theo out. I tried to seem as if I were thinking it over. "So I could stay looking like myself forever? I could even reconnect with my family once they knew what I was?"

He nodded.

"Okay, I agree. I'll help you with your Revelation."

Dread shook his head at me, seemingly more amused than exasperated. "You have to convince Vex of that, Allay. And I doubt he'll believe you so quickly."

"What do I have to do to convince him?"

He considered it, his eyes narrowed as he thought. "Maybe if you cooperate on another project with us, something short-term yet sincere, he'll believe you."

Was it his signature that made me feel as if I were standing on the edge of a slippery slope? "What kind of project?"

His hands clasped together on the table. "You must understand, Allay, that you don't have much time left."

Back to that again; my need to take on another demon's life force before I died. But I wanted answers and Dread was a very old demon; he would know the truth, if anyone did. "How long do you think I have?"

"Two weeks, perhaps. No longer than that."

"What? That soon?" I had gotten so good at suppressing the growing urgency inside of myself that I hadn't realized it was that dire. I was going to die if I didn't take another demon. Something deep inside my belly began to cramp, twisting me forward as it overwhelmed me with the need to take, take, take.... I forced it back down.

Dread was nodding sympathetically. "I may have a solution. Hybrids are much more fertile than other demons. If you cram yourself with energy, Allay, you can fission fairly quickly."

I grimaced. "You want me to eat my own offspring?"

"No—I will. Then I'll give you mine, which is sure to emerge afterward. You need it even more than I do, Allay. We can help each other. I . . . need your help."

He was being honest; he was letting his shields ease, reaching for my hands. But my disgust rang through my palms. To him it was a lovely offer, a gesture of trust and bonding. To me it was abhorrent.

Dread dropped my hands, trying to get away from my disgust. I couldn't have screamed, "No!" in his face any louder.

"If that's the way you feel about it." He rubbed the back of his hand against his mouth, as if I had slapped him.

"I . . . can't."

"I see that."

I didn't know what else to say. I wasn't going to live at the mercy of Dread and Vex, pushed this way and that according to their whim. I'd been owned all this time as surely as I owned Snowplow. But it was time for that to end.

My own death would solve my problems. But I needed to settle some things first. I could take responsibility for myself to the end, and go the way I had tried to live—proud and independent. It wasn't a bad way to go, after all: Human integrity and demonic pride were two pretty powerful statements to make to both races.

Dread saw it. "You're thinking about walking out, aren't

you? Once you renew yourself, you think you can keep on the run from everyone. You figure someday we'll find another possessed human, and we'll use that hybrid for our Revelation. Then you can come out of hiding because we won't need you anymore."

I was glad he hadn't guessed my real intentions. "Actually, I hadn't gotten past the running part, but thanks for the optimistic plan for my future."

His eyes narrowed. "It would be much better if we were friends. You want your friend released, and I need a demon to consume. Work with me, Allay."

I stood up, pushing the chair back. "Shouldn't you be wearing horns and a pointy little tail?"

"Don't walk out, Allay."

I turned on my heel and headed to the door. It was time to see how far Vex and Dread were willing to go.

I returned to the elevator without seeing another soul, but it was Sunday evening after all. The door was open and waiting, and the lobby button turned bright white under my finger. As I descended, I expected to take another uncontrolled ride down to the basement to face Montagna's squad.

But the door opened at the lobby, and when I stepped into the secured area between the elevators, none of the guards looked at me. They all seemed to be busy with something. I didn't recognize any of them—they hadn't been involved in the takedown of Theo.

The gate opened automatically and the stoic man standing next to it nodded to me as I went through. "Good evening, Ms. Meyers," he said.

There were lots of people hanging out in the lobby, reading or working on computers. One young mother was watching her two toddlers play next to a padded bench that encircled a raised planter.

It was all so ordinary, as if I had stepped into another world—the old world.

I walked through the lobby, wondering what they were doing to Theo. They could be beating him up or worse. If I hadn't stopped Vex, he could have sucked the life from him, leaving him a senseless husk. What would stop Vex from doing that now?

As I neared the glass door, horns were honking from the backed-up traffic waiting to get onto the Williamsburg Bridge. Construction crews had put up orange barriers blocking the outside lanes so they could work all night. Policemen would be over there directing traffic.

Nobody was running after me to stop me. Didn't they care about the stink I could make? But the Fellowship of Truth had a lot of influence in the city; Dread probably had dinner with the mayor on a regular basis. Maybe they could do anything they wanted to with Theo and get away with it.

Someone bumped into me, muttering in irritation. I realized I was standing in the middle of the sidewalk, not moving.

I couldn't leave Theo in their hands. I had to do something to bring down the Fellowship, and it had to work fast because I didn't have much time.

13

I called Revel as soon as I got into a cab and was heading over the bridge. When he answered, I asked, "Do you know what Vex plans to do with me?"

"Allay, is that you? What's wrong?"

"I'm going to ask only one more time, and then I'm hanging up. Did Vex tell you how he intends to use me for his church?"

"His church? What are you talking about, Allay? The only thing I know is that Vex wants you protected, so we did that, Shock and I. You haven't made it easy, you know. You have no security and you act as if you were invincible, taking risks when you could be safe. But we make sure that the other demons know what Vex will do to them if they step out of line."

"The Glory demons don't listen very well."

"Why didn't you tell us that? You should have heard Vex when he laid into me. He was livid. We could have done something to stop them, but you didn't give us a chance." His voice grew more eager. "But what does this have to do with the Fellowship, Allay?"

If he didn't know, then I wasn't about to tell him. "How's Shock doing?"

He knew better than to push me. "She's much better. Her aura is sound. She says she remembers the attack and she saw the demon, but there was no signature even as he drained her. I think that's frightened her more than she wants to admit. She hasn't even hinted at leaving here."

"So do you know who the stealth demon is? I need to find out."

"I'm doing the best I can, Allay. I've been research-ing this for centuries, but it's hard to say what's truth and what's myth. It's most likely more than one demon."

I sighed, wishing he could be more help. "You have to protect Shock from Vex and Dread. Can you do that? They may try to use her to manipulate me." I wasn't telling any secrets; everyone knew I'd do anything for Shock.

"I won't let that happen, Allay. But I have to know: What does Vex want from you?"

I hung up, and I didn't answer when he tried to call me back. I wasn't even sure it was safe for Shock to stay with Revel, but there was no other option right now. If she couldn't sense her attacker, then she couldn't be on the streets.

It wasn't safe for me, either.

I called Shock's cell and gave her the bad news about Vex's big plans for me—Revelation and all. She was almost monosyllabic, she was so stunned. "You aren't going to do it, Allay, are you?" Shock finally asked.

"No. I'm no messiah. I want nothing to do with this."

"You'd better not tell Vex that."

"Isn't that the truth. But I have to force him to let Theo go. I owe it to Theo for getting him involved in this. I'm on my way to the police now."

"Allay . . . you can't do that. Why don't you come here and we can talk it over, try to figure something out."

Revel was right; Shock was spooked. It must have been awful looking into the face of a demon you couldn't sense as your life force was drained away. "Revel says you saw him. The demon. Did he wear the same persona both times?"

Her voice was much lower. "Yeah, he was . . . bland. Male, twenty-five to forty, light brown hair, brown eyes. Allay, it could have been anyone. I knew he was a demon, but I felt nothing."

Her tone chilled me. "You stay at Revel's where you're safe, Shock. Don't tell him about Vex's plans for a Revelation, not yet. I'll call you when I find out who's behind this." As I hung up, I wished I could tell her I was closer to knowing the truth. But she was right; it could have been anyone.

It was time to play hardball with Vex.

The police station was a gray-green cement-block building on Avenue A that smelled strongly of Pine-Sol. I figured going local would give me more leverage since the cops there knew me, instead of reporting Theo's kidnapping to the Williamsburg police. I talked to Lieutenant Markman, whom I'd worked with on an assault case between two patrons in my bar. He took me seriously, asking probing questions: Why was my driver's license recorded by the Fellowship security guards, but not Theo Ram's? Why was I allowed to leave the Prophet's Center but Mr. Ram was detained? Why did we stay overnight at the Prophet's Center?

I found it difficult to answer. Like any good cop, he sensed I was hiding something when I explained that I went to see the prophet because I had just discovered the church owned my bar. Markman was older, rounded in the face and belly, with silver hair cut very short. But he had walked the streets and knew a thing or two about people. I didn't think I was able to pass off my stumbling words as anxiety for my friend, caught in the clutches of the Fellowship.

Once I reported the kidnapping, the bureaucracy took over with crushing force. After a lengthy wait, Markman reported back to me in his flat, cop monotone: The Brooklyn police had gone over to the Prophet's Center, where they were informed that there had been no visitors in the past week by the name of Theo Ram. However, one Emma Meyers was an honored guest with free access to anywhere in the complex. The police were told that I had come alone, and the security guards showed them footage that seemingly proved their assertions. *More doctored video.*

Meanwhile, Lieutenant Markman had pulled the police report from the incident with Pique at my bar Friday night and sent a car over to Theo's apartment. "Nobody of that name lives at apartment 3R at that address," Markman told me when I was finally called back to his desk after cooling my heels in the front. "A family by the name of Sanchez lives there and they've never heard of him. The boys asked around, but nobody knows the guy. There's no one by the surname Ram registered with the New York State driver's license bureau under any address or with the Taxi and Limousine Commission. In fact, there're no tax forms filed under any variation of the name Theo Ram in Manhattan."

"He lied?" That was the last thing I expected. It stunned me—all demons were natural lie-detectors. I had felt guilt from him, yes, but not deception.

Markman looked at me sternly. "I would like to remind you, Ms. Myers, that filing a false police report is a criminal misdemeanor. Are you sure you want to sign this complaint against Mr. Anderson?"

I was so confused that I stuttered a refusal and stumbled my way out of there. Then I went to East Tenth Street myself to ask some questions. It went from murky twilight to full dark as I searched around for someone who might know Theo. The cops had been there looking for him; that was the hottest information I found.

At a loss, I slowly headed downtown. Who was Theo? Why had he lied to me? More important, how could he have lied to me and I didn't see it in his aura? Was I so besotted that I couldn't trust myself with him?

I remembered how he had appeared out of nowhere during my fight with Pique. Maybe he was working for another demon; a spy planted outside my bar to watch, and even protect me. Since he had saved me from Pique, it could have been Revel. Or Vex. Or possibly Dread.

I stopped in my tracks. *Whoa* . . . That made a lot of sense, and answered a lot of questions.

That was why Theo had been so protective of me. That was why he felt guilty, because he couldn't tell me. And that was why he held back last night in the loft—he couldn't let his boss think *he* was seducing me. Maybe that was why Dread had discounted him so completely, because Theo was one of their own hired hands sent to watch over me.

The more I thought about Theo's emotions, that terrible well of despair bubbling deep inside of him, I knew that he worked for the church. They were destroying him, using him for ugly, cruel deeds, just as surely as they were destroying Phil Anchor inch by painful inch.

Stupid, stupid me. I should have realized it.

That changed everything. I wouldn't get any help from the police or by threat of media exposure. This was between me and Vex alone. Demon to demon; Vex would not be swayed by anything or anyone even remotely human. He would expect me to come in with my human sensibilities overwhelming demonic logic. Well, he was in for a surprise.

I looked up and realized my feet had automatically brought me home. My block looked exactly the same, but somehow it felt strange. The windows of the bar needed washing, but the sidewalk had been swept the way I liked it, and the flowers in the planter under the tree were freshly watered. There was a pile of black garbage bags sitting on a thrown-out couch in front of the building next door. My car was tucked behind the gate in the narrow alley, an old Karmen Ghia always packed with essentials and ready for a quick getaway.

But it seemed futile to run from trouble when the end was fast catching up with me.

I had to take care of my people and get them out of

harm's way. I would have to close down the bar. It belonged to Vex, so I couldn't stay here.

This was the end of the Den on C.

When I entered the bar, heads turned. Surprised and welcoming calls of greeting rang out from the Sunday night regulars. It was nearing ten o'clock, so Lolita was there.

Carl lifted both arms and cried out, "Woo-hoo! The queen returns! Now we can par-*tay*."

Lolita plunked down a glass on the bar and made a bee-line to the door. Her relief shifted to concern when she saw my worried expression. She gave me a long hug. "Are you okay? How's Jamie?"

"She's fine, almost completely recovered."

"That's good news, isn't it? What's wrong?"

I took a shaky breath. "We're going to have to close up early, Lo."

"Why? What happened?"

"Trouble with the owners. They're shutting us down." It was as good as any other excuse, and at least had a measure of truth.

"Allay, no. Not for good?"

"Yes. I'm so sorry, Lo." This would destroy her life al-most as much as mine. She and Darryl would have to find new jobs.

Lo's mouth formed a perfect *O*. For a second, I thought she was going to cry.

Then with a flip of her hand, her expression hardened. "Fuck 'em! We'll find another bar. How about a drink be-fore we close up?"

I started to smile. Leave it to Lolita to go out with class. I was worried about the danger to my patrons with my being here, but another twenty minutes probably wouldn't mat-ter. I raised my voice, calling out, "Drinks on the house, everyone!"

After that, Lolita and I were kept busy serving drinks to everyone. Old Jose managed to get one from each of us. There were only about twenty people in the bar, so our little rush was over too soon. As I pulled on the lever to pour a draft beer, I realized I would never do that again. I would never wipe down the bar with my towel or clean these glasses with the sink brushes. Even the feel of the honeycomb mats under my soles seemed poignant in that final light.

I went around to talk to everyone, telling them I was sorry, but we'd have to close up early. Over and over, I said, "We're shutting down the old place. It's been great serving you."

As a matter of principle and loyalty, I didn't feed off them, not a drop. I wanted it to be a clean good-bye. I wanted to be able to remember it with pride.

Some of the patrons said their good-byes and left, while others lingered at a complete loss, like old Jose, as if he couldn't get it through his head that he shouldn't show up tomorrow for happy hour. I accepted a hug from Maria Rodriguez, who shifted her ever-present toothpick to the other side of her mouth so as not to poke me in the eye. Her dark roots were several inches deep beneath her bronzed hair.

"You can't go away, Lah-lah," Maria said, using my nickname. She also called Lolita "Lo-Lo." "What will I do without you?"

I just smiled sadly and said good-bye to everyone. Somehow this had become everything to me, these people, this stinky old bar.

With a purring meow, Snowplow jumped up on the bar and rubbed his back against my face. I came up spitting fur, wiping my lips. He dived in for another strafing run, but I caught him and turned him upside down in my arms where he purred and drooled on himself, he was so glad to see me.

"You stupid cat," I whispered. "What am I going to do with you?"

I was tearing up, and the pain in my chest made it hard to breathe. So I concentrated on rubbing his ears until his eyes closed in ecstasy.

Lolita let the last person out, and together we drew the metal shutter down over the front and locked the door.

Now I felt marginally safer. But I had to get Lolita out of here before any demons showed up. I stopped her from gathering the glasses. "Lo, could you do me a huge favor?"

"Anything, you know that."

"Could you take care of Snowplow and Monkey for a while?" I would have to find something more permanent, especially if I didn't survive my final deadline in two weeks. "I know Snowplow gets on your nerves, but it will only be for—"

Lolita put her hand on mine. "As long as you need it, Allay. I'll take care of your cats. You know I love them. Only not while I'm working."

"Thank you. It's a huge load off my mind. Could you help me get them now? I've got carriers upstairs for them."

"Allay, you're not getting kicked out tonight, are you? Do you have a place to stay? You can come home with me."

The last place I could go was to Lo's apartment. I wanted to keep demons away from her, not attract them. "I'll stay here tonight; that's no problem. But I don't want to risk going out and having some idiot padlock the door with the cats shut in here."

Lo nodded seriously. "You know you're welcome to stay at my place, Allay. Anytime."

The lies spread between us, forming an impassable gulf. "I know."

I helped carry out the cat carriers with the two protesting cats, and signaled for a cab for Lolita. She was also carrying $2,153 in bar receipts that hadn't been deposited this weekend—all I had in the safe—with instructions to give one-third of it to Darryl, one-third to Pepe, and to keep the rest for herself. It was piss-poor severance pay, but maybe Michael could wrangle something more for them. I didn't want to promise Lolita anything I couldn't deliver.

I checked the padlock on the metal shutter, then retreated upstairs. Even with my heavy doors and a screw twisted through the holes to hold the skylight shut, I felt exposed in my own apartment. It was as if I were seeing everything with new eyes, looking at a memory, something that was already long gone.

My place was strewn with things I'd picked up and friends had given me. I went around, carefully touching a lei from my last birthday luau in the bar, the thorns on a squat, round cactus that sat on my front windowsill, and a pink porcelain piggy bank that matched the one my sister had gotten at Christmas when we were young. I could imagine the pig smashed in a Dumpster as a crew of men wearing breath masks gutted the interior of the bar for demolition. A narrow condo tower might go up in its place.

With sudden loathing, I stripped off the purple T-shirt and black pants that Vex had given me, and threw them in the trash can along with the Mary Janes. As I changed into my own familiar jeans and hoodie, I knew I couldn't stay long. I couldn't stay in a place Vex owned. This wasn't my home anymore.

I'd done the best I could for my people and my pets. What about Theo? Did I owe him anything? Not really, since he had lied to me. I could hardly be self-righteous about it when I was lying to him, too. But as it turned out, I hadn't dragged him into this. He was already deep in Vex's pocket when he showed up at my place and got knocked around. Now I knew why he had been so accommodating and understanding. He never even asked why a girl named Emma was nicknamed Allay. That was because he was being paid to infiltrate my life.

It had all been a lie—just like everything else.

Before I left, I took one long, last look around. This was it, the end.

I couldn't bear to say good-bye, so I rushed out quicker than I meant to. It felt too awful to linger.

Downstairs, I paused before opening the door, making sure I couldn't sense any demon signatures. Then I peeked out to check if there was anyone watching me, in the same way as Theo had been. But nobody was lingering in the doorways or sitting in parked cars. Traffic was fairly sparse this late on a Sunday night, with mostly locals out and about instead of people coming in from the outer boroughs and New Jersey.

I closed the door behind me, then headed over to the gated alleyway. As I unlocked the padlock and stepped back to open the gate, I practically collided with Phil Anchor. "Phil! I didn't see you."

Phil was breathing hard, as if he had run to catch me before I left. His finger pointed in my face. "You've been a baaaad girl, haven't you, Allay?"

"Hey, stop that," I ordered, backing away from his finger.

His worn leather coat creaked as he moved, and the smell of cigar smoke was strong on him. From his shaking hands and the way he kept wiping his mouth, I figured he was binging again. "What did you do with my drop, Allay? They said you missed the handover."

It took me a second to remember. "The USB? I gave it to the prophet. Yesterday." When he hesitated, I realized this was all some stupid coke drama. "I took it to Brooklyn myself. Haven't you talked to anyone since then? Didn't they tell you?"

He fumbled out his phone. "No messages. He told me to make a copy and wait for drop-off instructions."

"You're pathetic." I reached out to shove past him, but he wouldn't let me touch him, as usual. "They've twisted you, Phil. You call this a life? You'd do anything for a fix, wouldn't you? Even if it means helping somebody sneak into my place. All you care about is you."

He grimaced as if I had hit a nerve. "I didn't help anybody. You let that guy inside last night."

I was talking about my mysterious intruder, not Theo. "How do you know about Theo? Have you been watching me, Phil?"

"No, it's not like that. I came by a few times, but I couldn't . . . I thought there was another way. . . ." He trailed off, lost in his own thoughts, his eyelid twitching.

"You must know Theo. Or whatever his real name is. He works for the prophet, too."

Phil shook his head. "No, he doesn't."

I thought he was lying. "Of course not, just like you don't."

"No, really. Sebastian asked me to do a background check on Theo Ram yesterday." He was talking about Savor, so it must have been Dread's request after I had arrived at the Prophet's Center. "I haven't found anything. It's as if he doesn't exist. Sebastian says he's never seen him before—he's also come up with nada. My contact on the inside says the cops can't figure out who he is, either." Phil shrugged and tried to give me a winning smile, but his lips were chapped and cracked. "I thought I'd come over here and ask you about him. Come on, Allay, I need to give the boss something. So who is the guy?"

I realized I was standing there with my mouth open. "I don't know. From the way he acted, I thought he was hired to watch over me."

Phil nodded thoughtfully. "The question is, who cares about you enough to pay for it?"

Suddenly it made sense. It was my other sugar-daddy—Revel, the one who was responsible for protecting me. But I didn't say that.

Phil saw it in my face. "You know who sent him, don't you, Allay? Come on, give a guy a break. I really need this job."

"This isn't a job, Phil. You're messing with people's lives, digging up the dirt on them so the prophet can make them dance on his string. I don't know how you can live with yourself."

He pulled back. "You're a big one to talk. How long have they owned you, Miss Holier-than-thou?"

I smiled tightly. "I quit. You won't be coming to this bar anymore. I have nothing to lose, now. Maybe I should blow the whistle on the lot of you. If I thought anyone would believe me, I would. Maybe that would stop him."

Phil shook his head, confused. "You're going to tell? About me?" When I didn't reply, he insisted, "What did I ever do to you? You can't do that to me. *Allay* . . ."

I couldn't believe I had ever been attracted to him. But that guy in the past wasn't this Phil Anchor; it was someone who had squandered tons of potential and vitality. He'd taken this path and it had ruined him, just as it had ruined me.

I pushed open the gate. His voice got louder as he insisted that I couldn't rat on him. I finally snapped, "For Christ's sake, shut up, Phil. I've got much bigger things to deal with than your petty piss-ant crimes!"

He looked hurt for a moment, with hangdog blue eyes that had none of their former charm. He seemed to be debating whether to step in front of the bumper of my car to block me. The intensity of his reaction, the shame he was hiding, were sickening.

I got in and jammed the car into gear. As I edged out, Phil moved away. I backed into the street, watching for traffic. He shoved his hands into his pockets, hunching his shoulders under the lamppost, disappearing behind me as I road off.

I drove around for a while, turning abruptly and running red lights until I was sure nobody could have followed me. Then I pulled over to call Revel. I had to go through Ki to get to him, and the wait burned me up.

Instead of saying a standard hello, Revel demanded, "Why don't you answer your phone, Allay? I left you six messages."

"I was busy closing down the bar." I didn't want to hear his exclamation of joy over the fact that I had finally abandoned the old place. "Why didn't you tell me you knew Theo? Or whatever his real name is."

"Who? You mean your bodyguard? Do I know him?"

"You hired him to spy on me." Grudgingly I added, "To watch over me. He fought off Pique."

There was a beat. "I don't know what you're talking about—"

"You're lying. I'm going to hang up if I get any more lies from you, Revel."

He already knew I had information, juicy stuff that he could use. Plus, he was just plain curious about what was going on. "It was for your own good, Allay. I needed to be sure nobody hurt you. Vex would kill me if I was lax."

I sighed. "So who is he?"

"You think I know? I have an agency that takes care of security for me. It requires a lot of manpower to maintain round-the-clock coverage."

"Along with surveillance duties. I'm sure they sent you plenty of pretty pictures."

"It's part of the package—"

"I don't want to hear about it. But you should know that Vex has Theo, and I don't think he's going to let him go."

"Why would Vex care about the hired help?"

"Because . . ." *I care about him.* They knew exactly how much I cared about Theo from the way I had fought Montagna's goons in the basement. They probably had close-ups of my face as I held on to him.

I cared about him. It didn't matter why he was watching over me. He was being paid, but he was also trying to do a good thing by protecting me.

It was much worse than imagining that Theo had sold

his soul to the church like Phil. Vex would use Theo against me to get me to cooperate. Theo wouldn't have been hired to stand outside my bar and watch over me if I hadn't insisted on pretending I was an ordinary woman who could live like everyone else. Revel was right; I should have been secure in some penthouse fortress like him. Instead, real people had risked their lives to protect me.

But I couldn't explain that to Revel. "It doesn't matter why. Vex has him, and you have to make him let Theo go."

"I'm sure he already has. I'll have Ki contact the agency and check to see that all their men are accounted for."

I clenched my teeth. "Why don't you call Vex and ask him?"

"I thought you wanted me to protect Shock. If I start poking my neck out, Vex is going to take a swipe at me." His voice grew persuasive. "Why don't you come over, Allay? We need to sit down together and figure out our next move."

Actually, I sort of wished I could run up to his feathered nest and relax, even just for a moment. I wanted to check out, sleep for a long time, not think about anything for a while. But that was impossible.

I was responsible for Theo. I had to do whatever it took to get him away from Vex. I also needed to get some sort of leverage on Vex so that he wouldn't go after Shock.

But as hard as I considered it, I had nothing to hold over Vex. I could threaten to let myself die rather than do as he wanted, but he might just force me to absorb a demon essence somehow. I preferred to keep my intentions a secret because, in reality, it was my ultimate escape route if all else failed. Dying looked easy next to going through the charade Vex had in mind.

Vex's only weak spot was Dread. There must be some way to put pressure on him so they would turn on each other and concentrate on their own power struggles.

"Allay? Are you still there?" Revel asked. "Shock wants

to see you, and you shouldn't be out there alone. You don't have any protection right now."

I hung up on Revel, unwilling to admit my absurd dilemma. How could I make two of the most powerful demons in the world afraid of me?

Then I remembered Phil's face, and how afraid he was when he thought I would expose him. His eyes had bugged out as if I had jabbed my fingers into his throat. That was some way to get a guy's attention.

It gave me an idea—a really great idea. What if I blackmailed one of the big guys Dread had bribed, such as the planning and zoning commissioner? I could threaten to expose his dealings with the Fellowship. I would offer to keep my mouth shut only if he convinced the prophet to let Theo go. That would definitely put Dread at odds with Vex. He wouldn't want his pet civil servant to be upset.

If that wasn't enough, I could blackmail another one tomorrow, and another one after that. Hopefully the suffering Dread would go through was not worth keeping Theo, now that I had left the complex. It might even cause one of the bribed officials to turn evidence on the church. At the very least, I'd throw a wrench into their payola scam.

Theo was right about me—I couldn't just walk away. I had to do something to stop them.

I stashed the car in a garage down on Canal Street. There were several quick ways to get out of the city from Chinatown.

Then I ducked into an all-night Internet café, the kind with rows of tables with people staring at the monitors. This one offered a choice of hot Chinese tea or coffee, so I took tea and smelled it rather than drank it.

It took some searching to find out that the New York City Planning commissioner, Dennis Mackleby, lived in Battery Park City. He owned an apartment in one of the

high-rises filled with wealthy urban families. It wasn't far
from where I was sitting.

A search through the phone records yielded his home
number. I keyed it into my phone, but didn't press SEND until I was back out on the street. It was just after midnight—
no better time for a blackmailer to strike. The phone rang
six times before a sleepy voice picked up. "Mackleby residence."

It was a woman, perhaps his wife. My hands were sweating and I wasn't sure I could do this. "I need to speak to
Dennis Mackleby. It's an emergency."

"Who is this?" she asked more sharply.

"Tell him it's Allay from the Den on C. With bad news."

She repeated the words after me, and sooner than I
would have imagined, Dennis Mackleby was on the phone.
"Who is this? What is this about, calling me at this hour? I
won't stand for prank calls."

"Mr. Mackleby, we've never met, but I know your driver,
Nelson. He comes to my bar to pick up your bribe from
Prophet Anderson the first of every month."

That cut him off at the knees. It sounded as if he were
strangling; then he put his hand over the mouthpiece but
not quickly enough before I heard him give some excuse
to his wife. "Hold on," he said. Then the sound of the door
shutting preceded his terse demand. "You had better re-
think what you're doing. I'm not the kind of guy you want
to mess around with."

"Yes, it would be very messy. Splashed all over the
papers, exactly how those waterfront variances for the
Prophet's Arena were bought and paid for with regular
installments."

"I don't know what you're talking about," Mackleby
said. "You have nothing on me. This is a sick joke and you
should be ashamed of yourself."

But he didn't hang up. His breathing was harsh in my

ear. He was saying those things because he had to, in case I was taping him. He was hooked and on my line.

"I'll keep my mouth shut—forever—if you do one thing," I promised. "You have to convince the prophet to release the man known as Theo Ram. They're holding him in the Prophet's Center, and unless I see him free on the streets by tomorrow with my own eyes, I'm going public with my evidence. Remember, Theo Ram."

I hung up, shaking. I turned and hurried up Vesey Street. It was tragic, what I was reduced to. I think in that moment I gave up hope for myself as a human being.

I wouldn't subject myself to Revel's relentless questions, and I couldn't admit how much I cared about Theo out loud to anyone, not even Shock, so I spent the rest of the night riding around on the subway, changing from line to line. The clack-clack rhythm of the rocking car lulled me, as people came and went. The stations all began to look the same—the platforms, steel I-beams, and tiles stained with black, brown, and white residue seeping down from the streets.

I felt glimpses of other demons as the train stopped at the stations, but deep in the tunnels, the layers of concrete blocked all signatures. I felt relatively safe, knowing it would give time for Mackleby to pressure Dread, and for Dread to pressure Vex. It was anyone's bet what would happen next.

At every stop, I glanced at my phone as reception returned. Just as the morning rush hour picked up, my battery started running low. Vex liked to ride the subways during rush hour, irritating the cramped passengers, so I couldn't stay any longer. I decided to get my car and drive around for a while to charge up my cell. That would also keep any demons from detecting a pattern in my movements.

As I got out at Canal and Broadway, a message that wasn't from Revel finally beeped through. But it wasn't the message I was expecting. It was from Lolita. *Hi Allay. I hope everything's going okay. I talked to Darryl and Pepe, and I'm meeting with both of them this morning to give them their pay. Pepe said he was on his way over to the bar to clean up since we didn't get to it last night, so you may see him before I do. Give me a call when you get up and get this.*

My blood ran cold. Pepe was going to the bar. I called his home, but his wife said he had left a while ago. He didn't have a cell phone, so I couldn't intercept him.

I had to go back to the bar to tell him to go home. Nobody should go near that place. It was like nuclear waste, deadly. Any demon looking for me would start there, and Vex had made it clear with Theo that he wouldn't hesitate to hurt people to get to me.

The Monday morning rush hour didn't make it easy to get to the bar in a hurry. The subway would take me only halfway. Rather than wait on the crowded platform and shove into a full car, I sprinted up Broadway, heading north. I tried to grab a cab, but they were all full, or people were waiting to step into one as soon as somebody got out.

I had to run nearly thirty blocks to get back home, but I was glad I did when I saw the metal shutter on the bar was halfway up. Pepe was moving around inside, sweeping the floor.

I ducked under the shutter and went inside. With a glance, I saw he had gathered all the glasses we left out and stacked them neatly by the sink to be washed. The tables were wiped down. "Pepe! What are you doing here? Didn't Lolita tell you the bar is closed?"

Pepe didn't stop sweeping, smiling his slow grin. "It's my job to leave it clean. I'll leave it clean for the boss."

"We aren't working for him anymore," I said firmly. "Besides, this place will be torn down more than likely. Who cares if there're glasses on the tables?"

"I care." Pepe was looking straight at me. "I took care

of this place for ten years. I've been proud to do it. I know you're proud, too, Allay."

I looked around. This bar had been my refuge, my pearly conch shell of safety that I could retreat into and make my life my own. For a moment, I couldn't bear the thought of losing it all. But it was only an illusion.

"Come on, Pepe. We're not allowed to be here anymore." I gently took the broom from his hands, and he finally realized I wasn't going to let him finish his job.

Then something slammed against the metal shutter, making us both jump and cover our ears from the earsplitting echo. Then came more high-pitched popping. I saw Pepe's look of surprise, and there was nothing more as everything went dark.

14

As I slowly woke up, despite my body's best attempts at staying under, my head was ringing and it felt as if my lungs were scorched with every breath. I realized I was staring at the ceiling of the bar, its dust-covered ducts and pipes as familiar as the back of my hand.

For far too long I lay there dazed, unable to remember anything. It was disorienting, deeply frightening. I wasn't even sure of my own name.

The faint tinkling of glass and the harsher sound of gasps next to me got me moving. I turned my head and saw Pepe lying beside me. Blood was everywhere.

Everything came back in a rush. We were lying in the midst of a sea of glass and splintered wood. Someone had shot out the front windows of the bar.

I crawled over to Pepe, not even feeling the broken glass. He had been hit in the lower abdomen and the thigh. Blood poured sluggishly from the dark pits where the bullets had entered. His eyes were wide-open, shocked, and insensible.

My hands fumbled my phone out of my pocket, and I dialed 911, my bloody fingers slipping on the numbers. A perfunctory voice answered, and I managed to give the address of my bar. "A man's been shot. Send an ambulance as fast as you can."

I could hear keys clicking as she placed the request. "Are you injured, ma'am?" she replied.

"No. No. I'm fine. But he's been shot. You have to hurry!"

Dropping the phone, I looked for something to press down on the wounds to staunch the bleeding. I started to unzip my hoodie, figuring it was large enough to cover both holes, when I realized it was soaked in blood already.

Well, wouldn't you know it, I was hit. One charred hole was centered just below my heart, and the other two were lower down in my belly.

I had been killed.

Dread was right; I could come back to life after a mortal blow. So that was what it felt like. It was awful; I couldn't think straight, and my body couldn't function properly. I must have been out cold for a few minutes.

As I pulled off my hoodie, a bullet fell down. It must have been stopped by my ribs—I could feel the residual pain there—and been pushed out as I regenerated. My stomach was smeared with blood, its sharp demon scent, like that of the pool of blood around me, blending with the alcohol-infused wood in the bar.

Using the hoodie, I covered each of Pepe's wounds with my hands. Pepe groaned and flinched at the pressure, but I couldn't let him bleed like that. He was muttering in Spanish, so I assured him, "It'll be okay, Pepe. They're coming to help you."

The metal shutter was still pulled halfway down over the front. Shadows moved outside the bar, visible through the windows below the shutter. "Is somebody in there?" a man called through.

"Yes! A man's been shot!" I called back.

It turned out to be one of my neighbors, a guy with a tattoo on the front of his neck who walked his Chihuahua by the bar several times a day. He pushed up the metal grate and carefully climbed through the busted window. There was a huge piece of plate glass hanging from the other window frame like a guillotine waiting to fall. He crunched through the broken glass on the floor, using his foot to swipe clear a spot on the floor next to Pepe. He looked as shocked as I felt. I didn't know what to say; from friendly waves and casual talk on the street, to being caught up in attempted murder. It was too much.

I had no doubt I was the target. Poor Pepe had gotten in the way.

Other people were gathering, peering inside in appalled fascination. This was their block, where they lived, and an ordinary Monday morning had suddenly turned into the lead story on the evening news.

An ambulance pulled up with sirens and lights flashing. They seemed to have gotten here awfully quick, and they surrounded Pepe, ripping open his shirt and pants, giving him oxygen and lifting him onto a white-padded gurney. None of them associated me with Shock, for which I was grateful; I didn't need any special attention right now while I was so rattled.

I picked up the blood-soaked hoodie they dropped on the floor, and threw it into the garbage can behind the bar. I didn't want anyone looking at those bullet holes. But the tallest EMT noticed—he must have been right out of college, he was so baby-faced. His eyes went to my bare stomach, smeared with blood.

I realized for the first time that I was wearing only my black bra and jeans.

"Are you hurt anywhere?" he asked, joining me. "Here, sit down."

I sat down where I could watch them working on Pepe. "I'm okay."

His doubt was clear as he quickly checked me over with his gloved hands. He even probed the slices on the knees of my jeans from when I had knelt next to Pepe. I had cut myself, but I healed it before he noticed.

"Is Pepe going to be okay?" I asked.

"He's stable, but he's going to need surgery."

More sirens were approaching. The cops. *Perfect.*

The EMTs swept out with Pepe strapped to their rolling gurney as the police arrived. I wasn't surprised to see no-nonsense Lieutenant Markman among them. He came right up to me. *Fab-ulous.* This was just the cherry on the cake of my morning, round two with my local cop.

"Why don't you tell me what's really going on here, Ms. Meyers?" he asked.

"*God*, I wish I knew!" I meant every word.

Markman's aura turned the distinct orangey red of suspicion. "Just tell me what you do know. Who was the victim? Your employee? He was almost killed. Do you want that to happen to someone else?"

He could have been my own conscience speaking. For a wild moment, I almost wanted to confess everything—but I'd land up in Bellevue for fourteen days of observation. And wouldn't that be a sight if I imploded on them while under the glare of the hospital cameras? I'd be the star of the demon Revelation whether I wanted it or not.

Don't tell me it's fate! I don't believe in fate. . . .

So I did my best to live in the real world. "I quit yesterday, so I shut the place down. I have no idea why anyone would want to shoot me. I'm just a bartender. And Pepe's the janitor."

"Where were you when this happened?"

"I was in the cooler. Pepe was sweeping out here."

It took a lot more questions in the same vein before Lieutenant Markman was done with me. Clearly, I was under suspicion now, even though I was one of the victims. The cops were also interviewing people who had been on the street—someone had seen a man running away wearing a black bandana around his head.

I picked up my phone out of the glass when Markman

asked for the number for the owners. I gave him Michael's contact info as the management agent, and I called Michael right then.

He sounded tired when he answered. "Michael, here."

"Hi, it's me, Allay."

His gravelly voice grew much warmer. "Allay, dear, what's up?"

"Michael, there's been a . . . shooting." I almost said "accident," but it certainly had been intentional. "Pepe's hurt and they're taking him to the hospital. Someone shot through the front windows of the bar."

Instantly Michael was in take-charge mode. "Is he all right? What about you? Are you hurt?" In spite of my protests that I was fine, he insisted, "You should go to the hospital, Allay, and get checked out. You don't sound good."

"I'll go as soon as the police let me."

"Which hospital is it? I'll meet you there, and I can take care of the bills for Pepe."

"Thank you, Michael. You're the best."

"It's why we have good insurance, dear."

My throat closed at how kind he sounded. Why couldn't Revel be more like Michael? I never felt that Michael had an ulterior motive for helping me. Vex may have been paying him to manage the bar, but I knew his concern for me was genuine.

But I didn't want to question Michael in front of Lieutenant Markman, about why he hadn't told me that the prophet had bought the bar—or that I had quit and closed the place down. It was just as well, because my battery finally died, cutting our conversation short. As long as Pepe was taken care of, the rest didn't matter.

I wanted nothing more than to get out before demons started showing up en masse. But Lieutenant Markman would only allow me to go upstairs to change my clothes. He wouldn't let me go to the hospital to check on Pepe. I had to wait while the cops photographed the scene of the crime and gathered up evidence, such as the bullet that had my blood on it. I should have picked it up and kept it—what if they tested it and realized I'd been shot?

An ever-shifting crowd of curious onlookers gathered around outside watching. At one point, when I thought we were nearing the end of my little drama fest, I felt Savor approaching. I almost bolted away, to hell with the consequences. Emma Meyers was dead, anyway. That bullet had killed her as surely as if I had been human.

But Savor might be bringing word about Theo's release. She might even be bringing Theo himself, if Vex was smart.

So I waited on the edge of my chair. I recognized Savor immediately, though he was in a new male persona. This guise was an older gentleman with a good head of receding silvery hair and a perpetual golf tan, a little rough around the edges, someone who had built an industrial or mechanical empire.

Theo wasn't with him.

Savor waited until the cops were pulling out to approach the open door. "Ms. Meyers?" he said to me, in case anyone overheard. "I was sent to assess the damage and authorize repairs."

I joined Savor as he entered. "Michael called the Prophet? Figures." Lowering my voice so no one outside could hear through the broken windows, I added, "Did Dread send you? Or was it Vex?"

"Dread. He said shots had been fired but . . ." Savor didn't finish, shaking his head as he stared at the damage.

"Hmm . . . I wonder if Vex is in the loop. I see now why it's risky for him to let Dread control things. Vex must be dying to get back in charge."

Savor opened his arms wide at all the debris. "What are you thinking, Allay? Dread sent me over to Mackleby's this morning to try to calm the guy down. He practically had a stroke in front of me."

"I'll call the Internal Revenue auditor next. He took payments for years. You can tell Dread that. He's a nice juicy bug I can squish."

Savor was shaking his head as if I'd gone crazy. "You're upsetting Dread, Allay. You don't want him against you."

"Oh, I think it's a little too late for that." The name of the game was dissension in the ranks. And I was causing it.

By the time we made cursory rounds so Savor could fulfill his role, the cop cars had disappeared up the street. I went outside and drew down the metal shutter in front of all the lingering, curious eyes and padlocked it. As I walked away, my last sight of the bar was of streamers of yellow crime tape the cops used to hold people back, fluttering from the tree trunk into the gutter.

Savor caught up with me, muttering, "I knew you wouldn't run to Glory."

I gave him a look. "Glory wants me dead; why would I go to her?"

"Don't be so sure of that. You never know what people will do. Look at you—you're the last person I can imagine who would turn to blackmail."

That stung. "Tell Dread to let Theo go. If they don't cut him loose and keep out of his life, I'll report every dirty deal I've been involved in for the past decade. The fact that my bar was just strafed like some kind of gangster movie will lend me some credibility, don't you think?"

Savor smacked his forehead with a beefy hand. "Allay, Allay. You're in way over your head. My advice is for you to run away. As far and fast as you can."

I rounded the corner onto Houston, the busy crosstown street. "What do you think I'm doing? If you'll leave me alone, I can get on with it."

Before Savor could reply, I sensed other demons—

at least four, maybe five—approaching rapidly from the south.

I ran into Houston, my arm raised in a futile attempt to flag down a cab. A cab was safety, mobility, protection against demons. But the few cabs that went by were already hired, carrying people to work.

With the bombardment of signatures growing stronger, I continued running down Houston with Savor right on my heels. Turning onto the street behind me, I could feel the stinging of a hundred bees, the terrible sensation caused by Goad, dominating the other signatures. He was a Vex demon.

I really didn't want to see Goad. He was a sociopath on a leash, if I ever met one.

My ears were also ringing, which meant Stun was with them. Stun was Shock's offspring, but she had rarely spoken to him since he was born fifty years ago.

I realized Savor wasn't chasing me; he was running with me, also looking back to judge where the demons were coming from. His glance said that ten-to-one Goad and Stun were after me, but he wasn't taking any chances.

I ran across Clinton Street amid blaring horns, ignoring the DON'T WALK signs. I nearly killed myself again crossing to the other side of Houston against the light. Savor shouted at cars in his deep voice, banging on hoods to get their attention as we passed between them.

In the narrow streets of the Lower East Side, we ran down Suffolk against the traffic. I was about to veer onto Rivington, when the signatures came barreling at us from the west and a cargo van pulled up in front of us.

Five demons jumped out, dressed in white scrubs as if they were orderlies from a hospital. The van had a huge BELLEVUE decal on it.

One demon I could handle, even two—but not five, not even if Savor fought by my side.

I ran.

They caught me before the end of the block, piling on me in a tangle of arms and legs, ignoring my blows. They trussed me up in a thick leather straitjacket, wrapping my arms around me, and shackling my legs in heavy iron cuffs. Even for a demon, it would be hard to break free of that.

I knew because this wasn't the first time I'd been locked into a straitjacket. It brought back all those terrifying memories of when I was a teenager and just possessed by a demon. I had huddled in a straitjacket in a cell for hours, listening to distant, eerie cries and unable to scratch or wipe my runny nose or eyes. I felt that same hopelessness, unable to control myself, much less what happened, as lost as I could be.

The demons carried me facedown by my elbows and legs. Savor was hovering near the van, watching. He seemed reluctant to get too close in case they came after him next.

Goad was assuring a few passersby. "Everything's under control. The patient is fine now."

"Where are you taking me?" I gasped, trying to see with my face only inches from the sidewalk.

"Where you'll be safe," Goad said with a rough laugh as they tossed me into the back of the van.

15

I rattled around in the back of the truck, mostly faceup. It was clear where we were going when I saw the cables of the bridge—back to Brooklyn.

The van drove around the back of the Prophet's Center and through an open loading dock bay. A driveway circled down to the basement where a dozen other cars were parked. I was tossed onto the cement, and the van quickly returned up the ramp. Goad was the only demon who stayed with me.

I strained every muscle I could, willing myself to break free. Stitches on the leather began to pop. My tendons tore, but I pressed on. Goad kicked my back, and my breath exploded from me. I lay there gasping and glaring up at him.

Goad grinned and reached down to stroke my cheek, absorbing my flare of outrage. Because of Vex's protection, Goad had stayed away from me. But Shock said he was known for seeking out demon energy. "Such a sweet morsel . . . ," he murmured almost lovingly.

He drew harder, straining at my shields. His fingertips pressed into my skin as if he wanted to push his whole hand into me, to penetrate my defenses physically if he couldn't do it spiritually.

"Asshole!" I concentrated on holding my shields together. I wouldn't allow him to shake my will like Pique had done.

The elevator pinged, startling us both. Goad jerked back before he could be caught sampling the catch.

I saw the huge boots first, and though these were combat-style boots, it reminded me of the ones that had disappeared through my skylight. Looking up, I saw it was Montagna, Dread's chief of security. As she lifted me easily and dumped me in the little elevator, I wondered if maybe she was the human who'd helped the demon get into my apartment.

If so, that meant Dread was in control of the stealthy demon, or somehow he had learned how to hide his own signature. It made sense that a demon as old as Dread would be the one to discover a way to conceal it.

Goad stayed in the underground garage, giving me a wave of his fingertips good-bye. He had never gotten a taste of me before, but his intent expression said he would do whatever he could to feed off me again. Just what I needed—another demon stalking me. It was getting crowded in my personal corner of hell.

The elevator went up to the top floor, and the door opened into a small, enclosed foyer that I had never seen before. The foyer and elevator were private with no two-way mirrors or cameras peering down. I doubted there was any record of my being brought here.

Dread was close by, but I couldn't feel Vex in the Prophet's Center. I wasn't sure if that was good or bad.

Montagna dragged me through an open door. It closed behind us with a muffled sound, as if it sealed when it locked.

At the end of the narrow room was a huge, circular cage, five feet across and eight feet tall. At first sight it looked like a birdcage because of its peaked roof and decorative ironwork scrolls between the bars. The bars looked strong, plus they were spaced so closely that a demon wouldn't be able to shrink enough to squeeze through. Some demons could make themselves appear as young as a six-year-old, but even a little girl's head wouldn't fit through those bars.

Montagna opened the small door on the cage and shoved me inside, clanging it shut behind me. I fell to the floor, unable to keep my balance with my arms locked around myself in the straitjacket. My chin hit the smooth metal floor.

The door on the other side of the room opened, and Dread appeared. I struggled to roll over. There was no way I was lying like a beetle on my back in front of him.

By the time I got up on my knees, Montagna was gone. Dread and I were alone.

"What do you think you're doing?" I demanded. "You can't force me to play a part in your Revelation."

"After the assassination attempt this morning, Vex thought it would be better if you stayed here under our protection."

I let out a short laugh of disbelief. "Are you insane?"

Dread shrugged. "Vex's orders. He thinks you can be broken to heel, and he's willing to take as long as he needs in order to do it."

I seized at the crack that had formed in their foundation. "What about you, Dread? What do you think?"

"I think you're too independent to be broken so easily."

I sat back on my heels. "Maybe you're the smart one."

"That remains to be seen."

The door from the elevator opened and Montagna appeared. Theo was with her, his wrists in handcuffs that were locked to a belt around his waist. His shirt hanging in tatters, he was scraped up, bruised, but defiant nonetheless.

I had never been so glad to see anyone in my life.

Theo lurched forward, trying to get to the cage. "Allay! Are you all right? You're bleeding. What did they do to you?"

Montagna bashed him in the back of the leg, sending him down to his knees with a grunt. I couldn't wipe my face, but I could feel the blood drip from my chin. I hadn't even noticed it got busted open when I hit the floor of the cage. Now that he'd seen it, I couldn't heal it.

"Let him go to her," Dread ordered.

Theo crawled the last few feet to the bars of the cage. "Allay!"

I wiggled forward on my knees. "I'm okay, Theo. Have they hurt you?"

Dread interrupted. "You're famished, Allay. You need to eat." He didn't seem to care whether Montagna or Theo heard.

Theo was still incensed at seeing me trussed up. "You think torturing her will make her cooperate?"

"Oh, no. She's not the one who's going to be tortured." Dread gestured to Montagna. "You are."

Theo resisted as much as a man could with his wrists cuffed to his belly button. He got in a good swipe at Montagna's feet to throw her off balance, and his roundhouse kick just missed her chin. I was cheering him on for all I was worth.

Montagna's training showed as she danced out of the way, then darted back in. Grappling with him, she slammed him face-first against the cage. It was so heavy it didn't even budge, but it rang out horribly as his skull connected with the bars. With two quick motions, she hooked his restraining belt to the scrollwork between the bars. It held him close to the cage so that he had to lean forward, keeping his knees bent to hold himself up.

"Go ahead," Dread ordered. "Make it hurt."

"Dread, no!" I cried. "You can't!"

Montagna grabbed Theo's hair and jerked his head back. "I'm going to enjoy this," she hissed into his ear. There weren't any sexual undertones; she wasn't getting off on being able to beat him. It was darker than that, a predatory instinct unleashed.

Her fingers dug into his T-shirt and pulled down sharply. The worn threads shredded as she ripped the tattered remains off his back.

"Dread, stop her," I pleaded. "Don't do this or I'll never help you, I swear."

"Allay, don't make it worse," Theo warned. Then he looked away.

Her fist landed on his kidney, making him grunt in pain. Then her other fist pounded the other side.

"The police report said your ribs were broken," Montagna murmured. "How does that feel now?"

I tasted blood. My own lip was bleeding where I bit it. "You're sick," I hissed at her.

She used him like a punching bag, beating him in the lower back. He couldn't take a breath between the blows, they rained down on him so hard and fast. She varied her punches from place to place, even hitting him repeatedly in the ribs under his arm.

When Montagna finally stopped, she was breathing heavily. For a woman in such good shape, that said something. Theo was sagging from the restraining belt at his waist, cutting into his back unbearably but unable to stand in the violet haze of pain that engulfed his aura.

I was helpless, wrapped up in the straitjacket. I couldn't even touch him to take away his pain.

I stole a glance at Dread. He looked dissatisfied with what was happening. He didn't like pain. He wanted fear, that slow-burning eater of life. But Theo wasn't afraid in spite of the beating.

Montagna was definitely enjoying herself. She unhooked him from the cage, then used her truncheon to hit him sharply in his chest and the back of his legs as he curled into a defensive ball. "Lie still!"

She started to strip him, yanking at his shoe as he managed a weak kick or two, which she avoided; then she jerked his other shoe off. His jeans quickly followed.

Dread looked alarmed. "How bad is he?"

"Pretty bad. Blood on the lips means he could die," Montagna replied, her voice nonchalant. I hated her.

"That's enough then. Put him inside."

I strained as hard as I could at the straitjacket. One of

the buckles snapped off, and I felt more of the stitching let go.

But it wasn't enough. Dread used the ornate iron key to unlock the small door, and Montagna dragged Theo over and rolled him inside.

Dread slammed the cage door shut behind him, locking it and slipping the iron key into his pocket. "You know what to do, Allay. The more you resist, the worse it will be."

Dread's footsteps were followed silently by Montagna as they left the room, shutting the door behind them. Montagna was a killer, and I had no doubt that she worked for Dread, because she got what she needed. She probably didn't mind tenderizing his meat as long as she could finish off the leftovers.

I leaned over him. *"Theo . . ."*

There was blood smeared on his lips and trickling down one corner, bright red. His eyes were drawn in pain at each gasping breath, as if it were unbearable. His back and sides were inflamed bright red with patches of bloody flecks where his flesh had been pounded raw. There was a long, purpling bruise forming across his chest, where he had been hit with her truncheon. Other bruises marked the back of his legs.

He lifted his hand to grab on to the front of my jacket where my arms crossed. "Turn around," he rasped.

I shifted so he could reach the buckle in back to undo it. He didn't say anything about the other one I'd broken. He didn't have to undo the back of the jacket; I shrank my chest and arms and wiggled out easily once my arms were freed.

He groaned as he tried to raise himself, falling back down. I sat down so he could lie with his head on my lap. "Here, this will be better."

Theo eased back slowly, wincing as he curled on his side. He let out a ragged breath as he settled into place. The heat of his body was scorching, so solid and heavy against me, as if he were a fire I could warm myself over. The musky scent of him and the sheen of sweat on his bare skin made me think of twining my legs with his . . . thoughts that I was ashamed of. How could I lust after a man who was in such misery? I was an evil creature.

I touched his cheek with trembling fingers, brushing the scrapes he had gotten when the guards pushed him down in the basement. His eyes closed as I ran my hand through his thick hair, feeling the slight tug where the ends curled. I scooped off his pain, taking it as fast as I could to give him some relief. I did it to help him, but his suffering passed into my own body in the form of potent energy.

I resolutely refused to touch the bright streaks of euphoria that shot through his aura where I drew away the pain; those brief moments when he felt a hint of relief. The golden light was tantalizing, but it would be wrong to take even a drop.

Theo's gaze was so trusting and open. Why did he still look at me that way? I didn't deserve it. I'd proved in every way I didn't deserve it.

"That feels better." He sighed.

"I'm sorry. It's my fault."

"Would you believe that it's worth it to be with you?"

It made me sad to think I had glamoured him with my demon ways. My hand faltered. "No . . ."

"Well, it is."

Theo was worried about me. I could feel his concern and fear for me pouring off him in waves. But he wasn't scared for himself, despite his terrible pain. My fingers tingled with the medley of his emotions every time I stroked his hair.

He kept closing his eyes as if the simple touch were heaven. I was pulling off a great deal of his pain, so it wasn't surprising that endorphins were making him heady. Perhaps that explained his fearlessness.

"You're not like any man I've ever met, Theo."

His eyes were blue again, not black and dilated. "I would go to the ends of the earth for you, Allay."

I felt it, too. Like a dying wish, I wanted to escape all of this and run away with him. It was foolish—I barely knew him. But I'd never felt this way before.

Theo was exactly what I needed in a man; a partner, a lover, the perfect mate. In another world, we would have a big romance, then settle down and have kids, change and grow together, share our old age together. The Happily Ever After that everyone wanted. It was my wasted life's dream, a hope I had lost at eighteen, though it had taken until now for me to face it.

Living as I was, I was already dead. Hope and new possibilities were dead, because I had to live a lie.

That was why, in spite of myself, I thought about Vex's offer. Everything would change if I worked with him. I could tell everyone exactly who I was—something other than human, a creature of pure spirit. I could live in truth.

But I'd be a freak show, a perversion of religion, fool's gold for the shysters to sell.

It would be another dead imitation of life. No, the only way to live was the one promised in Theo's eyes—love and admiration, a tender caring that shrugged aside selfish needs, and the light of endless faith.

I couldn't have that life.

Tears filled my eyes, but I smiled to show him that it wasn't all pain. Oh, it was bittersweet, but at least I had gotten a taste of what I had lost, here at the end. I had been granted a glimpse into paradise, and it confirmed everything I knew already—there was nothing else worth living for.

A long time went by as Theo dozed off in a delirium. I watched him sleeping, drawing off his stronger twinges of pain with a light fingertip.

Eventually, the inner door opened, revealing a slice of black hardwood floor and towering windows—Dread's loft. I hadn't noticed that before. The light was coming in strongly, indicating it was late afternoon. How convenient it was for him to keep his victims caged up right next door; how liberal of Lash to allow it.

Looking at Theo, curled up and naked, made something snap inside of me. I wanted to tell him the truth about myself. He deserved to know it. But there were probably cameras in the room, and Vex would know if I did. Then they would definitely kill him.

Suddenly I realized Dread was in the room. I had been too distracted, and his signature was now tempered by another demon's. Vex was back, as well. It felt as if he were right next door, in Dread's loft.

As Dread walked over to the cage, my lip lifted as if I smelled something bad.

"We have all the time in the world," Dread assured me. "When this man dies, we'll get another one of your people so you can feed off them."

He was talking about Lolita and Darryl. Pepe. Maybe even Shock. They would let Montagna torture them. All of them. One by one in a parade, each suffering because of me.

Well, doesn't that just suck.

I stood up to confront Dread, clenching my hand around one of the bars. "You're disgusting."

"You'll give in eventually, Allay. Everyone does."

Theo shifted slightly, his knees drawn up in obvious pain. "Go fuck yourself! Allay, don't listen to him. You can't trust him."

"I won't," I told Theo. "I'll never do it. You hear that, Vex? Never."

Dread cocked his head, waiting. A few seconds later, Vex sauntered in, wearing his skateboarder guise. I wasn't expecting his first words: "I know who tried to kill Shock."

Next to me, Theo's head went up. But I was sure Vex was putting on a show. At this point, I figured the stealth demon was Vex himself, or barring that, Dread, especially since Phil Anchor and Savor had been distracting me both times the stealthy demon had struck.

"It was Abash, one of Glory's offspring," Vex said triumphantly. "Her signature is extremely mild, so I've suspected for some time that Glory's been using her as an assassin. She was spotted in your neighborhood on Saturday, and just now she appeared in the vicinity of Revel's apartment. She'll probably try to kill Shock or steal her away, if she can, to set a trap for you."

I couldn't trust him. "Did you tell Revel?"

"I just got off the phone with him. He's increasing his security, and I've sent a few of my people over there to help out."

Revel could be letting the viper into his bosom. Poor Shock. There was nothing I could do to help her while I was in this cage.

"I'm the only one who can protect you," Vex assured me. "And Shock, since you're so fond of her."

I gestured at the cage. "Thanks for the protection."

"You have no idea the lengths I'm going to for you, Allay. Tonight I'm launching a preemptive strike against Glory. If I'm lucky, I'll smash her entire entourage, along with the queen bee herself."

Dread stepped forward. "Tonight? You pulled that together quickly. . . ."

"Don't tell me you're having doubts." For an instant, the younger-looking man was clearly the one in charge, not the prophet, a disconcerting sight. "Lash betrayed us, and now she has to pay for it."

"Yes, of course," Dread agreed. "I just wasn't expecting it to be tonight."

Vex was going to kill them all—Glory's entire inner circle, including Lash—tonight. Then there would be no one to stop him from carrying out his Revelation.

Vex dismissed Dread with a slight lift of his hand, and the prophet fell back a step, the obedient lieutenant. "I'm taking care of you, Allay," Vex assured me. "I'll always take care of you. Just keep eating up and get that aura nice and strong. If you cooperate, we can talk about letting you out."

I felt as if I were in kindergarten again. I wanted to shout, "Never!" at him. But that wouldn't help Theo. I had to try to get him out of here. "I won't cooperate unless you let Theo go. Now."

"You need sustenance." Vex grimaced, shaking his head as he surveyed Theo's wounds and ordered Dread, "No need for all that mess. She'll feed without you hurting him."

Grudgingly Dread agreed. I rolled my eyes—as if I were going to buy that. Vex even smiled at me as he left the room. He was trying to break me down so that I would trust him. But I knew he was the one responsible for Theo's wounds.

Dread looked awfully bitter after Vex left.

From behind me, Theo said, "I guess the kid's running the show. Isn't it always that way?"

I actually smiled. He couldn't have poked Dread in the eye harder.

Dread came over to glare down at Theo. "His time will come. Sooner than he thinks."

"That sounds like a threat." My glance went to the cameras. "I don't think Vex will like that."

Dread frowned, shaking his head at himself. "I'll have to wipe the tapes," he muttered.

It was too bad Vex wasn't watching from Dread's loft. His aura was descending, moving away from us. It felt as if he were leaving the building again. It probably took a lot of work to launch a strike force against a bunch of demons.

"Clearly you're not needed for the plan tonight," I pointed out. "He probably put Goad in charge instead of you."

"Maybe I can use this . . . ," Dread murmured. He wasn't

looking at us; he was staring through the cage, lost in thought. His deadly tone would have frightened me more, but what he was considering didn't involve me.

He was thinking about the strike against Glory and Lash. What had Savor said just before I was kidnapped? They had expected me to run to Glory. Yet I was sure that Glory was the last person Vex wanted me to see. So why did Dread let me leave, hoping I'd go to Glory?

Dread tried to set up Vex. Using me.

It almost took my breath away. "You wanted me to tell Glory that Vex is ready to launch the Revelation." Dread's surprised look was all the confirmation I needed. "You want Glory to take on Vex. You're ready to break with him, aren't you? But you can't do it by yourself. You can't try to kill him—what if he beats you? But if you get Glory mad enough at him, she'll do the dirty work for you."

Dread actually smiled. "As a matter of fact, she will. Since you didn't do what you were supposed to, I'll find some other way. I can warn Glory about this preemptive strike. She doesn't even have to know it's me tipping her off." He looked regretful. "Though it's too bad . . . I'd love to see Lash get what she deserves."

His matter-of-factness chilled me to the heart. I stepped sideways to block his view of Theo, as I gripped the iron bar. The edges had been worn off over years of use. Dread must have put hundreds of people in this cage—and demons, too, no doubt. No wonder Vex had been so quick to suspect him of killing demons in his own line.

Dread suddenly grabbed on to my hand, pressing my fingers into the bar. The colored swirl around our hands rippled. "Too bad you weren't more useful, Allay. I'm afraid you aren't worth keeping around anymore."

He squeezed tighter, making me gasp at the burst of pain in my fingers. "Vex isn't going to like it if you hurt his patron saint," I pointed out.

"After tonight, Vex won't be around to care."

A bone snapped in my finger, firing off like a tiny shot. "You're hurting me!"

Theo moved so fast that I almost didn't see him as he reached through the bars to slam down on Dread's arm with a closed fist. Dread let go of me, rubbing his arm.

I pushed back against Theo with all of my strength, backing us both away from Dread. Theo was radiating intense hatred for the man. He was supporting me, despite the insanity of the past few days, despite the incomprehensible things he had just heard. There was no hesitation, no doubt in his feelings for me.

It was one of the sweetest moments of my life.

But the scraped flesh of his cheek and the livid bruises across his torso reminded me; I had sentenced him to death by bringing him here. "I'm sorry."

His arms tightened around me as he murmured, "So am I."

"Enough of that." Dread drew himself up, walking back to the door that led to his loft. But instead of leaving, he stopped by a small black fixture in the wall. He slid open a panel and spun the lock.

The safe door opened and Dread pulled out a gun. It had a long nozzle, as if there were a silencer on the end.

"No!" I choked out.

Theo thrust me away, leaving himself exposed, as I cried, "Don't, Theo!"

Dread took aim and the soft *whoot!* of the gun was my only warning. The high-pitched whistle was followed by an explosion that made my ears ring. Theo's hands jerked away as he lurched back against the bars.

Dread had shot him point-blank in the head.

16

I caught Theo as he started to slide down the bars, keeping him from keeling over. His eyes were partly open, but already clouding. His heart fluttered against my hand, trying to keep pace with the blood leaking out of the back of his blown-out skull.

He collapsed onto me, his head falling on my shoulder, spilling a thin stream of hot blood down my chest. The sharp tang of blood and gunpowder bit my throat. "Theo," I cried, choking.

I reached for that last spark of life inside of him, hoping to sustain him for a few moments more. But he died as I held him. His aura flickered out as if it had been doused with water.

Everything else vanished, and there was only this horror. I had been telling myself that Theo wouldn't make it out of this alive, trying to face up to what I had done to him. Now he was dead—gone. And it was my fault, from beginning to end.

I couldn't face it.

I held on to Theo, too shocked to cry, too ripped open to do anything but gasp every breath as if I were drowning. For a moment I thought I was also dying, that my essence was draining away at the same moment as his.

"Allay!" Dread shouted, running around to our side

of the cage. He must have thought I was dying, too, or he wouldn't have been so unguarded.

Ignoring Dread, I cradled Theo, closing his eyes with my shaking, blood-smeared hand. What would his family think when he never returned? Would his body be found somewhere, a victim of unknown violence? I hoped they didn't have to wait day after day, never getting word that he had died. His father must have been good for him to be so kind and true himself, despite how terrible he thought himself.

Dread grasped at my shoulder, making me lurch away, obeying a deeper instinct. The need in him to consume another demon was very strong. I finally saw what he wanted from me—he was going to steal my essence. With the scrape of the bolt, Dread unlocked the cage door with the iron key. It swung open with a squeak.

I scrabbled back, still holding on to Theo, crouching in the center of the cage.

Dread stepped into the cage, standing in front of the small door. I carefully eased Theo down, and stood up to face him.

It was much more frightening with Dread inside the cage. Suddenly the iron bars were too constraining. All I could do was prepare to protect myself the best I could, as the last spark of humanity I'd had left in the world lay dead at my feet.

Dread gave me one of his rare smiles. "Vex won't even know you're gone. He's too busy dealing with Glory to come back tonight. Glory will take care of him for me."

Dread took one careful step forward, keeping me from stepping out of his line. Then he took another, backing me against the bars. It was difficult to defend myself in such close quarters.

I parried Dread's first attempts to grab me, tripping over Theo's sprawled legs. Dread moved as if he were the one who invented Aikido and knew exactly what I would do to respond to him. Though I tried to deflect him, he had the advantage with cramped space. Once he got close, I tried to spin out from under him. But he rolled with me, pressing me into the bars to stop me.

His hand went around my throat, grabbing my wrist while pinning my other arm between us, pressing his body hard against mine. I struggled like a pinned butterfly, but I didn't have a fraction of his strength. Dread was bursting with power.

His thumb pressed into my throat, making it hard to breathe. "Your fear is so sweet. I knew it would be. Go ahead, fight me. I like it that way. . . ."

I wanted to gag. He was getting off on it, feeding on my terror. He pressed his groin into mine so I could feel the enormous rod of his erection. That made me struggle even more.

"I could rape you as I kill you," he murmured. "I used to make Lash watch me. . . ."

Despite my frantic attempts to shield myself, Dread reached right in and slurped up the pitiful remnants of my energy like a starving vampire bat. His hips bumped into me in a lewd imitation of sex. Wildly I wrenched my wrist free and scratched at his hand, trying to grab on to some leverage point to make him let go of my throat. But I was so weak, I could barely struggle anymore.

He was draining me.

Dimly, I realized this was the end. A wave of acceptance passed through me, and I relaxed. Dread grimaced as if my reaction were distasteful. I was glad. At least I had soured the milk for him.

My skin felt as if it were drying up from inside as I began to shrivel. Then Dread reached for my essence, to pull it into himself. I wanted to scream, the pain was so intense, but I couldn't. My inner flame wavered, flickering inside as it began to tilt toward him, ripping from its mooring in my soul.

Suddenly Theo rose up behind him. It seemed like a death vision, one last wild hope. Then Theo put his arm around Dread's neck and squeezed.

Dread let out a yelp in surprise, letting go of my throat. But Theo pushed Dread into me, pressing me back against the bars even harder. Even with Dread's hand no longer around my neck, I still wasn't able to breathe. I could barely see.

It couldn't be Theo. But his furrowed brow with rivulets of drying blood down his face left no doubt. He was alive.

How? How did he survive a bullet to the head? I couldn't think without air to breathe.

Theo was incredibly strong, holding Dread as easily as he had held me. And something else was happening. Energy was flowing into me—Dread's energy.

Theo was absorbing Dread's energy and somehow forcing it to flow into me. A realization crashed into me like the proverbial brick.

Theo is a demon.

But that was impossible—Theo's flesh burned as hot as a human's. He ate; he perspired; he had all those precious human flaws that my body now lacked. His energy felt distinctly like a human's, not a demon's. But nothing else could explain his resurrection.

Dread bucked underneath Theo in shock, smashing me into the bars. As his outrage continued to pour out, I absorbed as much as I could. My skin felt as if it were plumping back up under the onslaught, not as wrinkled and drawn. But I was light-headed from lack of oxygen, ready to pass out.

Finally, Theo rolled Dread off me, slamming him against the cage. He kept his legs locked around Dread's, shoving his face against the bars. Dread was as highly charged as a demon could get, but he had dropped his shields to absorb my essence, so it took only minutes for his energy to drain into Theo. Theo took him right down to the point where his flesh started to shrivel and his arms and legs began to curl inward. When Dread could hardly move, and there was only a drop or two of energy left inside of him, Theo finally let him go. Dread lolled on the floor, looking like a much smaller, older man.

It was so sudden, I couldn't seem to catch up.

Theo finally turned to me. I was staring at him in horror, my hands still at my throat. "Finish him, Allay. It will only take a second, and then you'll be renewed."

My voice cracked. *"Who are you?"*

He breathed a heavy sigh. "I'm a demon."

Silence spun between us, delicate as glass and hard as diamond. I could only stare at him, blinking. *"How* can you be a demon? You don't feel anything like a demon."

"I've fortified my shields. It's not something modern demons have mastered. I don't think Vex and Glory even know it can be done. I learned so I could kill Bedlam, the demon who birthed them. I was his progenitor. I've been watching their lines ever since, destroying the worst of their offspring. Demons can be the source of remarkable advances, but we're our own worst enemies, as you've discovered."

I couldn't believe it, even though I had watched him consume Dread. "Prove it."

Theo hesitated. "I haven't let down my shields in . . . centuries."

I was shaking my head, unable to accept it. He *felt* human.

"All right," he agreed. "If that's what it takes for you to trust me."

It was dazzling; one second Theo was standing within arm's reach, his expression so earnest and familiar, his na-ked body so battered. The next, he was nearly obscured by a rainbow glow around him. His signature suddenly thrummed through my body, as if I were speeding down a tunnel with the wind whistling around me. It was thrilling, heady, and scary, and about to go out of control at any second.

He was Ram.

I gasped, trying to get my bearings in the midst of his power. Unshielded, he felt older than dirt, like an ancient pyramid with its base buried in the sands of time. I could almost sense the desert wind in the palms, the scent of spices, and the cooling waters of the Euphrates lapping inside of him. He was eternal.

To think he could shield this, and make himself feel like an ordinary man!

Like an ordinary man ...

"It was *you*," I breathed. "You're the one who sneaked into my house to kill Shock!"

Ram's shields slammed back into place, cutting off the exotic reverberations. He looked caught. "Allay, we don't have time for this. You have to take Dread now. Before Vex returns."

I looked down at Dread, who was curling into a ball, his hands clenched into claws. He would be easy to take, and my need to regenerate was clamoring urgently, demanding that I do it. I would die—die soon—if I didn't.

I looked down at my hands and imagined myself touching Dread, sucking the life out of him, in the same way that Theo—no, Ram—had sucked the life out of Shock.

I couldn't get it through my head. *Theo is a demon. I should have known it. Shouldn't I?*

Looking back, I realized he was the only one in my apartment when Shock was attacked. And it explained why he never asked questions, accepting whatever happened, no matter how outlandish it was. No ordinary guy could have done that. But he gave me exactly what I had needed, so I ignored the warning signs.

Demons always give you what you want, so you give them what they want.

"Why Shock? What did she ever do to you?"

Now Ram really looked caught and even a little sheep-
ish, if that was possible. "Those demons she births every
half century are brutal. Do you know what Stun does to his
victims? Once I saw him hit an old lady with a baseball bat.
I would have killed him a long time ago, but there've been
others who are even worse, too many to keep up with. The
numbers are growing exponentially. Now I have to kill the
demons who birth too many offspring. It's the only way to
control our population."

He had used me to get to Shock. He had used me to try
to kill the one person I could be honest with. And I had
protected him and cared about him, while he lied to me.

I launched myself at him, with every intention of hurting
him. I felt like an animal, filled with mindless rage. "You
bastard!"

He kept me from punching him, easily holding me off.
Through his palms, he forced some of the energy he had
stolen from Dread into me, feeding me his concern and
admiration. He actually liked that I was fighting mad. "It
wasn't on purpose, Allay. I was hunting Pique. You would
have died if I hadn't jumped him outside your bar."

"That's why you had sex with me. You wanted to kill
Shock."

"It's true that's why I went upstairs with you. But, Allay, I never lied about how I feel about you. I've never met
a woman with such resolve to do right, with such force of
character and strength of will. What happened between us
had nothing to do with any other demon. Never. The only
lie is who I am."

My strength was growing by the second as he forced
more energy into me. "What are you doing?" I tried to jerk
my wrists away from him.

"Dread nearly killed you. You need to take in a lot of
energy fast, or you'll be defenseless."

"No." I tried to wrest my arms from his grasp, struggling
to raise my shields to keep him from giving me his stolen

energy. But I wasn't skilled or strong enough to block him. "Stop it. Let me go or I'll scream!"

"The guards are probably used to screams coming from this room," he said. But he let me go. My aura was glowing nicely now.

I edged away from Dread, avoiding his feet. He was in bad shape, his clawed hands drawn up to his pinched face. His eyes were heavy lidded. He was still murmuring; I don't know what. But it sounded more furious than pleading for his life. A demon like Dread had probably never imagined himself brought so low. Who had ever challenged Vex's second-in-command?

It was the height of irony that I, a possessed human, was supposed to do him in. I supposed for someone like Ram, it was easy. "How could you kill all those people?"

"I have to maintain the balance, Allay. I can't let demons overrun humanity; it would ruin everything. Take a look around you—even the poorest families live better than kings used to. If I hadn't culled the most dangerous, despicable demons over the centuries, that couldn't have happened. It's good for demons, too. Civilization has to flourish for us to survive. We die with them when they fall."

"The last time someone wanted mankind to make great leaps, it involved cutting off my head."

"Forget about all that." Ram pointed at Dread. "You have to consume him, Allay. We've got more than enough evidence that he tortures people, as well as demons, in this cage—"

Abruptly, he stopped. I felt it, too—the first tingles of Vex's signature. Vex was approaching quickly down below, outside the building. What if he had felt it when Ram lowered his shields?

"Vex is coming. We have to move fast," he said.

I clutched the bars behind me, still shaking my head.

"Allay, you have to take him. Now." Ram ran a hand through his hair in frustration. Naked, wounded, he looked like my familiar Theo, but somehow he was completely different. "I have to go wipe the tapes. I can't allow proof of demon existence to be linked to the death of the prophet. That would be catastrophic for civilization."

"What about Vex?"

"I'll take care of him. You do the right thing and finish off Dread."

Ram hurried to the door, but he paused on the threshold, looking back. I met his eyes, still angry and confused. Then I resolutely looked away.

The door closed and Ram was gone. I couldn't sense him now that he was shielded again. I had come to rely on my ability to sense other demons before I saw them. Avoiding them kept me alive. So the possibility that a demon could shield himself to the point that he felt completely human was terrifying. I had stopped thinking straight, or apparently, seeing straight. I had believed his line of bullshit, and accepted him for what he portrayed himself as—a man who had such a strong connection with me that he would give up everything to stand by my side in my hour of need.

That man didn't exist.

But Ram had saved me again—this time from death at Dread's hands. The energy he had forced me to take had been so satisfying . . . better than anything I had ever consumed. It had revived me from the brink of death. But getting drained had also intensified my aching need to take another demon, to renew my dying spark of life force.

Dread was within arm's reach. I slowly sank down to my knees next to him. He looked defenseless now, smaller and more fragile. His signature was a feeble thing, weaker than Shock's had been when I had found her.

It would take nothing, a brush of my finger to the back of his hand, and I could steal his essence away from him. I could see it glowing inside of him, vulnerable and ready to be taken. There was only a thin layer of energy keeping it from leaping into my core and it strained against those bounds, eager for my touch. I almost called to it, wanting it more than anything.

It was such a small thing to do to gain two centuries of life, to give me all that I would do and see. . . . I was sure I would be productive, generous, useful—not a corrupt, greedy bastard like Dread.

But I would be a murderer, a cannibal. People shouldn't kill other people to survive. It wasn't right, on the most fundamental level. It was what made demons evil.

Vex's signature was approaching, on this very floor. Vex was more attuned to Dread's signature than anyone else. What if he felt Dread's flickering signature and came to check it out?

I reached out for Dread again, pushed to the brink by self-preservation.

But Vex's signature began to recede as he walked past, down the hallway toward his loft at the other end of the building.

I pulled my hands back without touching Dread.

I was still myself.

It was a remarkable relief, despite the gnawing in my belly. And at least I could sense Vex. It was better than knowing Ram was right next door and I couldn't sense him.

Then I remembered seeing Theo and Vex grappling in the hallway. It suddenly took on new meaning. Ram had been trying to kill Vex, not the other way around. And I had interrupted him.

Ram, the self-professed assassin, proved how right I was to hold tight to my last remnants of humanity. I had scared myself with the fear of becoming a human serial killer, but the reality was much worse. How many of his offsprings' offspring had he eaten?

And he was proud of it.

I leaned in close to Dread's ear. "I could kill you, but I won't. You owe me one, Dread."

I got up and left the cage. The key was still in the lock, so I turned it—a final, irrevocable sound; then I pocketed the heavy iron key, leaving Dread curled like a small, empty husk on the floor. *There, nobody would be able to reach him and accidentally become possessed.*

It was my only choice. If anyone deserved to die, it was Dread. But I was no executioner.

17

Somewhere along the way, I had accepted that I wasn't getting out of this mess alive. *But who does? Life always ends in death.*

My only choice was in how I lived.

With Vex's signature pulsing strong at the other end of the building, I cautiously opened the door into Dread's loft. In a truly schizophrenic moment, I half feared, half hoped that Ram would be there.

But the enormous loft was empty. The shattered remains of a speaker lay in front of several open wall panels holding electronic equipment. The sleek black machines had been dragged out, trailing wires, their guts smashed. That had to be Ram's work, erasing the tapes of the torture chamber.

I glanced down at myself; I was sticky with drying blood from my chest to my fingertips: Ram's blood.

I sniffed the back of my hand. It was definitely demon blood. Why hadn't I recognized it when Ram was shot? I, of all people, shouldn't have doubted that a demon could shield his signature. I had seen those motorcycle boots with my own eyes and hadn't felt a signature. But still I hadn't truly believed it.

Feeling as if dogs were nipping at my heels, I shoved aside the bamboo screen and washed myself in the large sink. I took off my shirt and bloody bra and practically had to crawl inside to rinse myself, scrubbing my face, as well.

The water that ran off was pale scarlet, the color of old anger.

Then I started checking doors, looking for the closets. There were several private studies and sitting rooms, but no bedroom. One large room was lined with cabinets, shelves, and bars for hanging clothes. It looked as if a tornado had blown through and taken some of the stuff, leaving the rest dangling from hangers and spilling out of drawers and across the floor.

Lash had left in a hurry, it seemed.

Using the hand towel to dry off, I chose black leggings and a dark empire-waist dress with a pattern that looked something like irises down one side of the skirt. I didn't have much energy to spare to fully heal my throat, so I left the bruises alone. Then I fluffed up my hair and glanced in the mirror placed discreetly in a nook near the door.

I stopped short, caught by my wide eyes. I was a stranger to myself, just another desperate girl. The city was full of them.

Trying to calm myself, I reached for the door handle. I was plotting ways out of the Prophet's Center, but I realized something else had changed.

Vex's signature was not as strong.

I'd been thinking about running for the stairwell, but instead, a foreboding drew me down the long corridor. The door to Vex's loft had been left ajar.

I pushed it open and ducked inside to avoid the prying eyes of the security guards with their cameras in the hallway.

Vex's loft had the same sleeping mezzanine with a galley kitchen below, but his was decorated in industrial chic, black and silver. It was scattered with the paraphernalia of a skateboarding geek—video games, racing magazines, graphic novels of every kind. The lithographs and multimedia sculptures were bold, rough, grating on the senses. Neglect showed in the dust bunnies rolled against every wall in fat wads, as if the cleaning staff never entered.

The windows were streaky and clouded, obscuring the sweep of the suspension bridge that crossed right in front of me. Orienting myself, I realized that Dread's show office was one floor directly below.

The sun was setting, casting golden flares off the wires of the bridge. Beyond it was the park on top of the Prophet's Arena, along with the rooftops and towers of Brooklyn surrounding the bay of the old Navy Yard. Along the water's edge were towering cranes like prehistoric giraffes. Rows of the reflective round pools of the Red Hook sewage plant were on the far side of the bay.

I heard Vex gasp.

Looking in, I saw that Ram's arm was around Vex's neck, putting one of Vex's arms behind his back where it could do no harm. Ram had healed his body so there wasn't a trace of the burns or his black eye, or of the cut on his forehead, though the butterfly bandages were still where I'd placed them.

If this was a wrestling match, nobody would win. But Ram already had what he needed. He was pulling energy from Vex, drawing it through his strong shields one drop at a time.

With his face pressed into Ram's shoulder, Vex said breathlessly, "What are you?"

I could tell that Vex was trying to find an angle—by playing meek, he hoped to make Ram overconfident. But Ram replied, "I'm Bedlam's progenitor. I'm the one who killed him."

Vex seemed stunned. "No, that's impossible."

With dark clouds moving in ominously close, the light in the room faded quickly, leaving only the lights on the buildings punctuating the darkness. They were facing away from me, so I wasn't sure if they saw me or felt my signature in the midst of their battle.

Vex struggled, oblivious to bones cracking and muscles tearing. His face was pressed sideways so he couldn't bite into Ram's shoulder. He kept trying to twist away, and he expended inhuman strength to flip them over. But Ram's feet locked into his legs, keeping him from finding the leverage he needed. Vex was powerful after so many centuries, but Ram was thousands of years old and that much stronger. Ram also clearly knew a thing or two about shields.

"I've . . . felt you before," Vex choked out.

Ram hooked his feet into Vex's hips to keep him from slipping away again. "It's true. I lured Bedlam into kidnapping me off the street one night—in the persona of a harmless Sicilian boy. But instead of taking me himself, he gave me to you and Glory, so I could feed you. I let Bedlam lock me up between your boxes—those iron-bound coffins you and Glory had lived inside from the moment you were born. You both reached your arms through the holes, grasping on to my legs. You were near starved, kept alive only to preserve your essence until Bedlam needed it. I fed you both well before I broke the link on the chain and set myself free."

Vex struggled harder, but he couldn't budge Ram. The energy he was bleeding was starting to weaken him. His voice was strained from the head lock. "Glory told you that. She's been working with you. She sent you to stop me from launching the Revelation."

"Remember how I pulled the long iron pin from the hinges on the side of the box and opened it to find you first? The lid blocked us from her sight. I smiled at you and reached out my hand to help you. I was afraid you were going to attack me and I was going to have to reveal that I was a demon in order to fight you off. But after a moment, you took my hand and let me pull you up. You were blinking around at the room, and you were so shaky, you couldn't help me take out the pin on the lid to Glory's box. When I opened it, she leaped out like a wild cat. But she bounced

off me and scurried into a corner. I think you were as surprised as I was."

Vex let out his breath, as if he couldn't doubt anymore.
"I had seen only glimpses of that room through the hole:
the fresco on the wall of a woman reclining on a sofa eating
a banquet; piles of grapes; kneeling slaves presenting plat-
ters of roasted boar. We were being stored there, meat for
Bedlam to consume."

"Yes, and when Bedlam saw that I had gotten loose and
came in to investigate, you two bludgeoned him to death."

"Yes . . ."

"But you didn't take his essence."

Vex's voice was fainter. "We agreed it was best to never
speak of it. But it's affected everything we did. We protected ourselves, surrounding ourselves with our offspring,
preparing for his return. But he never appeared. I used to
sometimes wonder if it was Bedlam out there causing the
disappearances. Yet if he had lived, surely he would have
taken vengeance on us."

"You two were better than Bedlam. The best thing about
you was your détente with Glory. You've proved coopera-
tion begets prosperity for both demons and humans. But
for the sake of greed and power, you were ready to throw
that all away. You intended to impose chaos and supersti-
tion on the world again, warping the natural flow of society
by promising humans immortality."

"No, I understand now. Let this be the first step in our
negotiations. I'm willing to work with you, and with Glory,
too. Tell me what you want."

Vex's strength was waning now, and his struggles were
increasingly easy to subdue. I didn't think it was an act to
lull Ram. He had been draining off Vex's energy as hard
as he could for a while now. Vex's signature was weaken-
ing right in front of my eyes. I couldn't turn away from the
awful sight.

"Think of this as Judgment Day, Vex. I'm tallying up

your sins. The people you killed. The harm you inflicted. You were convenient for me, keeping your line in check. But you've lost control of them. Two hundred years ago no demon would have touched Allay if that was your order. Now I wonder if you have a full count of your own line."

"Shock's Petrify is the latest in my line. The last one before that was Slam. Was it you who killed him last month? But I admit . . . I could keep a better eye on my people. Your people, actually." He gasped a few times, trying to catch his breath. "You're our progenitor, Ram. We're part of your line. You deserve to hold your rightful place among us."

Ram sounded sickened. "If I wanted that, I would have taken it long ago. I've done nothing but pay for my useless pride, my stupidity in fighting Bedlam until everyone was dead. I'm complicit in the death of my own beloved progenitor. Nothing you could give me can change that."

The energy was pouring out faster now, as Vex's shields finally dropped. Ram soaked everything up as quickly as he could, swelling even bigger. He began to transform in small ways, trying to bleed off the excess energy, changing his hair color in rapid succession, growing his chest larger, his biceps bulkier, then back to normal again.

"Let me try," Vex whispered. "Let me try to serve you."

He was softening, slumping in on himself. Ram had to tighten his arm to keep hold as Vex began to compress inward. His chest caved as his skin shriveled, and his arms and legs began to draw up. It reminded me eerily of Dread. My own urgent need called out to the core exposed at the heart of Vex, only a last few drops of energy remaining.

The essence of his life was beautiful, sparkling like an enormous diamond, casting rainbows into my eyes. I took a step forward. I couldn't have torn myself away for anything. Vex's essence had been honed to a heightened brilliance over the centuries—alluring, hypnotic, irresistible. . . .

"I gave you life when I freed you from Bedlam," Ram whispered. "Now I take it back."

Ram drew in the essence that kept Vex alive, and absorbed it into himself. It slammed into him; though no bigger than his fist, it looked as if he had swallowed a blimp. It swelled inside of him, the power of life.

"*No!*" Vex let out a final breath, a moan of bewilderment.

His body quickly shrank in on itself, growing more intangible. Slowly the clothes collapsed onto Ram, and his arms weren't holding anything anymore. A long, thin form hung in the air, curling and collapsing, growing smaller by the second. Tendrils of smoke rose as it rolled into itself, disappearing with an audible pop.

There was a bad smell in the air, like burned oil—the unforgettable stench of dead demon.

18

It broke the spell that had held me frozen. Was it Ram's mesmerizing voice that had kept me standing by as he killed Vex? What kind of strange powers did he possess?

I hadn't done anything to try to stop him. I was complicit in Vex's death.

Ram turned, his expression filled with anguish. "I wish that hadn't been necessary."

He buried his head in his hands, swaying where he sat as if his ears were ringing. He had just absorbed a prodigious amount of energy. Even through his powerful shields, his signature was leaking out. It felt as if I were standing in a wind tunnel.

He stood up, dragging Vex's empty clothing off him. Bits of dust and dirt that had been clinging to Vex's body sifted down—ashes to ashes. . . .

Ram was glowing; a pearly luminescence from Vex's core emanated from him. But there was something more: He was pulsing.

Pulsing like Shock right before she gave birth.

No way . . . "Are you going to split in two?" I blurted out.

He turned around, with a faint look of surprise, but he was too far gone to reply. Keeping my distance, I watched as he struggled to shake out Vex's old clothes and pull them on. He shifted his guise to mimic Vex's persona of Tim Anderson. His sloppy brown hair fell into his eyes, obscuring his vision, and his limbs grew thin and rangy.

He staggered as he got his legs through the baggy jeans, wincing in disgust at the state of the clothing. But he could hardly leave without clothes on. Frankly, I was surprised the guards hadn't arrived already. I wondered who Ram had impersonated—buck naked—in order to get inside Vex's loft without raising the alarm.

Ram had to stop and grab hold of his stomach, much the same way Shock had done, as if trying to hold himself together. I could feel the cracks in his shields spreading wider, and could feel his deep reserves and the raging torrent that Vex's energy had created inside of him, as if a horse were about to burst out of him at any second.

I owed him nothing. In fact, I hated him for trying to kill Shock, for the lies he had told me.

But I couldn't let Ram fission in front of the church employees.

So as he moved toward the door, I went with him. I wasn't afraid; I doubted he was capable of attacking anyone at the moment. He had never tried to kill me, though he'd had plenty of opportunities.

Maybe I'd been too useful, like a Trojan horse, letting him get close to his victims.

He grabbed the skateboard leaning next to the front door, while I took one last look back. I knew what had happened here would rock the demon world to its foundations. For good or ill, Vex was dead.

I didn't say a word to him. And he didn't seem capable of speaking through his clenched jaw. I wanted to sympathize with his pain. But he wasn't Theo.

When we reached the door to the vestibule of the private elevator, Ram lifted his face to the camera. But he was struggling too hard to hold his guise and it didn't recognize him as Tim Anderson. Swearing and nearly overwhelmed, he ducked away, trying to pull himself together.

I took a chance and lifted my face. The door swung open, indicating that Vex hadn't rescinded my free pass throughout the complex.

I couldn't feel Dread in the room beyond with the cage. The door didn't have a handle on the outside, so there was no way for me to get in to check on him. After watching Ram absorb Vex, I was sure I had done the right thing. Only a demon could kill that easily.

I summoned the tiny elevator, as Ram slumped against the wall. He was shaking as if he were suffering from heroin withdrawal, banging the skateboard into his legs. He kept wiping the sweat from his forehead and neck, but he was perspiring so badly that his hair was dripping. It was so undemonlike, I still had a hard time believing he wasn't human. I remembered how flushed and moistened I'd been after sex with him, after I had absorbed his energy without even knowing it.

When the elevator came, I punched the basement level, hoping to avoid the guards at the front desk. I hoped my guess was correct and there were no cameras, because I failed completely at acting nonchalant. I jittered around, avoiding Ram, who could hardly stand up himself.

When we reached the bottom and the elevator dinged open, I was braced to face Montagna and her goons, like last time—or Goad and his horde. Ram held the skateboard ready to use as a weapon. I was prepared to break whatever I had to in order to escape this time.

But there was nothing but cinderblock walls and the dull roar of a distant furnace burning trash.

Ram weaved his way toward the glowing red sign of an exit door. I ran ahead and pushed it open with the crossbar, but from the interior of the stairwell it was locked. On the floor above were two doors at right angles to one another. The one directly ahead was a wide, steel double door with an arm at the top that shut it automatically.

The way out. I ran up and gave a sigh of relief when

it opened onto the street. The heavy clouds made it dark; maybe the sun had already set, as well. There were a few people hurrying by in the rain, hunched under umbrellas and hoods. The bridge loomed in the growing darkness at the end of the street.

It took Ram more time to climb the steps, but I remembered how I had helped him up to my apartment when he was stalking Shock and how good his hard stomach and heavy arm around my shoulders had felt. Now I didn't want to touch him. I made him climb up alone.

When he reached the top, he was pulsing even faster. "I can . . . hardly see, Allay. I have to get to cover now."

A guy ran past, his jacket over his head to ward off the rain. There were more running footsteps and exclamations of distress as pedestrians had to leap the growing puddle at the corner of the curb.

As much as I wanted to let Ram fission right on the church's doorstep, I couldn't let my own feelings get in the way. I couldn't risk Ram outing demons to humanity this way.

I needed to find someplace private before he made a spectacle of himself. It seemed that I was going to be a demon midwife once again.

A few blocks down to the edge of the river, I found a long stretch of chain-link fence against the massive stone base of the bridge. The waterfront street ran underneath, along the holding pen for delivery cube trucks. Since the bridge was split into two roadways, rain sluiced down in the middle, as well as on either side.

Ram reverted to his Theo guise. Hunched over his stomach, he was slogging through the water-filled gutters, holding on as hard as he could. Flashes of pulsing, pearly white light shot out of him. I was sure people could see it, but everyone was rushing to get through the driving rain, their heads mercifully down.

When we reached the fence under the roadway, I glanced around to check that nobody was nearby. Then I pulled on the gate, straining until the metal bent outward. There was enough of a gap that I could squeeze through. Ram went down on his knees and crawled in after me.

He didn't get far from the gate, weaving his way over to lean against a panel truck. We were both soaked to the skin from our dash down to the river, and the sound of pouring rain and wet tires rushing by on the bridge overhead drowned out everything else.

Now that Ram didn't have to hold himself together, I could see the ripples of pain spreading through him. Every muscle in his body clenched. He turned and pressed his forehead into the truck, trying to hide the glow in his face and hands. Vex's clothes damped the light, keeping him from shining like a radioactive man.

"I hate this." Ram panted, his teeth clenched in agony. "It's the last thing I wanted. But taking them both ... it was too much."

I stayed back, remembering the burst of energy that Shock had released. I wondered if he was thinking about her, that greedy girl and all of her offspring. "Maybe you're too quick to condemn demons whose only crime is being fertile. Demons like Shock."

His anguished blue-gray eyes were so familiar, Theo's eyes. But he wasn't Theo.

His back arched, and suddenly his shields fell. His signature thrummed out, like a deep-throated motorcycle rushing down the highway. Any demons within a few blocks would be able to feel his signature amplified by the fissioning.

"Maybe you should lie down—," I started to suggest.

He clenched his eyes shut against the brightness, stiffening against the side of the truck. Spasming, he let out a strangled cry as his insides tore their way out. Unlike Shock, he fought it every step of the way.

When the new demon ripped away from him, Ram was thrown back against the truck by the shock wave of expended energy. It rattled the chain-link fence, which I clung to so as not to lose my footing.

A fully-formed doppelganger staggered away from Ram.

Ram slid down, bracing himself against the truck. The new demon slipped and fell down in the mud, flailing a bit as it fought to get up. He looked vaguely like Theo, but his features quickly shifted, seemingly out of control. He was expending energy uselessly.

I eased back through the gate onto the sidewalk, feeling safer with a fence between us. Ram was sitting up but was clearly dazed by the birth.

It took a few moments for me to realize the new demon had the same signature as Ram; a racing, headlong sensation. It was odd, to say the least, to feel the same signature coming from two demons. But the new demon's power was only a fraction of Ram's.

Ram's shields snapped back up defensively. It left me in an echoing silence, with only the faint Ram-like signature coming from the new demon. It was a relief not to feel such a blast of sensation.

Ram looked amazed. "You feel like me."

At that moment, the demon's signature shifted and wavered, becoming something else. I felt as if I were floating in a featureless void, with no reference point to ground me. The demon was Mystify, born of Vex's utter surprise at Ram's existence and his own abrupt death.

"How did you do that?" I asked him through the fence. "You imitated Ram's signature."

Mystify shook his head. "I don't know." His signature was fluctuating again, briefly becoming Ram's. Then it was suddenly mine—a light, buoyant sensation. I knew it was my own because of the way it fit inside me, as if something that was usually a comfortable white noise in the background were suddenly echoing off a cliff. It was disorienting.

Then his signature returned to his own. I doubted Mystify was doing it on purpose; it was too chaotic, as if he were having trouble retaining a persona. He was a demon chameleon, assuming whoever's signature was nearby.

Ram got to his feet, smeared with mud from the ground. He was shaking off the worst of the effects. His shields were so tight that none of his demon energy leaked through. It felt as if I were standing under the bridge with only one other demon—Mystify.

Mystify took a threatening step toward Ram, his hands up as if wanting to feed off his energy. He took a stance that looked fairly competent, probably drawing on Ram's memory traces.

"Don't even think about it," Ram ordered. "I've reabsorbed every offspring I've birthed since I killed Bedlam. That was the only way to keep from revealing my existence. You'd be dead, too, right now but for one thing."

He was serious. I was hanging on every word, as was Mystify.

"My cover's blown," Ram said flatly. "Allay knows. And once one person knows, everyone knows. So I don't have to kill you."

"You've killed *all* of your offspring?" I asked in disbelief.

"There have only been a few. The last one was four hundred years ago, in Tuscany." He looked thoughtfully at Mystify. "But you're more fortunate than that."

"You've killed enough people today," I agreed, on the edge of hysterical laughter. I addressed Mystify. "Stay away from him, and you might survive."

Mystify hesitated, then took a step backward. He looked down at himself, naked and dirty from where he had fallen down on the ground. Then he glanced at the street.

"Here." Ram pulled off the long-sleeved, buttoned-down shirt that Vex had worn over a loose tank top. "Don't even ask about the pants."

Mystify snatched the shirt from Ram's hand and shrugged it on, buttoning it with clumsy fingers. The tails in front and back fell to the middle of his thighs, and as I watched, Mystify's persona shifted toward the decidedly feminine. I wasn't sure if it was to pull off the shirt as the lone garment, or if Mystify was going to prefer female personas.

With a long look at me—I wasn't sure why—Mystify ducked out of the gate and slipped past me, heading south along the waterfront.

Ram slowly slid back down to sit next to the truck. "There's so much I want to explain to you, Allay. I wish I could make you understand why it's necessary for me to kill. You don't know how terrible it could be if I didn't do this."

"So you think you're some kind of god?" I couldn't wrap my mind around living for four thousand years.

"No, not me. Never me. But Merge was worshiped as a god. Mithra's cult endured for thousands of years, through many different cultures. He thought we should cooperate with humans, and it transformed everything. But my own offspring destroyed that dream. Bedlam—" He grimaced and broke off. "Go away, Allay. I don't want you here if any demons come to investigate."

I took a step away, then halted. I cursed my human sensibilities. "Won't you go into a stupor now? Your shields will drop. You'll be defenseless."

"I can fight it off long enough to get underground, where it's safe. But it's too risky for you to come with me."

Apparently he had everything under control—as usual.

I took one step away, then another. Ram was watching me through slit eyes. His fingers gestured as if to urge me to go faster.

I walked away, turning the corner out of sight. It was

so ordinary, even though it felt as if I were crawling out of the mouth of hell. Could everyone see it on me? They should be pointing at me and warning small children to keep away.

I picked up speed as I headed up the street, bending my head against the rain. What if Zeal was coming this way now with Goad and his horde to investigate that strange, booming signature? Now that I was so close to escape, I couldn't bear it if a shout rose behind me and Montagna's guards gave chase, dragging me back to that iron cage.

I found myself running down the street as if fleeing the scene of a crime. Despite the slippery, wet sidewalk, I sprinted to the on-ramp to the bridge, where I finally had to stop to catch my breath.

Where can I go? I had no money, and I couldn't go home. This was it; I was on the run—for whatever amount of time I had left.

That brought clarity to my thoughts. If I couldn't kill Dread, I couldn't kill anyone. So that meant I had two weeks to live. The only thing I had to worry about now was protecting the people I cared about—and that meant protecting Shock.

I loved Shock; there was no doubt about it. She was my only companion, the only person I trusted who could also trust me. That was reason enough for me to do anything I could to save her.

But I had to be honest with myself at the end of my life. Shock was the only person who knew me, really knew me. If I died and Shock died, there would be nothing left of my life—nothing but Lolita's memory of me, and that was only a small part of who I really was. It would be as if I never existed.

It felt like my entire life would be defined by whether Shock lived or died. It was irrational, but it was the only thing I had left. Shock *had* to survive.

To make sure of that, first I needed to get out of Brooklyn.

I was drenched beyond wet as I walked across the Williamsburg Bridge. There was no roof over the suspended red cage that enclosed the pedestrian walkway. Despite the rain, a few other people were walking or biking across. Some had umbrellas, and a few unprepared souls like me hurried across miserably.

I was thankful for the darkening twilight, warily eyeing the Prophet's Center as I passed by high up on the bridge. The multipaned windows stared back at me blankly. There was no telling if anyone inside was watching.

Had Zeal found Dread? Or Montagna? My heart leaped as I wondered whether Dread's accomplice had a key. If she touched him, she could become a possessed human like me—or rather, worse than me. Now there was a comforting thought—a demon terminator waiting to happen.

I should have killed Dread for that reason alone. Regret stung at me. I only hoped Zeal found him first. She might steal his essence for herself.

Wasn't it just as bad to wish someone dead and not lift a hand to save him, rather than kill him outright? *Or is it only hypocrisy?*

I wondered if anyone would be looking for Vex tonight. Would Goad continue with the strike force against Glory with Vex missing? Everything could already be set in motion, as they prepared to launch their attack.

There could be more deaths in store tonight.

It took me more than twenty minutes to cross the river, loping along as fast as I could on the wet surface. The end of the bridge let me off on Delancey Street, only a few blocks away from the Den. But the bar was off-limits now.

I went to the subway entrance on Essex and stood at the top of the grimy concrete steps leading underground. Trying to get out of the rain under the metal shutter of a discount shoe store, I held out my hand and asked plaintively, "Could you help me get a ride home? My purse was stolen, and I live uptown."

I repeated my lies several times as people passed by without looking at me. But my genuine desperation helped, along with my soaking wet dress clinging to my body, which must have had an impact. Two women gave me change, and another guy donated a dollar bill. I almost had the price of a fare when another man offered, "Come on. I'll let you in with my metrocard."

Gratefully, I followed him downstairs into the station. He swiped his card to let me through the turnstile first, and I thanked him without getting too close. I kept straining to sense if he was a demon. Now that I knew it was possible for a demon to conceal his signature, I would never feel safe again.

I caught the first F train heading north and got off at Fourteenth Street, where the L line crossed. In the middle of the long platform, a pay phone was bolted to a steel I-beam. If this call went bad and my location was traced, I wanted maximum confusion about my destination; from this station I could literally get anywhere in the city with only one transfer.

I picked up the handset and, with a shaking hand, dialed the number. It rang twice as I clutched the phone to my ear. People were drifting onto the platform to wait for the next subway train, but I leaned my forehead against the thickly painted beam to avoid looking at them. Everything depended on this call.

Revel answered. I was glad I didn't have to go through one of his minions this time.

"Revel . . . ," I said, my voice husky. "Did you know Vex kidnapped me off the street and took me prisoner?"

"Allay! Thank God. Vex said you were in danger. He said he had to lock you up to keep you safe."

"Of course he did. And you believed every word."

"What did you expect me to do? Storm the bastions of the Fellowship? I told Vex I had to see you. When he seemed reluctant, I called in a favor. He agreed to let me see you tomorrow. Where are you now?"

Actually, that sounded plausible enough. "Did you tell Shock what happened to me?"

"Are you kidding? There would be no stopping her from doing something stupid, and then you'd never forgive me. Vex wouldn't take kindly to her interfering."

I wasn't about to tell Revel that Vex was no longer a threat. I needed to hoard my valuable information—it was all I had to trade. Everyone would find out soon enough. "I'm in the subway. I just escaped from Dread's giant iron cage where he tortures people. If you have Zeal's number, you should tell her to go check on Dread before someone finds him. I locked him in his own cage, nearly drained empty."

There was absolute silence on his end, a telling reaction. All I could hear was dank dripping and the distant noise of horns on the street above. Revel was a smart man; he would be assessing this information from every angle. "Allay, you're in serious danger. I'll come get you. I'll take you someplace out of the city, somewhere safe—"

"No, thanks." That wasn't what I needed from him.

"Allay, if you don't trust me, why did you call?" he asked in exasperation.

Revel might mean well, but he had only a limited amount of power and influence. Even with Vex out of the picture, I doubted he would fare well in a standoff with Dread. And there was certainly nothing he could do to stop Ram from getting to Shock. Ram could pose as a pool boy and kill her anytime he wanted to.

I needed to find a way to make Ram leave Shock alone. But how could I do that? He claimed he admired me, even cared about me, but he still justified himself in trying to kill someone I considered a sister. How could you convince someone like that? How could you influence someone who didn't have a conscience?

I had to find some reason, something that would keep him away from Shock even after I was gone. The first place to start was to find out if Ram had been telling Vex the truth about his past and why he killed his offspring. "What do you know about Mithra?" I asked Revel.

His surprise couldn't have been more complete. "Mithra? As in the Roman cult?"

"Earlier than that. Mesopotamian Mithra. Does that legend have anything to do with demons?"

The rising sound of clack-clacking as a subway train rushed into the station made me put my hand over the mouthpiece. I couldn't hear myself, much less Revel. "Wait a sec!"

The brakes of the train squealed as it ground to a halt, discharging people. The people who had gathered nearby entered the train, and the doors pinged to close. I couldn't hear again until it pulled out of the station, and everyone was streaming past me to the exit.

"Okay, go ahead," I told him, adding another quarter to the phone.

"There is something . . . the first recorded instance of a 'demon' was by the Sumarians around 1500 BC, in some of the earliest human writings. It describes an ancient myth, the Persian god Mithra, who lived for thousands of years and used his powers as an angelic mediator between heaven and Earth, as judge and preserver of the created world. When I examined the tablet, I saw another cuneiform figure combined with the name Mithra—it means 'come together.' "

"Merge," I breathed.

"Yes, I suppose. This symbol appears in more than one tablet. The most interesting may have been written by demons for other demons. Some attributes are clearly demon—he never sleeps, never eats, but is sustained on pure faith, a self-perpetuating, ephemeral being."

So Ram was telling the truth about his progenitor. "What was he like?"

"The mythology of Mithra echoes most creation myths. He was born from a rock, witnessed by shepherds. The sun god sent his messenger, the raven, to Mithra and ordered him to sacrifice a bull. Mithra did so reluctantly, turning his face away in sorrow. The white bull transformed into the moon, and Mithra's cloak became the vault of the sky. The plants and animals sprang from the bull's body. Seasons and time were created as the sun and moon began to alternate between light and darkness. The four elements came into being—air, fire, earth, and water. Creatures of the dark were also raised, starting the struggle between good and evil. Mithra supposedly joined the sun god and had a common meal, then drove with him to the end of the world. After that, Mithra returned to fight the forces of evil."

"That's not exactly helpful."

"If you tell me why you want to know, maybe I can narrow it down for you, Allay. Otherwise you're getting the wiki version."

Actually that was the one quality I still managed to admire about Revel; he was insatiably curious and always wanted to know more. I remembered grilling him like this for hours during our summer of love, asking him about demons and the odd words that rose in my memory, unbidden reminders of Plea. Revel could talk by the hour, by the day, long winding ruminations about where we came from and why we existed.

Was I ready to trust Revel again? I needed to trust him to bring him into my confidence.

"Do you know that Vex has plans for Glory?" I abruptly asked.

"No." His interest was piqued. "What is it? Tell me, Allay."

"You must have heard something."

There was shifting on the other end. "There's a lot of activity among the Vex demons; that's all I know. Four came through JFK earlier today. I think Goad's involved."

"But you don't know what's up?"

"No, but I bet you do," he said eagerly. "I've answered all your questions, Allay. Turnabout is fair play."

That told me what I needed to know. I was almost positive he knew nothing about the strike tonight against Glory, or he wouldn't be so flippant about everything.

That meant Revel wasn't part of Vex's inner circle. That meant he wasn't completely irredeemable.

"I know who the stealth demon is, the demon assassin. It was that guy, Theo Ram."

"Him?" Stunned silence filled the line. Then he added, "The agency did say they didn't have an employee who fit that description. I thought he worked for Vex."

"Nope, he has his own agenda." I gave him the short version of Ram's history and motivation for killing his distant progeny. "I need to know everything you can find out about him—and Merge—so I can stop him from killing Shock."

"Ram! As in the goat? Or ramming something? I guess it doesn't matter. It'll take time to run this through my database. Ram, Mithra, Merge, and Bedlam. That covers most of human history, Allay."

"I know, but do what you can. And please . . . I know that telling you this is like making a public broadcast, but if you could keep it under wraps, at least for another day, it could save Shock's life." It wasn't likely Mystify would talk about his progenitor anytime soon. He must know he should keep it secret for his own safety. That made it very valuable information, for the next little while.

He sounded worried again. "What are you going to do, Allay?"

"The only other person who may know more about Ram is Glory. Vex was convinced she was working with him. There's a chance that's true. She may know how to call him off Shock."

"Allay, you can't go to Glory. Vex says she's tried to kill you."

"It was Pique who tried to kill me. Who knows who he's taking orders from?" I bit my lip, about to add that it really didn't matter. I was already sitting on death row.

"You have to listen to me this time, Allay. You walked in off the street to see Vex on a whim, and look where you ended up! What makes you think Glory will be any kinder? She's never even met you."

"This time I have something the big boss needs— information that will save her life."

"It has to do with Vex and what Goad's planning," Revel said, as if he had me figured out.

"Stay out of it, Revel. Things got messed up last time because you called and warned Dread I was coming." That wasn't true, but I didn't want to let Mr. Busybody interfere again. I had to be the one to tell Glory about the attack planned for tonight. Was it rolling forward without Vex? Or would his death be enough to derail it?

"Let me help you," he insisted, partly exasperated and partly pleading.

A series of beeps warned me that we were being cut off. I had run through all my change, and the dollar bill was useless. "I'll call back as soon as I can. Tell Shock I'm taking care of it."

"Allay, where are—"

The dial tone cut him off. I held on to the receiver— it felt smooth with age and was comforting in my hand. I hoped I could trust Revel, but I couldn't rely on it.

He was right about one thing—I couldn't risk going straight to Glory. If Vex was right, she had already tried to kill me a couple of times. I had to approach her very carefully so she wouldn't shoot first and ask questions later.

The only demon of that lineage that I had anything in common with was Lash—surely I could convince Lash that I was telling the truth when it came to Dread.

I knew where to find Lash—she was living with Crave in his Harlem brownstone. I'd seen one of the *Post* headlines calling it the LOVE NEST ON 117TH STREET. The picture spread had included a close-up of the double door with its number, sixty-nine, making a visual double entendre between the address and the sexual shenanigans of the young artisan and his cougar mistress.

Time to make a trip to Harlem.

19

I caught the 3 train up to 116th Street. Glory's last residence had been in Hong Kong, where she'd been queen of the karaoke scene. When Hong Kong reverted to Chinese control in the mid-1990s, she had come to New York and chose the only large unclaimed territory left in Manhattan—Harlem. Glory had assumed the persona of a late-thirtysomething African American singer named Selma Brown. Selma invested in dozens of empty hulks of brownstones and restored them. Some had been sold and others were occupied by her demon cohorts, helping to initiate the wave of gentrification in central Harlem.

Only on brief, rare occasions throughout history had Vex and Glory lived in the same city. According to Revel, the first time was in Rome, and it had been sacked by the Visigoths because of them.

As the subway car rocked, whizzing through the dark tunnels, I hoped I was right about this.

I got brief flashes of other demons' signatures as the train stopped at the stations along the Upper West Side. There seemed to be a larger number of them than usual. After the Central Park North stop, the train entered Harlem, so the demons I sensed after that belonged to Glory.

At the 116th Street stop, I was ready and the first one through the doors. I ran down the concrete tunnel past the turnstiles and up the steps. I reached the sidewalk, which glistened from the rain, and rounded the corner without anyone calling out to me. On Lenox, the cracked and buckled asphalt gave my shoes a better grip. I darted across as soon as there was a break in traffic and turned down 117th Street at a dead sprint. An aggravated horn blared out behind me. A disgruntled cabbie or two were low on my list of priorities.

Then I sensed Crave and Lash—their identities were written in their signatures. Lash was a stinging sensation that made my skin hum, whereas Crave seemed to be at the center of a whirlpool, pulling me down to him.

I ran past nearly identical brownstones, one after the other. Those with lit-up facades had clearly been restored, while others had bricked-in windows and stone crumbling under the city pollution. I was amazed not to be stopped before I reached the long brownstone stoop with a heavy, carved railing leading up to Crave's house.

The element of surprise did have advantages. But I could feel other signatures overlapping as demons began to converge on me. They were starting to blur together, so I couldn't tell if Glory was among them.

I ran up and rang the doorbell repeatedly. The lamp cast a warm glow on the landing. "Lash, I need to see you." I called directly into the camera positioned over the intercom, hoping to get her full attention. "I've just escaped from Dread's cage."

People on the street were watching me. An entire family, including white-haired grandparents and a fat, shiny baby, filled the front steps two doors down, enjoying the fresh night air after the rain. Two demons were hurrying toward me from both ends of the block, closing in on Crave's house. They slowed, watching me warily as they approached. Another demon was coming up the other side of the street. Such a demon convergence, all for little ol' me.

"What do you want?" sounded a male voice from the intercom.

"I've come to warn you. Vex has sent Goad and his horde to attack Glory, including everyone in her line who lives in Harlem." I wasn't about to bring Ram into this, not until I was talking to Glory.

The demons on the street heard me, and they exchanged looks as if I must be crazy. The neighboring family was watching with frank interest, as if they were used to all kinds of goings-on at this house.

The heavy iron-work and glass door opened, revealing an old-fashioned tiled foyer. Crave glowered down at me. "I know you need to rekindle yourself, Allay, but you're far too weak to mount an attack on us. If you think to try, then try it with me."

I stared at him openmouthed. Power emanated from Crave; he seemed to exert a magnetic attraction. Maybe it was his seductive signature. He had an imposing presence, wearing black from his polished boots to his collared shirt, casually untucked from his pants. His persona had dusky skin and black hair, with big dark Latino eyes. But his aquiline nose and chiseled features harked back to a European origin.

I had to remind myself to answer him. "How on Earth could I hurt *you*?" My voice lowered so the family couldn't overhear. "Vex is dead. He ordered Goad and his horde to attack Harlem tonight. It may be too late to stop it."

This time it was Crave who gaped at me. I thought he looked even more appealing when he wasn't trying to be so fierce. "Vex is dead?"

"Saw it with my own eyes."

Lash appeared behind Crave. "My God, how did it happen?" She struck a dramatic pose, one hand clutching the mahogany jamb of the inner door. The long skirt of her white robe swirled around her high-heeled slippers—the kind that went out of style fifty years ago. Her pale blond ringlets were gathered loosely in an artful up-do. She

looked like a leading lady on American Movie Classics, except in color instead of black and white.

Then Lash got a good look at me and broke her pose,
exclaiming, "That's my Prada dress! What have you done
to it?"

I looked down at the filmy dress, the black, purple, and
green wash of colors that looked something like irises if
you squinted. It had mostly dried on my trip uptown, but
the bottom was looking a lot more bedraggled than when
I had put it on. "Sorry. I took it from your closet. My own
clothes were covered in blood."

Lash looked up at Crave. "That's definitely my dress."
Then she noticed the partially healed bruises on my neck.
Her lips narrowed in recognition. "Let her inside, Crave."

I followed them into the sumptuous parlor floor, decorated
with antique furniture of the same era as the pristine mold-
ings, tin ceilings, and fretwork in the archways. I settled
down on an ornate sofa, feeling very tired. Since demons
didn't sleep, I took it for a sign of my impending doom.
Without my core to power me, I would gradually fade
away.

To keep things simple, I started with Goad kidnapping
me off the street. I described how Dread had locked me in
the cage and tortured Theo Ram and me.

Lash wasn't the least bit surprised about the cage part,
but she didn't react to Ram's name. Perhaps Glory hadn't
told her about Ram. Meanwhile, Crave was indignant.
"That's ridiculous. We're forbidden from imprisoning other
demons. Glory and Vex wouldn't allow another Bedlam to
rise up."

Lash gave him a look as if he were a child. I'd seen Revel
look at Shock in the same way, and both of them treated
me like that in turn. There was a terrible ageism among the
demons measured in centuries rather than decades.

"He put your offspring in the cage, didn't he? Before he ate them," I asked Lash, "did he put you in the cage, too?"

Lash stiffened in outrage. "I wasn't one of his play toys." But she was too shocked and taken aback for it to be anything but a sham.

I had guessed her secret. "I thought so."

Lash's gaze finally broke from mine, her shoulders slumping. Her aura flared with conflicting emotions—fear, sadness, anger, pain. "Now everyone will know," she wailed. "They'll assume it because of who I am."

I couldn't help her there. There was no hiding it now. I'd already told Revel about Dread's cage. I'd also practically shouted it on the street.

Crave was also staring at Lash, his eyes narrowed. After a few moments, Lash protested, "It's not my fault I like to be forced. I was made that way. Dread needed my fear to satisfy him."

"The perfect symbiotic relationship," I agreed. "As long as it's consensual."

"It was; it was." Lash looked off to the side. "For a long time we were partners in everything. It wasn't all . . . erotic stimulation."

"I noticed that Dread calls you 'my wife' instead of by your name," I pointed out. "As though that's the most important thing about you."

Her face crumpled, as if I had made another direct hit. "Vex is the one who made Dread let me go. Otherwise he would have forced me back. Vex knew that if I told anyone about Dread's cage, everyone would be in an uproar. Now he'll finally get what he deserves."

A flash of Dread inside his cage, shrunken, diminished, made me swallow. Yeah, he'd gotten what he deserved, all right.

Crave waved that aside. "I want to know what happened to Vex. Dread killed him, didn't he? The student finally bested the master."

"That's ridiculous!" Lash denied. "Dread is too scared of Vex."

I had to keep them on track and off the track of Vex's killer. That was my prize bit of information—I was going to catch bigger game than these two with it. "With Vex dead, there's no way to know if the strike will go on. Goad's horde could be on its way right now."

"Dread will stop them," Lash said confidently. "He won't let them kill me. It's probably why he turned on Vex."

I raised my brows. There was no way I could cut through that mess of mistaken assumptions. "Are you willing to bet your life on it? What harm would it do to prepare yourselves just in case?"

"What harm, indeed?" Crave agreed. "We should warn Glory and the others."

They were still very suspicious. Lash stayed in the parlor to keep an eye on me, calling Glory to give her the news, while Crave directed the servants in locking down the house. I had no advice to offer, and I was cut out of the most important conversations, which took place in quick, whispered conferences in the hallway. A general malaise was overwhelming me, making the bustle of activity flow around me like slow syrup, easy and painless.

But I heard reports as the Glory demons shored up in their defensive positions. Crave instructed Milo, his driver and bodyguard, to remain out of sight on the ground floor where he would have immediate access to the front and the back of the house.

Lash took me upstairs, where she told me to sit down outside a small, interior room. It held the monitors for the cameras trained down on the street, the front stoop, the tiny front patio where the door led to the basement, along with various shots of the backyard and roof.

I hugged my knees to my chest, desperately hoping I hadn't set them off on a false alarm. Vex could have been lying about the strike to rile me up, or to provoke Dread.

Who knew? If nothing happened, then it would make a very bad first impression.

I may end up bargaining with Glory for my release.

My only distraction was watching the interaction between Crave and Lash. She tried to call the shots, but Crave wouldn't let her, countermanding some of her orders—like posting demons at the main entry points to Harlem to alert Goad that the surprise had been blown and possibly avert the strike. Lash tried to argue, but Crave insisted that they were much safer in their defensive positions.

Crave and Dread couldn't have been more different; Crave's dark, dangerous vibes were nothing like Dread's constrained coldness. Crave snapped back at her when Lash grew irritable. Finally he insisted, "Sit down, Lash. Everything is set. You'd do best to calm yourself."

She flounced out in a huff, but returned soon enough. She couldn't bear to be far from his side.

I held my breath, waiting.

We didn't have to wait long. We all felt it at the same time: an influx of demons too numerous to separate the signatures. They were moving in a wave up Harlem. That many signatures deafened my senses, as if we were being buried in a demon tsunami. I had to remind myself to breathe.

I scrambled up to see the monitors behind Crave and Lash. In seconds, a long black sedan stopped in front of the house.

Crave shot me a strangely victorious look for the start of a battle. Now he believed me. This many demons couldn't be anything less than an invasion force.

Stun's ear-ringing sensation separated from the others, unmistakable. The other demon signatures clashed together, drowning out one another. With Crave and Lash so close to me, I couldn't distinguish any of the others. But I wasn't surprised that Vex had planned to send Stun, one of his most loyal demons, after Crave and Lash. Goad was probably at Glory's house right now.

I wondered if Stun could sense me inside Crave's house. Since the Vex demons weren't looking for me, they might not notice my subtle signature among the others. Then again, they had every reason to be cautious. I wondered if they would kill me, too, if they got inside. Or would they take me back to the cage?

"Call 911," Crave ordered into his walkie-talkie. A burst of static carried back the affirmative.

"How's that going to help?" Lash drawled scornfully.

"I call 911 all the time," I said. "It's a hassle dealing with the police, whether you're a demon or a human." At her glare, I realized I had just sided with Crave against her. She was the kind of woman who wouldn't forget that.

On one of the screens, several dark figures appeared at the top of the fence and dropped down. They quickly assembled a black battering ram; then they each grabbed a handle and ran out of the frame. Crave alerted his people.

"Two demons, two humans," Crave muttered.

I scanned the different screens until I found the one over the back door pointing downward. There was no sound as the men rammed the door on the basement floor, shattering the wood frame. The door slammed back, cracked nearly in half.

Suddenly a shot rang out far down below. On the monitor, one of the men fell back, struck in the leg. The other three leaped out of range as another shot was fired from inside. There were flashes as the invaders fired back. But when the demons tried to get to their downed partner, another shot drove them off.

"Milo's in a good position," Crave murmured. "He could hold them forever."

"Look, there's more," I said, pointing at another screen. It was a view of the roof.

Crave alerted his man on the top floor to be prepared.

The demons smashed the glass of the skylight, but the servants had bolted a thick Plexiglas plate underneath. Their battering ram bounced off it without making a dent. Crave smiled at their confusion when they realized they wouldn't be able to get in that way.

"How many people did he send to kill me?" Lash exclaimed.

"Considering they've targeted all of us in Harlem, I'd say we each got a pair of demon assassins with human backup." Crave sounded bored. "Vex couldn't possibly round up any more loyalists than that willing to risk their own necks."

Lash clutched her fist to her chest, her eyes flashing. "To think Dread gave orders to kill me!"

"Actually, it was Vex," I reminded her.

"Dread could have stopped it!" Her voice quavered indignantly. "He should have."

Crave ignored her, focusing on the efforts of his people to repel the invaders. The man down in the backyard was writhing and calling out to the others. But they couldn't reach him with Milo keeping them pinned down. The two demons on the roof abandoned their quest to get inside and jumped down the three stories to break up the stalemate in the backyard, laying down covering fire as they retreated. They had to leave their wounded man behind or risk being shot by Milo.

It was over soon, and the signatures of the demons receded, soon to be replaced by fleeting signatures as Vex demons fled from Harlem. Their retreat was not nearly as organized as their attack.

Then the police arrived with blaring lights. The city's finest were certainly quick when there were reports of shots being fired. Too bad I had learned that firsthand.

I spent many long hours holed up in one of the rooms on the third floor. It was in the center of the house, so I couldn't see out the front or the back, but I knew it was still dark out, the quiet before dawn with only a distant siren stirring the air. The room was decorated in red, like a bordello nightmare with tassels and fringe. The wide sofa was large enough for two people to recline easily, as if it were designed for seduction. If my experience with Revel was any guide, that made it likely I was being recorded.

The cops searched the entire place, of course, taking the wounded man away along with the evidence of an attempted burglary, but there were a thousand procedures that had to be followed. Crave had suggested we conceal my presence in his house—and I agreed. I'd had enough of cops this week. I could only imagine Lieutenant Markman's reaction if my name got mixed up in yet another shooting. So I swallowed my pride and crouched in a built-in hidey-hole inside the back of the closet until they were done.

The fact that Crave was Mark Cravet, the notorious jewelry designer who had stolen the affections of the prophet's wife, made it even more sensitive. I had already declared to the police that the prophet had kidnapped my friend.

Lash reappeared as the sun was rising. "That man who was shot used to be Dread's driver. The investigators think the prophet is retaliating against us because of our affair. How could he be so stupid?"

I was tired of pointing out that Dread had nothing to do with the attack. "Are the police outside?"

"Yes, along with the paparazzi. They started showing up as soon as it hit the police radios. Those bloodsucking vermin."

"Uh-oh. I'll have to sneak out somehow...."

"Glory wants to speak to you first. She's got some questions for you."

Of course she did. Lash must have told Glory that Vex was dead. "That's why I came here."

Lash was clenching her fists and furrowing her brow as she paced back and forth in the small room. Her agitation marred her celebrity-staged appearance. I was certain she managed the effect of full makeup by sheer will alone. "I still can't believe Dread wants me dead."

Since that was true, I couldn't deny it. "You did leave him. Rather abruptly, from what I saw. He was shocked. And really put out that it was Crave you left him for."

"He never respected Crave. But he's never seen in him the things I have."

"Crave *is* alluring. And very dominant. I can understand why a woman like you enjoys being with him."

Lash lifted her eyes to heaven. "I've never loved anyone like I love Crave. I've known him practically since he was born, right before the Civil War. It was as if my heart opened up at his first words. But I convinced myself that it was his signature, that drawing-in effect."

I nodded. "It is mesmerizing."

"I tried to ignore it, and I laughed at the women who fell for him. Sometimes I laughed about it with him. We always flirted. It was an unspoken thing between us; our eyes would meet across the room. We spoke to each other whenever we could."

I didn't point out that there was a world of difference between lust and love.

"Dread knew nothing about it—nor did anyone else. Everyone was surprised when I left. But when Crave came to Harlem with Glory, I started seeing him out every week. It was the first time we've lived in the same city, moved in the same social circles. He plays the games I adore, making me push against him, spar with him, that glorious struggle of wills. . . ."

She was lost in the rush of new romantic energy, though she had known the man for more than a century and a half.

"So that's why you left Dread? Because you fell in love with Crave?"

Lash hesitated. "I was too entwined with Dread to ever leave him. How do you throw away sixteen hundred years together?" She shook her head ruefully. "But that night I left, something happened. It wasn't shocking or huge. Sometimes I think it's the most trivial thing, but it was too much for me. I finally saw Dread for who he really is."

I was trying to win her sympathy. "What happened?"

She frowned, turning away. "It was nothing much. What matters is that I left."

Disappointed, I realized I would get nothing more out of her. I reclined back on the sofa, watching Lash pace back and forth for a while. The red haze of her fury had eased, but her serious expression was far more frightening because it held less drama and more determination.

Several hours later, I wanted desperately to talk to Shock. But after I'd seen Crave's security system, I couldn't tell her the most important thing—that it was Ram who had tried to kill her. I was starting to think it was my own paranoia, induced by Revel's twisted tastes, but I had the feeling people were listening in on everything I said. I couldn't even risk calling Michael to find out how Pepe was; the less these demons knew about my friends, the better.

To relieve my boredom after Lash left, I opened my door to better hear the bass voices of the cops echo up the stairway. When that finally went quiet, there was an eerie silence in the house. Occasionally there were footsteps pattering up or down below, and the sound of doors closing softly.

Then I heard Lash's voice, rising high and strident.

I hurried out into the hallway, leaning over the banister to hear. She was shouting about suing someone for defamation. Crave replied shortly and pointedly, sending her off on a higher tirade.

I quietly descended two flights, staying on the inside of the steps where they wouldn't creak. With every step, I got to hear Lash read out loud as she rattled a newspaper in anger. "It's a two-page banner headline! THE PROPHET

STRIKES BACK! What are we, aliens? This isn't journalism; it's not even yellow—it's puce! How did they get this printed so fast?"

"You really must join the computer age, darling," Crave drawled.

"Don't they have laws that prevent this from happening? See, here, they say our 'love nest was violated.' They say the injured robber performed odd jobs for the church—odd jobs! And they're saying you're the one who shot him, or at least they're implying you did it. Look at this: 'Mark Cravet, the infamous playboy, defended his love . . .'!"

"Nice shot of my house," Crave said.

Lash sounded angry, but she also seemed to be enjoying herself. She was the center of attention. She poured over the photographs, noting how well she looked in the one where she was snuggled under Crave's arm. She also read the fawning description of Mark Cravet, how he was considered an artist for his fanciful pavé designs using gems he cut into extraordinary shapes.

By crouching at the top of the stairs, I could see down into the parlor. The room was shadowed from the shutters pulled over the front windows. Lash was wearing a formal dress again, a pale blue halter with an empire waist, showing off her shoulders, long neck, and décolleté.

She was fingering her necklace, a delicate, gem-studded chain. The studied tilt of her head, setting off her eyes and seductive mouth, showed that all the world was a stage to Lash, including her intimacies. "You are brilliant, darling. I never want to take this off."

Crave seemed more irritated than pleased by her flattery. "The servants are going to catch you one day," he told her, letting his eyes linger on her flushed cheeks.

She *was* looking rather youthful and vibrant with glossy blond hair and blushing skin. In public, she had to stay faithful to the persona she had created of the prophet's aging wife. Clearly she wasn't satisfied with that role while she was enchanting him. But Crave was right; someone was going to notice how young and dewy Lash was looking these days.

Lash shrugged, flicking out the fingers of her hand lightly as if to toss away any concern about that. "I do it to please you, because I know you see beautiful young women every day, and I know how they tempt you."

"You knew who I was when you came to me. You can't keep getting jealous every time a woman speaks to me."

"I know, Crave. I'll do whatever you want. I didn't object, did I, when you brought home those whores last week? I know what you are, and I love you for it."

"That's not likely to happen now, what with the reporters camped on our sidewalk. I'll be cast as the devil in this little drama of yours, just you see."

Lash took his hand, closing her eyes as she soaked up his irritation. The flashing of her aura lit up the darkened room as she pulled on him hard, as if she hadn't fed since yesterday.

Crave impatiently shoved her hand away. "You must learn to feed from others. I can't sustain you on my own."

Lash was almost panting to be torn away from him as he castigated her—her favorite emotion. "It's hard! You know how I've lived my life. He would only let me feed from him. It feels too . . . intimate to do it with someone I don't love."

Crave looked away from her. But he allowed her to take hold of his hand, letting her soak up his annoyance.

The silence roiled with tension. Then he ordered quietly, "Get down."

She trembled as she shed her shame and desire for him. Slowly she knelt, humbling herself to him. Her flush of embarrassment was so strong that I could see the deep teal streaks in her aura.

She clung to his hand. He touched her hair to absorb her longing for him, her thrill at his touch, the spike in her desire. Her lips parted as if to say she would do anything he asked if he would only touch her again. Her breasts strained against the halter of her dress as she leaned closer to him.

"Show me how much you want it," he said.

She kissed his hand fervently. I felt like a voyeur now, as if I should back away slowly. I didn't want to watch them feed each other. It felt like watching them have sex.

Crave shook his head. "That's not good enough. I think you need to be lying on the floor while you do that."

Confused, she looked down, then put her hand to her mouth, realizing what he wanted.

Nothing could have torn me away. . . . Did he want her to kiss his feet?

He did! Lash slowly bent down, putting her face to the toe of his slipper. Her lips pressed in firmly so he would feel it through the leather.

"I love you," she murmured, pressing her lips against him again.

"What do you want?" he asked her.

"To touch you," she instantly replied, her face still near his foot.

"Then do it."

She hesitated, and I didn't understand at all. But then she removed his leather slipper, pulling it from his foot.

I wondered if Dread had ever debased her like this. Surely Dread had wanted her fear, not her humiliation. But perhaps Crave knew better that physical wounds had little effect on demon bodies, and were quickly shed and gone. The psychic barbs he struck Lash with were better aimed to cut to her heart.

Her desire surged for him, her need to abandon herself to his wishes. Crave's eyes closed as he soaked it up, as her lips pressed against his foot. It was so strong that it washed through the room. It hit me like a contact high—she practically swooned from his sudden desire to push her away from him, despite everything she was giving him. There was never a more thorough masochist than Lash.

"Tell me why you left Dread," he said quietly.

She froze in the act of kissing his foot, her lips pressed against his skin. I was also caught off guard. He had been listening to us talk. He must have heard what she said in the bordello room.

Lash pulled back, her eyes downcast. "I left him for you, Crave."

"No." He smiled a little. "That's the pretty story we tell everyone. But it's time I know *why* you decided to leave him that night. What happened, Lash?"

Her hands were still holding on to his foot as she knelt in front of him, exposed and vulnerable. Her eyes were glazed.

He grabbed her arm, ready to pull her off him, to force her to let go. "Tell me now, Lash. Or—"

"All right!" She took a deep breath, looking up at him. "Something . . . happened while I was getting ready to go out that night. My back was turned to Dread, and I was holding up a hand mirror to check my hair. He walked by and cast me a look of . . . I can only call it contempt. His lip curled up, as if disgusted by the sight of me. It was pure luck I saw it in the mirror. When I turned, there was nothing in his expression to suggest he wasn't listening to every word I was saying, just like any other time."

She looked down at her hand as if remembering the mirror in her palm, and the image of his disdain emblazoned across it. "He tried to put me in the cage that night, and I panicked. I couldn't do it. I lost trust in him. What else was he hiding from me? Had he been lying all those years? He was furious, but Vex intervened. I grabbed what I could and came here to you."

"You left because he looked at you wrong?" Crave asked in disbelief.

Her eyes shifted away. "You should have seen it. He

was so cold, so contemptuous. As if he hated me. But when I turned around, he looked like he always did, attentive, cherishing. I realized that face I knew so well, that love he showed me, it was all fake—a mask he wore for me. He never really loved me. He just needed me."

She was hating every second of it, while she squirmed with wild pleasure at being forced to reveal her darkest secret. Crave was soaking it up as fast as she was feeding off him, passing the flare of energy back and forth between them, an incestuous generation of power.

"But darling," he drawled, "I feel contempt for you from time to time. Look at you down on the floor kissing my feet...."

Her eyes shone, and for the first time she really looked at him. "Yes, but with you I feel your love. You want me to be happy. I know you say and do all of these awful things for me, to give me what I need, because you love me."

Crave stared at her. I could read it on his face—he didn't love her.

But Lash couldn't see it. She bent to kiss his hand again. How could she not see that their relationship was a rapidly passing fad on Crave's part?

And now he knew that Lash hadn't really left Dread for him. No wonder Lash didn't understand the depths of Dread's jealousy. She hadn't left because of Crave; she had left because of Dread. She must have expected Dread to try to get her back, to woo her. His need for vengeance was baffling her.

Crave abruptly pulled away from Lash. She cried out wordlessly, but he walked out the back door.

I hastily withdrew, tiptoeing up the stairs to the bordello room as silently as I could.

Perhaps Lash could see that Crave didn't love her. But she thought she had an eternity to bind him to her.

20

My first indication that something was about to happen came from the tickling of a new signature. The demon approached slowly, so I had time to feel the lifting, swirling sensation grow in strength and clarity. My own signature was buoyant, but this was like being carried into the sky in an ecstatic rush.

Glory was coming. Finally.

Lash came to get me; she didn't have to say a word. I followed her down to the parlor as Glory arrived. Lash looked irritable, as if she hadn't fed enough. Crave had been sucking off her energy as fast as she drank from him. I knew what it was like to be on starvation rations.

To avoid the reporters, Glory came in from the garden. She was alone, confident that her network of loyal offspring were patrolling the borders of her territory. Her Selma Brown persona was in her forties now, full figured and boundlessly self-assured. She was wearing a yellow print dress and sandals, with her head wrapped in a brown and gold scarf. I could easily imagine her on the stage, singing backup in a sequined evening gown.

Crave went to stand in front of the shuttered bow window with his hands clasped behind his back. Lash stood on the other side, in the archway to the library. I felt surrounded.

I stood up, nodding to Glory. "Nice to meet you."

"I don't have time for that nonsense." Glory came right up to me. "You tell me what's going on here, Allay. What happened to Vex? Why did those demons attack me last night? You seem to know more about this than anyone else."

The time for hoarding my information was over. If I wanted to survive and save Shock, I needed Glory's help. "Vex thought you were trying to kill me. Is it true, Glory? Did you sic Pique on me? And your *other* assassin?"

"*You?* Kill you? Vex never said a word about you to me. Why would he care so much that he'd break an agreement we've had forever?"

I was a little surprised. "Don't you know about Vex's Revelation that he was planning?" At their blank looks, I added, "Using me as the star attraction."

Glory shook her head. "It sounds to me like you're babbling. What revelation?"

"Vex intended to cut off my head on television so I could resurrect and prove I'm immortal. He called it 'the Revelation.' He said you were trying to kill me to stop him from doing it. That's why he sent Goad's horde against you. To kill you first."

Glory turned on Lash. "Do you know anything about this?"

Lash had her hands to her mouth. "Vex always said he had big plans, but I didn't know it was *this*." She considered it a moment. "But when I think of what they've done, it does make sense. Dread had a possessed human for a while, a member of the church. He tended to that man like a father. But he eventually had to be put down. He was too unstable and dangerous. He almost killed Zeal."

"They tried to create a hybrid to be their puppet," I said. "Then Dread decided he could be their new messiah. But Vex couldn't let Dread get hold of that much power. He claimed that Dread's background wouldn't hold up to scrutiny, and that I had to do it."

"But why?" Crave asked. "Why would they expose us all?"

"There's been a technological development—it's called the ERI. It shows the difference between humans and demons. Dread said soon they'll be used everywhere as metal and bomb detectors, in airports, government buildings. . . ." From their appalled expressions, they understood the problem. "You didn't know anything about this?" I asked Lash, unable to believe it. Vex had been so convinced she was a spy.

But I had heard for myself the much more mundane reason why she had left Dread.

Lash turned to Glory. "I had *no* idea. You don't think I'd hide something like this from you?"

Glory smiled blandly, but she might also consider the timing odd that Lash had defected to her line at this moment.

I was more concerned about making my point. "Vex's plan was to expose us first, in a way that would benefit him, so the Fellowship of Truth could take over the world."

Glory gave me a hard look. "You told Lash that Vex was dead."

I took a deep breath. "Ram killed Vex."

Confusion flickered in her face as she tried to figure out what I meant. I could feel her suspicion, as if she thought I was trying to pull a fast one. "Who did?" Glory asked.

"Ram. You know, the stealth demon. The one who's been causing all the mysterious deaths."

For the first time I saw a glimmer of recognition. "You mean Malaise. You know who killed Malaise?"

"It was Ram."

Lash let out an irritated sound. "You keep saying that, but it means nothing. Who is Ram?"

"Glory should know better than anyone. Vex said he was working with you. To destroy his line." I watched her carefully, reaching out with my senses.

Her suspicion was growing. "Either you're a liar or he was. Why would he accuse me of working against him?"

There was no tinge of deception in her aura or the way she reacted. Then again, I would never trust myself after Ram had fooled me so completely. Even if I was touching Glory, I might not be able to tell if she was hiding a long-standing relationship with Ram.

I had to know for sure. "I don't think Vex knew about Ram until he was being consumed. Ram was Merge's off-spring, the progenitor of Bedlam. You didn't kill Bedlam, did you, Glory? Neither did Vex. Ram killed him after you both escaped."

"Vex and I killed Bedlam," Glory insisted quickly. "We beat him to death with the iron rods that held our coffins closed."

She said it so calmly that it reaffirmed my opinion of these ancient demons—they had no conscience. "You killed his body, but you didn't take his essence."

For the first time, Glory looked uncertain, as if she had tried so hard to convince herself and everyone else that Bedlam was truly dead, that he was never coming back. The lie they had told was so old that it had calcified into stone inside of her.

"Bedlam isn't coming back because Ram killed him that day he set you free." I explained how Ram had learned to fortify his shields and told them word for word what Ram had said to Vex. Glory believed it; every word of it rang true with what had happened to her.

"You never knew you'd been helped by a demon?" I had to ask. "You never suspected Ram existed?"

"I thought . . . in weak moments I thought that Bedlam was killing the demons in my line, that he was preying on us." Her lips clamped shut, as if even now it was difficult for her to speak about it.

"If it's true, then who knows where Ram is?" Lash

said, coming forward. "If we can't sense him, he could be anywhere!"

"A secret killer among us," Glory murmured.

"You didn't know about this?" Crave asked Glory, as if he had never doubted her before. Glory ignored him, lost in thought.

Lash repeated herself, her voice rising higher. "He could be anyone!"

"You said that," Crave pointed out.

Lash shot him a frown. "I mean, it could be Milo, and we wouldn't know it."

"If it's Milo, he's doing a good job of keeping us safe."

Glory glanced from one to the other. There was a tightening in her eyes that said she didn't like what she was seeing. What did she think of this love match? At this point she probably wished Lash was by Dread's side, keeping watch over him instead of playing sex games with Crave.

Clearly Vex had been wrong about Glory; he had been running from shadows. Glory wasn't scheming to stop his Revelation. She wasn't working with Ram against him; she didn't even know Ram. And since she didn't know him, then she couldn't tell me anything useful to stop him.

Now how can I keep him from killing Shock?

Glory abruptly turned to me. "You're dying, honey."

I admired her bluntness. "Yes, I know."

"Why didn't you take Dread's essence? He was defenseless, from what I hear."

I wondered who her spy was in the Fellowship. "I'm no murderer."

Glory raised her brows. "It's your business if you want to extinguish yourself. I won't protest, seeing as you could be coerced into becoming a religious miracle."

"That won't happen, I can assure you. Dread understood that, even if Vex didn't."

Glory considered me long and hard. "Your shields aren't very good, Allay, and you wear your emotions for everyone to see. But I don't know what you expect from me."

"I want to make sure Shock is safe. Ram says she's too fertile. He said there're too many demons, that we're multiplying too fast for him to keep up with."

"Interesting . . . maybe we can make it a bit harder for him," Glory said. "We could use more demons in the world. If we took better care of our newbies . . . Well, it's something to consider."

"We need to find out more about Ram."

"Believe me, I'm going to talk to everyone. If anyone has information about Ram, I'll know it. In fact, it's a damn good thing Vex is dead or I would have killed him myself after that stunt last night. No, I'm only just getting started. Dread has to man up now that Vex is gone, and he had better not step out of line again."

"Will you help me protect Shock from Ram?" I didn't add, *in the time I have left*. It was too morbid.

Her gaze sharpened. "I think you should worry about yourself, Allay. He may seek you out again, now that he's exposed himself to you. He may want to silence you."

"Maybe." There was no telling what he was capable of.

"If I were you, I'd charge myself up." Glory lifted her admonishing finger to keep me from speaking. "Depleted as you are right now, you're a sitting duck. You wouldn't be able to defend yourself from anyone in this state."

"Seems like everyone lately has been trying to feed me." But I wasn't averse to the idea, now that I wasn't being stuffed like a Thanksgiving turkey for Dread's pleasure. "If I really bulk up, how long do I have left?"

Glory leaned over and patted my leg. "Two days, maybe three. You'd better be sure this is the path you want to be on, Allay."

"I thought I had weeks left."

"You've been sorely taxed, taken to the brink of death,

if I'm not mistaken. There are limits to the soul, and you've found yours."

I nodded, struck to the core. *I'm going to die. Day after tomorrow.*

Glory gestured to Crave. "Give Allay some energy, Crave. You're burning so bright, you're hurting my eyes."

Crave hesitated, glancing over at Lash. She was offended by Glory's suggestion.

"I can find someone else," I quickly assured Glory.

"Nonsense! Crave is busting out with more than enough. He could give you half and you'd both be up for anything." Glory's voice grew firmer. "So do it."

"What if she tries to steal Crave's essence when he opens to her?" Lash demanded. "What if this is some kind of elaborate ruse . . . ?"

Nobody was buying that, and Lash trailed off.

"All I'm talking about is a little power exchange," Glory said, exasperated. "I'm not telling you to fuck her."

Her voice rang in the air, and I felt myself blush like I hadn't since I was a teenager. But I did want to take what Crave could give me. I needed to fully heal myself now that I had only a limited number of hours left. I had to work fast to take care of Shock.

Crave sat down next to me on the sofa and held out his hand. I silently took it, accepting the energy he began pumping into me. His palm was firm and square, his fingers light on mine.

Lash shot daggers at him, refusing to meet my gaze. She began pacing again, swishing her skirt from side to side like an angry cat. I felt quite detached from Crave even though his power began to course through me, lighting me up like a Christmas tree. It felt like sparklers tingling across my skin instead of something that drove deep inside of me, like Ram's energy. Crave was a devastatingly handsome man with an undeniable magnetism, but I'd been burned black around my heart where Ram had touched me.

Glory sat back, a huge grin on her face, clasping her hands across her thick waist. "I'm a betting woman, Allay, and I think you're not going to let yourself die. I think you and I can work together."

An hour later, we had agreed to a mutual nonaggression pack. Glory agreed to help Shock, if she could, though she didn't sound too confident. I wasn't, either. If Ram wanted to get to Shock, Glory wouldn't be able to stop him. Glory asked me to keep quiet about the ERI machine until she could explain it to her own demons and figure out what they would do about it.

It seemed like such a faraway concern, months in the future, way beyond what I needed to worry about. I was almost glad I wouldn't have to be part of the debacle that was sure to come when demons were outed to the world.

With nothing else to gain, I was ready to leave Harlem. I wasn't about to share everything I knew with Glory—such as the fact that Revel was already scouring recorded history to find out more about Merge. Now Revel was my only hope. *How sad was that?*

I rubbed my hands together, but I couldn't erase the feel of Crave's palm. I was more charged up than I'd ever been. Lash was glaring at me as if I had stolen the food off her plate and eaten it in front of her. She had insisted on taking back the Prada dress, practically ripping it off me. But Crave finally let her feed from him, chastised by Glory's sharp order to give the "poor girl" a break. That quelled Lash until I could change into her reluctant donation of an expensive pair of slacks and a cashmere shell, the most casual clothes she owned. Lash hated every second of my negotiation with Glory, not that she distrusted me. Her jealousy burned too brightly for any of us to ignore.

When Glory left through the back door, I went with her. To avoid the paparazzi, I followed her over the short chain-link fences that separated the gardens. At the end of the block was a larger apartment building with a yard surrounded by an old wooden fence. It was easy to get over using the thick crossbeams, though it was funny watching a forty-something, full-figured woman climbing over it so nonchalantly. I landed in a grassy patch with some scraggly bushes along one side. A walkway and a gate led out to the street. There wasn't anyone in sight.

Glory stopped me. "Where are you going now?"

"To see Shock. I have to tell her about Ram. I don't know what she's going to do."

"You should take care of yourself, Allay. I think you're distracting yourself from what you really need to do. Worrying about Shock is a lot easier than dealing with your own problems."

She was right. But I didn't have to listen to her.

Glory gave me a cheery wave good-bye, completely at odds with the importance of her position and the gravity of the situation. She was timeless, that way. As if nothing could really touch her. "It's a breath of fresh air to meet someone like you, Allay. And I'm not just talking about that lovely flavor you have. I can feel it without even touching you. No wonder you try to lie low. But I don't think that will be possible anymore."

Sadly, I agreed. I was quickly becoming notorious in demon circles, burning out as I was like a meteor. . . .

She went north, while I caught a cab going downtown. I settled into the back and took stock of my situation. Glory had given me a credit card and some cash, enough to last a few weeks. It showed her confidence that I would somehow be able to do the terrible deed. She'd advised that I get out of the city immediately to avoid Dread while the effects from Vex's death shook down. She even gave me the locations of a few rogue demons who would be easy prey.

Shock and I should both leave, get out of New York, and disappear.

The cab pulled up on Park Avenue, across the boulevard from Revel's place. I couldn't sense his signature, but Shock was far up above. Surely she could feel me, too.

I was waiting on the corner for the light to cross, when someone tapped my elbow. Startled, I looked at the balding, middle-aged man. "Yes?" I asked.

"May I speak to you for a moment?"

He shielded his face with a hand, and his features morphed into Theo Ram.

I let out a screech in spite of myself.

"Allay, wait!" He grabbed on to my arm as I almost bolted away. His determination to speak to me, to explain, to make everything right again, poured into me through his touch.

It stopped me in my tracks. "What are you doing sneaking up on me? That's not right."

"Allay, why didn't you take Dread's essence?" There was anguish in his voice. "You're dying."

Suddenly I realized that the woman who had gotten out of the cab behind mine was now loitering by the window of the bookstore. She was young, wearing low-rise jeans and large, gold hoop earrings—like any other teenager you saw in the city. But they usually traveled in packs, not alone, and definitely not in cabs.

Glory had put a tail on me.

In a weird way, that made me feel better. Someone was watching out for me. "Come on," I said to Ram. I took him into the Starbucks around the corner.

The strong, overlapping scents of coffee, spices, and flavorings assaulted my nose. There were strollers and moms gathered to one side, and people with open laptops seated here and there. It was late for breakfast and early for lunch, so there were empty seats.

I sat down at a table near the back. Ram kept his Theo Ram face on, which I thought was odd. If he was so keen on hiding, why was he wearing a guise that other demons would associate with him?

Ram started to reach out to me, but I pulled back. "I'd never hurt you, Allay. You don't need to be afraid of me."

"Are you here to kill Shock?"

He met my eyes. "No. I'm sorry, Allay. I'm sorry I hurt you. I convinced myself it was in your best interest because Shock wasn't taking care of you properly."

"You know how much I love her."

"Not then, I didn't. Not until our cab ride up to Revel's. I could have killed Shock as I carried her up in the elevator." My heart seized, thinking of it. "But I didn't because I realized you would be bereft without her. I won't try to hurt Shock again. In fact, I won't kill any demon just because they're fertile, if it will make you happy."

My heart leaped. "You won't?"

"No. That's why I let Mystify go. I knew you wouldn't like it if I consumed him. From now on, I'll only target demons who hurt people."

I frowned. "Who hasn't hurt people? You hurt me. Who are you to judge everyone else?"

"I'm talking about Pique and Stun, the evil, vicious ones. And Dread, who's been hurting people all along, without my knowing it. You could have put an end to that yourself."

So casual, his talk of killing. "You're exactly what I don't want to become."

Ram flinched. "If I fail, civilization will fall. I have to be this way."

"So you're uncivilized in defending civilization?"

"I'm fighting against the forces of chaos, imbalance, and impurity. I've been battling this war for eons, Allay. I was the first to spread the seeds of civilization. I left my people and my home, where I had everything, and I traveled around the world giving people the tools to band together, and the knowledge of how to create something far larger than individuals could do alone. I carried iron with me, and I lived among them, teaching them how to mine and work the iron into strong tools capable of more than bronze.

"Everywhere I went, I found demons living among the humans. I've seen what happens when a population is overrun by too many demons. Chaos reigns and the citizens scatter. The demons die off because there's not enough emotional energy to go around. It proves Merge's belief that balance is key."

It still seemed like a massive justification for murder, but I was feeling much more relieved now that he had sworn he wouldn't kill Shock. I wanted to be sure he would stick to his word. So I listened closely, remembering how he had blamed himself for the death of his progenitor. "What happened to Merge?"

He looked so much like the old Theo, holding back his pain by sheer will, but there was a difference. Ram was showing me his weariness, his great age. He might have looked like Theo Ram, but he wasn't pretending to be an ordinary cabbie's son anymore.

"By the time I had returned home, around 800 BC, the demon war had killed Merge and most of our line. I gathered the remnants together and fought to help the cities in the Fertile Crescent. But Bedlam was supporting the descendants of the Aegeans, their aggressive warrior cultures, dominated by autocrats."

"That doesn't make you responsible for Merge's death."

"I wasn't there when he needed me." He met my gaze. "I left because of Hope. I let her drive me away for hundreds of years, just when Merge needed me the most. He didn't want me to go. He thought I was overreacting. But Hope and I . . . we never could make it right. She was a possessed human, like you."

I felt as if I'd been pricked with a needle. Is that what I was to him? A replay of an old romance?

That certainly explains a few things. . . .

"There were legends about Hope; some are still known today. The maiden who lived half in the light and half in the darkness. The bride who is forced to go to the underworld for part of the year. That's you, Allay."

"What happened to Hope?" I asked, quickly diverting him away from me.

"She survived my absence, as I knew she would. She had taken on the guise of a goddess for too long to be anyone's pawn. She reached out to me. I began to trust her again, to feel we might yet love each other. Then she betrayed me." His mouth worked, as if he weren't sure he would finish. But he went on. "I had made a map of the world with all the cities I had started, all the seeds I had planted. Hope took it from me and gave it to Bedlam."

"Why? How could she do that to you?"

His eyes slid off mine. "She had her reasons. You might even sympathize with her. But the effect was disastrous. Bedlam set out to destroy everything I had built. He traveled with a war band and killed every demon and disrupted every civilization he could find, going to every place I had carefully marked on the map. I retaliated by killing every demon who ever worked with Bedlam."

Dared I ask? "Including . . . Hope?"

Ram just looked at me. He didn't have to say it. Of course he had killed Hope. No wonder he was racked by guilt. No wonder he needed a confessor.

"We interfered in human destiny trying to destroy each other," he admitted. "I think that's what plunged the world into the dark age. Vex would have done the same if I hadn't stopped him. I'm not going to let that happen again. I had to wait a long time for the Renaissance and Humanitarian movement to catch hold and flower. But humanity has been well rewarded, don't you think? Why can't you see that my intentions are honorable?"

"How can good come from killing someone?"

He raised his hands, as if he couldn't understand me.

"You ate meat when you were human, didn't you? You have to kill to survive in this world. By the way, where did you get all that energy?"

I hesitated; then I was mad at myself. "Crave."

His response was immediate and unexpected. A surge of jealousy shot orange and green spikes through his aura. Crave's reputation was well deserved, and Ram must know that.

"Glory told Crave to feed me." I lifted my chin. "I warned her about Goad's horde last night, so they were prepared to fight off the demons."

"You told Glory about me."

"You knew I wouldn't stay quiet and let you keep on killing people."

He scrubbed a hand through his hair. I wondered if that familiar gesture was truly his or that of his persona. "That doesn't matter. The most urgent thing is your condition, Allay. You must take another demon. Today. Now."

"You can't understand what I'd have to give up." I refused to meet his eyes.

He reached out again, as if to stroke my arm. It was the last thing I expected. He had used me, been intimate with me to get where he needed to be.

His feelings were so strong because I reminded him of Hope, his one great love.

I pushed back my chair as far as I could go. I couldn't stand it. "I don't care what you want from me. I'm not playing *that* game again."

Ram stood up. His voice was husky. "I'll always care about you, Allay."

Part of me thought he was telling the truth, but he had already proved that he could manipulate me into doing anything he wanted. And he had killed the last possessed human he got involved with!

Ram accepted my rebuff as if it were his due. He turned silently, and from the corner of my eye, I watched him leave and disappear down the sidewalk. It was eerie. I couldn't feel him, so he could have been anyone—any man on the street.

"I'll always care about you." His voice, the way he said it so low and raw, kept repeating in my head. So he admitted he had used me, but somewhere along the way he had started to really care about me?

Could it be possible?

He was a murderer who had almost killed Shock. He was like Revel, a pathological liar who would say whatever it took to control me. The similarities were too stark to ignore. Revel had said he loved me during our summer together. But he had seduced me with an ulterior motive, just like Ram.

I sat there with my stomach churning. I should have been glad—Ram said he would stay away from Shock. But I felt too many other things to feel good.

When I finally felt Revel's signature approaching, I was a mass of confusion. So far Revel had proved himself to me. Maybe I could trust him, and that bothered me, because a few days ago I would have sworn he was completely untrustworthy. *I don't know the truth anymore.*

Revel zoomed past in a limo service car and disappeared into the parking garage by the time I got to the sidewalk. I caught the eye of the black woman at the bookstore; she nodded discreetly, returning to the shelf she was perusing. She definitely belonged to Glory—a spy keeping an eye on me, she was not someone I had to be concerned about at the moment. My life, what remained of it, was an open book. I would tell Glory later that Ram had sought me out to say he wouldn't target Shock anymore.

I crossed the street and went into the fancy lobby of Revel's apartment building. I gave my name and was instantly ushered to the elevator that was waiting open for me.

When I reached the penthouse, Revel was standing in

the magnificent stained-glass gallery. The afternoon light cast patches of brilliant blue, green, and purple on the carved marble, making me feel as if I were underwater.

"There she is," Revel announced, clapping his hands slowly in admiration. "The girl who toppled a power structure that's lasted since the Roman Empire. Nice to see you looking all charged up, Allay."

"I'm not the one who killed Vex."

He gave me a hard look. "I can tell, or you wouldn't be in such dire need of replenishment. But the word is you warned Glory about the strike, and they ambushed Goad's horde."

"Wow, you demons have this grapevine stuff down."

"'You demons,'" he repeated with a laugh. "Haven't you ever heard of texting? A list of Vex demons who took part in the attack on Harlem is circulating. Some were flown in from as far away as China. Glory has demanded they return to their territories immediately. Luckily, they seem to be madder at Dread than you. They figure Dread must have made some kind of bargain with you before you ran off to warn Glory."

"Great, so now I'm supposed to be on Dread's side."

"Zeal told me what happened after she found him. She was able to bring him back from the brink of death. He's apparently still out of it."

I raised my brows. "I didn't know you were so close to her."

"We aren't. But there may be possibilities there. She owes me big-time for alerting her about Dread. Thank you very much for that, by the way."

I rolled my eyes and headed to the stairs. But as I neared Revel, he drew back instinctively. I noticed it because he usually tried to sidle closer to me so he could touch me. That was one reason I wouldn't let him come to the bar.

He could see how badly I needed to take another demon.

"Allay. I didn't realize it was this critical."

"I'm not going to attack you, if that's what you're worried about."

He frowned. "You need to get that taken care of."

I started down the stairs. "I'm going to assume you're being sarcastic."

Revel followed me. "Seriously, Allay, I can help you—"

I preferred it when he was sarcastic. "I need to talk to Shock."

By the time I reached the bottom of the marble stairs and turned into the grand living room, Shock dashed through the door to meet me. She looked strong and well charged, with her buzzed white hair and baggy street clothes exactly the same as usual.

"Why didn't you ring up?" she demanded. "I could feel you down there, but the stupid staff wouldn't let me go down, not without Revel's permission." Shock stopped awkwardly at a distance from me, giving me her usual half smile. "Am I glad to see you!"

Then her eyes narrowed, as she sensed my dire need. "Allay! You're about to—"

"Not here," I warned her. I didn't want to get into it in front of Revel.

Revel was watching us both. "I'm glad you're here, Allay. It's not safe out there. Goad is refusing to do as Dread says. Since Dread has contributed no offspring, Goad's line makes up nearly one-third of the Vex demons, and he controls most of them."

"That has nothing to do with us," Shock said dismissively. "We're not in Goad's line."

"Some are sure to hold a grudge against Allay for her part in this."

It all seemed so minor when I wouldn't be around to enjoy the real fireworks. "The important thing is Ram. Did Revel tell you everything, Shock?"

She nodded. "We found a lot of references to gods called

'Ram' or variations on that theme. You'll have to tell us if any of it is helpful."

I took a deep breath. "I think we're okay now. I just saw Ram downstairs."

Shock drew into herself, shuddering. Revel's lips parted, as if trying to remember feeling anything that would have tipped him off that a demon was so close. I knew how unnerving it was. Demons were their signatures; to know there was one out there who didn't have a signature was . . . disconcerting.

"Ram promised he wouldn't hurt you, Shock. He says he won't hurt any demon for simply being fertile. But he will continue to kill the ones who hurt people."

Shock asked me, "Do you believe him?"

"I think so, yes. There's no reason for him to lie about it. If he wants to kill us, he could do it whenever he wants."

"Good point." Shock considered it briefly, coming to her decision. "I'm sick of living in fear, holed up here like a mummy stuck in a coffin. There's nothing I can do to stop him. I have to accept that. I'm not staying here a minute longer."

"You're welcome," Revel said with a huff.

Shock ignored him. "But what about you?" she asked me. "Maybe you should stay, Allay. It sounds as if you've made a lot of enemies."

Revel agreed. "Vex's order of protection is gone now that he's dead. It'll be open season on hybrids."

"What I really want is to go home." My sudden, sharp yearning to retreat to my cozy apartment and the familiar faces in the bar almost overwhelmed me. "But the bar belongs to Vex."

"No, it doesn't," Shock said. "The Den belongs to you. I didn't want Vex coercing you into something because you lived and worked in their business. So I made him put it into a trust for you. You can't sell it, but it's yours until you die, and then it reverts back to Michael."

Allay turned to Revel. "You said Vex could take the bar away from me."

"I didn't know it was put in trust for you," Revel said. "Shock didn't tell me that."

Shock grimaced. "It was my idea. I knew you would leave, Allay, if you thought you owed Vex for the bar. Putting it into a trust meant we didn't have to involve you in the legal stuff. I didn't want you to feel obligated to him, but I thought the bar would be the safest place for you. In hindsight, I should have told you."

"Michael knows," I said with sudden realization.

Shock nodded. "Yes, he set the trust up and manages it. I'm sorry."

"It doesn't matter, Shock. Vex owned me, anyway. He was just biding his time before he plucked me off the street." I felt an easing of the fist clutching my insides ever since I had found Shock almost dead on my sofa. "So I can go home."

"Are you crazy?" Revel protested. "Your front windows were shot out. You can't go back there."

"I know who did that." I wasn't ready to tell Revel about my poor attempt at blackmailing Commissioner Mackleby, with his thug for a driver and his empire of licenses and permits. A demon would have known the uselessness of such a drive-by shooting against me, so I could discount my real enemies. "I can call him off. All I need is a phone."

Shock was jittering up and down. "If you want to leave, Allay, then let's go. I can make it to work on time if we hurry."

I smiled at Revel to lessen our abrupt departure; then I ran up the steps after Shock. Revel caught up as we stepped into the elevator. "Call me if you need help." He said it to both of us, but he was looking at me.

I said something I thought I never would. "Thank you, Revel. You really came through for me."

His dark eyes looked huge. "That's what I'm here for," he said as the elevator door closed.

*   *   *

Once Shock and I were ensconced in the back of a cab, protected by the Plexiglas barrier and heading south to more-familiar territory, I asked, "How was it staying with Revel?"

Shock made a face, scrunching up her delicate nose. "Like living on candy, all sweetness and light. I was hard-pressed to find even the most trivial suffering in that place. I can't wait to get back to work."

Her hands were clenching and unclenching, like an addict looking for her fix. It made her even more admirable that no matter how badly she needed it, she would never inflict harm on others to feed off their pain—unlike Dread.

I did notice that she stayed on the far side of the seat. Both Shock and Revel instinctively wouldn't come close to me. But Ram had reached out for me—several times. He wanted to touch me, even while I was in this desperate need of a new essence. He wasn't afraid deep down that I was going to snap and try to kill him. Then again, he was the uber-predator—he wasn't afraid of anyone.

As if reading my mind, Shock said, "What are you going to do about your situation, Allay?"

"I don't know," I admitted.

"You have to take a demon tonight. It can't wait any longer. I'll help you. It's supposed to be easier if there're two to one."

I groaned, putting my hands to my head. "I've been over this so many times. I'm no murderer."

"Huh." Shock looked out at the buildings and cars whizzing by. "If I'm going to die, I'd rather it be someone like you who kills me."

"What? Why would I kill my best friend?"

"I'm just saying—it's better than someone like Dread. Or Stun. He's my own offspring, I know, but he's awful. Would you want their face to be the last thing you see? Would you want to give them more life?"

"I'd be no better than them if I killed someone."

Shock considered that seriously. "I don't think so, Allay. You're nothing like them."

I knew it wasn't her fault she couldn't understand the moral issues at stake. "How do you plan on picking a demon when your time comes?"

"I never thought about it. I may go look up Stun. It would sure catch him by surprise." Shock laughed thinking about it.

I didn't.

We were silent all the way down until we reached the East Village. I thought it was prudent when Shock instructed the driver to turn into Alphabet City. I wasn't going to walk anywhere without someone at my back. I never wanted Goad's horde chasing me in their psych-ward van again. I turned to look at the cabs following us and wondered which one held Glory's spy.

The driver pulled up in front of the bar. "Don't stop the meter," I told him. "Shock's going on downtown."

"Come with me, Allay. You can stay at work until I get off; then we'll find you someone. I'm not going to let you go out like a light because you're too finicky to do what needs to be done."

"You say that as if I were refusing to eat my broccoli."

"You are. You'll just have to get over it." Shock gave me an admiring glance. "By the way, you look great all charged up like this. You should do it more often."

I opened the door and got out. It was no use arguing with Shock. She made it sound so easy that it made me feel sick.

"I'll come by later," Shock called after me. "Don't you dare go out until I get back."

21

It was weird seeing the bar closed up at the height of happy hour, with the metal shutter down over the front and the windows of my apartment dark up above. There was trash strewn across the sidewalk, and someone had dumped a six-pack of empty beer bottles at the base of the tree, leaving broken glass scattered on the sidewalk.

I stood looking up at the building. *My place.* I almost wanted to cry. All along, the bar had belonged to me. Somehow it felt different, so perfect yet awful at the same time, because now I didn't have time to enjoy it.

Mail was strewn across the floor of the foyer—bills, invoices, several red Netflix envelopes, and lots of junk mail. There were no dirty packets of money waiting to be handed off. I was done with that forever.

I hesitated at the inner door to the bar, dreading what I would see. But the phone was in there, and I needed to find out how Pepe was doing.

It was dark inside, with only the silvered east light coming from the windows in the back. Tables were pushed into odd clusters and some of the chairs were down.

I stepped inside carefully, but found no crunching glass. Flipping on the light revealed the front windows had been repaired with new plate glass, and the floor had been scrubbed clean of blood. The bar looked as if it could be opened right now. Michael had taken care of everything, getting it fixed in record time.

I really wanted to open up. I was tempted to throw one last huge party, but it would be too dangerous for my patrons.

I called Michael. He answered on the first ring. "Allay? Is that you?"

"Hi, Michael. Yes, I'm back at the bar."

His voice was so familiar, like a father's. "I'll be right there, Allay. Don't you go anywhere!"

I tried to protest, to say I just wanted to check in, but Michael was already heading out his door. So I waited in the cool, shadowed bar, the muted sounds of the street making it seem as if I were far away from everything, suspended in a bubble in a teeming ocean.

I could have sat there forever.

But it wasn't long before Michael came knocking at my door. He gave me a big hug right there in the foyer. He was an aging bear of a man, solid and reassuring. He looked as if he hadn't gotten much sleep last night. He worried too much about everything, including me.

How could I have ever doubted him?

"It's so good to see you," I told him.

"My dear, what happened to you?" He held me away and gave me a good look up and down. "Were you hurt in the shooting? You disappeared and nobody knew where you were."

How could I lie and say I was fine when I was dying? "I'm sorry, I should have called you sooner. This whole thing has been a big mess. My cell is gone, so don't try that number."

"I have. Too many times."

I led him into the bar to a table at the back. Through the windows I could see the tree next door hanging down over my yard. "How's Pepe?"

"He's recovering well. He should be able to get out of

the hospital tomorrow. He had to have his bowel resected, but his health is good and the doctors say he's healing fine."

"Thank goodness." My relief knew no bounds. It was my fault Pepe had been shot. "Is his family all right? Do they need money?"

"All taken care of. I've made sure they'll get disability payments, and the medical bills are coming directly to me."

"Thank you, Michael. And thank you for fixing the bar up. The new windows look great."

"That's what I'm here for."

That was what Revel had said. Funny.

I had to talk to him about it. "Shock told me about the trust. Why didn't you ever tell me you don't own the bar?"

His tone grew more serious. "Allay, from the moment I met you, I thought you deserved a break. When your sister got Mr. Anderson to buy the bar for you, well, I was thrilled. Who wouldn't be? I knew you would take care of this old girl. And I was glad to still be able to manage the financials, to make sure you didn't get off track."

Michael shook his head, remembering. "But as I got to know you better, I told Mr. Anderson that you should be informed. I didn't like lying about it. He refused, and your sister agreed with him. She came to my office to convince me to leave well enough alone. She said you were too proud, that you wouldn't want to be beholden to anyone. I knew how happy you were here, and selfishly, I didn't want you to leave. Did I do wrong?"

"No, you meant well. And it doesn't matter in the end."

Michael frowned. "I don't like the sound of that. The end of what? The police said you reported a friend of yours was kidnapped by the prophet. Is that true? Don't tell me Mr. Anderson was involved in the shooting."

"No, I don't think so."

"The police don't have any leads that I know of. They've

been asking for you. They want to talk to you. Follow-up questions, they say."

I groaned. "I suppose I have to do it. But not tonight. I need one night of peace; that's all I ask for."

Michael was still concerned. "Where have you been, Allay?"

"I went to see the prophet when I found out he bought the bar from you. Things got . . . a little out of hand." I hated lying to him. "It turns out the guy I thought they kidnapped was actually lying to me all along."

"How are things between you and Mr. Anderson?"

I left him lying on the floor of his own cage, nearly dead. Dread should be supremely grateful that I had spared his life. But he was arrogant enough to want to kill me for seeing him brought so low. "That's yet to be determined."

"Well, he doesn't have any control over you or this bar. So it doesn't matter whether you're on friendly terms with him or not."

"So I really do own the bar?"

"All right and tight. For the rest of your life."

The thought of my life lasting barely longer than tomorrow ended the pleasant mood Michael had put me in. I arranged to meet him at the precinct to speak to Lieutenant Markman the next morning. I hoped I'd have a coherent story put together by then.

When I disappeared, there were going to be a lot of questions asked. Shock would have to be prepared to deal with that.

In fact, I could leave a few pointers for the police right now. With Shock safe from Ram, my biggest concern was making sure Dread didn't revive Vex's plan and stage a religious resurrection with himself as the star. I could atone for my part in the fraud and bribery committed by the church by exposing them through my death. There was a certain poetic justice in that.

After I went missing, the cops would pull my phone

records. They would see that I had called Commissioner Mackleby from my cell the night before the shooting, and if I called him now from the bar, that might help the cops make the link between him and the church.

I also had something to say to Mackleby.

So I called him, hardly expecting him to be home at seven thirty on a Wednesday evening. Most men of his stature were out having dinner or at a social function.

The woman who answered quickly muffled the phone with her hand. When Mackleby came on, he knew exactly who I was. His caller ID probably said the Den on C.

"I told you never to call me again," he snarled. "I don't care what you think you know; I don't talk to blackmailers."

"You missed me," I told him.

"Miss you? What kind of bullshit is this, lady?"

"I won't be calling you again," I assured him. "Whatever you said to the prophet worked. He let Theo Ram go, so I'm now satisfied. As far as I'm concerned, this is over."

"You don't know what over is," he muttered.

"Yes, I get your threat. If I die of some violent or mysterious means, or I disappear, an envelope containing all the evidence I have of your acceptance of bribes will go to the police and media. This envelope will stay sealed forever, as long as you leave me alone from now on."

"Me leave *you* alone? Lady, you're nuts. You've done nothing but harass me in my own home. Stop calling me."

He hung up. He was good. If his phone was being tapped, or mine for that matter, he had plenty of plausible deniability.

But I would get him in the end, along with Dread.

Upstairs, my apartment felt deserted without the cats. I wanted to call Lolita to ask how she was putting up with the Snow-monster and his minion, but I didn't want to drag her into my problems.

It seemed too cruel to pop up briefly before disappearing again. I had already said my good-byes.

I also didn't think I'd be fetching my car from the Canal Street garage anytime soon. It seemed futile to run from trouble when the end was fast catching up with me. Besides, I would have to go alone. I could see now that Shock would never run away from the city with me. She needed her fix too badly. And being back home, I was inclined to agree that I belonged right here.

I stripped off Lash's expensive clothing and threw it in the trash on top of the Mary Janes that Vex had given me. Enough of other people's clothes! I filled up the old, deep, scratched, claw-foot tub with steaming hot water. Pouring in the last of the fragrant sea salt, I sank under the water to relax. It turned pale pink as the remnants of the dried blood dissolved from my skin.

What would it be like to kill someone?

I'm considering it, I slowly realized.

I didn't want to die. I wanted to grab every moment and truly live. I wanted to find a man who made me feel the way Theo made me feel; only this time it would be real. I could forge my own alliances with other demons. *No more living like a hermit for me.*

But to live, I would have to go out with Shock tonight and hunt down and kill a demon. At this moment, surrounded by everything I would lose, I tried to find some way that would be possible. Maybe I could learn to live with myself afterward. I could pick someone really bad, like Stun, and justify it that way.

Maybe I would lose my human side; then it would be my death either way. But I could at least try to live as a real demon, someone who enjoyed sucking the life out of people to survive.

But if I was capable of murder, I would have killed Petrify. It had been impulsive, a thing of the moment. I almost did it, but something inside of me had stopped me cold despite my mindless compulsion to take his essence. And now, after days of mulling it over, I was convinced it was wrong to kill to survive. There seemed no getting past it.

Shock could present me with a demon all tied up with a bow, but I was the one who had to kill him. Or her.

It was full dark by the time I gave up on adding hot water to the mix. But it was soothing to simply relax there, as if I were supported by my floating signature, forgetting everything including my impossible dilemma.

I finally got out and dried off. I was pulling on a pair of sweatpants when I felt him. Savor was coming.

Leaving the lights off in the front room, I went to the window. At first, I wasn't sure which person walking up the block was Savor. A group of young people paused by the bar in confusion—obviously they were coming to the Den and didn't even recognize it with the shutter down. They kept looking up the street at the signs, puzzling it out and asking one another if this was right.

When they finally moved on, a young woman was left behind. She looked no more than eighteen with pale silvery-blond hair and waiflike features. She could have been a hothouse student from Julliard or one of the ballet companies; she was even wearing black slippers.

It was Savor. She rang my doorbell, then backed up to look at my windows.

I unlocked the gate and pushed it aside so I could open the window. I looked up and down the street, but I didn't see Glory's spy. Maybe someone new had taken over. There was a skinny guy with a bad complexion hanging out near the fajita place, but that wasn't unusual. Regardless, I knew somebody was watching me.

Leaning onto the sill, I said, "How did you know I was here? Did you get a text?"

She glanced at the people passing by. "Hey, Allay. Can I come in?"

"No. You can't."

"Allay ... don't be angry at me. I had nothing to do with Goad taking you like that. I got into trouble with Dread for going to see you."

"You stood by while they threw me in the van." A guy passing by looked up at me, startled. I had never seen him before, so I shrugged it off. "As far as I'm concerned, you were the first wave in the horde sent to get me."

"That's not true. I came to warn you to get out of the city. Don't you remember?" Savor's angelic face was stricken. She was trying to manipulate me with her looks. Most demons thought I'd fall for that because I was human, so they used the same tricks on me that they used on their prey.

"What do you want, Savor?"

She came up close to the building. We were near enough that if I reached down, I could have touched her outstretched fingertips. Savor gave a slight jump in excitement. "I knew it! You didn't kill Vex. I didn't think you had it in you."

"I never said I did."

Looking from side to side, Savor waited until nobody was nearby. "Only the fact that you didn't kill Dread saved you from a death order. He says you did his 'dirty work' for him. I'm thinking he means Vex."

"Feel free to tell him I didn't do it."

"So it was Ram—Dread's people felt him when he dropped his shields. Everyone's talking about him."

"Good for them. Is there anything else I can do for you, Savor?"

"I came here to thank you, Allay, for not ratting me out. You didn't tell Dread that I'm the one who spilled the beans that you were supposed to run to Glory. I appreciate—" She broke off as a couple approached.

"It's nothing. It doesn't matter." I watched them pass by. "Is that all?"

Savor shrugged.

"Then go report back to Dread. I won't be seeing you again. Good-bye, Savor."

I started to shut the window, but she lifted her hand. "Don't be so quick to assume that, Allay. I have interests uptown, too."

It took me a second to realize what she was saying. I mouthed the word, "Glory?"

Savor nodded, grinning wickedly. I couldn't believe it. Savor was a double agent, working for Glory, as well as Dread. Savor was Glory's spy in the Fellowship.

And to think her pretty butt had been planted on my barstool all this time and I didn't know it. I had always seen Savor as the bottom of the barrel in Dread's organization, but maybe that was enough for her to get valuable information for Glory.

My astonishment showed. "I had no idea."

"Not very flattering," Savor said, and for a moment I saw a glimpse of her favorite persona, Sebastian with his supercilious manners.

I laughed. "I guess I will be seeing you around. But you still can't go out with Lolita. You understand?" As soon as I said it, I remembered that the bar wasn't going to reopen unless I killed a demon tonight.

I didn't see how that was going to happen.

But Savor was too pleased with herself to notice my discomfort. As I closed the window and relocked the gate, I wondered if I had let Savor in, would she have avoided me like Revel and Shock did?

Even worse, would I have been tempted to consume her?

My desperate need was burning, really starting to hurt now. Would it become all-consuming? Would I lose my reason and all control, and attack any demon who happened to be nearby? Or would I struggle with this until I died?

I had a bad feeling I was waiting until I couldn't help myself, taking the coward's way out.

22

It was getting late and only a few people were around when I ventured out to clean up the broken bottles on the sidewalk. I couldn't stand looking down at the mess. I would be able to see anyone coming down the block or driving up in a car, and get inside before they arrived.

I just finished sweeping up the broken bits when I felt Ram approaching. He was unshielded and letting his signature fly free, approaching from downtown.

My heart began beating faster. I wasn't afraid. I couldn't quite identify what I was feeling.

Then a few seconds later, I felt another signature weaving through, becoming more dominant: Pique's abrasive signature. He was chasing Ram.

Straining up on my toes, I tried to see down the block. A dark-haired man veered across the street, right in front of a car. A shout went up as he turned down Second Street, disappearing out of the light of the streetlamps, heading toward the East River.

Pique came loping after him in one of his nerdy personas. He kept pushing his glasses up on his nose and his long gait was fast. He was highly charged and clearly determined to run Ram down.

My first thought was that Ram was pulling something on Pique, maybe even luring him past the bar to trick me into taking him. But then Ram wouldn't have turned away so soon.

That was when I realized I was wrong. It wasn't Ram. The signature wasn't nearly strong enough. *It was Mystify.*

Ram's offspring must have come over the bridge from Brooklyn and had the misfortune to run straight into Pique.

I remembered what Glory had said about helping our newbie demons, rather than abandoning them to their fate like so many baby turtles running a gauntlet of hungry seagulls. Pique had probably already killed Petrify this week, and he would consume Mystify without hesitation if he got his hands on the poor kid.

I couldn't stand there and watch Mystify get slaughtered.

I ran to catch up with them, passing by a series of ramshackle tenements and a new, glass-fronted condo building that had recently sprouted in a vacant lot.

I knew it was dangerous, what I was doing. But did it really matter? I had nothing left to lose.

At the end of the block, I faced the projects. I couldn't feel either of their signatures. I ran up Avenue D to Fourth, then back down to Houston Street, but nothing but cars and headlights glared in my eyes.

"Damn!" I was angry at myself for losing them.

When the light changed, I hurried across the street into the projects. The sidewalks curved and crisscrossed between the redbrick apartment towers. The buildings were identical, with rows of small windows rising fifteen stories high. These were the Wild Houses, one of dozens of projects for low-income residents in the city, with the Baruch Houses being an even larger complex right below Houston Street.

The sidewalk was bordered by a three-foot-high wrought-iron fence to protect the narrow grass plots. The trees were mature, and the grass was nice and thick behind the fences.

The housing authority kept it clean, and I liked the neighborhood feel, so I often walked around the Wild, watching the kids in the little playgrounds and the basketball courts between the buildings. Most of the Spanish I had picked up, I had learned here, not in Orange County.

I neared the upper edge on Sixth Street, at the back corner by the narrow FDR highway that ran along the edge of Manhattan. I felt the prickling of Pique at the edge of my extended senses. He was on the other side of the highway, in the narrow strip of the East River Park that bordered the river.

I ran up the turquoise ramp of the pedestrian overpass. A few boys were lingering at one end, watching the cars on the FDR speed by underneath. Their fingers were laced in the chain-link fence as if they wished they were going somewhere, too.

I came down on the other side, and turned past the old-fashioned stucco restrooms. Iron lampposts cast pools of light as I ran down the cobblestone lane. On either side were towering trees, and a wide grass border next to the concrete barriers of the highway. Squashed between the highway and the river was a grassy, oval track field surrounded by a tall chain-link fence.

Pique was still ahead of me, moving south. If I could feel him, then he could feel me. But he was focused on easier prey.

There were people in the park despite the late hour; joggers and bikers kept up with me while others idled on the benches or walked in the cool night air in sedate couples. I passed by a lane that ran at right angles a short distance to the river. Benches lined both sides, and the trees arched together overhead, making a dark tunnel. The river gleamed at the end, reflecting the lights from Brooklyn on the other side.

Then I felt Ram's signature, closer to the river. For a second, I wondered whether it really was Ram. But it lacked the depth of the power he had, unique from every other demon I'd met.

I veered off the lane and ran between the trees, ignoring the marked pathways through the grass.

Ahead was another high chain-link fence, this time protecting a soccer field. Like the track circle, the field had been closed for the night and the floodlights were turned off.

A flare of energy alerted me. Mystify and Pique were nearby. The closer I got, the more staccato the "Ram" signature became, as if Mystify were having trouble maintaining it, as if he were under stress. Maybe they didn't sense my delicate signature while they were so close to each other.

Sped by urgency, I grabbed on to the chain-link fence and quickly scaled its eight-foot height. My strength helped me stay quiet, and I counted on the darkness under the trees to prevent any passersby from seeing me.

I swung my legs over the top and lightly jumped down, remembering how those demons had jumped from the roof of Crave's house. I had never attempted anything that high before, but it was nice to know it could be done.

I darted into the shadows of several bushes. There was only an iron-bar fence between me and the edge of the river, with the bank reinforced by short bulkheads disappearing into the water. The river sparkled under the artificial lights, stretching across to the Domino Sugar refinery.

Circling, I finally saw Mystify and Pique in the shadows of another cluster of bushes at the edge of the soccer field. They were wrestling against each other, their legs braced wide. The energy swirled around them in prismatic colors, flashing scarlet with fury where their hands gripped each other.

Pique was taking Mystify's energy by force.

I didn't even think; I ran into them, slamming against Pique and throwing him off balance. Pique didn't let go of Mystify, and we all three went down in a tangle of arms and legs.

Pique continued drawing energy out of Mystify. His snarl showed that he was not going to be denied. His fingers dug into Mystify's arm like claws, tearing his flesh.

"Let go of him!" I screamed, beating at Pique's face. He didn't seem to care.

Mystify was gasping in my ear. "Get off me!" He shoved me until I rolled over onto Pique.

Then Mystify kicked Pique in the throat, finally breaking his hold.

The moment he did, his signature changed. It was no longer a racing, driving rhythm. Instead, I felt as if I were suspended in a blank void with nothing to grasp on to. It was baffling.

I had felt this sudden switch before. But Pique lay there stunned, staring at Mystify openmouthed.

Then in an instant, Mystify's signature changed to Pique's. The grating, rasping, rough sensation couldn't be mistaken. My lips formed Pique's name when I looked at Mystify.

Now Pique was even more confused. If I hadn't felt it myself, I wouldn't have believed it.

"Watch out!" Mystify called as he darted away.

I realized I should be running, too. As I turned away, I was jerked to a halt when Pique grabbed my ankle. I struggled to pull away, but he swiped my feet from under me.

As I kicked and tried to roll away, he crawled up my body. He was grimacing, showing his teeth, but it couldn't be called a grin. There was no merriment in it.

Pique was pressing me down so I couldn't buck him off. He got his hands on my throat. But he left himself open, unlike Dread, and I was able to grab a finger and pull sharply downward, breaking his hold enough to breathe. Still holding on to his finger, I lifted one hip and used my leverage to roll him off.

My shirt ripped as I got away, standing up to face him, prepared for another attack.

His fingers twitched, as if urging me to go for him, to attack.

"I'm not falling for that again," I told him.

He lunged for me, and I stepped out of his line and spun him away from me.

Pique was coughing when he got up, and he spit out blood. My elbow had hit him, though that hadn't been my intention. His focus was hard on me.

It was always this way when I confronted Pique. Some demons taunted me, trying to psych me out. But with Pique, I felt as if I were being stalked by a lion or a hawk, with each move ruled by cold calculation.

I'm getting tired of running.

I suddenly realized I'd been right that night I fought with Pique at the bar—it was time for me to stop getting pushed around. My mistake was that I'd been too cocky, charged up with Petrify's energy. But standing up to this psychopath was the right idea.

Pique tried to grab me, and I smoothly evaded him, making him stumble past me with a nudge of his shoulder.

He kept coming, and I kept deflecting his strikes and using his leverage points against him. I was always reacting; this time I didn't strike out at him, reflecting the true spirit of Aikido. Most people thought the style had a balletic beauty, but was worthless in a real fight. However, I was living proof that it worked.

I wouldn't make the same mistake again.

He had caught me by surprise in our last fight because I made an aggressive move and it backfired on me. This time I stuck to what I did best, stepping away every time he charged and wearing him down. Again and again I threw Pique, letting go of him at the point of maximum trajectory. He came up, shaking his head and staggering. I wasn't being easy in my takedowns, and even a demon could take only so much pounding. Even I winced when he wrenched his knee, snapping the ligaments with loud popping sounds.

His charges began to slow. He was bleeding in several places, while I wasn't even breathing heavily.

"I'm not running anymore," I told him.

Pique was fairly charged-up, as usual. He could have kept hammering at me in hopes that I would slip up again as I had in front of the Den. But the predator assessed me, seeing how I glowed with energy, more than ever before. I wasn't backing down.

This time I didn't look like easy pickings.

Pique backed up a step. I went forward one. "You'd *better* run."

He backed up another step, still assessing me. But there was doubt in his stance. Then he made his decision and began walking away, picking up speed.

Abruptly a shadow separated from the dark mound of bushes. Pique was keeping an eye on me as he retreated, so he didn't see the man emerge.

Pique could turn on him in an instant. "Get away!" I called out in warning.

When he stepped fully forward, I saw it was Ram. He was back in his Theo-guise.

I hated not being able to sense him. "I need to bell that cat," I muttered.

Ram expertly tackled Pique, taking him down. Pique was already so battered from the hard falls that he flailed uselessly. Ram got him into a headlock and held him face-down in the dirt.

I ran up next to them. "Ram! What are you doing?"

He exerted a bit more pressure, popping Pique's shoulder out of joint. His cry of pain made Ram grimace in satisfaction. Now Pique wasn't resisting as hard. "You can't let him go, Allay. You need to take him."

"I'm not going to kill Pique!"

"He's the one, Allay. It's time for you to face up to this."

I backed up a few steps, on the verge of running into the

darkness. "Don't you think I wish it were that easy! Don't you think I want to live?"

"Then do it; do it now. I'll hold his shields open for you—it'll go much faster that way."

I shook my head, tears stinging my eyes, warring in my heart, my soul, my body, my mind. . . . "I can't do it! It's not right to kill someone to survive."

Ram let out a growl of frustration, kneeling against Pique as he held him down on the ground. "It *is* the right thing for demons, Allay. You're a demon now, whether you believe it or not."

"If I die without killing, I'll still be human."

"You'll die by your own hand. There's a sin in that, I'm told."

"I'm not committing suicide, Ram. It's completely different. I'm refusing to commit murder."

"Allay, nobody's immortal but the gods. We aren't gods—I should know that better than anyone. Like every other living creature, we're supposed to die someday, to pass our energy on to the next generation. You keep thinking of demons in human terms. Humans shouldn't be killed because they're so fragile; they die of such insignificant things—a bee sting, a virus, a scratch from a rusty nail. But the only thing that can kill a demon is another demon. Along with fissioning, it's the only way our essence is passed on. It's how we live on in spite of our death."

I had to admit that he was convincing. I had never considered that demons died only by the hand of other demons. It *was* the natural order of things, as far as demon life went. But did I really want to be a demon?

Slowly, I said, "I had no choice when I was turned. If I do this, I'll be making a choice to be something other than human."

"You *are* something other than human, Allay. It's time for you to stop hiding from yourself and the world. You even deny the memories in your own head. That's no way to live."

The truth stung. "It was the only way I could survive."

"You did that. Now it's time to start living again. I know you're hurt by what I did to you. Lying to you. I never meant to ruin your life. I'm trying to help you now, so you can move on and find what you want. Live how you want."

"But to do that, I have to end someone else's life. Who's to say that Pique is going to be this way forever? He's hardly been alive a month. I was certifiably insane after I was turned. Who am I to judge and condemn him?"

I looked down at Ram struggling to hold on to Pique, who was now fighting back with everything he had. It felt wrong to stand there and watch, just as I had watched Ram kill Vex. I was culpable in that, an accessory to murder. Could I take the next step?

Ram got Pique under control again, shoving his face deeper into the grass. "Believe me, Allay, I know what kind of demon Pique is. He lives for suffering, and it will save the world a lot of hurt if he's gone. You can end it here. Think of it as snuffing out a disease or a deadly virus."

"He must have more to him than that. He's a person, not a sickness. He must have at least one redeeming quality."

Ram gave me a hard look, to be sure I really meant it. "There is one thing I've seen. . . ."

"Yes?" I urged, looking for anything that could stop this from happening.

"You know how he likes to wear glasses?"

"Yeah, it's weird. He doesn't need them to see."

"No, but he steals them from people; he seeks out victims who wear them. I saw why last week. When he's not being a first-rate prick, he'll sit on a bench or a curb and stare at the simplest things for hours. Leaves. Pictures from magazines. Even plain water. His pupils change shape, as if he were using the lenses to see down to microscopic levels. You could say it's his only hobby."

I wished I hadn't asked. It made Pique seem more real than the bogeyman who lurked outside my bar. But it was so peculiar, as well. He wasn't even a reasonable facsimile of a human being. He didn't have a home or people he loved. He was a demon, and his only reason for existence was to prey on people.

Pique's face was smashed into the grass as he muttered, "Do *something* already or let me go."

My eyes opened wide. I'd never heard Pique speak before. I wasn't sure he could. But he must taunt people since he liked to provoke them.

"Who's your progenitor?" I demanded, curious why nobody had claimed him.

The silence stretched so long that I thought he wouldn't answer, even with Ram exerting pressure on his arm.

"Don't do that—," I started to protest.

But Pique blurted out, "Lash!"

"Lash?" I stared between him and Ram. "But Dread said Lash gave her offspring to Crave. That was her old ritual with him. The thought of it drove him crazy."

"Maybe Pique got away before Crave could take him. What happened?" Ram demanded, giving Pique a shake. "Tell us what happened."

But Pique refused to speak again. Now I understood why he was formed this way; he was born of Lash's twisted relationship with Crave. I wondered who started that rumor that Lash gave Crave her offspring? She must have consumed Crave's offspring in order to replenish herself, but the circle had been broken there.

It felt as if I had Pique's life in a nutshell. It hadn't been much of one so far.

Ram dug his knee in Pique's back to keep him from struggling. "Face it, Allay. Pique is dead. I'm not letting him go even if you walk away. He's been hurting a lot of people, killing them from the inside out. And you need his essence. You have to take him, Allay."

I felt a cold, hard certainty growing inside of me. Something was saying, "Do it! Do it!"

It was that dying core in my belly, the demon heart of me, speaking louder than any of my human qualms. I had died when I was shot by Mackleby's henchmen; then I came back to life. No human could do that.

I was a demon.

If being a demon meant killing another demon every two hundred years, then that was what I had to do. I expected my decision to feel like rotten maggots and worms turning in my underbelly, but instead a sparkling clarity filled my mind. I could survive.

I was going to kill Pique. I was glad it was this honest, this unequivocal. No justifications. I was going to take his essence and use it to save myself.

It was time for Pique to die.

I knelt down next to his head and looked up at Ram. "He's shielded."

Ram's expression didn't change. "Brace yourself." He dropped his shields, letting loose the aggressive thrumming of his signature to echo around us. It was a hundred times stronger than Mystify's pale imitation. Despite his recent fissioning, Ram had a depth of energy reserves that was stunning.

I sat back on my heels. It nearly took my breath away, he was so powerful. Now with his shields down I could see the finer gradations of his emotions—concern for me, relief that I agreed, confusion over his own strong feelings, and a hard, watchful edge that was never blunted.

Concentrating hard, Ram forced a spike of his own aura into Pique, a cone of deep midnight blue spearing straight toward his core.

I was glad to see it was the color of regret. There was a certain respect in that.

Pique squirmed under Ram's hold as the spike penetrated. I realized it wasn't really hurting him, but it disrupted his flow. His energy rippled in and out now instead of swelling like a balloon around him.

"Touch him," Ram urged, his teeth gritted to hold his own energy deep inside of Pique.

I reached out and grasped the back of Pique's greasy neck. He flinched under my hand. His shields were nonexistent, as if he couldn't hold himself together coherently with Ram interfering in his energy flow.

"Do it quickly, Allay."

I tugged on Pique's outrage and his blossoming fear at finding he was stripped of his defenses. His emotions flooded into me, with no restraints on his side because of Ram's spike. I absorbed his power as quickly as I could, as if I were taking huge gulps of him. . . .

The ultimate selfish act, killing to save myself. I never thought I'd do it.

Pique spat in fury, "You're no better than I am!"

"Shut up," Ram muttered, wrenching his arms higher.

Pique cried out in pain.

"Don't, Ram," I begged, my pace slackening. How could this be right?

"Mine! All mine!" Pique sputtered. "You sucking scum! Let go of me . . . I'll show you all!"

Ram looked worried, but oddly enough, Pique's outburst made me feel calmer. Pique *was* a ruthless predator, and I was going to transform him into renewed life for me. The bile and fury that spewed from him choked me, but I couldn't stop. I had denied my need for too long, and it took over relentlessly.

Swelling uncomfortably, I pressed on. His neck began to soften sickeningly under my fingers, his head slumping; I kept absorbing his energy. Ram had to adjust his hold as Pique quickly shrank. His back suddenly caved in as the skin on his arms shriveled.

Ram let go of him and rolled away, leaving only me touching him.

Pique was screaming now, his voice high-pitched from his shrinking chest. It was the worst sound I had ever heard.

It cut directly to my heart. I would never be able to get it out of my mind.

Abruptly I saw the flame of life deep within him. There was no energy left to surround and protect his core. His essence pulsed with fractured colors, calling to me, perfect and blameless.

My entire being responded. I needed life, so I took it, drawing it into myself.

His essence shone with hope and time, the most beautiful thing I had ever felt. I took it inside of me, and it welcomed me home as the life force suffused me, filling me with an ecstatic rush.

I fell back from the impact as the heat and flame swelled inside of me. All I could see was a blinding white brightness. But as the darkness returned, I saw a ghostly shadow turning next to Ram. He pulled away as the shape rose higher as it curled into itself.

With a popping sound that hurt my ears, Pique disappeared in a burst of smoke. The oily stench made me gag, but I was so bursting full of energy that I couldn't. It was taking all of my concentration to hold on to everything.

Every emotion I had ever felt was screaming inside of me, as if the world were spinning out of control.

23

I rolled away from where Pique had lain. The awful rancid smell of his death clung to everything it touched; but the fresh wind blowing upriver helped carry away the last remnants of the smoke.

I was lying on my back on the grass, looking up. The clouds were hanging low overhead, shining rosy with light that reflected from the buildings. The trees in the park concealed us from the hundreds of lit windows in the project towers of the Wild, while the lights on the other side of the river were even farther away. We were isolated in the midst of the city.

I slowly realized that Ram's shields were back up and his signature had disappeared. It felt as if I were alone on the edge of the river.

My arms wrapped around my stomach.

"Are you okay?" Ram asked, coming closer.

"No . . . I feel . . . awful."

Ram touched my arm. "You're pulsing! You're going to fission, Allay."

"What?" My head came up sharply. "How? I didn't take that much, did I?"

"Enough for a hybrid." He stroked my arm. "You're on the path, but not barreling down it as I was with Mystify. My guess is, it'll happen in a few hours."

I was appalled. That was the last thing I wanted. "Can't I stop it? Bleed off energy somehow?"

Ram shook his head. "It's too late. Don't worry, I'll help you through it."

I moaned, dropping my head back to the grass. "I can't birth a demon. It'll be vile, like Pique. All those awful emotions he fed me . . . the demon will embody what he last felt, won't it? I feel sick. . . ."

Ram hesitated, then reached out and trailed his finger down the back of my hand. I saw the longing in his gaze.

He took my hand, twining his fingers in mine. For once he felt cool, while I burned hot.

I sighed as I absorbed his sweet relief that I had consumed Pique. He was glowing like the sun, he was so happy. There was no regret in him now, not a drop. It bothered me, but he was being honest.

It was hard touching Ram like this, knowing that he was a demon. Knowing that "Theo Ram," the guy I'd started to fall for, was a phantom.

He felt my reluctance to touch him, but he murmured, "Take it. For your offspring, Allay. For the sake of humanity. Don't let Pique sire another fiend."

I shuddered, feeling as if everything had gone dreadfully wrong. Now I was hurtling down the precipice without anything to break my fall.

Ram's hand was an anchor.

But I couldn't trust him. How could I?

"Relax," he urged. "Don't fight it. Don't fight me."

Despite the swirling of my head, I moaned, "Oh God! You make it sound like I'm the drunk girl at a frat party."

His guilt seeped through. "I'm sorry I took advantage of you. Truly, I am. But I didn't have to make love to you that first night. You had already brought me into your home. I kissed you because I wanted to. And then . . ."

"Then I threw myself at you." I didn't want to ask, but

I had to. "Why didn't you make a move on me the other night in the loft?"

"I felt terrible for deceiving you. I've never felt bad about that before. But with you . . . I couldn't push myself on you. I was determined to take only what you gave me and not a single bit more. I saw how you do that with the people you care about."

We must have both been thinking of how he went down on me, how I writhed under him. A burst of lust shot through him, curling and stretching, growing like a living vine spreading through his body.

I felt it, and almost let go. But I was tingling, too, thinking of how he had licked and kissed me to ecstasy. Nothing had ever felt so good. . . .

My lips parted in surprise. My response was instant. I accepted his burgeoning lust, staining his aura the deepest green of passion, as mine also began to turn verdant.

He leaned over me, cupping my cheek with his hand. I closed my eyes briefly as he softly stroked me, then traced my lips with his fingertip.

We stared into each other's eyes for a long time, our faces close together. Everything else whirled around me, the river rushing by glinting silver and black, the pink sky and the wind in the trees, the crushed grass beneath me. . . .

Only he was solid, real. Everything else had been reduced to pure energy, the chaos beyond.

I would have been terrified without him there. How could he fake the feelings I sensed in him? He was so tender and caring. He wanted me with a devouring need. It consumed him, but he held back, unwilling to take advantage of me while I was so disoriented. He was restraining himself by force of will.

Maybe he really did care about me.

I pulled his face down closer so I could kiss him. I pressed my lips to his cheek, then the corner of his lips, then full on his mouth. Ram returned my kiss, as if savoring my taste.

Through our lips, I could delve even deeper into his feelings; his fierce desire for me, his need to hold me, his giddy relief that I would live. I glutted myself in him, kissing without restraint and wallowing in his tremendous power. My own emotions flooded out—my fear and confusion, my need to ground myself in something, anything . . . the burgeoning pain from the pressure of too much energy swelling inside of me. It swirled back and forth in a dizzying loop until I didn't know where he ended and I began.

Ram pulled me against him, his hand tightening on the neck of my T-shirt. He clearly wanted to rip it off, to get rid of everything that separated us. But then his glance caught my dazed eyes, and he stopped cold.

My fingers tightened on him as he pulled away. "What's wrong, Ram?"

"I should get you home where you'll be safe."

"Is someone coming?" I asked.

"Not yet. But with my shields up, I can feel only what's in the immediate area."

"Drop your shields, Ram. I need to feel you with me. It's so confusing . . . not knowing what's real and what isn't." I knew it didn't make sense, but that was what I felt. The sensations were completely alien, the demon side of me I had denied for so long.

He held me close and buried his face in my neck, dropping his shields.

When his shields fell, I knew it was the right thing to do. Despite my bewilderment and the spiraling chaos that Pique had filled me with, Ram's driving signature gave focus to the movement inside me. My buoyancy gave him relief.

"Ah . . . much better." I sighed.

"It is." He was trembling, feeling exposed from letting down his shields. He had lived hidden for too long.

But a golden joy coursed through him at my acceptance. I latched on to him eagerly; it was much better than the pain and confusion I was feeling. I'd rather feel what he felt. I wanted him to carry me along. "Yes, let yourself go," I murmured. "Oh, this feels better."

His hands tightened on me as he kissed my neck up to my jaw and cheek. "I'll rip this shirt off you if I do."

"Yes, skin," I agreed. Skin-to-skin touch would help ground me.

With Ram's help, I managed to snake my shirt up over my head. He kissed me, sliding it slowly off my face. Then he pulled off his own shirt. He hugged me close to him, rolling back in the grass. My bare breasts pressed against his chest as the breeze off the river sent shivers across my skin.

It all narrowed to this—where we touched, where my fingers dug into his hard arms, where our energy flowed together, meshing and joining. I kissed him and rolled again, finding myself lying on the fragrant grass with Ram's weight on top of me.

He got our pants off with an ease that only a demon could manage. Then his hips pressed into me, rubbing against me. My head was spinning, and I didn't know how much was lust and how much was the impending birth. I didn't care.

Right now, all I cared about was the deep resonance between us, which was keeping me from spiraling out of my mind.

"Are you sure?" he asked, hesitating even now.

But I wanted all of him, now. I lifted my hips for him, letting him enter me. He slowly sank inside me, feeling every trembling muscle in my body.

He murmured my name, his tone achingly tender.

I strained up to him, wrapping my legs around his to lock him against me. He rocked slightly, feeling he could go no farther, filling me completely. It cut the swelling pain inside of me as I cried out in release, euphoric waves washing through me. Our energy swirled together, merging.

Ram could hold back no longer. His hips thrust into me as I arched along with him, opening myself fully to him.

"*Allay!*" he cried as he emptied into me.

24

The waves of bliss seemed to go on for an eternity, lost as I was in the midst of my own pleasure.

Finally, almost painfully, Ram pulled away from me. I was burning up, panting and limp from my climax.

"Allay, try to relax." Ram was out of breath, but he tried to sound as reassuring as possible. "You're going to fission now. Don't worry, I'll be right here with you."

"Now?" I cried out, my fingers clutching at the grass, staring sightlessly into the clouds.

"You'll be fine. Trust me, Allay."

I reached for him, no longer able to see. I couldn't feel him anymore; he was shielded again. If only I could touch him, that would stop the sickening, whirling world.

"Lie back," Ram's voice told me. "Don't try to touch me now. You've got what you need. I don't want to ruin it by feeding you more."

I couldn't understand what he meant. The words were meaningless. A jumble. Did I trust him? I thought so. Then I remembered he had lived a lie throughout recorded history. How could a creature steeped in deception know what was the truth?

I panted, staring up at the pink glow. It was all I had left.

My contracting muscles were making me practically

rigid. I shook my head back and forth on the grass, balling my hands into fists.

Too far away, Ram urged, "Relax into it, Allay. Don't tense up."

"I'm . . . bursting," I managed to get out.

"It only feels like you're about to explode. You won't, I promise. The more you fight it, the more painful it is. Don't try to stop it."

I bit my lip, twisting in agony. How could I relax when my body was trying to tear itself apart? Shit, if I survived this, I was going to start a Lamaze class for demons. No one should go into this blind.

"Let it out," he murmured. He sounded closer, but not close enough to touch. "You don't have to keep quiet. There's nobody around."

My panting grew harsher. He could sense the pain building inside of me. I gave a cry as something tore within me and then again, as if my moorings were ripping loose deep in my essence.

"That's it; let go," he urged.

I screamed. "It's killing me!"

"I promise, you won't die. I won't let you, remember? I'll take care of you, Allay." He kept murmuring his assurances.

There was nothing else like fissioning—no human analogy could properly describe it. The spirit tore in half. It felt as if I were losing something precious and irrevocable.

Then there was nothing left but a howling wall of noise. It felt as if I were being diced alive, as if every atom inside of me were being split. There was no inside/outside—there were only tiny pieces of me floating loosely together.

Gradually, I realized there were two people living in the diffuse universe inside of me. We bumped and jostled each other, unable to fit in the too-small space within my skin. Which was me—both, none?

Then the other one lifted her arm away. Where my arm was left felt slack and empty.

The pain intensified as she tugged on my chest and head. I could hear it tearing inside my head, echoing inside of me as the other demon separated from me.

I curled on my side, groaning. Lying next to me was the pearly white form of a naked girl. Her short black hair went light, then dark again. Her expression mirrored my own—a round *O* of a mouth and dark pits for eyes.

I was grateful when Ram finally pulled me into his arms. His touch chased away the fear.

But I tensed up again when he held out one hand to ward off the new demon. He was radiating defensiveness. "Go away!"

"No, Ram," I begged. "You're scaring her."

"Allay, demons are born hungry. They'll attack anything that moves."

The new demon sat up on her knees, watching us warily. "I don't want to attack you. But I am hungry."

I felt the demon's name in her signature, an uplifting sensation, as if she were a feather being wafted on the breeze. . . . "Bliss," I said in recognition.

Ram was still tense. "That's certainly fitting. It would have been different if I had touched you during the birth. I was so anxious watching for other demons, it would have ruined that imprint."

"I feel much better now." I sighed, relaxing back against him. "That wasn't fun."

But Ram wouldn't let me lie down. "We have to go, Allay. We're too exposed here."

I tried to cooperate, getting to my feet like a shaky colt. Where was all my newfound strength? Inside of Bliss. She looked perky enough for both of us.

"I'm hungry," Bliss repeated more insistently.

"Get out of here," Ram ordered.

I tried to pull away from him, remembering Glory's words, and feeling, of all things, maternal. "Don't be that way, Ram. She doesn't mean any harm."

"She's a demon, Allay. You can't take any chances." Ram held on to me, not letting me get any closer to Bliss.

I watched her sitting there so calmly, crossing her legs to get comfortable. The initial shifting of her features had finally stopped, and she had settled back into my persona. It was a little disconcerting, like looking into a distorted mirror.

What would happen to her? The thought of baby turtles and their desperate dash to the sea haunted me.

Extending my senses as much as I could, I found a demon signature at the farthest extent of my reach. I couldn't tell who it was, but he might have been drawn by the birth of Bliss. Demons must have sensed Ram's strong signature while he was unshielded.

"Do you feel it?" I asked Ram.

"Two demons in the projects, and one farther down by Houston Street."

He had a much longer reach than I did, but that made sense, seeing as how old he was. "Bliss won't be able to get past them."

"I'm more worried about getting *you* past them before you fall into a stupor."

I felt the tug of unconsciousness trying to draw me down, but I resisted. I couldn't let Ram push Bliss out of the nest to die.

"She's coming with us," I said.

"I am?" Bliss asked happily. Her smile was exactly like mine.

"Yes," I said over Ram's protest. "Of course you are."

"I'm hungry," Bliss repeated plaintively.

"*Allay*," Ram warned, "she's acting okay right now, but she could go psycho any second. New demons are changeable until they settle into themselves. You're trusting her because she looks like you and she came from you. But that's no way to judge a demon."

"Let's just get back to the bar. We'll deal with judging everyone later." He was propping me up, but I toppled over as I tried to reach for my clothes.

Ram stopped arguing and helped me get dressed, his hands gentle even as he shot Bliss hard looks.

"You can put on Pique's clothes," I told Bliss.

She nudged then with her bare toe. "They're nasty."

"You'll only have to deal with it for a few minutes. You can change at the bar."

Bliss carefully picked up each article of clothing, shaking them with a brisk snap to dislodge the rancid stench. But nothing but a good burning would help Pique's clothes. She screwed up her nose and complained about the smell, getting dressed far too slowly. I offered to trade with her, but Ram wouldn't hear of it.

Finally Bliss got the button-up shirt closed, and she had to hold up the jeans with one hand until she expanded her hips to a generous size. Now she looked like me with an extra twenty pounds.

Bliss tied the laces of her shoes with the same delight only a four-year-old could muster. She joined us with a slight bounce of excitement. "I'm ready."

Everything seemed to spin around in a big loop—trees, ground, sky. I almost fell down. But Ram was supporting me, so I hardly had to make an effort to take each step. When he realized I was only going through the motions, he swept me up in his arms to carry me.

My head fell against his shoulder. I briefly closed my eyes, wishing I could let go. But I had to stay alert. It would attract attention if Ram had to carry me while I was passed out.

It was getting harder to reach out with my senses. The demon in the projects hadn't moved. He could be confused by the way Ram's signature kept coming and going.

It would be smart of the others to be wary of him. I would bet on Ram even five against one.

Ram didn't like that Bliss was following us. But it turned out I would never have made it up and over the chain-link fence without her help. Ram had to balance with me on top and carefully lower me down to her after she had climbed over. I felt like a useless bag of potatoes, but my muscles were shutting down despite my best efforts.

As I struggled to keep my eyes open, I was also grateful to have a girl walking beside us with a huge, sunny grin on her face. It certainly helped deflect suspicion. A pair of cops stationed at the end of the pedestrian walkway asked what was wrong as we approached, but I murmured, "I'm just dizzy. Too much sake with dinner. They're taking me home."

"This your sister?" one of the cops asked, staring from me to Bliss.

Bliss giggled, but I quickly agreed, and they let us by. I wondered what would have happened if I hadn't been able to talk to them.

As we walked across the pedestrian bridge, passing over the highway, Ram said, "I'm going to unshield myself. I think that's the best way to blast through these two demons up ahead. If they don't give way, Bliss, you carry Allay back to the bar. I'll take care of the demons."

His matter-of-fact viciousness made me stiffen. I didn't like it. It was his worst side. He killed his own progeny. And he thought that was a good thing.

What was evil? Knowingly doing harm?

If that was true, then I had done evil by killing Pique. Even if it saved thousands of people from suffering, it was still a harmful act. Pique was gone because of me. How quickly regret was catching up to me.

I hung on to Ram grimly as he carried me down the winding sidewalks between the towers of the project. Most people took one look at Bliss skipping alongside us and

figured things were under control. A few catcalls and offers
of help were easily turned aside.

The whole time, Ram continued to radiate his signature
unshielded. I was grateful beyond measure when the other
demons gave way as they felt his approach. I couldn't sense
who they were through Ram's thrumming sensation. They
had probably never felt such a strong signature before, and
apparently had the good sense not to test him without further investigation.

But the final block to the bar almost did me in. I was
wavering in and out of a daze, lulled to sleep by the rhythm
of Ram's stride.

"The keys are in my pocket," I mumbled as we turned
the corner.

Ram stopped dead. "Oh, no. Shock's here."

I turned to see, as Shock darted across the street, nearly
getting hit by a cab. "Hey, you! Put her down now!"

"It's all right," I tried to say, but Shock was yelling at
Ram so loudly that she didn't hear me.

Ram finally set me down, and was pushed back into a
wall by Shock. She tried to shove him farther down the
street. It was well after midnight, so there weren't many
people around to see.

"He helped me, Shock." I grabbed on to her leg, tasting her righteous anger—and fear. "He was bringing me
home."

Now that Ram, his hands held up, had backed off, Shock
subsided. She crouched next to me, warily looking from me
to Bliss. She could see the truth in my pearly glow, and the
familiar persona that Bliss wore.

"You did it," Shock realized. She gave me an awkward
hug. "You did it, Allay. You're not dying anymore."

"No, I only feel like it."

She clearly wanted to know whom I had consumed, but
she could tell with one look that I felt bad about it. I wasn't

sure I had done the right thing following Ram's lead. I was grateful, yes, but I wasn't sure.

"You birthed this one?" Shock asked, though it was clear Bliss belonged to me.

It only took a moment longer for Shock to connect Bliss's name with Ram's presence. Her expression was so hurt and disapproving, I felt bad. Ram had tried to kill Shock, and now I was sleeping with him?

Shock was too good to say it out loud. Still, I heard it through our touch. "I'm sorry," I murmured.

I could hardly hold up my head. I was going to pass out and leave everything a horrible mess.

"I've got to get you inside," Shock said, picking me up herself. It must have looked odd, such a small delicate girl muscling me up with such ease. Her arms around me felt deceptively thin.

"Bliss! She has to come," I insisted, reaching out for her.

"*No*," both Shock and Ram protested at the same time. Then they stared at each other, distrust in every line of their bodies.

"I'm hungry," Bliss repeated plaintively.

"Then go eat," Shock said dismissively. She waited for a cab to pass by, then started across the avenue.

"Come with us, Bliss," I called. To Shock, I pleaded, "Please take care of her, Shock. Feed her for me. Just till I wake up."

"Allay!" Shock protested, appalled that I would ask.

"It's too dangerous to take her into the bar," Ram agreed. "You won't be shielded, Allay. It will take only a minute for her to drain you dry. Shock, you can't let her—"

"*Don't* tell me what to do!" Shock glared at him. "I never intended to bring that creature in with us."

"You can't leave her out here to die," I protested, or at least I tried to. I'm not sure what came out. If only I had more strength. If only I could stand on my own two feet and argue them down.

But my head was swimming, and blackness was creeping into my vision. I heard voices, but I couldn't tell what they were saying anymore. My fight against the stupor was over, and it was winning.

Poor Bliss would be left on the curb like the broken bottles.

25

When I finally opened my eyes and stretched, I wallowed in the luxury of waking up. I hadn't woken up in ten years, and it felt even better than I remembered. I was lying on my daybed looking at my favorite view; the light was shining the color of love through the rustling leaves of the acacia tree.

Shock was watching me from the chaise. "You've been out for fifteen hours."

"That long?" I stretched again, smiling lazily.

"How do you feel?"

It was a good question. I pushed myself up, testing everything. The persistent ache in my belly, like a deadly tumor, was gone now that I had replenished myself. "Good. Back to normal."

Shock finally smiled. "That's a relief. Allay, why did you go out without me? You could have been killed."

"Pique was chasing Mystify, and I had to do something to help him."

"Wait a second—who's Mystify?"

"Ram's offspring. He birthed Mystify after he consumed Vex." That was when I remembered. "Bliss! What happened to Bliss?"

"She's downstairs in the bar. With Ram." Shock's sour expression said all she needed to say about that.

"You left her with him?" I wasn't sure if I liked that.

Straining, I could barely sense her floating-feather feeling. She had a light signature, like me. If I didn't know what I was looking for, I wouldn't have known a demon was down in my bar.

"You wanted us to bring her in," Shock said with a shrug. "Ram agreed to feed her. I certainly wasn't going to bring her up here while you were unshielded."

On second thought, Ram knew I would never forgive him if he hurt Bliss. He was probably taking good care of her. I should be grateful.

So why did I feel worried instead?

Shock gave me a hand to help me up. "He said you took Pique. Good choice."

I didn't want to talk about it. When I thought about Pique, that nice floaty feeling in my stomach turned to lead. "Let's go downstairs and see what's up with those two."

Shock stopped me. "The question is, what's up with you and Ram? Did you really have sex with him, Allay?"

"I did when I thought he was human. And again in the park after I killed Pique. I don't know what came over me. I was about to fission, and he was there, so strong and steady...."

"Did he take advantage of you?" she demanded.

"No, nothing like that. It started innocently. He was giving me energy to counteract Pique's bile—it was awful going down. Really awful. I felt tainted. And Ram was being so sweet to me. It just ... snowballed."

"Into public sex in the park?" Shock's doubts were clear. "Allay, you have to stay away from him. He's dangerous. He's manipulating you, playing you like a fiddle. From what you've said, he's been around for almost four thousand years. You pick up a thing or two about human psychology when you're that old."

"He could have let me die in that cage, Shock. Dread was killing me. But Ram revealed himself to save me. Why would he do that if he didn't care about me a little bit?" I heard the pleading in my own voice and despised myself for it.

"He found out about the ERI machine, so he knew he wouldn't be able to hide any longer. Like all of us. You told him, didn't you?"

"No. I don't think he knows about that." I would have to tell him. I owed him that.

Shock grumbled. "He uses people. He used you over and over again. Who knows what he wants from you?"

I didn't like it, but it made sense. Ram had an ulterior motive from the first moment he had met me. "I'll be careful," I promised. "I don't want to get involved with him, that's for sure. I only just got free from Vex."

"Good." Shock finally looked relieved. "I thought you were losing it for a second there."

Maybe I was. I didn't know what to think of Ram.

Together Shock and I went downstairs. Opening the door, I heard the clink of the balls on the pool table. It was midafternoon, so enough light came through the windows that we didn't need to switch on the overheads.

Ram turned as soon as he heard the bolt click. I had to adjust my eyes to see his shadowed face. His expression was cautious, hopeful. It made my heart twist traitorously.

Bliss finished her shot, crying out in glee when the ball went into the pocket. "So you're finally up," she said over her shoulder. "I was getting sick of waiting. But the big guy here wouldn't let me leave."

Bliss didn't look like me anymore—her hair was longer, blonder, and curling in a mass down her back. Her eyes were bigger and blue, exaggerated for a striking effect, as was her figure. I wondered what they had been doing all these hours. That much pool would get awful tiresome.

"I'm glad you're here," I told her. "It's not safe for a rogue demon on the streets."

Bliss smiled, genuinely happy. "But there's so much I want to see."

"I know you're dying to leave. But you can always come back if you need a safe place to hang out," I offered.

"Allay!" Shock protested. "You can't keep her here. New demons are unstable. There's no telling what she might do."

"Why not? I'm up and shielded now. She's not going to be able to hurt me."

I noticed Ram wasn't saying anything. Bliss took her next shot and missed. Her pout was worthy of a photo shoot. Ram moved around the table and lined up his own shot. He made it with a bank into the corner pocket.

"Ram has to go, too," Shock insisted, her hands on her hips. "Revel called. He says there's talk of forming a posse to take him down. If they find out he's here, they'll storm the place."

Smoothly, Ram sank the eight ball. "I'm not going to endanger Allay. It's time for me to be leaving, anyway. I just wanted to wait until she was up."

Bliss clapped her hands at his win, as excited as if she were the victor. "You're really good, Ram."

"I've had lots of practice," he said.

That reminded me of what Shock had said. Ram was ancient. How could I tell what his true motives were?

I wanted to thank him for helping me, but the words stuck in my throat. He had helped me kill Pique. It had saved me, yes. But I wasn't sure if it hadn't destroyed me, too. I couldn't pretend to be human anymore. I had birthed a demon.

To Bliss, I said, "Why don't you stay here for a while until I talk to Dread? I want to see where we stand with the Vex demons."

I wanted to offer the same thing to Ram, but I couldn't. He didn't need my protection.

"I'd like it a lot better if the bar was open," Bliss said thoughtfully.

Shock grimaced. "That reminds me—the police came by earlier. I didn't answer the door. We should get your story straight before you talk to them."

I had intended to ensnare the prophet after I was gone. Perhaps I could still swing something. . . . Surely exposing Dread's machinations was the best way to keep him too busy to pull a demon Revelation. Now I had all the time in the world to deal with him.

I giggled, then giggled some more at their expressions. "I know. I can't help it. But I'm not going to die. I can hardly believe it."

"You don't know how glad I am about that," Shock said fervently.

"Me, too," Ram said quietly.

"What about the bar?" Bliss asked.

The Den was *my* bar. I could hardly believe it. I touched the curved back of a chair, worn smooth through the years by many hands. I could get Lolita and Darryl and Pepe to come back. My patrons would gather around me again.

"Okay, Bliss. We'll open up after I deal with the cops." And make sure Mackleby wouldn't try another drive-by.

"Are you sure you're ready?" Shock asked. "What if you get rushed by Goad's horde?"

"Then we'll deal with it, like I always have. Come on, Shock. It'll be fun. Let's celebrate my return from the dead."

Shock smiled in spite of herself. "Well, then, I'm calling in sick. I'm not leaving you alone here with only *her* for backup."

It was a sign of her devotion that she was willing to give up work for me. There was no need for it, but I wanted Shock here for my celebration.

Ram was the only one who wasn't smiling. He put away

his pool cue. "It's time for me to go. I'll head out the back in case anyone's watching."

I wanted to ask him to stay, but Shock was clearly unsettled by him. No wonder. She had spent the past few days remembering the terror of a demon attacking her with no warning, with no hope of resistance. Ram had come within seconds of killing her. Only blind luck had saved her.

So I nodded helplessly. I lifted my hand in a wave goodbye. It seemed like too much and not nearly enough at the same time, especially with Shock shooting daggers of hatred at him.

As the back door closed behind Ram, she let out a noisy sigh. "Thank the Lord, he's gone! Tell him to stay away from you, Allay. No good can come of him."

"He can come back anytime," Bliss said philosophically. "We wouldn't be able to sense him. He could be anyone."

Shock looked stricken, and I felt bad that Bliss had reminded her. It wasn't something I could forget. Not now. "Don't worry, Shock. He promised he won't target any demon unless they hurt humans."

"I don't see why you believe him," Shock said.

I thought about it: the way he had looked at me the first time we made love, such intimate strangers; the way he had saved me from Dread; how he had given me his tenderness in the park so I wouldn't birth a monster.

"I do believe him," I finally said.

"But you can't trust him, Allay. Don't tell me you trust him."

I hesitated, and it was Bliss who blurted out, "Of course she trusts him. I should know better than anyone."

"I don't know," I equivocated, unsure in the face of Shock's disbelief—and hurt.

"You can't dictate to the heart," Bliss said philosophically. "The heart wants what it wants."

"Does your heart want him?" Shock asked in dismay.

"I don't know. I barely know him. But he did save my

life. Three times, if you count helping me consume Pique."
I wasn't sure whether I regretted that or not.

Bliss nodded agreement, while Shock was silenced. She
didn't like it, but in truth, there was nothing we could do
about Ram. He would go where he wanted and do what he
wanted. Because of him, everything had changed in the demon world. We would have to wait to see what happened.

I would see Ram again; I was sure of it. Meanwhile, I
had all the time in the world to figure him out.

I also had time to forge the alliances I would need to
protect myself. I already had Shock and Revel on my side.
Somewhere in the past few days, I'd learned to trust Revel
again. And I thought Bliss might turn out to be an ally, as
well. Maybe I could bring Mystify into the fold. He owed
me one for saving him, and it could be useful to have a demon around who could mimic others.

With a solid group of demons working together, we
could even repel a horde if we needed to. We could make
our own way without having to be beholden to some over-
bearing overlord.

I was ready. It was finally time to start living again.

ABOUT THE AUTHOR

S. L. Wright has lived in New York City for more than twenty years, exploring every part of the city, from rooftops to underground tunnels. She moved to Manhattan to get her master's degree in fine arts, and not long afterward met her husband, Kelly Beaton. Together they have spent the past decade restoring a big brick house on the edge of Bushwick, Brooklyn. Wright is an activist at heart, saving wild cats in the city as well as helping people who are persecuted for their personal choices.

TRICK OF THE LIGHT

A Trickster Novel

by

ROB THURMAN

Las Vegas bar owner Trixa Iktomi deals in information. And in a city where unholy creatures roam the neon night, information can mean life or death. Not that she has anything personal against demons. They can be sexy as hell, and they're great for getting the latest gossip—but they also steal human souls and thrive on chaos. So occasionally Trixa has to teach them some manners.

When Trixa learns of a powerful artifact known as the Light of Life, she knows she's hit the jackpot. Both sides—angel and demon—would give anything for it. But first she has to find it. And as Heaven and Hell ready for an apocalyptic throwdown, Trixa must decide where her true loyalty lies—and what she's ready to fight for.

Available wherever books are sold or at penguin.com

THE ULTIMATE IN
SCIENCE FICTION AND FANTASY!

From magical tales of distant worlds to stories of
technological advances beyond the grasp of man, Penguin has
everything you need to stretch your imagination to its limits.

penguin.com

ACE

Get the latest information on favorites like
William Gibson, T.A. Barron, Brian Jacques,
Ursula K. Le Guin, Sharon Shinn, Charlaine Harris,
Patricia Briggs, and Marjorie M. Liu,
as well as updates on the best new authors.

ROC

Escape with Jim Butcher, Harry Turtledove, Anne Bishop,
S.M. Stirling, Simon R. Green, E.E. Knight, Kat Richardson,
Rachel Caine, and many others—plus news on the
latest and hottest in science fiction and fantasy.

DAW

Patrick Rothfuss, Mercedes Lackey, Kristen Britain,
Tanya Huff, Tad Williams, C.J. Cherryh, and many more—
DAW has something to satisfy the cravings of any
science fiction and fantasy lover.
Also visit dawbooks.com.

*Get the best of science fiction and fantasy
at your fingertips!*

Penguin Group (USA) Online

What will you be reading tomorrow?

Tom Clancy, Patricia Cornwell, W.E.B. Griffin,
Nora Roberts, William Gibson, Robin Cook,
Brian Jacques, Catherine Coulter, Stephen King,
Dean Koontz, Ken Follett, Clive Cussler,
Eric Jerome Dickey, John Sandford,
Terry McMillan, Sue Monk Kidd, Amy Tan,
J. R. Ward, Laurell K. Hamilton,
Charlaine Harris, Christine Feehan...

You'll find them all at
penguin.com

*Read excerpts and newsletters,
find tour schedules and reading group guides,
and enter contests.*

Subscribe to Penguin Group (USA) newsletters
and get an exclusive inside look
at exciting new titles and the authors you love
long before everyone else does.

PENGUIN GROUP (USA)
us.penguingroup.com